" WALLACE STATIONED HIMSELF IN THE CUTTER, SIGNALLING THE SHIP TO COME ON "—PAGE 383

JACK TIER

THE FLORIDA REEF

JAMES FENIMORE COOPER

Fredonia Books
Amsterdam, The Netherlands

Jack Tier:
The Florida Reef

by
James Fenimore Cooper

ISBN: 1-4101-0346-3

Reprinted from the 1896 edition

Fredonia Books
Amsterdam, The Netherlands
http://www.fredoniabooks.com

PREFACE.

THIS work has already appeared in *Graham's Magazine*, under the title of "Rose Budd." The change of name is solely the act of the author, and arises from a conviction that the appellation given in this publication is more appropriate than the one laid aside. The necessity of writing to a name, instead of getting it from the incidents of the book itself, has been the cause of this departure from the ordinary rules.

When this book was commenced, it was generally supposed that the Mexican War would end after a few months' of hostilities. Such was never the opinion of the writer. He has ever looked forward to a protracted struggle; and, now that Congress has begun to interfere, sees as little probability of its termination, as on the day it commenced. Whence honorable gentlemen have derived their notions of the Constitution, when they advance the doctrine that Congress is an American Aulic Council, empowered to encumber the movements of armies, and, as old Blucher expressed it in reference to the diplomacy of Europe, " to spoil with the pen the work achieved by the sword," it is difficult to say more than this, that they do not get them from the Constitution itself. It has generally been supposed that the present executive was created in order to avoid the very evils of a distracted and divided council, which this new construction has a direct tendency to revive. But a presidential election has ever proved, and probably will ever prove stronger than any written fundamental law.

We have had occasion to refer often to Mexico in these

pages. It has been our aim to do so in a kind spirit ; for, while we have never doubted that the factions which have possessed themselves of the government in that country have done us great wrong,—wrong that would have justified a much earlier appeal to arms,—we have always regarded the class of Mexicans who alone can properly be termed the " people," as mild, amiable, and disposed to be on friendly terms with us. Providence, however, directs all to the completion of its own wise ends. If the crust which has so long encircled that nation, inclosing it in bigotry and ignorance, shall now be irretrievably broken, letting in light, even Mexico herself may have cause hereafter to rejoice in her present disasters. It was in this way that Italy has been, in a manner, regenerated ; the conquests of the French carrying in their train the means and agencies which have, at length, aroused that glorious portion of the earth to some of its ancient spirit. Mexico, in certain senses, is the Italy of this continent ; and war, however ruthless and much to be deplored, may yet confer on her the inestimable blessings of real liberty, and a religion released from " *feux d'artifice*," as well as all other artifices.

A word on the facts of our legend. The attentive observer of men and things has many occasions to note the manner in which ordinary lookers on deceive themselves, as well as others. The species of treason portrayed in these pages is no uncommon occurrence ; and it will often be found that the traitor is the loudest in his protestations of patriotism. It is a pretty safe rule to suspect the man of hypocrisy who makes a parade of his religion, and the partisan of corruption and selfishness, who is clamorous about the rights of the people. Captain Spike was altogether above the first vice ; though fairly on level, as respects the second, with divers patriots who live by their deity.

JACK TIER.

CHAPTER I.

"*Pros.* Why, that's my spirit !
          But was not this nigh shore ?
Ariel. Close by, my master.
Pros.   But are they, Ariel, safe ?
Ariel. Not a hair perished."

Tempest.

"D' YE hear, there, Mr. Mulford ?" called out Captain Stephen Spike, of the half-rigged, brigantine Swash, or Molly Swash, as was her registered name, to his mate, "we shall be dropping out as soon as the tide makes, and I intend to get through the Gate, at least, on the next flood. Waiting for a wind in port is lubberly seamanship, for he that wants one should go outside and look for it."

This call was uttered from a wharf of the renowned city of Manhattan, to one who was in the trunk-cabin of a clipper-looking craft, of the name mentioned, and on the deck of which not a soul was visible. Nor was the wharf, though one of those wooden piers that line the arm of the sea that is called the East River, such a spot as ordinarily presents itself to the mind of the reader, or listener, when an allusion is made to a wharf of that town which it is the fashion of the times to call the commercial emporium of America— as if there might very well be an emporium of any other character. The wharf in question had not a single vessel of any sort lying at, or indeed very near it, with the excep-

1

tion of the Molly Swash. As it actually stood on the eastern side of the town, it is scarcely necessary to say that such a wharf could only be found high up, and at a considerable distance from the usual haunts of commerce. The brig lay more than a mile above the Hook (Corlaer's, of course, is meant—not Sandy Hook) and quite near to the old Almshouse, far above the ship-yards, in fact. It was a solitary place for a vessel, in the midst of a crowd. The grum topchain voice of Captain Spike had nothing there to mingle with, or interrupt its harsh tones, and it instantly brought on deck Harry Mulford, the mate in question, apparently eager to receive his orders.

"Did you hail, Captain Spike?" called out the mate, a tight, well-grown, straight-built, handsome sailor-lad of two- or three-and-twenty, one full of health, strength, and manliness.

"Hail! If you call straining a man's throat until he's hoarse, hailing, I believe I did. I flatter myself, there is not a man north of Hatteras that can make himself heard further in a gale of wind than a certain gentleman who is to be found within a foot of the spot where I stand. Yet, sir, I've been hailing the Swash these five minutes, and thankful am I to find some one at last who is on board to answer me."

"What are your orders, Captain Spike?"

"To see all clear for a start as soon as the flood makes. I shall go through the Gate on the next young flood, and I hope you'll have all the hands aboard in time. I see two or three of them up at the Dutch beer-house, this moment, and can tell 'em, in plain language, if they come here with their beer aboard *them*, they'll have to go ashore again."

"You have an uncommonly sober crew, Captain Spike," answered the young man, with great calmness. "During the whole time I have been with them, I have not seen a man among them the least in the wind."

"Well, I hope it will turn out that I've an uncommonly sober mate in the bargain. Drunkenness I abominate, Mr. Mulford, and I can tell you, short metre, that I will not stand it."

"May I inquire if you ever saw me, the least in the world, under the influence of liquor, Captain Spike?" demanded the mate, rather than asked, with a very fixed meaning in his manner.

"I keep no log-book of trifles, Mr. Mulford, and cannot say. No man is the worse for bowsing out his jib when off duty, though a drunkard's a thing I despise. Well, well—remember, sir, that the Molly Swash casts off on the young flood, and that Rose Budd and the good lady, her aunt, take passage in her, this v'y'ge."

"Is it possible that you have persuaded them into that, at last !" exclaimed the handsome mate.

"Persuaded ! It takes no great persuasion, sir, to get the ladies to try their luck in that brig. Lady Washington herself, if she was alive and disposed to a sea-v'y'ge, might be glad of the chance. We 've a ladies' cabin, you know, and it 's suitable that it should have some one to occupy it. Old Mrs. Budd is a sensible woman, and takes time by the forelock. Rose is ailin'—pulmonary they call it, I believe, and her aunt wishes to try the sea for her constitution—"

"Rose Budd has no more of a pulmonary constitution than I have myself," interrupted the mate.

"Well, that 's as people fancy. You must know, Mr. Mulford, they 've got all sorts of diseases nowadays, and all sorts of cures for 'em. One sort of a cure for consumption is what they tarm the Hyder-Ally—"

"I think you must mean hydropathy, sir—"

"Well it 's something of the sort, no matter what; but cold water is at the bottom of it, and they do say it 's a good remedy. Now Rose's aunt thinks if cold water is what is wanted, there is no place where it can be so plenty as out on the ocean. Sea-air is good, too, and by taking a v'y'ge, her niece will get both requisites together and cheap."

"Does Rose Budd think herself consumptive, Captain Spike?" asked Mulford, with interest.

"Not she ; you know it will never do to alarm a pulmonary, so Mrs. Budd has held her tongue carefully on the subject before the young woman. Rose fancies that her

aunt is out of sorts, and that the v'y'ge is tried on her account ; but the aunt, the cunning thing, knows all about
it.''

Mulford almost nauseated the expression of his commander's countenance while Spike uttered the last words.
At no time was that countenance very inviting, the features
being coarse and vulgar, while the color of the entire face
was of an ambiguous red, in which liquor and the seasons
would seem to be blended in very equal quantities.   Such
a countenance, lighted up by a gleam of successful management, not to say with hopes and wishes that it will hardly
do to dwell on, could not but be revolting to a youth of
Harry Mulford's generous feelings, and most of all to one
who entertained the sentiments which he was quite conscious of entertaining for Rose Budd.   The young man
made no reply, but turned his face toward the water, in
order to conceal the expression of disgust that he was
sensible must be strongly depicted on it.

The river, as the well-known arm of the sea in which
the Swash was lying is erroneously termed, was just at that
moment unusually clear of craft, and not a sail, larger than
that of a boat, was to be seen between the end of Blackwell's Island and Corlaer's Hook, a distance of about a
league. This stagnation in the movement of the port, at
that particular point, was owing to the state of wind and
tide. Of the first, there was little more than a southerly
air, while the last was about two thirds ebb. Nearly everything that was expected on that tide, coast-wise, and by
the way of the Sound, had already arrived, and nothing
could go eastward, with that light breeze and under canvas,
until the flood made. Of course it was different with the
steamers, who were paddling about like so many ducks,
steering in all directions, though mostly crossing and re-
crossing at the ferries. Just as Mulford turned away from
his commander, however, a large vessel of that class shoved
her bows into the view, doubling the Hook, and going eastward. The first glance at this vessel sufficed to drive even
Rose Budd momentarily out of the minds of both master
and mate, and to give a new current to their thoughts.

Spike had been on the point of walking up the wharf, but he now so far changed his purpose as actually to jump on board of the brig and spring up alongside of his mate, on the taffrail, in order to get a better look at the steamer. Mulford, who loathed so much in his commander, was actually glad of this, Spike's rare merit as a seaman forming a sort of attraction that held him, as it might be against his own will, bound to his service.

" What will they do next, Harry ? " exclaimed the master, his manner and voice actually humanized, in air and sound at least, by this unexpected view of something new in his calling. " What *will* they do next ? "

" I see no wheels, sir, nor any movement in the water astern, as if she were a propeller," returned the young man.

" She's an out-of-the-way sort of a hussy ! She's a man-of-war, too ; one of Uncle Sam's new efforts."

" That can hardly be, sir. Uncle Sam has but three steamers, of any size or force, now the Missouri is burned ; and yonder is one of them, lying at the Navy Yard, while another is, or was lately, laid up at Boston. The third is in the Gulf. This must be an entirely new vessel, if she belong to Uncle Sam."

" New ! She's as new as a governor, and they tell me they 've got so now that they choose five or six of *them*, up at Albany, every fall. That craft is sea-going, Mr. Mulford, as any one can tell at a glance. She's none of your passenger-hoys."

" That's plain enough, sir, and she's armed. Perhaps she's English, and they 've brought her here into this open spot to try some new machinery. Ay, ay ! she's about to set her ensign to the navy men at the yard, and we shall see to whom she belongs."

A long, low, expressive whistle from Spike succeeded this remark, the colors of the steamer going up to the end of a gaff on the sternmost of her schooner-rigged masts, just as Mulford ceased speaking. There was just air enough, aided by the steamer's motion, to open the bunting, and let the spectators see the design. There were the Stars and Stripes, as usual, but the last ran perpendicularly, instead of in a horizontal direction.

"Revenue, by George!" exclaimed the master, as soon as his breath was exhausted in the whistle. "Who would have believed they could screw themselves up to doing such a thing in that bloody service?"

"I now remember to have heard that Uncle Sam was building some large steamers for the revenue service, and, if I mistake not, with some new invention to get along with, that is neither wheel nor propeller. This must be one of these new craft, brought out here, into open water, just to try her, sir."

"You're right, sir, you're right. As to the natur' of the beast, you see her buntin', and no honest man can want more. If there's anything I *do* hate, it is that flag, with its unnat'-ral stripes, up and down, instead of running in the true old way. I *have* heard a lawyer say, that the revenue flag of this country is onconstitutional, and that a vessel carrying it on the high seas might be sent in for piracy."

Although Harry Mulford was neither Puffendorf, nor Grotius, he had too much common-sense, and too little prejudice in favor of even his own vocation, to swallow such a theory, had fifty Cherry Street lawyers sworn to its justice. A smile crossed his fine, firm-looking mouth, and something very like a reflection of that smile, if smiles *can* be reflected in one's own countenance, gleamed in his fine, large dark eye.

"It would be somewhat singular, Captain Spike," he said, "if a vessel belonging to any nation should be seized as a pirate. The fact that she is national in character would clear her."

"Then let her carry a national flag, and be d——d to her," answered Spike, fiercely. "I can show you law for what I say, Mr. Mulford. The American flag has its stripes fore and aft by law, and this chap carries his stripes parpen-dic'lar. If I commanded a cruiser, and fell in with one of these up and down gentry, blast me if I wouldn't just send him into port, and try the question in the old Almshouse."

Mulford probably did not think it worth while to argue

the point any further, understanding the dogmatism and stolidity of his commander too well to deem it necessary. He preferred to turn to the consideration of the qualities of the steamer in sight, a subject on which, as seamen, they might better sympathize.

" That 's a droll-looking revenue cutter, after all, Captain Spike," he said, " a craft better fitted to go in a fleet, as a lookout vessel, than to chase a smuggler in-shore."

" And no goer in the bargain ! I do not see how she gets along, for she keeps all snug under water ; but, unless she can travel faster than she does just now, the Molly Swash would soon lend her the Mother Cary's chickens of her own wake to amuse her."

" She has the tide against her, just here, sir ; no doubt she would do better in still water."

Spike muttered something between his teeth, and jumped down on deck, seemingly dismissing the subject of the revenue entirely from his mind. His old, coarse, authoritative manner returned, and he again spoke to his mate about Rose Budd, her aunt, the "ladies' cabin," the " young flood," and "casting off," as soon as the last made. Mulford listened respectfully, though with a manifest distaste for the instructions he was receiving. He knew his man, and a feeling of dark distrust came over him, as he listened to his orders concerning the famous accommodations he intended to give to Rose Budd and that "capital old lady, her aunt," his opinion of " the immense deal of good sea-air and a v'y'ge would do Rose," and how " comfortable they both would be on board the Molly Swash."

" I honor and respect Mrs. Budd, as my captain's lady, you see, Mr. Mulford, and intend to treat her accordin'ly. She knows it—and Rose knows it—and they both declare they 'd rather sail with *me*, since sail they must, than with any other shipmaster out of America."

" You sailed once with Captain Budd yourself, I think I have heard you say, sir ? "

" The old fellow brought me up. I was with him from my tenth to my twentieth year, and then broke adrift to see fashions. We all do that, you know, Mr. Mulford, when we are young and ambitious, and my turn came as well as another's."

"Captain Budd must have been a good deal older than his wife, sir, if *you* sailed with him when a boy," Mulford observed a little dryly.

"Yes; I own to forty-eight, though no one would think me more than five or six-and-thirty, to look at me. There was a great difference between old Dick Budd and his wife, as you say, he being about fifty, when he married, and she less than twenty. Fifty is a good age for matrimony, in a man, Mulford; as is twenty in a young woman."

"Rose Budd is not yet nineteen, I have heard her say," returned the mate with emphasis.

"Youngish, I will own, but that's a fault a liberal-minded man can overlook. Every day, too, will lessen it. Well, look to the cabins, and see all clear for a start. Josh will be down presently with a cart-load of stores, and you'll take 'em aboard without delay."

As Spike uttered this order, his foot was on the plank-sheer of the bulwarks, in the act of passing to the wharf again. On reaching the shore, he turned and looked intently at the revenue steamer, and his lips moved, as if he were secretly uttering maledictions on her. We say maledictions, as the expression of his fierce, ill-favored countenance too plainly showed that they could not be blessings. As for Mulford, there was still something on his mind, and he followed to the gangway ladder and ascended it, waiting for a moment when the mind of his commander might be less occupied to speak. The opportunity soon occurred, Spike having satisfied himself with the second look at the steamer.

"I hope you don't mean to sail again without a second mate, Captain Spike?" he said.

"I do though, I can tell you. I hate dickies; they are always in the way, and the captain has to keep just as much of a watch with one as without one."

"That will depend on his quality. You and I have both been dickies in our time, sir; and my time was not long ago."

"Ay, ay, I know all about it; but you didn't stick to

it long enough to get spoiled. I would have no man aboard the Swash who made more than two v'y'ges as second officer. As I want no spies aboard my craft, I'll try it once more without a dicky.''

Saying this in a sufficiently positive manner, Captain Stephen Spike rolled up the wharf, much as a ship goes off before the wind, now inclining to the right, and then again to the left. The gait of the man would have proclaimed him a sea-dog, to any one acquainted with that animal, as far as he could be seen. The short squab figure, the arms bent nearly at right angles at the elbow, and working like two fins with each roll of the body, the stumpy, solid legs, with the feet looking in the line of his course and kept wide apart, would all have contributed to the making up of such an opinion. Accustomed as he was to this beautiful sight, Harry Mulford kept his eyes riveted on the retiring person of his commander, until it disappeared behind a pile of lumber, waddling always in the direction of the more thickly peopled parts of the town. Then he turned and gazed at the steamer, which, by this time, had fairly passed the brig, and seemed to be actually bound through the Gate. The steamer was certainly a noble-looking craft, but our young man fancied she struggled along through the water heavily.

She might be quick at need, but she did not promise as much by her present rate of moving. Still, she was a noble-looking craft, and as Mulford descended to the deck again, he almost regretted he did not belong to her; or, at least, to anything but the Molly Swash.

Two hours produced a sensible change in and around that brigantine. Her people had all come back to duty, and what was very remarkable among seafaring folk, sober to a man. But as has been said, Spike was a temperance man, as respects all under his orders at least, if not strictly so in practice himself. The crew of the Swash was large for a half-rigged brig of only two hundred tons, but, as her spars were very square, and all her gear as well as her mould seemed constructed for speed, it was probable more hands than common were necessary to work her with facility and expedition. After all, there were not many persons

to be enumerated among the "people of the Molly Swash,"
as they called themselves ; not more than a dozen, including those aft, as well as those forward. A peculiar feature
of this crew, however, was the circumstance that they were
all middle-aged men, with the exception of the mate, and
all thorough-bred sea-dogs. Even Josh, the cabin-boy, as
he was called, was an old, wrinkled, gray-headed negro, of
near sixty. If the crew wanted a little in the elasticity of
youth, it possessed the steadiness and experience of their
time of life, every man appearing to know exactly what to
do, and when to do it. This indeed composed their great
merit ; an advantage that Spike well knew how to appre-
ciate.

The stores had been brought alongside of the brig in a
cart, and were already stowed in their places. Josh had
brushed and swept, until the ladies' cabin could be made no
neater. This ladies' cabin was a small apartment beneath
the trunk, which was, ingeniously enough, separated from
the main cabin by pantries and double doors. The arrangement was unusual, and Spike had several times hinted that
there was a history connected with that cabin ; though what
the history was Mulford never could induce him to relate.
The latter knew that the brig had been used for a forced
trade on the Spanish Main, and had heard something of her
deeds in bringing off specie, and proscribed persons, at different epochs in the revolutions of that part of the world,
and he had always understood that her present commander
and owner had sailed in her, as mate, for many years before
he had risen to his present station. Now, all was regular
in the way of records, bills of sale, and other documents,
Stephen Spike appearing in both the capacities just named.
The register proved that the brig had been built as far
back as the last English war, as a private cruiser, but recent and extensive repairs had made her "better than new,"
as her owner insisted, and there was no question as to her
sea-worthiness. It is true the insurance offices blew upon
her, and would have nothing to do with a craft that had
seen her two score years and ten ; but this gave none who
belonged to her any concern, inasmuch as they could

scarcely have been underwritten in their trade, let the age of the vessel be what it might. It was enough for them that the brig was safe and exceedingly fast, insurances never saving the lives of the people, whatever else might be their advantages. With Mulford it was an additional recommendation, that the Swash was usually thought to be of uncommonly just proportions.

By half-past two, P.M., everything was ready for getting the brigantine under way. Her fore-topsail—or fore-*taw*sail as Spike called it—was loose, the fasts were singled, and a spring had been carried to a post in the wharf, that was well forward of the starboard bow, and the brig's head turned to the southwest, or down the stream, and consequently facing the young flood. Nothing seemed to connect the vessel with the land but a broad gangway plank to which Mulford had attached life-lines, with more care than it is usual to meet with on board of vessels employed in short voyages. The men stood about the decks with their arms thrust into the bosoms of their shirts, and the whole picture was one of silent, and possibly of some-that uneasy expectation. Nothing was said, however; Mulford walking the quarter-deck alone, occasionally looking up the still little tenanted streets of that quarter of the suburbs, as if to search for a carriage. As for the revenue steamer, she had long before gone through the southern passage of Blackwell's, steering for the Gate.

"Dat's dem, Mr. Mulford," Josh at length cried from the lookout he had taken in a stern-port, where he could see over the low bulwarks of the vessel. "Yes, dat's dem, sir. I know dat old gray horse dat carries his head so low and sorrowful like, as a horse has a right to do dat has to drag a cab about this big town. My eye! what a horse it is, sir!"

Josh was right, not only as to the gray horse that carried his head "sorrowful like," but as to the cab and its contents. The vehicle was soon on the wharf, and in its door soon appeared the short, sturdy figure of Captain Spike, backing out, much as a bear descends a tree. On top of the vehicle were several light articles of female appliances, in the shape of bandboxes, bags, etc., the trunks having previously arrived in the cart. Well might that over-driven gray horse appear sorrowful, and travel with a lowered head. The cab, when it gave up its contents discovered a load of no less than four persons besides the driver, all of weight, and of dimensions in proportion, with the exception of the pretty and youthful Rose Budd. Even she was plump, and of a well-rounded person ; though still slight and slender. But her aunt was a fair picture of a shipmaster's widow ; solid, comfortable, and buxom. Neither was she old, nor ugly. On the contrary, her years did not exceed forty, and being well preserved, in consequence of never having been a mother, she might even have passed for thirty-five. The great objection to her appearance was the somewhat indefinite character of her shape, which seemed to blend too many of its charms into one. The fourth person, in the fare, was Biddy Noon, the Irish servant and *factotum* of Mrs. Budd, who was a pock-marked, red-faced, and red-armed single woman, about her mistress' own age and weight, though less stout to the eye.

Of Rose we shall not stop to say much here. Her deep-blue eye, which was equally spirited and gentle, if one can use such contradictory terms, seemed alive with interest and curiosity, running over the brig, the wharf, the arm of the sea, the two islands, and all near her, including the Almshouse, with such a devouring rapidity as might be expected in a town-bred girl, who was setting out on her travels for the first time. Let us be understood ; we say town-bred, because such was the fact ; for Rose Budd had been both born and educated in Manhattan, though we are far from wishing to be understood that she was either very well-born or highly educated. Her station in life may be inferred from that of her aunt, and her education from her station. Of the two, the last was, perhaps, a trifle the highest.

We have said that the fine blue eye of Rose passed swiftly over the various objects near her, as she alighted from the cab, and it naturally took in the form of Harry

Mulford, as he stood in the gangway, offering his arm to aid her aunt and herself in passing the brig's side. A smile of recognition was exchanged between the young people, as their eyes met, and the color, which formed so bright a charm in Rose's sweet face, deepened, in a way to prove that that color spoke with a tongue and eloquence of its own. Nor was Mulford's cheek mute on the occasion, though he helped the hesitating, half-doubting, half-bold girl along the plank with a steady hand and rigid muscles. As for the aunt, as a captain's widow, she had not felt it necessary to betray any extraordinary emotions in ascending the plank, unless, indeed, it might be those of delight on finding her foot once more on the deck of a vessel!

Something of the same feeling governed Biddy, too, for, as Mulford civilly extended his hand to her also, she exclaimed,—

"No fear of me, Mr. Mate; I came from Ireland by wather, and knows all about ships and brigs, I do. If you could have seen the times we had, and the saas we crossed, you'd not think it nadeful to say much to the likes iv me."

Spike had tact enough to understand he would be out of his element in assisting females along that plank, and he was busy in sending what he called "the old lady's dunnage" on board, and in discharging the cabman. As soon as this was done, he sprang into the main-channels, and thence *viâ* the bulwarks, on deck, ordering the plank to be hauled aboard. A solitary laborer was paid a quarter to throw off the fasts from the ring-bolts and posts, and everything was instantly in motion to cast the brig loose. Work went on as if the vessel were in haste, and it consequently went on with activity. Spike bestirred himself, giving his orders in a way to denote he had been long accustomed to exercise authority on the deck of a vessel, and knew his calling to its minutia. The only ostensible difference between his deportment to-day and on any ordinary occasion, perhaps, was in the circumstance that he now seemed anxious to get clear of the wharf, and that in a way which might have attracted notice in any suspicious and attentive observer. It is possible that such a one was not very distant, and that Spike was aware of his presence, for a respectable-looking, well-dressed, middle-aged man *had* come down one of the adjacent streets, to a spot within a hundred yards of the wharf, and stood silently watching the movements of the brig, as he leaned against a fence. The want of houses in that quarter enabled any person to see this stranger from the deck of the Swash, but no one on board her seemed to regard him at all, unless it might be the master.

"Come, bear a hand, my hearty, and toss that bow-fast clear," cried the captain, whose impatience to be off seemed to increase as the time to do so approached nearer and nearer. "Off with it, at once, and let her go."

The man on the wharf threw the turns of the hawser clear of the post, and the Swash was released forward. A smaller line, for a spring, had been run some distance along the wharves, ahead of the vessel, and brought in aft. Her people clapped on this, and gave way to their craft, which, being comparatively light, was easily moved, and was very manageable. As this was done, the distant spectator who had been leaning on the fence moved toward the wharf with a step a little quicker than common. Almost at the same instant, a short, stout, sailor-like looking little person waddled down the nearest street, seeming to be in somewhat of a hurry, and presently he joined the other stranger and appeared to enter into conversation with him ; pointing toward the Swash as he did so. All this time, both continued to advance toward the wharf.

In the meanwhile, Spike and his people were not idle. The tide did not run very strong near the wharves and in the sort of a bight in which the vessel had lain ; but, such as it was, it soon took the brig on her inner bow, and began to cast her head off shore. The people at the spring pulled away with all their force, and got sufficient motion on their vessel to overcome the tide, and to give the rudder an influence. The latter was put hard a-starboard, and helped to cast the brig's head to the southward.

Down to this moment, the only sail that was loose on

board the Swash was the fore-topsail, as mentioned. This still hung in the gear, but a hand had been sent aloft to overhaul the buntlines and clewlines, and men were also at the sheets. In a minute the sail was ready for hoisting. The Swash carried a whapper of a fore-and-aft mainsail, and, what is more, it was fitted with a standing gaff, for appearance in port. At sea, Spike knew better than to trust to this arrangement; but in fine weather, and close in with the land, he found it convenient to have this sail haul out and brail like a ship's spanker. As the gaff was now aloft, it was only necessary to let go the brails to loosen this broad sheet of canvas, and to clap on the outhauler, to set it. This was probably the reason why the brig was so unceremoniously cast into the stream, without showing more of her cloth. The jib and flying-jibs, however, did at that moment drop beneath their booms, ready for hoisting.

Such was the state of things as the two strangers came first upon the wharf. Spike was on the taffrail, overhauling the main-sheet, and Mulford was near him, casting the fore-topsail braces from the pins, preparatory to clapping on the halyards.

"I say, Mr. Mulford," asked the captain, "did you ever see either of them chaps afore? These jokers on the wharf, I mean."

"Not to my recollection, sir," answered the mate, looking over the taffrail to examine the parties. "The little one is a burster! The funniest-looking little fat old fellow, I 've seen in many a day."

"Ay, ay, them fat little bursters, as you call 'em, are sometimes full of the devil. I don't like either of the chaps, and am right glad we are well cast, before they got here."

"I do not think either would be likely to do us much harm, Captain Spike."

"There 's no knowing, sir. The biggest fellow looks as if he might lug out a silver oar at any moment."

"I believe the silver oar is no longer used, in this country at least," answered Mulford, smiling. "And if it were, what have we to fear from it? I fancy the brig has paid her reckoning."

"She don't owe a cent, nor ever shall for twenty-four hours after the bill is made out, while I own *her*. They call me ready-money Stephen, round among the ship-chandlers and caulkers. But I don't like them chaps, and what I don't relish I never swallow, you know."

"They'll hardly try to get aboard us, sir; you see we are quite clear of the wharf, and the mainsail will take now, if we set it."

Spike ordered the mate to clap on the outhauler, and spread that broad sheet of canvas at once to the little breeze there was. This was almost immediately done, when the sail filled, and began to be felt on the movement of the vessel. Still, that movement was very slow, the wind being so light, and the *vis inertiæ* of so large a body remaining to be overcome. The brig receded from the wharf, almost in a line at right angles to its face, inch by inch, as it might be, dropping slowly up with the tide at the same time. Mulford now passed forward to set the jibs, and to get the topsail on the craft, leaving Spike on the taffrail, keenly eying the strangers, who, by this time, had got down nearly to the end of the wharf, at the berth so lately occupied by the Swash. That the captain was uneasy was evident enough, that feeling being exhibited in his countenance, blended with a malignant ferocity.

"Has that brig any pilot?" asked the larger and better-looking of the two strangers.

"What's that to you, friend?" demanded Spike, in return. "Have you a Hell-Gate branch?"

"I may have one, or I may not. It is not usual for so large a craft to run the Gate without a pilot."

"Oh! my gentleman's below, brushing up his logarithms. We shall have him on deck to take his departure before long, when I'll let him know your kind inquiries after his health."

The man on the wharf seemed to be familiar with this sort of sea-wit, and he made no answer, but continued that close scrutiny of the brig, by turning his eyes in all directions, now looking below, and now aloft, which had in truth occasioned Spike's principal cause for uneasiness.

"Is not that Captain Stephen Spike, of the brigantine Molly Swash?" called out the little, dumpling-looking person, in a cracked, dwarfish sort of a voice, that was admirably adapted to his appearance. Our captain fairly started; turned full toward the speaker; regarded him intently for a moment; and gulped the words he was about to utter, like one confounded. As he gazed, however, at little dumpy, examining his bow-legs, red broad cheeks, and coarse snub nose, he seemed to regain his self-command, as if satisfied the dead had not really returned to life.

"Are you acquainted with the gentleman you have named?" he asked, by way of answer. "You speak of him like one who ought to know him."

"A body is apt to know a shipmate. Stephen Spike and I sailed together twenty years since, and I hope to live to sail with him again."

"*You* sail with Stephen Spike? when and where, may I ask, and in what v'y'ge, pray?"

"The last time was twenty years since. Have you forgotten little Jack Tier, Captain Spike?"

Spike looked astonished, and well he might, for he had supposed Jack to be dead fully fifteen years. Time and hard service had greatly altered him, but the general resemblance in figure, stature, and waddle, certainly remained. Notwithstanding, the Jack Tier that Spike remembered was quite a different person from this Jack Tier. That Jack had worn his intensely black hair clubbed and curled, whereas this Jack had cut his locks into short bristles, which time had turned into an intense gray. That Jack was short and thick, but he was flat and square; whereas this Jack was just as short, a good deal thicker, and as round as a dumpling. In one thing, however, the likeness still remained perfect. Both Jacks chewed tobacco, to a degree that became a distinct feature in their appearance.

Spike had many reasons for wishing Jack Tier were not resuscitated in this extraordinary manner, and some for being glad to see him. The fellow had once been largely in his confidence, and knew more than was quite safe for any one to remember but himself, while he might be of great use to him in his future operations. It is always convenient to have one at your elbow who thoroughly understands you, and Spike would have lowered a boat and sent it to the wharf to bring Jack off, were it not for the gentleman who was so inquisitive about pilots. Under the circumstances, he determined to forego the advantages of Jack's presence, reserving the right to hunt him up on his return.

The reader will readily enough comprehend, that the Molly Swash was not absolutely standing still while the dialogue related was going on, and the thoughts we have recorded were passing through her master's mind. On the contrary, she was not only in motion, but that motion was gradually increasing, and by the time all was said that has been related, it had become necessary for those who spoke to raise their voices to an inconvenient pitch in order to be heard. This circumstance alone would soon have put an end to the conversation, had not Spike's pausing to reflect brought about the same result, as mentioned.

In the meantime, Mulford had got the canvas spread. Forward, the Swash showed all the cloth of a full-rigged brig, even to royals and flying jib; while aft, her mast was the raking, tall, naked pole of an American schooner. There was a taunt topmast, too, to which a gaff-topsail was set, and the gear proved that she could also show, at need, a staysail in this part of her, if necessary. As the Gate was before them, however, the people had set none but the plain, manageable canvas.

The Molly Swash kept close on a wind, luffing athwart the broad reach she was in, until far enough to weather Blackwell's when she edged off to her course, and went through the southern passage. Although the wind remained light, and a little baffling, the brig was so easily impelled, and was so very handy, that there was no difficulty in keeping her perfectly in command. The tide, too, was fast increasing in strength and velocity, and the movement from this cause alone was getting to be sufficiently rapid.

As for the passengers, of whom we have lost sight in order to get the brig under way, they were now on deck again. At first, they had all gone below, under the care of Josh, a somewhat rough groom of the chambers, to take possession of their apartment, a sufficiently neat, and exceedingly comfortable cabin, supplied with everything that could be wanted at sea, and what was more, lined on two of its sides with state-rooms. It is true, all these apartments were small, and the state-rooms were very low, but no fault could be found with their neatness and general arrangements, when it was recollected that one was on board a vessel.

"Here ebberyt'ing heart can wish," said Josh, exultingly, who, being an old-school black, did not disdain to use some of the old-school dialect of his caste. "Yes, ladies, ebberyt'ing. Let Cap'n Spike alone for dat! He won'erful at accommodation! Not a bed-bug aft—know better dan come here; jest like de people in dat respects, and keep deir place forrard. You nebber see a pig come on de quarter-deck, nudder."

"You must maintain excellent discipline, Josh," cried Rose, in one of the sweetest voices in the world, which was easily attuned to merriment, "and we are delighted to learn what you tell us. How do you manage to keep up these distinctions, and make such creatures know their places so well?"

"Nuttin easier, if you begin right, miss. As for de pig, I teach dem wid scaldin' water. Wheneber I sees a pig come aft, I gets a little water from de copper, and just scald him wid it. You can't t'ink, miss, how dat mend his manners, and make him squeal fuss, and t'ink arter. In dat fashion I soon get de old ones in good trainin', and den I has no more trouble with dem as comes fresh aboard; for de old hog tell de young one, and 'em won'erful cunnin', and know how to take care of 'emself."

Rose Budd's sweet eyes were full of fun and expectation, and she could no more repress her laugh than youth and spirits can always be discreet.

"Yes, with the pigs," she cried, "that might do very well; but how is it with those—other creatures?"

"Rosy, dear," interrupted the aunt, "I wish you would

say no more about such shocking things. It's enough for
us that Captain Spike has ordered them all to stay forward
among the men, which is always done on board well dis-
ciplined vessels. I've heard your uncle say a hundred
times, that the quarter-deck was sacred, and that might be
enough to keep such animals off it.''

It was barely necessary to look at Mrs. Budd in the face
to get a very accurate general notion of her character.
She was one of those inane, uncultivated beings who seem
to be protected by a benevolent Providence in their pilgrimage on earth, for they do not seem to possess the power
to protect themselves. Her very countenance expressed
imbecility and mental dependence, credulity and a love of
gossip. Notwithstanding these radical weaknesses, the good
woman had some of the better instincts of her sex, and
was never guilty of anything that could properly convey
reproach.

She was no monitress for Rose, however, the niece much
oftener influencing the aunt, than the aunt influencing the
niece. The latter had been fortunate in having had an
excellent instructress, who, though incapable of teaching
her much in the way of accomplishments, had imparted a
great deal that was respectable and useful. Rose had
character, and strong character, too, as the course of our
narrative will show ; but her worthy aunt was a pure picture of as much mental imbecility as at all comported with
the privileges of self-government.

The conversation about "those other creatures" was
effectually checked by Mrs. Budd's horror of the "animals," and Josh was called on deck so shortly after as to
prevent its being renewed. The females stayed below a
few minutes, to take possession, and then they reappeared
on deck, to gaze at the horrors of the Hell-Gate passage.
Rose was all eyes, wonder and admiration of everything
she saw. This was actually the first time she had ever
been on the water, in any sort of craft, though born and
brought up in sight of one of the most thronged havens in
the world. But there must be a beginning to everything,
and this was Rose Budd's beginning on the water. It is

true the brigantine was a very beautiful, as well as an exceedingly swift vessel ; but all this was lost on Rose, who
would have admired a horse-jockey bound to the West
Indies, in this the incipient state of her nautical knowledge.
Perhaps the exquisite neatness that Mulford maintained
about everything that came under his care, and that included everything on deck, or above-aboard, and about which
neatness Spike occasionally muttered an oath, as so much
senseless trouble, contributed somewhat to Rose's pleasure ;
but her admiration would scarcely have been less with anything that had sails, and seemed to move through the water
with a power approaching that of volition.

It was very different with Mrs. Budd. She, good woman,
had actually made one voyage with her late husband, and
she fancied that she knew all about a vessel. It was her
delight to talk on nautical subjects, and never did she really
feel her great superiority over her niece so very unequi-
vocally, as when the subject of the ocean was introduced,
about which she did know something, and touching which
Rose was profoundly ignorant, or as ignorant as a girl
of lively imagination could remain with the information
gleaned from others.

"I am not surprised you are astonished at the sight of
the vessel, Rosy," observed the self-complacent aunt at one
of her niece's exclamations of admiration. "A vessel is a
very wonderful thing, and we are told what extr'orny beings
they are that 'go down to the sea in ships.' But you are to
know this is not a ship at all, but only a half-jigger rigged
which is altogether a different thing."

"Was my uncle's vessel, the Rose in Bloom, then, very
different from the Swash ?"

"Very different indeed, child ! Why, the Rose in Bloom
was a full-jiggered ship, and had twelve masts ; and this is
only a half-jiggered brig, and has but two masts. See, you
may count them—one—two !"

Harry Mulford was coiling away a top-gallant-brace,
directly in front of Mrs. Budd and Rose, and at hearing
this account of the wonderful equipment of the Rose in
Bloom, he suddenly looked up, with a lurking expression

about his eye that the niece very well comprehended, while he exclaimed, without much reflection, under the impulse of surprise,—

"Twelve masts! Did I understand you to say, ma'am, that Captain Budd's ship had twelve masts?"

"Yes, sir, *twelve!* and I can tell you all their names, for I learnt them by heart—it appearing to me proper that a shipmaster's wife should know the names of all the masts in her husband's vessel. Do you wish to hear their names, Mr. Mulford?"

Harry Mulford would have enjoyed this conversation to the top of his bent, had it not been for Rose. She well knew her aunt's general weakness of intellect, and especially its weakness on this particular subject, but she would suffer no one to manifest contempt for either, if in her power to prevent it. It is seldom one so young, so mirthful, so ingenuous and innocent in the expression of her countenance, assumes so significant and rebuking a frown as did pretty Rose Budd when she heard the mate's involuntary exclamation about the "twelve masts." Harry, who was not easily checked by his equals, or any of his own sex, submitted to that rebuking frown with the meekness of a child, and stammered out, in answer to the well-meaning, but weak-minded widow's question,—

"If you please, Mrs. Budd—just as you please, ma'am; only twelve is a good many masts"—Rose frowned again— "that is, more than I 'm used to seeing—that 's all."

"I dare say, Mr. Mulford, for you sail in only a half-jigger; but Captain Budd always sailed in a full-jigger, and *his* full-jiggered ship had just twelve masts; and, to prove it to you, I 'll give you the names: first, then, there were the fore, main, and mizzen masts—"

"Yes, yes, ma'am," stammered Harry, who wished the twelve masts and the Rose in Bloom at the bottom of the ocean, since her owner's niece still continued to look coldly displeased; "that 's right, I can swear!"

"Very true, sir, and you 'll find I am right as to all the rest. Then, there were the fore, main, and mizzen top-masts—they make six, if I can count, Mr. Mulford?"

"Ah!" exclaimed the mate, laughing in spite of Rose's frowns, as the manner in which the old sea-dog had quizzed his wife became apparent to him. "I see how it is; you are quite right, ma'am; I dare say the Rose in Bloom had all these masts, and some to spare."

"Yes, sir; I knew you would be satisfied. The fore, main, and mizzen top-gallant masts make nine; and the fore, main, and mizzen royals make just twelve. Oh, I'm never wrong in anything about a vessel, especially if she is a full-jiggered ship."

Mulford had some difficulty in restraining his smiles each time the full-jigger was mentioned, but Rose's expression of countenance kept him in excellent order; and she, innocent creature, saw nothing ridiculous in the term, though the twelve masts had given her a little alarm. Delighted that the old lady had got through her enumeration of the spars with so much success, Rose cried, in the exuberance of her spirits,—

"Well, aunty, for my part, I find a half-jigger vessel so very, very beautiful, that I do not know how I should behave were I to go on board a *full*-jigger."

Mulford turned abruptly away, the circumstance of Rose's making herself ridiculous giving him sudden pain, though he could have laughed at her aunt by the hour.

"Ah, my dear, that is on account of your youth and inexperience; but you will learn better in time. I was just so myself, when I was of your age, and thought the fore-rafters were as handsome as the squared-jiggers, but soon after I married Captain Budd I felt the necessity of knowing more than I did about ships, and I got him to teach me. He did n't like the business, at first, and pretended I would never learn; but, at last, it came all at once like, and then he used to be delighted to hear me 'talk ship,' as he called it. I 've known him laugh, with his cronies, as if ready to die, at my expertness in sea-terms, for half an hour together; and then he would swear—that was the worst fault your uncle had, Rosy—he *would* swear, sometimes, in a way that frightened me, I do declare!"

"But he never swore at you, aunty?"

"I can't say that he did exactly do that, but he would swear all round me, even if he did n't actually touch me, when things went wrong ; but it would have done your heart good to hear him laugh ! he had a most excellent heart, just like your own, Rosy dear ; but, for that matter, all the Budds have excellent hearts, and one of the commonest ways your uncle had of showing it was to laugh, particularly when we were together and talking. Oh, he used to delight in hearing me converse, especially about vessels, and never failed to get me at it when he had company. I see his good-natured, excellent-hearted countenance at this moment, with the tears running down his fat, manly cheeks as he shook his very sides with laughter. I may live a hundred years, Rosy, before I meet again with your uncle's equal."

This was a subject that invariably silenced Rose. She remembered her uncle, herself, and remembered his affectionate manner of laughing at her aunt, and she always wished the latter to get through her eulogiums on her married happiness, as soon as possible, whenever the subject was introduced.

All this time the Molly Swash kept in motion. Spike never took a pilot when he could avoid it, and his mind was too much occupied with his duty, in that critical navigation, to share at all in the conversation of his passengers, though he did endeavor to make himself agreeable to Rose by an occasional remark, when a favorable opportunity offered.

As soon as he had worked his brig over into the south or weather passage of Blackwell's, however, there remained little for him to do, until she had drifted through it, a distance of a mile or more ; and this gave him leisure to do the honors. He pointed out the castellated edifice on Blackwell's as the new penitentiary, and the hamlet of villas, on the other shore, as Ravenswood, though there is neither wood nor ravens to authorize the name. But the "Sunswick," which satisfied the Delafields and Gibbses of the olden time, and which distinguished their lofty halls and broad lawns, was not elegant enough for the cockney tastes of these latter days, so " wood " must be made to usurp the place of cherries and apples, and " ravens " that of gulls, in order to satisfy its cravings. But all this was lost on Spike. He remembered the shore as it had been twenty years before, and he saw what it was now, but little did he care for the change. On the whole, he rather preferred the Grecian Temples, over which the ravens would have been compelled to fly, had there been any ravens in that neighborhood, to the old-fashioned and highly respectable residence that once alone occupied the spot. The point he did understand, however, and on the merits of which he had something to say, was a little farther ahead. That, too, had been re-christened—the Hallet's Cove of the mariner being converted into Astoria—not that bloody-minded place at the mouth of the Oregon, which has come so near bringing us to blows with our " ancestors in England," as the worthy denizens of that quarter choose to consider themselves still, if one can judge by their language. This Astoria was a very different place, and is one of the many suburban villages that are shooting up, like mushrooms in a night, around the great commercial emporium. This spot Spike understood perfectly, and it was not likely that he should pass it without communicating a portion of his knowledge to Rose.

" There, Miss Rose," he said, with a didactic sort of air, pointing with his short, thick finger at the little bay which was just opening to their view ; " there 's as neat a cove as a craft need bring up in. That *used to be* a capital place to lie in, to wait for a wind to pass the Gate ; but it has got to be most too public for my taste. I 'm rural, I tell Mulford, and love to get in out-of-the-way berths with my brig, where she can see salt-meadows, and smell the clover. You never catch me down in any of the crowded slips, around the markets, or anywhere in that part of the town, for I *do* love country air. That 's Hallet's Cove, Miss Rose, and a pretty anchorage it would be for us, if the wind and tide did n't sarve to take us through the Gate."

" Are we near the Gate, Captain Spike ? " asked Rose, the fine bloom on her cheek lessening a little, under the apprehension that formidable name is apt to awaken in the breasts of the inexperienced.

"Half a mile, or so. It begins just at the other end of this island on our larboard hand, and will be all over in about another half mile, or so. It 's no such bad place, a'ter all, is Hell-Gate, to them that 's used to it. I call myself a pilot in Hell-Gate, though I *have* no branch."

"I wish, Captain Spike, I could teach you to give that place its proper and polite name. We call it Whirl-Gate altogether now," said the relict.

"Well, that 's new to me," cried Spike. "I *have* heard some chicken-mouthed folk say *Hurl*-Gate, but this is the first time I ever heard it called Whirl-Gate; they 'll get it to Whirligig-Gate next. I don't think that my old commander, Captain Budd, called the passage anything but honest up and down Hell-Gate."

"That he did—that he did; and all my arguments and reading could not teach him any better. I proved to him that it was Whirl-Gate, as any one can see that it ought to be. It is full of whirlpools, they say, and that shows what Nature meant the name to be."

"But, aunty," put in Rose, half reluctantly, half anxious to speak, "what has *gate* to do with whirlpools? You will remember it is called a gate—the gate to that wicked place, I suppose is meant."

"Rose, you amaze me! How can *you*, a young woman of only nineteen, stand up for so vulgar a name as Hell-Gate!"

"Do you think it as vulgar as Hurl-Gate, aunty?" To me it always seems the most vulgar to be straining at gnats."

"Yes," said Spike, sentimentally, "I 'm quite of Miss Rose's way of thinking—straining at gnats is very ill-manners, especially at table. I once knew a man who strained in this way, until I thought he would have choked, though it was with a fly to be sure; but gnats are nothing but small flies, you know, Miss Rose. Yes, I 'm quite of your way of thinking, Miss Rose; it *is* very vulgar to be straining at gnats and flies, more particularly at table. But you 'll find no flies or gnats aboard here, to be strain-

ing at, or brushing away, or to annoy you, Stand by
there, my hearties, and see all clear to run through Hell-
Gate. Don't let me catch *you* straining at anything
though it should be the fin of a whale!"

The people forward looked at each other, as they listened to this novel admonition, though they called out the
customary "Ay, ay, sir," as they went to the sheets,
braces, and bowlines. To them the passage of no Hell-
Gate conveyed the idea of any particular terror, and with
the one they were about to enter, they were much too familiar
to care anything about it.

The brig was now floating fast, with the tide, up abreast
of the east end of Blackwell's and in two or three more
minutes she would be fairly in the Gate. Spike was aft,
where he could command a view of everything forward,
and Mulford stood on the quarter-deck, to look after the
head-braces. An old and trustworthy seaman, who acted
as a sort of boatswain, had the charge on the forecastle,
and was to tend the sheets and tack. His name was Rove.

"See all clear," called out Spike. "D'ye hear there
for'ard! I shall make a half-board in the Gate, if the
wind favor us, and the tide prove strong enough to hawse
us to wind'ard sufficiently to clear the Pot—so mind
your—"

The captain breaking off in the middle of this harangue,
Mulford turned his head, in order to see what might be
the matter. There was Spike, levelling a spy-glass at a
boat that was pulling swiftly out of the north channel, and
shooting like an arrow directly athwart the brig's bows into
the main passage of the Gate. He stepped to the captain's
elbow.

"Just take a look at them chaps, Mr. Mulford," said
Spike, handing his mate the glass.

"They seem in a hurry," answered Harry, as he adjusted the glass to his eye, "and will go through the Gate
in less time than it will take to mention the circumstance."

"What do you make of them, sir?"

"The little man who called himself Jack Tier is in the
stern-sheets of the boat, for one," answered Mulford.

"And the other, Harry, what do you make of the other?"

"It seems to be the chap who hailed to know if we had a pilot. He means to board us at Riker's Island, and make us pay pilotage, whether we want his services or not."

"Blast him and his pilotage too! Give me the glass"— taking another long look at the boat, which by this time was glancing, rather than pulling, nearly at right angles across his bows. "I want no such pilot aboard here, Mr. Mulford. Take another look at him; here, you can see him, away on our weather bow, already."

Mulford did take another look at him, and this time his examination was longer and more scrutinizing than before.

"It is not easy to cover him with the glass," observed the young man; "the boat seems fairly to fly."

"We're forereaching too near the Hog's Back, Captain Spike," roared the boatswain, from forward.

"Ready about—hard a lee," shouted Spike. "Let all fly, for'ard; help her round, boys, all you can, and wait for no orders! Bestir yourselves—bestir yourselves!"

It was time the crew should be in earnest. While Spike's attention had been thus diverted by the boat, the brig had got into the strongest of the current, which, by setting her fast to windward, had trebled the power of the air, and this was shooting her over toward one of the greatest dangers of the passage on a flood tide. As everybody bestirred themselves, however, she was got round and filled on the opposite tack, just in time to clear the rocks. Spike breathed again, but his head was still full of the boat. The danger he had just escaped as Scylla met him as Charybdis. The boatswain again roared to go about. The order was given as the vessel began to pitch in a heavy swell. At the next instant she rolled until the water came on deck, whirled with her stern down the tide, and her bows rose as if she were about to leap out of water. The Swash had hit the Pot Rock.

CHAPTER II.

"*Watch*. If we know him to be a thief, shall we not lay hands on him?

Dogb. Truly, by your office, you may; but I think they that touch pitch will be defiled; the most peaceable way for you, if you do take a thief, is, to let him show himself what he is, and steal out of your company."

Much Ado About Nothing.

WE left the brigantine of Captain Spike in a very critical situation, and the master himself in great confusion of mind.

A thorough seaman, this accident would never have happened, but for the sudden appearance of the boat and its passengers,—one of whom appeared to be a source of great uneasiness to him. As might be expected, the circumstance of striking a place as dangerous as the Pot Rock in Hell-Gate, produced a great sensation on board the vessel. This sensation betrayed itself in various ways, and according to the characters, habits, and native firmness of the parties. As for the shipmaster's relict, she seized hold of the main-mast, and screamed so loud and perseveringly, as to cause the sensation to extend itself into the adjacent and thriving village of Astoria, where it was distinctly heard by divers of those who dwelt near the water. Biddy Noon had her share in this clamor, lying down on the deck in order to prevent rolling over, and possibly to scream more at her leisure, while Rose had sufficient self-command to be silent, though her cheeks lost their color.

Nor was there anything extraordinary in females betraying this alarm, when one remembers the somewhat astound-

ing signs of danger by which these persons were surrounded.
There is always something imposing in the swift movement
of a considerable body of water. When this movement is
aided by whirlpools and the other similar accessories of an
interrupted current, it frequently becomes startling, more
especially to those who happen to be on the element itself.
This is peculiarly the case with the Pot Rock, where, not
only does the water roll and roar as if agitated by a mighty
wind, but where it even breaks, the foam seeming to glance
up stream, in the rapid succession of wave to wave. Had
the Swash remained in her terrific berth more than a second
or two, she would have proved what is termed a " total
loss " ; but she did not. Happily, the Pot Rock lies so low
that it is not apt to fetch up anything of a light draught of
water, and the brigantine's fore-foot had just settled on its
summit, long enough to cause the vessel to whirl round and
make her obeisance to the place, when a succeeding swell
lifted her clear, and away she went down stream, rolling as
if scudding in a gale, and, for a moment, under no command
whatever. There lay another danger ahead, or it would be
better to say astern, for the brig was drifting stern foremost,
and that was in an eddy under a bluff, which bluff lies at an
angle in the reach, where it is no uncommon thing for craft
to be cast ashore, after they have passed all the more imposing and more visible dangers above. It was in escaping this
danger, and in recovering the command of his vessel, that
Spike now manifested the sort of stuff of which he was
really made, in emergencies of this sort. The yards were
all sharp up when the accident occurred, and springing to
the lee braces, just as a man winks when his eye is menaced,
he seized the weather fore-brace with his own hands, and
began to round in the yard, shouting out to the man at the
wheel to " port his helm " at the same time. Some of the
people flew to his assistance, and the yards were not only
squared, but braced a little up on the other tack, in much
less time than we have taken to relate the evolution. Mulford attended to the main-sheet, and succeeded in getting the
boom out in the right direction. Although the wind was in
truth very light, the velocity of the drift filled the canvas,

and taking the arrow-like current on her lee bow, the Swash, like a frantic steed that is alarmed with the wreck made by his own madness, came under command, and sheered out into the stream again, where she could drift clear of the apprehended danger astern.

"Sound the pumps!" called out Spike to Mulford, the instant he saw he had regained his seat in the saddle. Harry sprang amidships to obey, and the eye of every mariner in that vessel was on the young man, as, in the midst of a death-like silence, he performed this all-important duty. It was like the physician's feeling the pulse of his patient before he pronounces on the degree of his danger.

"Well, sir?" cried out Spike impatiently, as the rod reappeared.

"All right, sir," answered Harry, cheerfully, "the well is nearly empty."

"Hold on a moment longer, and give the water time to find its way amidships, if there be any."

The mate remained perched up on the pump, in order to comply, while Spike and his people, who now breathed more freely again, improved the leisure to brace up and haul aft, to the new course.

"Biddy," said Mrs. Budd considerately, during this pause in the incidents, "you need n't scream any longer. The danger seems to be past, and you may get up off the deck now. See, I have let go of the mast. The pumps have been sounded, and are found tight."

Biddy, like an obedient and respectful servant, did as directed, quite satisfied if the pumps were tight. It was some little time, to be sure, before she was perfectly certain whether she were alive or not—but, once certain of this circumstance, her alarm very sensibly abated, and she became reasonable. As for Mulford, he dropped the sounding rod again, and had the same cheering report to make.

"The brig is as tight as a bottle, sir."

"So much the better," answered Spike. "I never had such a whirl in her before in my life, and I thought she was

going to stop and pass the night there. That's the very
spot on which the Hussar frigate was wrecked.''

"So I have heard, sir. But she drew so much water
that she hit slap against the rock, and started a butt. We
merely touched on its top with our fore-foot and slid
off.''

This was the simple explanation of the Swash's escape,
and, everybody being now well assured that no harm had
been done, things fell into their old and regular train again.
As for Spike, his gallantry, notwithstanding, was upset for
some hours, and glad enough was he when he saw all three
of his passengers quit the deck to go below. Mrs. Budd's
spirits had been so much agitated that she told Rose she
would go down into the cabin and rest a few minutes on its
sofa. We say sofa, for that article of furniture, nowadays, is far more common in vessels than it was thirty years
ago in the dwellings of the country.

"There, Mulford,'' growled Spike, pointing ahead of the
brig, to an object on the water that was about half a mile
ahead of them, ''there's that bloody boat—d'ye see? I
should like of all things to give it the slip. There's a chap
in that boat I don't like.''

"I don't see how that can be very well done, sir, unless
we anchor, repass the Gate at the turn of the tide, and go to
sea by the way of Sandy Hook.''

"That will never do. I've no wish to be parading the
brig before the town. You see, Mulford, nothing can be
more innocent and proper than the Molly Swash, as you
know from having sailed in her these twelve months.
You'll give her that character, I'll be sworn?''

"I know no harm of her, Captain Spike, and hope I
never shall.''

"No, sir; you know no harm of her, nor does any one
else. A nursing infant is not more innocent than the
Molly Swash, or could have a clearer character if nothing
but truth was said of her. But the world is so much
given to lying, that one of the old saints, of whom we
read in the good book, such as Calvin and John Rogers,
would be vilified if he lived in these times. Then, it must

be owned, Mr. Mulford, whatever may be the raal innocence
of the brig, she has a most desperate wicked look.''

"Why, yes, sir ; it must be owned she is what we sailors
call a wicked-looking craft. But some of Uncle Sam's
cruisers have that appearance also.''

"I know it—I know it, sir, and think nothing of looks
myself. Men are often deceived in me, by *my* looks,
which have none of your long-shore softness about 'em,
perhaps; but my mother used to say I was one of the
most tender-hearted boys she had ever heard spoken of—
like one of the babes in the woods, as it might be. But
mankind go so much by appearances that I don't like to
trust the brig too much afore their eyes. Now, should we
be seen in the lower bay, waiting for a wind, or for the
ebb tide to make, to carry us over the bar, ten to one but
some philotropic or other would be off with a complaint to
the district attorney that we looked like a slaver, and have
us all fetched up to be tried for our lives as pirates. No,
no—I like to keep the brig in out-of-the-way places, where
she can give no offence to your 'tropics, whether they be
philos, or of any other sort.''

"Well, sir, we are to the eastward of the Gate, and all's
safe. That boat cannot bring us up.''

"You forget, Mr. Mulford, the revenue craft that
steamed up, on the ebb. That vessel must be off Sands'
Point by this time, and *she* may hear something to our dis-
paragement from the feller in the boat, and take it into
her smoky head to walk us back to town. I wish we were
well to the eastward of that steamer ! But there's no use
in lamentations. If there is really any danger, it's some
distance ahead yet, thank Heaven !''

"You have no fears of the man who calls himself Jack
Tier, Captain Spike?''

"None in the world. That feller, as I remember him,
was a little bustlin' chap that I kept in the cabin, as a sort
of steward's mate. There was neither good nor harm in
him, to the best of my recollection. But Josh can tell us
all about him—just give Josh a call.''

The best thing in the known history of Spike was the

fact that his steward had sailed with him for more than twenty years. Where he had picked up Josh no one could say, but Josh and himself, and neither chose to be very communicative on the subject. But Josh had certainly been with him as long as he had sailed the Swash, and that was from a time actually anterior to the birth of Mulford. The mate soon had the negro in the council.

"I say, Josh," asked Spike, "do you happen to remember such a hand aboard here as one Jack Tier?"

"Lor' bless you, yes, sir—'members he as well as I do the pea soup that was burnt, and which you t'rowed all over him, to scald him for punishment."

"I've had to do that so often, to one careless fellow or other, that the circumstance does n't recall the man. I remember him—but not as clear as I could wish. How long did he sail with us?"

"Sebberal v'y'ge, sir, and got left ashore down on the main, one night, when 'e boat were obliged to shove off in a hurry. Yes, 'members little Jack, right well I does."

"Did you see the man that spoke us from the wharf, and hailed for this very Jack Tier?"

"I see'd a man, sir, dat was won'erful Jack Tier built like, sir, but I did n't hear the conwersation, habbin' the ladies to 'tend to. But Jack was oncommon short in his floor timbers, sir, and had no length of keel at all. His beam was won'erful for his length, altogedder—what you call jolly-boat, or bum-boat build, and was only good afore 'e wind, Cap'n Spike."

"Was he good for anything aboard ship, Josh? Worth heaving-to for, should he try to get aboard of us again?"

"Why, sir, can't say much for him in dat fashion. Jack *was* handy in the cabin, and capital feller to carry soup from the gally, aft. You see, sir, he was so low-rigged that the brig's lurchin' and pitchin' could n't get him off his pins and he stood up like a church in the heaviest wea'der. Yes, sir, Jack was right good for *dat*."

Spike mused a moment—then he rolled the tobacco over in his mouth, and added, in the way a man speaks when his mind is made up,—

"Ay, ay! I see into the fellow. He'll make a handy lady's maid, and we want such a chap just now. It's better to have an old friend aboard, than to be pickin' up strangers, 'long shore. So, should this Jack Tier come off to us, from any of the islands or points ahead, Mr. Mulford, you'll round to and take him aboard. As for the steamer, if she will only pass out into the Sound where there's room, it shall go hard with us but I get to the eastward of her, without speaking. On the other hand, should she anchor this side of the fort, I'll not attempt to pass her. There is deep water inside most of the islands, I know, and we'll try and dodge her in that way, if no better offer. I've no more reason than another craft to fear a government vessel, but the sight of one of them makes me oncomfortable; that's all."

Mulford shrugged his shoulders and remained silent, perceiving that his commander was not disposed to pursue the subject any further. In the meantime, the brig had passed beyond the influence of the bluff, and was beginning to feel a stronger breeze, that was coming down the wide opening of Flushing Bay. As the tide still continued strong in her favor, and her motion through the water was getting to be four or five knots, there was every prospect of her soon reaching Whitestone, the point where the tides meet, and where it would become necessary to anchor; unless, indeed, the wind, which was now getting to the southward and eastward, should come round to the south. All this Spike and his mate discussed together, while the people were clearing the decks, and making the preparations that are customary on board a vessel before she gets into rough water.

By this time it was ascertained that the brig had received no damage by her salute of the Pot Rock, and every trace of uneasiness on that account was removed. But Spike kept harping on the boat, and "the pilot-looking chap who was in her." As they passed Riker's Island, all hands expected a boat would put off with a pilot, or to demand pilotage; but none came, and the Swash now seemed released from all her present dangers, unless some might still be connected with the revenue steamer. To retard her advance, however, the wind came out a smart working breeze from the southward and eastward, compelling her to make "long legs and short ones" on her way towards White-stone.

"This is beating the wind, Rosy dear," said Mrs. Budd, complacently, she and her niece having returned to the deck a few minutes after this change had taken place. "Your respected uncle did a great deal of this in his time, and was very successful in it. I have heard him say, that in one of his voyages between Liverpool and New York, he beat the wind by a whole fortnight, everybody talking of it in the insurance offices, as if it was a miracle."

"Ay, ay, Madam Budd," put in Spike, "I'll answer for that. They're desperate talkers in and about them there insurance offices in Wall Street. Great gossips be they, and they think they know everything. Now just because this brig is a little old or so, and was built for a privateer in the last war, they'd refuse to rate her as even B, No. 2, and my blessing on 'em."

"Yes, B, No. 2, that's just what your dear uncle used to call me, Rosy—his charming B, No. 2, or Betsy, No. 2 ; particularly when he was in loving mood. Captain Spike, did you ever beat the wind in a long voyage?"

"I can't say I ever did, Mrs. Budd," answered Spike, looking grimly around, to ascertain if any one dared to smile at his passenger's mistake ; "especially for so long a pull as from New York to Liverpool."

"Then your uncle used to boast of the Rose in Bloom's wearing and attacking. She would attack anything that came in her way, no matter who; and as for wearing, I think he once told me she *would* wear just what she had a mind to, like any human being."

Rose was a little mystified, but she looked vexed at the same time, as if she distrusted all was not right.

"I remember all my sea education," continued the unsuspecting widow, "as if it had been learnt yesterday. Beating the wind and attacking ship, my poor Mr. Budd used to say, were nice manœuvres, and required most of his tactics, especially in heavy weather. Did you know, Rosy dear, that sailors weigh the weather, and know when it is heavy and when it is light?"

"I did not, aunt; nor do I understand now how it can very well be done."

"Oh! child, before you have been at sea a week, you will learn so many things that are new, and get so many ideas of which you never had any notion before, that you'll not be the same person. My captain had an instrument he called a thermometer, and with that he used to weigh the weather, and then he would write down in the log-book 'to-day, heavy weather, or to-morrow, light weather,' just as it happened, and that helped him mightily along in his voyages."

"Mrs. Budd has merely mistaken the name of the instrument; the 'barometer' is what she wished to say," put in Mulford, opportunely.

Rose looked grateful, as well as relieved. Though profoundly ignorant on these subjects herself, she had always suspected her aunt's knowledge. It was, consequently, grateful to her to ascertain that, in this instance, the old lady's mistake had been so trifling.

"Well, it may have been the barometer, for I know he had them both," resumed the aunt. "Barometer, or thermometer, it don't make any great difference; or quadrant, or sextant. They are all instruments, and sometimes he used one, and sometimes another. Sailors take on board the sun, too, and have an instrument for that, as well as one to weigh the weather with. Sometimes they take on board the stars, and the moon, and 'fill their ships with the heavenly bodies,' as I've heard my dear husband say, again and again! But the most curious thing at sea, as all sailors tell me, is crossing the line, and I do hope we shall cross the line, Rosy, that you and I may see it."

"What is the line, aunty, and how do vessels cross it?"

"The line, my dear, is a place in the ocean where the earth is divided into two parts, one part being called the North Pole, and the other part the South Pole. Neptune lives near this line, and he allows no vessel to go out of one pole into the other, without paying it a visit. Never! never!—he would as soon think of living on dry land as think of letting even a canoe pass, without visiting it."

"Do you suppose there is such a being, really, as Neptune, aunty?"

"To be sure I do; he is king of the sea. Why should n't there be? The sea must have a king, as well as the land."

"The sea may be a republic, aunty, like this country; then, no king is necessary. I have always supposed Neptune to be an imaginary being."

"Oh, that's impossible—the sea is no republic; there are but two republics, America and Texas. I 've heard that the sea is a highway, it is true—the ' highway of nations,' I believe it is called, and that must mean something particular. But my poor Mr. Budd always told me that Neptune was king of the seas, and *he* was always so accurate, you might depend on everything he said. Why, he called his last Newfoundland dog Neptune; and do you think, Rosy, that your dear uncle would call his dog after an imaginary being—and he a man to beat the wind, and attack ship, and take the sun, moon, and stars aboard! No, no, child; fanciful folk may see imaginary beings, but solid folk see solid beings."

Even Spike was dumfounded at this, and there is no knowing what he might have said, had not an old sea-dog, who had just come out of the fore-topmast cross-trees, come aft, and, hitching up his trowsers with one hand while he touched his hat with the other, said with immovable gravity,—

"The revenue steamer has brought up just under the fort, Captain Spike."

"How do you know that, Bill?" demanded the captain, with a rapidity that showed how completely Mrs. Budd and all her absurdities were momentarily forgotten.

"I was up on the fore-topgallant yard, sir, a bit ago, just to look to the strap of the jewel-block, which wants some sarvice on it, and I see'd her over the land, blowin' off steam and takin' in her kites. Afore I got out of the cross-trees, she was head to wind under bare-poles, and if she had not anchored, she was about to do so. I'm sartin 't was she, sir, and that she was about to bring up.''

Spike gave a long, low whistle, after his fashion, and he walked away from the females, with an air of a man who wanted room to think in. Half a minute later, he called out,—

"Stand by to shorten sail, boys. Man fore-clew-garnets, flying jib down haul, topgallant sheets, and gaff-topsail gear. In with 'em all, my lads—in with everything, with a will.''

An order to deal with the canvas in any way, on board ship, immediately commands the whole attention of all whose duty it is to attend to such matters, and there was an end of all discourse while the Swash was shortening sail. Everybody understood, too, that it was to gain time, and prevent the brig from reaching Throg's Neck sooner than was desirable.

"Keep the brig off,'' called out Spike, "and let her ware —we're too busy to tack just now.''

The man at the wheel knew very well what was wanted, and he put his helm up, instead of putting it down, as he might have done without this injunction. As this change brought the brig before the wind, and Spike was in no hurry to luff up on the other tack, the Swash soon ran over a mile of the distance she had already made putting her back that much on her way to the Neck. It is out of our power to say what the people of the different craft in sight thought of all this, but an opportunity soon offered of putting them on a wrong scent. A large coasting schooner, carrying everything that would draw on a wind, came sweeping under the stern of the Swash, and hailed.

"Has anything happened on board that brig?'' demanded her master.

"Man overboard,'' answered Spike; "you have n't seen his hat, have you?''

"No—no,'' came back, just as the schooner, in her onward course, swept beyond the reach of the voice. Her people collected together, and one or two ran up the rigging a short distance, stretching their necks, on the lookout for the "poor fellow,'' but they were soon called down to "'bout ship.''

In less than five minutes, another vessel, a rakish coasting sloop, came within hail.

"Did n't that brig strike the Pot Rock, in passing the Gate?" demanded her captain.

"Ay, ay! and a devil of a rap she got, too."

This satisfied *him*; there being nothing remarkable in a vessel's acting strangely that had hit the Pot Rock in passing Hell-Gate.

"I think we may get in our mainsail on the strength of this, Mr. Mulford," said Spike. "There can be nothing oncommon in a craft's shortening sail, that has a man overboard, and which has hit the Pot Rock. I wonder I never thought of all this before."

"Here is a skiff trying to get alongside of us, Captain Spike," called out the boatswain.

"Skiff be d——d! I want no skiff here."

"The man that called himself Jack Tier is in her, sir."

"The d——l he is!" cried Spike, springing over to the opposite side of the deck to take a look for himself. To his infinite satisfaction he perceived that Tier was alone in the skiff, with the exception of a negro, who pulled its sculls, and that this was a very different boat from that which had glanced through Hell-Gate, like an arrow darting from its bow.

"Luff, and shake your topsail," called out Spike. "Get a rope there to throw to this skiff."

The orders were obeyed, and Jack Tier, with his clothesbag, was soon on the deck of the Swash. As for the skiff and the negro, they were cast adrift the instant the latter had received his quarter. The meeting between Spike and his quondam steward's mate was a little remarkable. Each stood looking intently at the other, as if to note the changes which time had made. We cannot say that Spike's hard, red, selfish countenance betrayed any great feeling, though such was not the case with Jack Tier's. The last, a lymphatic, puffy sort of a person at the best, seemed really a little touched, and he either actually brushed a tear from his eye, or he affected so to do.

"So you are my old shipmate, Jack Tier, are ye?" ex-

claimed Spike, in a half-patronizing, half-hesitating way—
and you want to try the old craft ag'in? Give us a leaf of
your log, and let me know where you have been this many
a day, and what you have been about? Keep the brig
off, Mr. Mulford. We are in no particular hurry to reach
Throg's, you 'll remember, sir."

Tier gave an account of his proceedings, which could have
no interest with the reader. His narrative was anything but
very clear, and it was delivered in a cracked, octave sort of
a voice, such as little dapper people not unfrequently enjoy
—tones between those of a man and a boy. The substance
of the whole story was this. Tier had been left ashore, as
sometimes happens to sailors, and, by necessary connection,
was left to shift for himself. After making some vain endeavors to rejoin his brig, he had shipped in one vessel after
another, until he accidentally found himself in the port of
New York, at the same time as the Swash. He know'd he
never should be truly happy ag'in until he could once more
get aboard the old hussy, and had hurried up to the wharf,
where he understood the brig was lying. As he came in
sight, he saw she was about to cast off, and, dropping his
clothes-bag, he had made the best of his way to the wharf,
where the conversation passed that has been related.

"The gentleman on the wharf was about to take boat,
to go through the Gate," concluded Tier, " and so I begs a
passage of him. He was good-natured enough to wait until
I could find my bag, and as soon a'terwards as the men
could get their grog we shoved off. The Molly was just
getting in behind Blackwell's as we left the wharf, and, having four good oars, and the shortest road, we come out into
the Gate just ahead on you. My eye! what a place that
is to go through in a boat, and on a strong flood! The
gentleman, who watched the brig as a cat watches a mouse,
says you struck on the Pot, as he called it, but I says ' No,'
for the Molly Swash was never know'd to hit rock or shoal
in my time aboard her."

" And where did you quit that gentleman, and what has
become of him ? " asked Spike.

"He put me ashore on that point above us, where I see'd

a nigger with his skiff, who I thought would be willin' to 'arn his quarter by giving me a cast alongside. So here I am, and a long pull I 've had to get here."

As this was said, Jack removed his hat and wiped his brow with a handkerchief, which, if it had never seen better days, had doubtless been cleaner. After this, he looked about him, with an air not entirely free from exultation.

This conversation had taken place in the gangway, a somewhat public place, and Spike beckoned to his recruit to walk aft, where he might be questioned without being overheard.

"What became of the gentleman in the boat, as you call him?" demanded Spike.

"He pulled ahead, seeming to be in a hurry."

"Do you know who he was?"

"Not a bit of it. I never saw the man before, and he did n't tell me his business, sir."

"Had he anything like a silver oar about him?"

"I saw nothing of the sort, Captain Spike, and knows nothing consarning him."

"What sort of a boat was he in, and where did he get it?"

"Well, as to the boat, sir, I *can*. say a word, seein' it was so much to my mind, and pulled so wonderful smart. It was a light ship's yawl, with four oars, and came round the Hook just a'ter you had got the brig's head round to the eastward. You must have seen it, I should think, though it kept close in with the wharves, as if it wished to be snug."

"Then the gentleman, as you call him, expected *that* very boat to come and take him off?"

"I suppose so, sir, because it *did* come and take him off. That 's all I knows about it."

"Had you no jaw with the gentleman? You was n't mum the whole time you was in the boat with him?"

"Not a bit of it, sir. Silence and I does n't agree together long, and so we talked most of the time."

"And what did the stranger say of the brig?"

"Lord, sir, he catechised me like as if I had been a child at Sunday-school. He asked me how long I had sailed in her; what ports we'd visited, and what trade we'd been in. You can't think the sight of questions he put, and how cur'ous he was for the answers."

"And what did you tell him in your answers? You said nothin' about our call down on the Spanish Main, the time you were left ashore, I hope, Jack?"

"Not I, sir. I played him off surprisin'ly. He got nothin' to count upon out of me. Though I *do* owe the Molly Swash a grudge, I'm not goin' to betray her."

"You owe the Molly Swash a grudge! Have I taken an enemy on board her, then?"

Jack started, and seemed sorry he had said so much; while Spike eyed him keenly. But the answer set all right. It was not given, however, without a moment for recollection.

"Oh, you knows what I mean, sir. I owe the old hussy a grudge for having desarted me like; but it's only a love quarrel atween us. The old Molly will never come to harm by my means."

"I hope not, Jack. The man that wrongs the craft he sails in can never be a true-hearted sailor. Stick by your ship in all weathers is my rule, and a good rule it is to go by. But what did you tell the stranger?"

"Oh! I told him I'd been six v'y'ges in the brig. The first was to Madagascar—"

"The d——l you did? Was he soft enough to believe that?"

"That's more than I knows, sir. I can only tell you what I *said*; I don't pretend to know how much he *believed*."

"Heave ahead; what next?"

"Then I told him we went to Kamschatka for gold dust and ivory."

"Whe-e-ew! What did the man say to that?"

"Why, he smiled a bit, and a'ter that he seemed more cur'ous than ever to hear all about it. I told him my third v'y'ge was to Canton, with a cargo of broom-corn, where

we took in salmon and dun-fish for home. A'ter that we
went to Norway with ice, and brought back silks and money.
Our next run was to the Havana, with salt and 'nips—''

" ' Nips ! what the devil be they ? ''

"Turnips, you knows, sir. We always calls 'em 'nips
in cargo. At the Havana I told him we took in leather
and jerked beef, and came home. Oh ! he got nothin'
from me, Captain Spike, that 'll ever do the brig a morsel
of harm ! ''

" I am glad of that, Jack. You must know enough of
the seas to understand that a close mouth is sometimes
better for a vessel than a clean bill of health. Was there
nothing said about the revenue steamer ? ''

" Now you name her, sir, I believe there was ; ay, ay,
sir, the gentleman *did* say, if the steamer fetched up to the
westward of the fort, that he should overhaul her without
difficulty, on this flood.''

" That 'll do, Jack ; that 'll do, my honest fellow. Go
below, and tell Josh to take you into the cabin again, as
steward's mate. You 're rather too Dutch built, in your
old age, to do much aloft.''

One can hardly say whether Jack received this remark
as complimentary, or not. He looked a little glum, for a
man may be as round as a barrel, and wish to be thought
genteel and slender ; but he went below, in quest of Josh,
without making any reply.

The succeeding movements of Spike appeared to be
much influenced by what he had just heard. He kept the
brig under short canvas for near two hours, sheering about
in the same place, taking care to tell everything which
spoke him that he had lost a man overboard. In this
way, not only the tide, but the day itself, was nearly spent.
About the time the former began to lose its strength, however, the fore-course and the main-sail were got on the
brigantine, with the intention of working her up toward
Whitestone, where the tides meet, and near which the
revenue steamer was known to be anchored. We say near,
though it was, in fact, a mile or two more to the eastward,
and close to the extremity of the Point.

Notwithstanding these demonstrations of a wish to work to windward, Spike was really in no hurry. He had made up his mind to pass the steamer in the dark, if possible, and the night promised to favor him ; but, in order to do this, it might be necessary not to come in sight of her at all ; or, at least, not until the obscurity should in some measure conceal his rig and character. In consequence of this plan, the Swash made no great progress, even after she had got sail on her, on her old course. The wind lessened, too, after the sun went down, though it still hung to the eastward, or nearly ahead. As the tide gradually lost its force, moreover, the set to windward became less and less, until it finally disappeared altogether.

There is necessarily a short reach in this passage, where it is always slack water, so far as current is concerned. This is precisely where the tides meet, or, as has been intimated, at Whitestone, which is somewhat more than a mile to the westward of Throgmorton's Neck, near the point of which stands Fort Schuyler, one of the works recently erected for the defence of New York. Off the pitch of the point, nearly mid-channel, had the steamer anchored, a fact of which Spike had made certain, by going aloft himself, and reconnoitring her over the land, before it had got to be too dark to do so. He entertained no manner of doubt that this vessel was in waiting for him, and he well knew there was good reason for it ; but he would not return and attempt the passage to sea by way of Sandy Hook. His manner of regarding the whole matter was cool and judicious. The distance to the Hook was too great to be made in such short nights ere the return of day, and he had no manner of doubt he was watched for in that direction, as well as in this. Then he was particularly unwilling to show his craft at all in front of the town, even in the night. Moreover, he had ways of his own for effecting his purposes, and this was the very spot and time to put them in execution.

While these things were floating in his mind, Mrs. Budd and her handsome niece were making preparations for passing the night, aided by Biddy Noon. The old lady

was factotum, or factota, as it might be most classical to
call her, though we are entirely without authorities on the
subject, and was just as self-complacent and ambitious of
seawomanship below decks, as she had been above board.
The effect, however, gave Spike great satisfaction, since it
kept her out of sight, and left him more at liberty to carry
out his own plans. About nine, however, the good woman
came on deck, intending to take a look at the weather,
like a skilful marineress as she was, before she turned in.
Not a little was she astonished at what she then and there
beheld, as she whispered to Rose and Biddy, both of whom
stuck close to her side, feeling the want of good pilotage,
no doubt, in strange waters.

The Molly Swash was still under her canvas, though
very little sufficed for her present purposes. She was directly off Whitestone, and was making easy stretches
across the passage, or river, as it is called, having nothing
set but her huge fore-and-aft mainsail and the jib. Under
this sail she worked like a top, and Spike sometimes fancied
she travelled too fast for his purposes, the night air having
thickened the canvas as usual, until it " held the wind as a
bottle holds water." There was nothing in this, however,
to attract the particular attention of the shipmaster's widow,
a sail, more or less, being connected with observation much
too critical for her schooling, nice as the last had been. She
was surprised to find the men stripping the brig forward,
and converting her into a schooner. Nor was this done in
a loose and slovenly manner, under favor of the obscurity.
On the contrary, it was so well executed that it might have
deceived even a seaman under a noonday sun, provided the
vessel were a mile or two distant. The manner in which
the metamorphosis was made was as follows : the studding-
sail booms had been taken off the topsail-yard, in order to
shorten it to the eye, and the yard itself was swayed up
about half-mast, to give it the appearance of a schooner's
fore-yard. The brig's real lower yard was lowered on the bulwarks, while her royal yard was sent down altogether, and the
topgallant-mast was lowered until the heel rested on the topsail-yard, all of which, in the night, gave the gear forward

very much the appearance of that of a fore-topsail schooner instead of that of a half-rigged brig, as the craft really was. As the vessel carried a try-sail on her foremast it answered very well, in the dark, to represent a schooner's foresail. Several other little dispositions of this nature were made, about which it might weary the uninitiated to read, but which will readily suggest themselves to the mind of a sailor.

These alterations were far advanced when the females reappeared on deck. They at once attracted their attention, and the captain's widow felt the imperative necessity, as connected with her professional character, of proving the same. She soon found Spike, who was bustling around the deck, now looking around to see that his brig was kept in the channel, now and then issuing an order to complete her disguise.

"Captain Spike, what *can* be the meaning of all these changes? The tamper of your vessel is so much altered that I declare I should not have known her!"

"Is it, by George! Then she is just in the state I want her to be in."

"But why have you done it; and what does it all mean?"

"Oh, Molly's going to bed for the night, and she's only undressing herself; that's all."

"Yes, Rosy dear, Captain Spike is right. I remember that my poor Mr. Budd used to talk about the Rose in Bloom having her clothes on, and her clothes off, just as if she was a born woman! But don't you mean to navigate at all in the night, Captain Spike? Or will the brig navigate without sails?"

"That's it; she's just as good in the dark, under one sort of canvas, as under another. So, Mr. Mulford, we'll take a reef in that mainsail; it will bring it nearer to the size of our new foresail, and seem more ship-shape and Brister fashion; then I think she'll do, as the sight is getting to be rather darkish."

"Captain Spike," said the boatswain, who had been set to look out for that particular change, "the brig begins to feel the new tide, and sets to windward."

"Let her go then; now is as good a time as another. We've got to run the gauntlet, and the sooner it is done the better."

As the moment seemed propitious, not only Mulford, but all the people, heard this order with satisfaction. The night was starlight, though not very clear at that. Objects on the water, however, were more visible than those on the land, while those on the last could be seen well enough even from the brig, though in confused and somewhat shapeless piles. When the Swash was brought close by the wind, she had just got into the last reach of the "river," or that which runs parallel with the Neck for near a mile, doubling where the Sound expands itself, gradually to a breadth of many leagues. Still the navigation at the entrance of this end of the Sound was intricate and somewhat dangerous, rendering it indispensable for a vessel of any size to make a crooked course. The wind stood at southeast, and was very scant to lay through the reach with, while the tide was so slack as barely to possess a visible current at that place. The steamer lay directly off the Point, mid-channel, as mentioned, showing lights, to mark her position to anything which might be passing in or out. The great thing was to get by her without exciting her suspicion. As all on board, the females excepted, knew what their captain was at, the attempt was made amid an anxious and profound silence; or, if any one spoke at all, it was only to give an order in a low tone, or its answer in a simple monosyllable.

Although her aunt assured her that everything which had been done already, and which was now doing, was quite in rule, the quick-eyed and quick-witted Rose noted these unusual proceedings, and had an opinion of her own on the subject. Spike had gone forward, and posted himself on the weather-side of the forecastle, where he could get the clearest look ahead, and there he remained most of the time, leaving Mulford on the quarter-deck, to work the vessel. Perceiving this, she managed to get near the mate, without attracting her aunt's attention, and at the same time out of ear-shot.

"Why is everybody so still and seemingly anxious.

Harry Mulford?" she asked, speaking in a low tone herself, as if desirous of conforming to a common necessity.
" Is there any new danger here? I thought the Gate had
been passed altogether, some hours ago?"

"So it has. D' ye see that large dark mass on the water,
off the Point, which seems almost as huge as the fort, with
lights above it? That is a revenue steamer which came out
of York a few hours before us. We wish to get past her
without being troubled by any of her questions."

" And what do any in this brig care about her questions?
They can be answered, surely."

" Ay, ay, Rose, they *may* be answered, as you say, but
the answers sometimes are unsatisfactory. Captain Spike,
for some reason or other, is uneasy, and would rather not
have anything to say to her. He has the greatest aversion
to speaking the smallest craft when on a coast."

" And that 's the reason he has undressed his Molly, as he
calls her, that he might not be known."

Mulford turned his head quickly toward his companion,
as if surprised by her quickness of apprehension, but he
had too just a sense of his duty to make any reply. Instead
of pursuing the discourse, he adroit y contrived to change
it, by pointing out to Rose the manner in which they were
getting on, which seemed to be very successfully.

Although the Swash was under much reduced canvas,
she glided along with great ease and with considerable
rapidity of motion. The heavy night air kept her canvas
distended, and the weatherly set of the tide, trifling as it
yet was, pressed her up against the breeze, so as to turn
all to account. It was apparent enough, by the manner in
which objects on the land were passed, that the crisis was
fast approaching. Rose rejoined her aunt, in order to await
the result, in nearly breathless expectation. At that moment she would have given the world to be safe on shore.
This wish was not the consequence of any constitutional
timidity, for Rose was much the reverse from timid, but it
was the fruit of a newly-awakened and painful, though still
vague, suspicion. Happy, thrice happy was it for one of
her naturally confiding and guileless nature, that distrust

4

was thus opportunely awakened, for she was without a guardian competent to advise and guide her youth, as circumstances required.

The brig was not long in reaching the passage that opened to the Sound. It is probable she did this so much the sooner because Spike kept her a little off the wind, with a view of not passing too near the steamer. At this point, the direction of the passage changes at nearly a right angle, the revenue steamer lying on a line with the Neck, and leaving a sort of bay, in the angle, for the Swash to enter. The land was somewhat low in all directions but one, and that was by drawing a straight line from the Point, through the steamer, to the Long Island shore. On the latter, and in that quarter, rose a bluff of considerable elevation, with deep water quite near it ; and, under the shadows of that bluff, Spike intended to perform his nicest evolutions. He saw that the revenue vessel had let her fires go down, and that she was entirely without steam. Under canvas, he had no doubt of beating her hand over hand, could he once fairly get to windward ; and then she was at anchor, and would lose some time in getting under way, should she even commence a pursuit. It was all-important, therefore, to gain as much to windward as possible, before the people of the government vessel took the alarm.

There can be no doubt that the alterations made on board the Swash served her a very good turn on this occasion. Although the night could not be called positively dark, there was sufficient obscurity to render her hull confused and indistinct at any distance, and this so much the more when seen from the steamer outside, or between her and the land. All this Spike very well understood, and largely calculated on. In effect he was not deceived ; the lookouts on board the revenue craft could trace little of the vessel that was approaching beyond the spars and sails which rose above the shores, and these seemed to be the spars and sails of a common fore-topsail schooner. As this was not the sort of craft for which they were on the watch, no suspicion was awakened, nor did any reports go from the quarter-deck to the cabin. The steamer had her quarter watches, and officers of the deck, like a vessel of war, the discipline of which was fairly enough imitated, but even a man-of-war may be over-reached on an occasion.

Spike was only great in a crisis, and then merely as a sea-man. He understood his calling to its minutiæ, and he understood the Molly Swash better than he understood any other craft that floated. For more than twenty years had he sailed her, and the careful parent does not better understand the humors of the child, than he understood exactly what might be expected from his brig. His satisfaction sensibly increased, therefore, as she stole along the land, toward the angle mentioned, without a sound audible but the gentle gurgling of the water, stirred by the stem, and which sounded like the ripple of the gentlest wave, as it washes the shingle of some placid beach.

As the brig drew nearer to the bluff, the latter brought the wind more ahead, as respected the desired course. This was unfavorable, but it did not disconcert her watchful commander.

"Let her come round, Mr. Mulford," said this pilot-captain, in a low voice, "we are as near in as we ought to go."

The helm was put down, the head sheets started, and away into the wind shot the Molly Swash fore-reaching famously in stays, and, of course, gaining so much on her true course. In a minute she was round, and filled on the other tack. Spike was now so near the land, that he could perceive the tide was beginning to aid him, and that his weatherly set was getting to be considerable. Delighted at this, he walked aft, and told Mulford to go about again as soon as the vessel had sufficient way to make sure of her in stays. The mate inquired if he did not think the revenue people might suspect something, unless they stood further out toward mid-channel, but Spike reminded him that they would be apt to think the schooner was working up under the southern shore, because the ebb first made there. This reason satisfied Mulford, and, as soon as they were half-way between the bluff and the steamer, the Swash was again tacked, with her head to the former. This manœuvre was executed when the brig was about two hundred yards from the steamer, a distance that was sufficient to preserve, under all the circumstances, the disguise she had assumed.

"They do not suspect us, Harry!" whispered Spike to his mate. "We shall get to windward of 'em, as sartain as the breeze stands. That boatin' gentleman might as well have stayed at home, as for any good his hurry done him or his employers!"

"Whom do you suppose him to be, Captain Spike?"

"Who! A feller that lives by his own wicked deeds. No matter who he is. An informer, perhaps. At any rate he is not the man to outwit the Molly Swash, and her old stupid, foolish master and owner, Stephen Spike. Luff, Mr. Mulford, luff. Now 's the time to make the most of your leg. Luff her up and shake her. She is setting to windward fast, the ebb is sucking along that bluff like a boy at a molasses hogshead. All she can drift on this tack is clear gain; there is no hurry, so long as they are asleep aboard the steamer. That 's it; make a half-board at once, but take care and not come round. As soon as we are fairly clear of the bluff, and open the bay that makes up behind it, we shall get the wind more to the southward, and have a fine long leg for the next stretch."

Of course Mulford obeyed, throwing the brig up into the wind, and allowing her to set to windward, but filling again on the same tack, as ordered. This, of course, delayed her progress toward the land, and protracted the agony, but it carried the vessel in the direction she most wished to go, while it kept her not only end on to the steamer, but in a line with the bluff, and consequently in the position most favorable to conceal her true character. Presently, the bay mentioned, which was several miles deep, opened darkly toward the south, and the wind came directly out of it, or more to the southward. At this moment the Swash was near a quarter of a mile from the steamer, and all that distance dead to windward of her as the breeze came out of the bay. Spike tacked his vessel himself now, and got her head up so high that she brought the steamer on her lee quarter, and looked away toward the island which lies north-wardly from the Point, and quite near to which all vessels of any draught of water are compelled to pass, even with the fairest winds.

"Shake the reef out of the mainsail, Mr. Mulford," said Spike, when the Swash was fairly in motion again on this advantageous tack. "We shall pass well to windward of the steamer, and may as well begin to open our cloth again."

"Is it not a little too soon, sir?" Mulford ventured to remonstrate; "the reef is a large one, and will make a great difference in the size of the sail."

"They 'll not see it at this distance. No, no, sir, shake out the reef, and sway away on the topgallant-mast rope; I 'm for bringing the Molly Swash into her old shape again, and make her look handsome once more."

"Do you dress the brig, as well as undress her, o' nights, Captain Spike?" inquired the shipmaster's relict, a little puzzled with this fickleness of purpose. "I do not believe my poor Mr. Budd ever did that."

"Fashions change, madam, with the times; ay, ay, sir, —shake out the reef, and sway away on that mast-rope, boys, as soon as you have manned it. We 'll convart our schooner into a brig again."

As these orders were obeyed, of course, a general bustle now took place. Mulford soon had the reef out, and the sail distended to the utmost, while the topgallant-mast was soon up and fidded. The next thing was to sway upon the fore-yard, and get that into its place. The people were busied at this duty, when a hoarse hail came across the water on the heavy night air.

"Brig ahoy!" was the call.

"Sway upon that fore-yard," said Spike, unmoved by this summons; "start it, start it at once."

"The steamer hails us, sir," said the mate.

"Not she. She is hailing a brig; we are a schooner yet."

A moment of active exertion succeeded, during which the fore-yard went into its place. Then came a second hail.

"Schooner ahoy!" was the summons this time.

"The steamer hails us again, Captain Spike."

"The devil a bit. We're a brig now, and she hails a schooner. Come, boys, bestir yourselves, and get the canvas on Molly for'ard. Loose the fore-course before you quit the yard there, then up aloft and loosen everything you can find."

All this was done as ordered, and done rapidly, as is ever the case on board a well-ordered vessel when there is occasion for exertion. That occasion now appeared to exist in earnest, for while the men were sheeting home the topsail, a flash of light illuminated the scene, when the roar of a gun came booming across the water, succeeded by the very distinct whistling of its shot. We regret that the relict of the late Captain Budd did not behave exactly as became a shipmaster's widow, under fire. Instead of remaining silent and passive, even while frightened, as was the case with Rose, she screamed quite as loud as she had previously done that very day in Hell-Gate. It appeared to Spike, indeed, that practice was making her perfect; and, as for Biddy, the spirit of emulation became so powerful in her bosom, that, if anything, she actually outshrieked her mistress. Hearing this, the widow made a second effort, and fairly recovered the ground some might have fancied she had lost.

"Oh! Captain Spike," exclaimed the agitated widow, "do not—do not, if you love me, do not let them fire again!"

"How am I to help it!" asked the captain, a good deal to the point, though he overlooked the essential fact, that, by heaving-to, and waiting for the steamer's boat to board him, he might have prevented a second shot, as completely as if he had the ordering of the whole affair. No second shot was fired, however. As it afterward appeared, the screams of Mrs. Budd and Biddy were heard on board the steamer, the captain of which, naturally enough, supposing that the slaughter must be terrible where such cries had arisen, was satisfied with the mischief he had already done, and directed his people to secure their gun and go to the capstan-bars in order to help lift the anchor. In a word, the revenue vessel was getting under way, man-of-war fashion, which means somewhat expeditiously.

Spike understood the sounds that reached him, among which was the call of the boatswain, and he bestirred himself accordingly. Experienced as he was in chases and all sorts of nautical artifices, he very well knew that his situation was sufficiently critical. It would have been so, with a steamer at his heels, in the open ocean ; but, situated as he was, he was compelled to steer but one course, and to accept the wind on that course as it might offer. If he varied at all in his direction it was only in a trifling way, though he did make some of these variations. Every moment was now precious, however, and he endeavored to improve the time to the utmost. He knew that he could greatly outsail the revenue vessel, under canvas, and some time would be necessary to enable her to get up her steam ; half an hour at the very least. On that half hour, then, depended the fate of the Molly Swash.

" Send the booms on the yards, and set stun'sails at once, Mr. Mulford," said Spike, the instant the more regular canvas was spread forward. " This wind will be free enough for all but the lower stun'sail, and we must drive the brig on."

" Are we not looking up too high, Captain Spike ? The Stepping-Stones are ahead of us, sir."

" I know that very well, Mulford. But it 's nearly high water, and the brig 's in light trim, and we may rub and go. By making a short cut here, we shall gain a full mile on the steamer ; that mile may save us."

" Do you really think it possible to get away from that craft, which can always make a fair wind of it, in these narrow waters, Captain Spike."

" One don't know, sir. Nothin' is done without tryin', and by tryin' more is often done than was hoped for. I have a scheme in my head, and Providence may favor me in bringing it about."

Providence ! The religionist quarrels with the philosopher if the latter happen to remove this interposition of a higher power, even so triflingly as by the intervention of secondary agencies, while the biggest rascal dignifies even his success by such phrases as Providential aid! But it is not surprising men should misunderstand terms, when they make such sad confusion in the acts which these terms are merely meant to represent. Spike had his Providence as well as a priest, and we dare say he often counted on its succor, with quite as rational grounds of dependence as many of the Pharisees, who are constantly exclaiming: "The temple of the Lord, the temple of the Lord are these."

Sail was made on board the Swash with great rapidity, and the brig made a bold push at the Stepping-Stones. Spike was a capital pilot. He insisted if he could once gain sight of the spar that was moored on those rocks for a buoy, he should run with great confidence. The two lights were of great assistance, of course; but the revenue vessel could see these lights as well as the brig, and *she*, doubtless, had an excellent pilot on board. By the time the studding-sails were set on board the Swash, the steamer was aweigh, and her long line of peculiar sails became visible. Unfortunately for men who were in a hurry, she lay so much within the bluff as to get the wind scant, and her commander thought it necessary to make a stretch over to the southern shore, before he attempted to lay his course. When he was ready to tack, an operation of some time with a vessel of her great length, the Swash was barely visible in the obscurity, gliding off upon a slack bowline, at a rate which nothing but the damp night air, the ballast-trim of the vessel, united to her excellent sailing qualities, could have produced with so light a breeze.

The first half hour took the Swash completely out of sight of the steamer. In that time, in truth, by actual superiority in sailing, by her greater state of preparation, and by the distance saved by a bold navigation, she had gained fully a league on her pursuer. But, while the steamer had lost sight of the Swash, the latter kept the former in view, and that by means of a signal that was very portentous. She saw the light of the steamer's chimneys, and could form some opinion of her distance and position.

It was about eleven o'clock when the Swash passed the lights at Sands' Point, close in with the land. The wind stood much as it had been. If there was a change at all, it was half a point more to the southward, and it was a little fresher. Such as it was, Spike saw he was getting, in that smooth water, quite eight knots out of his craft, and he made his calculations thereon. As yet, and possibly for half an hour longer, he was gaining, and might hope to continue to gain on the steamer. Then her turn would come. Though no great traveller, it was not to be expected that, favored by smooth water and the breeze, her speed would be less than ten knots, while there was no hope of increasing his own without an increase of the wind. He might be five miles in advance, or six at the most; these six miles would be overcome in three hours of steaming, to a dead certainty, and they might possibly be overcome much sooner. It was obviously necessary to resort to some other experiment than that of dead sailing, if an escape was to be affected.

The Sound was now several miles in width, and Spike, at first, proposed to his mate, to keep off dead before the wind, and by crossing over to the north shore, let the steamer pass ahead, and continue a bootless chase to the eastward. Several vessels, however, were visible in the middle of the passage, at distances varying from one to three miles, and Mulford pointed out the hopelessness of attempting to cross the sheet of open water, and expect to go unseen by the watchful eyes of the revenue people.

"What you say is true enough, Mr. Mulford," answered Spike, after a moment of profound reflection, "and every foot that they come nearer, the less will be our chance. But here is Hempstead Harbor a few leagues ahead; if we can reach *that* before the blackguards close, we may do well enough. It is a deep bay, and has high land to darken the view. I don't think the brig could be seen at midnight by anything outside, if she was once fairly up that water a mile or two."

"That is our chance, sir!" exclaimed Mulford cheerfully. "Ay, ay, I know the spot, and everything is favorable—try that, Captain Spike; I'll answer for it that we go clear."

Spike did try it. For a considerable time longer he stood on, keeping as close to the land as he thought it safe to run and carrying everything that would draw. But the steamer was on his heels, evidently gaining fast. Her chimneys gave out flames, and there was every sign that her people were in earnest. To those on board the Swash these flames seemed to draw nearer each instant, as indeed was the fact, and just as the breeze came fresher out of the opening in the hills, or the low mountains, which surround the place of refuge in which they designed to enter, Mulford announced that by aid of the night-glass he could distinguish both sails and hull of their pursuer. Spike took a look, and throwing down the instrument, in a way to endanger it, he ordered the studding-sails taken in. The men went aloft like cats, and worked as if they could stand in air. In a minute or two the Swash was under what Mrs. Budd might have called her "attacking" canvas, and was close by the wind, looking on a good leg well up the harbor. The brig seemed to be conscious of the emergency, and glided ahead at capital speed. In five minutes she had shut in the flaming chimneys of the steamer. In five minutes more Spike tacked, to keep under the western side of the harbor, and out of sight as long as possible, and because he thought the breeze drew down fresher where he was than more out in the bay.

All now depended on the single fact whether the brig had been seen from the steamer or not, before she hauled into the bay. If seen, she had probably been watched; if not seen, there were strong grounds for hoping that she might still escape. About a quarter of an hour after Spike hauled up, the burning chimneys came again into view. The brig was then half a league within the bay, with a fine dark background of hills to throw her into shadow. Spike ordered everything taken in but the try-sail, under which the brig was left to set slowly over toward the western side of the harbor. He now rubbed his hands with delight and pointed out to Mulford the circumstance that the steamer kept on her course directly athwart the harbor's mouth! Had she seen the Swash, no doubt she would have turned into the bay also. Nevertheless, an anxious ten minutes succeeded, during which the revenue vessel steamed fairly past, and shut in her flaming chimneys again by the eastern headlands of the estuary.

succeeded, during which the travelling vessel showed fairly past, and shut in by a flaring entrance again by the eastern headlands of the estuary.

CHAPTER III.

" The western wave was all a flame,
The day was well nigh done,
Almost upon the western wave
Rested the broad bright sun ;
When the stranger ship drove suddenly
Betwixt us and the sun."

The Ancient Mariner.

AT that hour on the succeeding morning, when the light of day is just beginning to chase away the shadows of night, the Molly Swash became visible within the gloom of the high land which surrounds so much of the bay of Hempstead, under easy sail, backing and filling, in order to keep within her hiding-place, until a look could be had at the state of things without. Half an hour later, she was so near the entrance of the estuary, as to enable the lookouts aloft to ascertain that the coast was clear, when Spike ordered the helm to be put up, and the brig to be kept away to her course. At this precise moment, Rose appeared on deck, refreshed by the sleep of a quiet night, and with cheeks tinged with a color even more delicate than that which was now glowing in the eastern sky, and which was almost as brilliant.

"We stopped in this bit of a harbor for the night, Miss Rose, that is all ;" said Spike, observing that his fair passenger was looking about her, in some little surprise, at finding the vessel so near the land and seemingly so much out of her proper position. "Yes, we always do that, when we first start on a v'y'ge, and before the brig gets used to travelling—don't we, Mr. Mulford?"

Mr. Mulford, who knew how hopeless was the attempt

60

to mystify Rose, as one might mystify her credulous and weak-minded aunt, and who had no disposition to deal any way but fairly by the beautiful, and in one sense now help-less young creature before him, did not see fit to make any reply. Offend Spike he did not dare to do, more es-pecially under present circumstances; and mislead Rose he would not do. He affected not to hear the question, therefore, but issuing an order about the head-sails, he walked forward as if to see it executed. Rose herself was not under as much restraint as the young mate.

"It is convenient, Captain Spike," she coolly answered for Mulford, "to have stopping-places, for vessels that are wearied, and I remember the time when my uncle used to tell me of such matters, very much in the same vein; but, it was before I was twelve years old."

Spike hemmed, and he looked a little foolish, but Clench, the boatswain, coming aft to say something to him in confidence, just at that moment, he was enabled to avoid the awkwardness of attempting to explain. This man Clench, or Clinch, as the name was pronounced, was deep in the captain's secrets; far more so than was his mate, and would have been filling Mulford's station at that very time, had he not been hopelessly ignorant of navigation. On the present occasion, his business was to point out to the captain two or three lines of smoke, that were visible above the water of the Sound, in the eastern board; one of which he was apprehensive might turn out to be the smoke of the revenue craft, from which they had so recently escaped.

"Steamers are no rarities in Long Island Sound, Clench," observed the captain, levelling his glass at the most suspected of the smokes. "That must be a Providence, or Stonington chap, coming west with the Boston train."

"Either of *them* would have been farther west, by this time, Captain Spike," returned the doubting, but watchful boatswain. "It's a large smoke, and I fear it is the rev-enue fellow coming back, after having had a look well to the eastward, and satisfying himself that we are not to be had in that quarter.

Spike growled out his assent to the possibility of such a conjecture, and promised vigilance. This satisfied his subordinate for the moment, and he walked forward, or to the place where he belonged. In the meantime, the widow came on deck, smiling, and snuffing the salt air, and ready to be delighted with anything that was maritime.

"Good morning, Captain Spike," she cried; "are we in the offing, yet?—you know I desired to be told when we are in the offing, for I intend to write a letter to my poor Mr. Budd's sister, Mrs. Sprague, as soon as we get to the offing."

"What is the offing, aunt?" inquired the handsome niece.

"Why *you* have hardly been at sea long enough to understand me, child, should I attempt to explain. The offing, however, is the place where the last letters are always written to the owners, and to friends ashore. The term comes, I suppose, from the circumstance that the vessel is about to be off, and it is natural to think of those we leave behind, at such a moment. I intend to write to your aunt Sprague, my dear, the instant I hear we are in the offing; and what is more, I intend to make *you* my amanuensis."

"But how will the letter be sent, aunty? I have no more objections to writing than any one else, but I do not see how the letter is to be sent. Really, the sea *is* a curious region, with its stopping-places for the night, and its offings to write letters at!"

"Yes, it's all as you say, Rose, a most remarkable region is the sea! You'll admire it, as I admire it, when you come to know it better; and as your poor uncle admired it, and as Captain Spike admires it, too. As for the letters, they can be sent ashore by the pilot, as letters are always sent."

"But, aunty, there *is* no pilot in the Swash, for Captain Spike refused to take one on board."

"Rose! You don't understand what you are talking about! No vessel ever yet sailed without a pilot, if indeed any *can*. It's opposed to the law, not to have a pilot; and now I remember to have heard your dear uncle say it wasn't a voyage if a vessel didn't take away a pilot."

"But if they take them away, aunty, how can they send the letters ashore by them?"

"Poh, poh! child; you don't know what you're saying; but you'll overlook it, I hope, Captain Spike, for Rose is quick, and will soon learn to know better. As if letters couldn't be sent ashore by the pilot, though he was a hundred thousand miles from land! But, Captain Spike, you must let me know when we are about to get off the Sound, for I know that the pilot is always sent ashore with his letters, before the vessel gets off the Sound."

"Yes, yes," returned the captain, a little mystified by the widow, though he knew her so well, and understood her so well, "you shall know, ma'am, when we get off soundings, for I suppose that is what you mean."

"What is the difference? Off the Sound, or off the soundings, of course, must mean the same thing. But, Rosy, we will go below and write to your aunt at once, for I see a light-house yonder, and light-houses are always put just off the soundings."

Rose, who always suspected her aunt's nautical talk, though she did not know how to correct it, was not sorry to put an end to it, now, by going below, and spreading her own writing materials, in readiness to write, as the other dictated. Biddy Noon was present, sewing on some of her own finery.

"Now write, as I tell you, Rose," commenced the widow:

"My dear sister Sprague,—Here we are at last, just off the soundings with light-houses all round us, and so many capes and islands in sight, that it does seem as if the vessel never *could* find its way through them all. Some of these islands must be the West Indies—"

"Aunty, that can *never* be!" exclaimed Rose; "we left New York only yesterday."

"What of that? Had it been old times, I grant you several days might be necessary to get a sight of the West Indies, but, now, when a letter can be written to a friend in Boston, and an answer received in half an hour, it requires no such time to go to the West Indies. Besides, what other islands are there in this part of the world? they can't be England—"

"No—no," said Rose, at once seeing it would be pref-

erable to admit they were in the West Indies ; so the letter
went on :—

"Some of these islands must be the West Indies, and it
is high time we saw some of them, for we are nearly off the
Sound, and the light-houses are getting to be quite numerous. I think we have already seen four since we left the
wharf. But, my dear sister Sprague, you will be delighted
to hear how much better Rose's health is already becoming—"

"My health, aunty ! Why, I never knew an ill day in
my life !"

"Don't tell me that, my darling ; I know too well what
all these deceptive appearances of health amount to. I
would not alarm you for the world, Rosy dear, but a careful
parent—and I'm your parent in affection, if not by nature—
but a careful parent's eye is not to be deceived. I know
you *look* well, but you are ill, my child ; though, Heaven be
praised, the sea air and hydropathy are already doing you
a monstrous deal of good."

As Mrs. Budd concluded, she wiped her eyes, and appeared really glad that her niece had a less consumptive
look than when she embarked. Rose sat, gazing at her
aunt, in mute astonishment. She knew how much and
truly she was beloved, and that induced her to be more
tolerant of her connection's foibles than even duty demanded. Feeling was blended with her respect, but it was
almost too much for her, to learn that this long, and in
some respects painful voyage, was undertaken on her account, and without the smallest necessity for it. The vex-
ation, however, would have been largely increased, but for
certain free communications that had occasionally occurred
between her and the handsome mate, since the moment of her
coming on board the brig. Rose knew that Harry Mulford
loved her, too, for he had told her as much with a seaman's
frankness ; and though she had never let him know that his
partiality was returned, her woman's heart was fast inclining
toward him with all her sex's tenderness. This made the
mistake of her aunt *tolerable*, though Rose was exceedingly
vexed it should ever have occurred.

"Why, my dearest aunt," she cried, "they told me it was on *your* account that this voyage was undertaken!"

"I know they did, poor, dear Rosy, and that was in order not to alarm you. Some persons of delicate constitutions—"

"But my constitution is not in the least delicate, aunt; on the contrary, it is as good as possible; a blessing for which, I trust, I am truly grateful. I did not know but you might be suffering, though you do look so well, for they all agreed in telling me you had need of a sea-voyage."

"I, a subject for hydropathy! Why, child, water is no more necessary to me than it is to a cat."

"But going to sea, aunty, is not hydropathy—"

"Don't say that, Rosy; do not say that, my dear. It is hydropathy on a large scale, as Captain Spike says; and when he gets us into blue water, he has promised that you shall have all the benefits of the treatment."

Rose was silent and thoughtful; after which she spoke quickly, like one to whom an important thought had suddenly occurred.

"And Captain Spike, then, was consulted in my case?" she asked.

"He was, my dear, and you have every reason to be grateful to him. He was the first to discover a change in your appearance, and to suggest a sea-voyage. Marine hydropathy, he said, he was sure would get you up again; for Captain Spike thinks your constitution good at the bottom though the high color you have proves too high a state of habitual excitement."

"Was Dr. Monson consulted at all, aunt?"

"Not at all. You know the doctors are all against hydropathy, and mesmerism, and the magnetic telegraph, and everything that is new; so we thought it best not to consult him."

"And my aunt Sprague?"

"Yes, *she* was consulted after everything was settled, and when I knew her notions could not undo what had been already done. But she is a seaman's widow, as well as myself, and has a great notion of the virtue of sea air."

5

"Then it would seem that Doctor Spike was the principal adviser in my case!"

"I own that he was, Rosy dear. Captain Spike was brought up by your uncle, who has often told me what a thorough seaman he was. 'There's Spike, now,' he said to me one day, 'he can almost make his brig talk'—this very brig too, your uncle meant, Rosy, and, of course, one of the best vessels in the world to take hydropathy in."

"Yes, aunty," returned Rose, playing with the pen, while her air proved how little her mind was in her words. "Well, what shall I say next to my aunt Sprague?"

"Rose's health is already become *confirmed*," resumed the widow, who thought it best to encourage her niece by as strong terms as she could employ, "and I shall extol hydropathy to the skies, as long as I live. As soon as we reach our port of destination, my dear sister Sprague, I shall write you a line to let you know it, by the magnetic telegraph—"

"But there is no magnetic telegraph on the sea, aunty," interrupted Rose, looking up from the paper with her clear, serene, blue eyes, expressing even *her* surprise, at this touch of the relict's ignorance.

"Don't tell me *that*, Rosy, child, when everybody says the sparks will fly round the whole earth, just as soon as they will fly from New York to Philadelphia."

"But they must have something to fly on, aunty; and the ocean will not sustain wires, or posts."

"Well, there is no need of being so particular; if there is no telegraph, the letter must come by mail. You can say telegraph here, and when your aunt gets the letter, the postmark will tell her how it came. It looks better to talk about telegraphic communications, child."

Rose resumed her pen, and wrote at her aunt's dictation, as follows: "By the magnetic telegraph, when I hope to be able to tell you that our dear Rose is well. As yet, we both enjoy the ocean exceedingly; but when we get off the Sound, into blue water, and have sent the pilot ashore, or discharged him, I ought to say, which puts me in mind of telling you that a cannon was discharged at us only last night, and that the ball whistled so near me, that I heard it as plain as ever you heard Rose's piano."

"Had I not better first tell my aunt Sprague what is to be done when the pilot is discharged?"

"No; tell her about the cannon that was discharged, first, and about the ball that I heard. I had almost forgot that adventure, which was a very remarkable one, was it not, Biddy?"

"Indeed, missus, and it was! and Miss Rose might put in the letter how we both screamed at that cannon, and might have been heard as plainly, every bit of it, as the ball."

"Say nothing on the subject, Rose, or we shall never hear the last of it. So, darling, you may conclude in your own way, for I believe I have told your aunt all that comes to mind."

Rose did as desired, finishing the epistle in a very few words, for rightly enough, she had taken it into her head there was no pilot to be discharged, and consequently that the letter would never be sent. Her short but frequent conferences with Mulford were fast opening her eyes, not to say her heart, and she was beginning to see Captain Spike in his true character, which was that of a great scoundrel. It is true, that the mate had not long judged his commander quite so harshly; but had rather seen his beautiful brig, and her rare qualities, in her owner and commander, than the man himself; but jealousy had quickened his observation of late, and Stephen Spike had lost ground sensibly with Harry Mulford, within the last week. Two or three times before, the young man had thought of seeking another berth, on account of certain distrusts of Spike's occupations; but he was poor, and so long as he remained in the Swash, Harry's opportunities of meeting Rose were greatly increased. This circumstance, indeed, was the secret of his still being in the "Molly," as Spike usually called his craft; the last voyage having excited suspicions that were rather of a delicate nature. Then the young man really loved the brig, which, if she could not be literally made to talk, could be made to do almost everything else. A vessel, and a small vessel, too, is rather contracted as to space, but those who wish to converse can contrive to speak together often, even in such narrow limits. Such had been the fact with Rose Budd and the handsome mate. Twenty times since they sailed, short as that time was, had Mulford contrived to get so near to Rose, as to talk with her, unheard by others. It is true, that he seldom ventured to do this, so long as the captain was in sight, but Spike was often below, and opportunities were constantly occurring. It was in the course of these frequent but brief conversations, that Harry had made certain dark hints touching the character of his commander, and the known recklessness of his proceedings. Rose had taken the alarm, and fully comprehending her aunt's mental imbecility her situation was already giving her great uneasiness. She had some undefined hopes from the revenue steamer; though, strangely enough as it appeared to her, her youngest and most approved suitor betrayed a strong desire to escape from that craft, at the very moment he was expressing his apprehensions on account of her presence in the brig. This contradiction arose from a certain *esprit de corps*, which seldom fails, more or less, to identify the mariner with his ship.

But the writing was finished, and the letter sealed with wax, Mrs. Budd being quite as particular in that ceremony as Lord Nelson, when the females again repaired on deck. They found Spike and his mate sweeping the eastern part of the Sound with their glasses, with a view to look out for enemies; or, what to them, just then, was much the same thing, government craft. In this occupation, Rose was a little vexed to see that Mulford was almost as much interested as Spike himself, the love of his vessel seemingly overcoming his love for her, if not his love of the right—she knew of no reason, however, why the captain should dread any other vessel, and felt sufficiently provoked to question him a little on the subject, if it were only to let him see that the niece was not as completely his dupe as the aunt. She had not been on deck five minutes, therefore, during which time several expressions had escaped the two sailors touching their apprehensions of vessels seen in the distance, ere she commenced her inquiries.

"And why should we fear meeting with other vessels?" Rose plainly demanded, "here in Long Island Sound, and within the power of the laws of the country?"

"Fear?" exclaimed Spike, a little startled, and a good deal surprised at this straight-forward question, "fear, Miss Rose! You do not think we are afraid, though there are many reasons why we do not wish to be spoken by certain craft that are hovering about. In the first place, you know it is war time; I suppose you know, Madam Budd, that America is at war with Mexico?"

"Certainly," answered the widow, with dignity; "and that is a sufficient reason, Rose, why one vessel should chase, and another should run. If you had heard your poor uncle relate, as I have done, all his chasings and runnings away in the war times, child, you would understand these things better. Why, I've heard your uncle say that, in some of his long voyages, he has run thousands and thousands of miles, with sails set on both sides, and all over his ship!"

"Yes, aunty, and so have I, but that was 'running before the wind,' as he used to call it."

"I s'pose, however, Miss Rose," put in Spike, who saw that the niece would soon get the better of the aunt, "I s'pose, Miss Rose, that you'll acknowledge that America is at war with Mexico?"

"I am sorry to say that such is the fact, but I remember to have heard you say, yourself, Captain Spike, when my aunt was induced to undertake this voyage, that you did not consider there was the smallest danger from any Mexicans."

"Yes, you did, Captain Spike," added the aunt; "you did say there was no danger from Mexicans."

"Nor is there a bit, Madam Budd, if Miss Rose, and your honored self, will only hear me. There is no danger, because the brig has the heels of anything Mexico can send to sea. She has sold her steamers, and, as for anything else under her flag, I would not care a straw."

"The steamer from which we ran, last evening, and which actually fired off a cannon at us, was not Mexican, but American," said Rose with a pointed manner that put Spike to his trumps.

"Oh! that steamer"—he stammered—"that was a race—only a race, Miss Rose, and I would n't let her come near me, for the world. I should never hear the last of it, in the insurance offices, and on 'change, did I let *her* overhaul us. You see, Miss Rose—you see, Madam Budd"— Spike ever found it most convenient to address his mystifying discourse to the aunt, in preference to addressing it to the niece—"you see, Madam Budd, the master of that craft and I are old cronies—sailed together when boys, and set great store by each other. We met only last evening, just a'ter I had left your own agreeable mansion, Madam Budd, and says he, 'Spike, when do you sail?' 'To-morrow's flood, Jones,' says I—his name is Jones— Peter Jones, and as good a fellow as ever lived. 'Do you go by the Hook, or by Hell-Gate—'"

"Hurl-Gate, Captain Spike, if you please—or Whirl-Gate, which some people think is the true sound; but the other way of saying it is awful."

"Well, the captain, my old master, always called it Hell-Gate, and I learned the trick from him—"

"I know he did, and so do all sailors; but genteel people, nowadays, say nothing but Hurl-Gate, or Whirl-Gate."

Rose smiled at this, as did Mulford; but neither said anything, the subject having once before been up between them. As for ourselves, we are still so old-fashioned as to say, and write, Hell-gate, and intend so to do, in spite of all the Yankees that have yet passed through it, or who ever shall pass through it, and that is saying a great deal. We do not like changing names to suit their uneasy spirits.

"Call the place Hurl-Gate, and go on with your story," said the widow, complacently.

"Yes, Madam Budd. 'Do you go by the Hook, or by Whirl-Gate?' said Jones. 'By Whirl-a-Gig-Gate,' says I. 'Well,' says he, 'I shall go through the Gate myself, in the course of the morning. We may meet somewhere to the eastward, and, if we do, I 'll bet you a beaver,' says he, 'that I show you my stern.' 'Agreed,' says I, and we shook hands upon it. That 's the whole history of our giving the steamer the slip, last night, and of my not wishing to let her speak me.''

"But you went into a bay, and let her go past you,'' said Rose, coolly enough as to manner, but with great point as to substance. "Was not that a singular way of winning a race?''

"It does seem so, Miss Rose, but it 's all plain enough when understood. I found that steam was too much for sails, and I stood up into the bay to let them run past us, in hopes they would never find out the trick. I care as little for a hat as any man, but I do care a good deal about having it reported on 'change that the Molly was beat, by even a steamer.''

This ended the discourse for the moment, Clench again having something to say to his captain in private.

"How much of that explanation am I to believe, and how much disbelieve?'' asked Rose, the instant she was left alone with Harry. "If it be all invention it was a ready and ingenious story.''

"No part of it is true. He no more expected that the steamer would pass through Hell-Gate, than I expected it myself. There was no bet, or race, therefore; but it was our wish to avoid Uncle Sam's cruiser, that was all.''

"And why should *you* wish any such thing?''

"On my honor, I can give you no better reason, so far as I am concerned, than the fact that, wishing to keep clear of her, I do not like to be overhauled. Nor can I tell you why Spike is so much in earnest in holding the revenue vessel at arm's length; I know he dislikes all such craft, as a matter of course, but I can see no particular reason for it just now. A more innocent cargo was never stuck into a vessel's hold.''

"What is it?''

"Flour; and no great matter of that. The brig is not half full, being just in beautiful ballast trim, as if ready for a race. I can see no sufficient reason, beyond native antipathy, why Captain Spike should wish to avoid any craft, for it is humbug his dread of a Mexican, and least of all, here, in Long Island Sound. All that story about Jones is a tub for whales."

"Thank you for the allusion; my aunt and myself being the whales."

"You know I do mean—can mean nothing, Rose, that is disrespectful to either yourself or your aunt."

Rose looked up, and she looked pleased. Then she mused in silence, for some time, when she again spoke.

"Why have you remained another voyage with such a man, Harry?" she asked earnestly.

"Because, as his first officer, I have had access to your house, when I could not have had it otherwise; and because I have apprehended that he might persuade Mrs. Budd, as he had boasted to me it was his intention to do, to make this voyage."

Rose now looked grateful; and deeply grateful did she feel, and had reason to feel. Harry had concealed no portion of his history from her. Like herself, he was a shipmaster's child, but one better educated and better connected than was customary for the class. His father had paid a good deal of attention to the youth's early years, but had made a seaman of him, out of choice. The father had lost his all, however, with his life in a shipwreck; and Harry was thrown upon his own resources, at the early age of twenty. He had made one or two voyages as a second mate, when chance threw him in Spike's way, who, pleased with some evidences of coolness and skill, that he had shown in a foreign port, on the occasion of another loss, took him as his first officer; in which situation he had remained ever since, partly from choice and partly from necessity. On the other hand, Rose had a fortune; by no means a large one, but several thousands in possession, from her own father, and as many more in reversion from her uncle. It was this money, taken in connection with the credulous imbecility of the aunt, that had awakened the cupidity, and excited the hopes of Spike. After a life of lawless adventure, one that had been checkered by every shade of luck, he found himself growing old, with his brig growing old with him, and little left beside his vessel and the sort of half cargo that was in her hold. Want of means, indeed, was the reason that the flour-barrels were not more numerous.

Rose heard Mulford's explanation favorably, as indeed she heard most of that which came from him, but did not renew the discourse, Spike's conference with the boatswain just then terminating. The captain now came aft, and began to speak of the performances of his vessel in a way to show that he took great pride in them.

"We are travelling at the rate of ten knots, Madam Budd," he said exultingly, "and that will take us clear of the land, before night shuts in ag'in. Montauk is a good place for an offing; I ask for no better."

"Shall we then have *two* offings, this voyage, Captain Spike?" asked Rose, a little sarcastically. "If we are in the offing now, and are to be in the offing when we reach Montauk, there must be two such places."

"Rosy, dear, you amaze me!" put in the aunt. "There is no offing until the pilot is discharged, and when he's discharged there is nothing but offing. It's all offing. On the Sound, is the first great change that befalls a vessel as she goes to sea; then comes the offing; next the pilot is discharged—then—then—what comes next, Captain Spike?"

"Then the vessel takes her departure; an old navigator like yourself, Madam Budd, ought not to forget the departure."

"Quite true, sir. The departure is a very important portion of a seaman's life. Often and often have I heard my poor dear Mr. Budd talk about his departures. His departures, and his offings and his—"

"Land-falls," added Spike, perceiving that the shipmaster's relict was a little at fault.

"Thank you, sir; the hint is quite welcome. His landfalls, also, were often in his mouth."

"What is a land-fall, aunty?" inquired Rose. "It appears a strange term to be used by one who lives on the water."

"Oh! there is no end to the curiosities of sailors! A

'land-fall,' my dear, means a shipwreck, of course. To fall on the land, and a very unpleasant fall it is, when a vessel should keep on the water. I 've heard of dreadful land-falls in my day, in which hundreds of souls have been swept into eternity, in an instant."

"Yes, yes, Madam Budd; there are such accidents truly, and serious things be they to encounter," answered Spike, hemming a little to clear his throat, as was much his practice whenever the widow ran into an unusually extravagant blunder, "yes, serious things to encounter. But the land-fall that I mean is a different sort of thing; being, as you well know, what we say when we come in *sight* of land, a'ter a v'y'ge; or, meaning the land we may happen first to see. The departure is the beginning of our calculation when we lose sight of the last cape or head-land, and the land-fall closes it, by letting us know where we are at the other end of our journey, as you probably remember."

"Is there not such a thing as clearing out in navigation?" asked Rose quickly, willing to cover a little confusion that was manifest in her aunt's manner.

"Not exactly in navigation, Miss Rose, but clearing out, with honest folk, ought to come first, and navigation a'ter-wards. Clearing out means going through the Custom-house, accordin' to law.."

"And the Molly Swash has cleared out, I hope?"

"Sartain, a more lawful clearance was never given in Wall Street; it 's for Key West and a market. I did think of making it Havana and a market, but port-charges are light-est at Key West."

"Then Key West is the place to which we are bound?"

"It ought to be, agreeable to papers; though vessels sometimes miss the ports for which they clear."

Rose put no more questions; and her aunt, being conscious that she had not appeared to advantage in the affair of the "land-fall" was also disposed to be silent. Spike and Mulford had their attention drawn to the vessel, and the conversation dropped.

The reader can readily suppose that the Molly Swash

had not been standing still all this time. So far from this, she was running "down Sound," with the wind on her quarter, or at southwest, making great head-way, as she was close under the south shore, or on the island side of the water she was in. The vessel had no other motion than that of her speed, and the females escaped everything like sea-sickness, for the time being. This enabled them to attend to making certain arrangements necessary to their comforts below, previously to getting into rough water. In acquitting herself of this task, Rose received much useful advice from Josh, though his new assistant, Jack Tier, turned out to be a prize indeed, in the cabins. The first was only a steward; but the last proved himself not only a handy person of his calling, but one full of resources— a genius, in his way. Josh soon became so sensible of his own inferiority, in contributing to the comforts of females, that he yielded the entire management of the "ladies' cabin," as a little place that might have been ten feet square, was called, to his uncouth-looking, but really expert deputy. Jack waddled about below, as if born and brought up in such a place, and seemed every way fitted for his office. In height, and in build generally, there was a surprising conformity between the widow and the steward's deputy, a circumstance which might induce one to think they must often have been in each other's way, in a space so small; though, in point of fact, Jack never ran foul of any one. He seemed to avoid this inconvenience by a species of nautical instinct.

Towards the turn of the day, Rose had everything arranged, and was surprised to find how much room she had made for her aunt and herself, by means of Jack's hints, and how much more comfortable it was possible to be, in that small cabin, than she had at first supposed.

After dinner, Spike took his siesta. He slept in a little state-room that stood on the starboard side of the quarter-deck, quite aft; as Mulford did in one on the larboard. These two state-rooms were fixtures; but a light deck overhead, which connected them, shipped and unshipped, forming a shelter for the man at the wheel, when in its place, as well as for the officer of the watch, should he see fit to use it, in bad weather. This sort of cuddy, Spike termed his "coach-house."

The captain had no sooner gone into his state-room, and closed its window, movements that were understood by Mulford, than the latter took occasion to intimate to Rose, by means of Jack Tier, the state of things on deck, when the young man was favored with the young lady's company.

"He has turned in for his afternoon's nap, and will sleep for just one hour, blow high, or blow low," said the mate, placing himself at Rose's side on the trunk, which formed the usual seat for those who could presume to take the liberty of sitting down on the quarter-deck. "It's a habit with him, and we can count on it, with perfect security."

"His doing so, now, is a sign that he has no immediate fears of the revenue steamer?"

"The coast is quite clear of her. We have taken good looks at every smoke, but can see nothing that appears like our late companion. She has doubtless gone to the eastward, on duty, and merely chased us, on her road."

"But _why_ should she chase us, at all?"

"Because we ran. Let a dog run, or a man run, or a cat run, ten to one but something starts in chase. It is human nature, I believe, to give chase; though I will admit there was something suspicious about that steamer's movements—her anchoring off the Fort, for instance. But let her go, for the present; are you getting things right, and to your mind, below decks?"

"Very much so. The cabin is small, and the two state-rooms the merest drawers that ever were used, but, by putting everything in its place, we have made sufficient room, and no doubt shall be comfortable."

"I am sorry you did not call on me for assistance. The mate has a prescriptive right to help stow away."

"We made out without your services," returned Rose, slightly blushing; "Jack Tier, as he is called, Josh's assistant, is a very useful person, and has been our adviser and manager. I want no better for such services."

"He is a queer fellow, all round. Take him altogether, I hardly ever saw so droll a being! As thick as he's long, with a waddle like a duck, a voice that is cracked, hair like bristles, and knee high; the man might make a fortune as a show. Tom Thumb is scarcely a greater curiosity."

"He is singular in 'build,' as you call it," returned Rose, laughing, "but, I can assure you that he is a most excellent fellow in his way, worth a dozen of Josh. Do you know, Harry, that I suspect he has strong feelings towards Captain Spike; though whether of like or dislike, friendship or enmity, I am at a loss to say."

"And why do you think that he has any feeling at all? I have heard Spike say he left the fellow ashore, somewhere down the Spanish Main, or in the Islands, quite twenty years since; but a sailor would scarce carry a grudge so long a time, for such a thing as that."

"I do not know—but feeling there is, and much of it, too, though, whether hostile or friendly, I will not undertake to say."

"I'll look to the chap, now you tell me this. It is a little odd, the manner in which he got on board us, taken in connection with the company he was in, and a discovery may be made. Here he is, however; and, as I keep the keys of the magazine, he can do us no great harm, unless he scuttles the brig."

"Magazine! Is there such a thing here?"

"To be sure there is, and ammunition enough in it to keep eight carronades in lively conversation for a couple of hours."

"A carronade is what you call a gun, is it not?"

"A piece of a one—being somewhat short, like your friend, Jack Tier, who is shaped a good deal like a carronade."

Rose smiled, nay, half laughed, for Harry's pleasantries almost took the character of wit in her eyes, but she did not the less pursue her inquiries.

"Guns! And where are they, if they be on this vessel?"

"Do not use such a lubberly expression, my dear Rose, if you respect your father's profession. *On* a vessel, is a new-fangled Americanism, that is neither fish, flesh, nor red-herring, as we sailors say; neither English nor Greek.''

"What should I say, then? My wish is not to parade sea-talk, but to use it correctly, when I use it at all.''

"The expression is hardly 'sea-talk,' as you call it, but every-day English—that is, when rightly used. On a vessel is no more English than it is nautical; no sailor ever used such an expression.''

"Tell me what I ought to say, and you will find me a willing, if not an apt scholar. I am certain of having often read it, in the newspapers, and that quite lately.''

"I 'll answer for that, and it 's another proof of its being wrong. *In* a vessel is as correct as *in* a coach, and *on* a vessel as wrong as can be; but you can say *on board* a vessel, though not 'on the boards of a vessel;' as Mrs. Budd has it.''

"Mr. Mulford!''

"I beg a thousand pardons, Rose, and will offend no more, though she does make some very queer mistakes.''

"My aunt thinks it an honor to my uncle's memory, to be able to use the language of his professional life, and if she does sometimes make mistakes that are absurd, it is with motives so respectable that no sailor should deride them.''

"I am rebuked forever. Mrs. Budd may call the anchor a silver spoon, hereafter, without my even smiling. But, if the aunt has this kind remembrance of a seaman's life, why cannot the niece think equally well of it?''

"Perhaps she does,'' returned Rose, smiling again, "seeing all its attractions through the claims of Captain Spike.''

"I think half the danger from him gone, now that you seem so much on your guard. What an odious piece of deception, to persuade Mrs. Budd that you were fast falling into a decline!''

"One so odious that I shall surely quit the brig at the first port we enter, or even in the first suitable vessel that we may speak.''

"And Mrs. Budd—could you persuade her to such a course?"

"You scarce know us, Harry Mulford. My aunt commands, when there is no serious duty to perform, but we change places when there is. I can persuade her to anything that is right, in ten minutes."

"You might persuade a world!" cried Harry, with strong admiration expressed in his countenance; after which he began to converse with Rose, on a subject so interesting to themselves, that we do not think it prudent to relate any more of the discourse, forgetting all about the guns.

About four o'clock, of a fine summer's afternoon, the Swash went through the Race, on the best of the ebb, and with a staggering southwest wind. Her movement by the land, just at that point, could not have been less than at the rate of fifteen miles in the hour. Spike was in high spirits, for his brig had got on famously that day, and there was nothing in sight to the eastward. He made no doubt, as he had told his mate, that the steamer had gone into the Vineyard Sound, and that she was bound over the shoals.

"They want to make political capital out of her," he added, using one of the slang phrases, that the "business habits" of the American people are so rapidly incorporating with the common language of the country, "they want to make political capital out of her, Harry, and must show her off to the Boston folk, who are full of notions. Well, let them turn her to as much account in that way as they please, so long as they keep her clear of the Molly. Your sarvant, Madam Budd," addressing the widow, who just at that moment came on deck; "a fine a'ternoon, and likely to be a clear night to run off the coast in."

"Clear nights are desirable, and most of all at sea, Captain Spike," returned the relict, in her best, complacent manner, "whether it be to run *off* a coast, or to run *on* a coast. In either case, a clear night, or a bright moon must be useful."

Captain Spike rolled his tobacco over in his mouth, and cast a furtive glance at the mate, but he did not presume to hazard any further manifestations of his disposition to laugh.

"Yes, Madam Budd," he answered, "it is quite as you say, and I am only surprised where you have picked up as much of what I call useful nautical knowledge."

"We live and learn, sir. You will recollect that this is not my first voyage, having made one before, and that I passed a happy, happy, thirty years, in the society of my poor, dear husband, Rose's uncle. One must have been dull, indeed, not to have picked up, from such a companion much of a calling that was so dear to him, and the particulars of which were so very dear to him. He actually gave me lessons in the 'sea dialect,' as he called it, which probably is the true reason I am so accurate and general in my acquisitions."

"Yes, Madam Budd; yes—hem—you are—yes, you are wonderful in that way. We shall soon get an offing now, Madam Budd; yes, soon get an offing, now."

"And take in our departure, Captain Spike," added the widow, with a very intelligent smile.

"Yes, take our departure. Montauk is yonder, just coming in sight; only some three hours' run from this spot. When we get there, the open ocean will lie before us; and give me the open sea, and I'll not call the king my uncle."

"Was he your uncle, Captain Spike?"

"Only in a philanthropic way, Madam Budd. Yes, let us get a good offing, and a rapping to'gallant breeze, and I do not think I should care much for *two* of Uncle Sam's new-fashioned revenue craft, one on each side of me."

"How delightful do I find such conversation, Rose! It's as much like your poor, dear uncle's, as one pea is like an other. 'Yes,' he used to say, too, 'let me only have one on each side of me, and a wrapper round the topgallant sail to hold the breeze and I'd not call the king my uncle. Now I think of it, *he* used to talk about the king as his uncle, too."

"It was all talk, aunty. He had no uncle, and, what, is more, he had no king."

"'That's quite true, Miss Rose," rejoined Spike, attempting a bow, which ended in a sort of jerk. "It *is* not very becoming in us republicans to be talking of kings, but a habit is a habit. Our forefathers had kings, and we drop into their ways without thinking of what we are doing. Fore-topgallant-yard, there!"

"Sir."

"Keep a bright lookout, ahead. Let me know the instant you make anything in the neighborhood of Montauk."

"Ay, ay, sir."

"As I was saying, Madam Budd, we seamen drop into our forefathers' ways. Now, when I was a youngster, I remember, one day, that we fell in with a ketch—you know, Miss Rose, what a ketch is, I suppose?"

"I have not the least notion of it, sir."

"Rosy, you amaze me!" exclaimed the aunt, "and you a shipmaster's niece, and a shipmaster's daughter! A catch is a trick that sailors have, when they quiz landsmen."

"Yes, Madam Budd, yes; we have them sort of catches, too; but I now mean the vessel with a peculiar rig, which we call a ketch, you know."

"Is it the full-jigger, or the half-jigger sort, that you mean?"

Spike could hardly stand this, and he had to hail the top-gallant-yard again, in order to keep the command of his muscles, for he saw by the pretty frown that was gathering on the brow of Rose, that she was regarding the matter a little seriously. Luckily, the answer of the man on the yard diverted the mind of the widow from the subject, and prevented the necessity of any reply.

"There's a light, of course, sir, on Montauk, is there not, Captain Spike?" demanded the seaman who was aloft.

"To be sure there is; every headland, hereabouts, has its light; and some have two."

"Ay, ay, sir; it's that which puzzles me; I think I see one light-house, and I'm not certain but I see two."

"If there is anything like a second, it must be a sail. Montauk has but one light."

Mulford sprang into the fore-rigging, and in a minute was on the yard. He soon came down, and reported the light-house in sight, with the afternoon's sun shining on it but no sail near.

6

"My poor, dear Mr. Budd used to tell a story of his being cast away on a light-house, in the East Indies," put in the relict, as soon as the mate had ended his report, "which always affected me. It seems there were three ships of them together, in an awful tempest directly off the land—"

"That was comfortable, anyhow," cried Spike; "if it must blow hard, let it come off the land, say I."

"Yes, sir, it was directly off the land, as my poor husband always said, which made it so much the worse you must know, Rosy; though Captain Spike's gallant spirit would rather encounter danger than not. It blew what they call a Hyson, in the Chinese seas—"

"A what, aunty? Hyson is the name of a tea, you know."

"A Hyson, I'm pretty sure it was; and I suppose the wind is named after the tea, or the tea after the wind."

"The ladies do get in a gale, sometimes, over their tea," said Spike, gallantly. "But I rather think, Madam Budd must mean a typhoon."

"That's it; a typhoon, or a Hyson, there is not much difference between them, you see. Well, it blew a typhoon, and they are always mortal to somebody. This my poor Mr. Budd well knew, and he had set his chronometer for that typhoon—"

"Excuse me, aunty, it was the barometer that he was watching; the chronometer was his watch."

"So it was—his watch on deck *was* his chronometer, I declare. I *am* forgetting a part of my education. Do you know the use of a chronometer, now, Rose? You have seen your uncle's often, but do you know how he used it?"

"Not in the least, aunty. My uncle often tried to explain it, but I never could understand him."

"It must have been, then, because Captain Budd did not try to make himself comprehended," said Mulford, "for I feel certain nothing would be easier than to make *you* understand the uses of the chronometer."

"I should like to learn it from *you*, Mr. Mulford," answered the charming girl, with an emphasis so slight on the

' you,' that no one observed it but the mate, but which was clear enough to him, and caused every nerve to thrill.

" I can attempt it," answered the young man, " if it be agreeable to Mrs. Budd, who would probably like to hear it herself."

" Certainly, Mr. Mulford, though I fancy you can say little on such a subject that I have not often heard already from my poor, dear Mr. Budd."

This was not very encouraging, truly ; but Rose continuing to look interested, the mate proceeded.

"The use of the chronometer is to ascertain the longitude," said Harry, " and the manner of doing it is simply this : A chronometer is nothing more nor less than a watch made with more care than usual, so as to keep the most accurate time. They are of all sizes, from that of a clock, down to this which I wear in my fob, and which is a watch in size and appearance. Now, the nautical almanacs are all calculated to some particular meridian—"

" Yes," interrupted the relict, " Mr. Budd had a great deal to say about meridians."

" That of London, or Greenwich, being the meridian used by those who use the English Almanacs, and those of Paris or St. Petersburg, by the French and Russians. Each of these places has an observatory, and chronometers that are kept carefully regulated, the year round. Every chronometer is set by the regulator of the particular observatory or place to which the almanac used is calculated."

" How wonderfully like my poor, dear Mr. Budd, all this is, Rosy ! Meridians, and calculated, and almanacs ! I could almost think I heard your uncle entertaining me with one of his nautical discussions, I declare !"

" Now the sun rises earlier in places east, than in places west of us."

" It rises earlier in the summer, but later in the winter, everywhere, Mr. Mulford."

" Yes, my dear Madam ; but the sun rises earlier every day, in London, than it does in New York."

" That is impossible," said the widow, dogmatically—

"Why should not the sun rise at the same time in England and America?"

"Because England is east of America, aunty. The sun does not move, you know, but only appears to us to move because the earth turns round from west to east, which causes those who are farthest east to see it first. That is what Mr. Mulford means."

"Rose has explained it perfectly well," continued the mate. "Now the earth is divided into 360 degrees, and the day is divided into 24 hours. If 360 be divided by 24 the quotient will be 15. It follows that, for each fifteen degrees of longitude, there is a difference of just one hour in the rising of the sun, all over the earth, where it rises at all. New York is near five times 15 degrees west of Greenwich, and the sun consequently rises five hours later at New York than at London.

"There *must* be a mistake in this, Rosy," said the relict, in a tone of desperate resignation, in which the desire to break out in dissent was struggling oddly enough with an assumed dignity of deportment. "I've always heard that the people of London are some of the latest in the world. Then, I've been in London, and know that the sun rises in New York, in December, a good deal earlier than it does in London, by the clock—yes, by the clock."

"True enough, by the clock, Mrs. Budd, for London is more than ten degrees north of New York, and the farther north you go, the later the sun rises in winter, and the earlier in summer."

The relict merely shrugged her shoulders, as much as to say that she knew no such thing; but Rose, who had been well taught, raised her serene eyes to her aunt's face, and mildly said,—

"All true, aunty, and that is owing to the fact that the earth is smaller at each end than in the middle."

"Fiddle-faddle with your middles and ends, Rose; I've been in London, dear, and know that the sun rises later there than in New York, in the month of December, and that I know by the clock, I tell you."

"The reason of which is," resumed Mulford, "because

the clocks of each place keep the time of that place. Now, it is different with the chronometers; they are set in the observatory of Greenwich, and keep the time of Greenwich. This watch chronometer was set there, only six months since; and this time, as you see, is near nine o'clock, when in truth it is only about four o'clock here, where we are."

" I wonder you keep such a watch, Mr. Mulford ! "

" I keep it," returned the mate, smiling, " because I know it to keep good time. It has the Greenwich time; and, as your watch has the New York time, by comparing them together, it is quite easy to find the longitude of New York."

" Do you, then, keep watches to compare with your chronometers?" asked Rose, with interest.

" Certainly not ; as that would require a watch for every separate part of the ocean, and then we should only get known longitudes. It would be impracticable, and load a ship with nothing but watches. What we do is this : We set our chronometers at Greenwich, and thus keep the Greenwich true time wherever we go. The greatest attention is paid to the chronometers, to see that they receive no injuries; and usually there are two, and often more of them, to compare one with another, in order to see that they go well. When in the middle of the ocean, for instance, we find the true time of the day at that spot, by ascertaining the height of the sun. This we do by means of our quadrants, or sextants ; for, as the sun is always in the zenith at twelve o'clock, nothing is easier than to do this, then the sun can be seen, and an arc of the heavens measured. At the instant the height of the sun is ascertained by one observer, he calls to another, who notes the time on the chronometer. The difference in these two times, or that of the chronometer and that of the sun, gives the distance in degrees and minutes, between the longitude of Greenwich and that of the place on the ocean where the observer is ; and that gives him his longitude. If the difference is three hours and twenty minutes, in time, the distance from Greenwich is fifty degrees of longitude, because the sun rises three hours and twenty minutes sooner in London, than in the fiftieth degree of west longitude."

"A watch is a watch, Rosy," put in the aunt, doggedly "and time is time. When it's four o'clock at our house it's four o'clock at your aunt Sprague's, and it's so all over the world. The world may turn round—I'll not deny it, for your uncle often said as much as *that*, but it cannot turn in the way Mr. Mulford says, or we should all fall off it, at night, when it was bottom upwards. No, sir, no; you've started wrong. My poor, dear, late Mr. Budd, always admitted that the world turned round, as the books say; but when I suggested to him the difficulty of keeping things in their places, with the earth upside down, he acknowledged candidly—for he was all candor, I must say that for him—and owned that he had made a discovery by means of his barometer, which showed that the world did not turn round in the way you describe, or by rolling over, but by whirling about, as one turns in a dance. You must remember your uncle's telling me this, Rose?"

Rose did remember her uncle's telling her aunt this, as well as a great many other similar prodigies. Captain Budd had married his silly wife on account of her pretty face, and when the novelty of that was over, he often amused himself by inventing all sorts of absurdities, to amuse both her and himself. Among other things, Rose well remembered his quieting her aunt's scruples about falling off the earth, by laying down the theory that the world did not "roll over," but "whirl round." But Rose did not answer the question.

"Objects are kept in their places on the earth by means of attraction," Mulford ventured to say, with a great deal of humility of manner. "I believe it is thought there is no up or down, except as we go from or towards the earth and that would make the position of the last a matter of indifference, as respects objects keeping on it."

"Attractions are great advantages, I will own, sir, especially to our sex. I think it will be acknowledged there has been no want of them in our family, any more than there has been of sense and information. Sense and information we pride ourselves on; attractions being gifts from God, we try to think less of them. But all the at-

tractions in the world could not keep Rosy, here, from falling off the earth, did it ever come bottom upwards. And,
mercy on me, where would she fall to !''

Mulford saw that argument was useless, and he confined
his remarks, during the rest of the conversation, to showing
Rose the manner in which the longitude of a place might
be ascertained, with the aid of the chronometer, and by
means of observations to get the true time of day, at the
particular place itself. Rose was so quick-witted, and already so well instructed, as easily to comprehend the principles ; the details being matters of no great moment to one
of her sex and habits. But Mrs. Budd remained antago-
nist to the last. She obstinately maintained that twelve
o'clock was twelve o'clock ; or, if there *was* any difference,
"London hours were notoriously later than those of New
York."

Against such assertions arguments were obviously useless, and Mulford, perceiving that Rose began to fidget, had
sufficient tact to change the conversation altogether.

And still the Molly Swash kept in swift motion. Montauk was by this time abeam, and the little brigantine began to rise and fall on the long swells of the Atlantic which
now opened before her in one vast sheet of green and rolling waters. On her right lay the termination of Long
Island ; a low, rocky cape, with its light, and a few fields
in tillage, for the uses of those who tended it. It was the
"land's end" of New York, while the island that was heaving up out of the sea at a distance of about twenty miles
to the eastward, was the property of Rhode Island, being
called Block Island. Between the two, the Swash shaped
her course for the ocean.

Spike had betrayed uneasiness as his brig came up with
Montauk ; but the coast seemed clear, with not even a distant sail in sight, and he came aft, rubbing his hands with
delight, speaking cheerfully.

"All right, Mr. Mulford," he cried ; "everything ship-
shape and Brister-fashion ; not even a smack fishing hereaway, which is a little remarkable. Ha! what are you
staring at, over the quarter, there?''

"Look here, sir, directly in the wake of the setting sun which we are now opening from the land—is not that a sail?"

"Sail! Impossible, sir. What should a sail be doing in there, so near Montauk? no man ever saw a sail there in his life. It's a spot in the sun, Madam Budd, that my mate has got a glimpse at, and, sailor-like, he mistakes it for a sail! Ha, ha, ha—yes, Harry, it's a spot in the sun."

"It is a spot *on* the sun, as you say, but it's a spot made by a vessel; and here is a boat pulling towards her, might and main; going from the light, as if carrying news."

It was no longer possible for Spike's hopes to deceive him. There was a vessel, sure enough; though, when first seen, it was so directly in a line with the fiery orb of the setting sun, as to escape common observation. As the brig went foaming on towards the ocean, however, the black speck was soon brought out of the range of the orb of day and Spike's glass was instantly levelled at it.

"Just as one might expect, Mr. Mulford," cried the captain, lowering his glass, and looking aloft to see what could be done to help his craft along; "a bloody revenue cutter, as I'm a wicked sinner! There she lies, sir, within musket shot of the shore, hid behind the point as it might be in waiting for us, with her head to the southward, her helm hard down, topsail aback, and foresail brailed; as wicked-looking a thing as Free Trade and Sailors' Rights ever ran from. My life on it, sir, she's been put in that precise spot, in waiting for the Molly to arrive. You see, as we stand on, it places her as handsomely to windward of us as the heart of man could desire."

"It *is* a revenue cutter, sir; now she's out of the sun's wake, that is plain enough. And that is her boat, which has been sent to the light to keep a lookout for us. Well, sir, she's to windward; but we have everything set for our course, and as we are fairly abeam, she must be a great traveller to overhaul us."

"I thought these bloody cutters were all down in the Gulf," growled the captain, casting his eyes aloft again, to see that everything drew. "I'm sure the newspapers have mentioned as many as twenty that are down there, and here is one, lying behind Montauk, like a snake in the grass !''

" At any rate, by the time he gets his boat up we shall get the start of him—ay, there he fills and falls off, to go and meet her. He 'll soon be after us, Captain Spike, at racing speed."

Everything occurred as those two mariners had foreseen. The revenue cutter, one of the usual fore-top-sail schooners that are employed in that service, up and down the coast had no sooner hoisted up her boat, than she made sail, a little off the wind, on a line to close with the Swash. As for the brig, she had hauled up to an easy bowline, as she came round Montauk, and was now standing off south-south-east, still having the wind at southwest. The weatherly position of the cutter enabled her to steer rather more than one point freer. At the commencement of this chase, the vessels were about a mile and a half apart, a distance too great to enable the cutter to render the light guns she carried available, and it was obvious from the first, that everything depended on speed. And speed it was, truly ; both vessels fairly flying ; the Molly Swash having at last met with something very like her match. Half an hour satisfied both Spike and Mulford that, by giving the cutter the advantage of one point in a freer wind, she would certainly get alongside of them, and the alternative was therefore to keep off.

" A starn chase is a long chase, all the world over," cried Spike ; " edge away, sir ; edge away, sir, and bring the cutter well on our quarter."

This order was obeyed ; but to the surprise of those in the Swash, the cutter did not exactly follow, though she kept off a little more. Her object seemed to be to maintain her weatherly position, and in this manner the two vessels ran on for an hour longer, until the Swash had made most of the distance between Montauk and Block Island. Objects were even becoming dimly visible on the last, and the light on the point was just becoming visible, a lone star above a waste of desert, the sun having been

down now fully a quarter of an hour, and twilight beginning to draw the curtain of night over the waters.

"A craft under Block," shouted the lookout, that was
still kept aloft as a necessary precaution.

"What sort of a craft?" demanded Spike, fiercely; for
the very mention of a sail, at that moment, aroused all his
ire. "Are n't you making a frigate out of an apple-or-
chard?"

"It 's the steamer, sir. I can now see her smoke.
She 's just clearing the land, on the south side of the island
and seems to be coming around to meet us."

A long, low, eloquent whistle from the captain, succeeded
this announcement. The man aloft was right. It *was* the
steamer, sure enough; and she had been lying hid behind
Block Island, exactly as her consort had been placed behind
Montauk, in waiting for their chase to arrive. The result
was, to put the Molly Swash in exceeding jeopardy, and
the reason why the cutter kept so well to windward was
fully explained. To pass out to sea between these two
craft was hopeless. There remained but a single alternative from capture by one or by the other,—and that Spike
adopted instantly. He kept his brig dead away, setting
studding-sails on both sides. This change of course brought
the cutter nearly aft, or somewhat on the other quarter,
and laid the brig's head in a direction to carry her close to
the northern coast of the island. But the principal advantage was gained over the steamer, which could not keep
off, without first standing a mile or two, or even more, to
the westward, in order to clear the land. This was so
much clear gain to the Swash, which was running off at
racing speed, on a northeast course, while her most dangerous enemy was still heading to the westward. As for
the cutter, she kept away; but it was soon apparent that
the brig had the heels of her, dead before the wind.

Darkness now began to close around the three vessels;
the brig and the schooner soon becoming visible to each
other principally by means of their night-glasses; though
the steamer's position could be easily distinguished by
means of her flaming chimney. This latter vessel stood to

the westward for a quarter of an hour, when her commander appeared to become suddenly conscious of the ground he was losing, and he wore short round, and went off before the wind, under steam and canvas; intending to meet the chase off the northern side of the island. The very person who had hailed the Swash, as she was leaving the wharf, who had passed her in Hell-Gate, with Jack Tier in his boat, and who had joined her off Throgmorton's was now on her deck, urging her commander by every consideration not to let the brig escape. It was at his suggestion that the course was changed. Nervous, and eager to seize the brig, he prevailed on the commander of the steamer to alter his course. Had he done no more than this, all might have been well; but so exaggerated were his notions of the Swash's sailing, that, instead of suffering the steamer to keep close along the eastern side of the island, he persuaded her commander of the necessity of standing off a long distance to the northward and eastward, with a view to get ahead of the chase. This was not bad advice, were there any certainty that Spike would stand on, of which, however, he had no intention.

The night set in dark and cloudy; and, the instant that Spike saw, by means of the flaming chimney, that the steamer had wore, and was going to the eastward of Block, his plan was laid. Calling to Mulford, he communicated it to him, and was glad to find that his intelligent mate was of his own way of thinking. The necessary orders were given, accordingly, and everything was got ready for its execution.

In the meantime, the two revenue craft were much in earnest. The schooner was one of the fastest in the service, and had been placed under Montauk, as described, in the confident expectation of her being able to compete with even the Molly Swash successfully, more especially if brought upon a bowline. Her commander watched the receding form of the brig with the closest attention, until it was entirely swallowed up in the darkness, under the land, towards which he then sheered himself, in order to prevent the Swash from hauling up, and turning to windward, close in under the shadow of the island. Against this manœuvre, however, the cutter had now taken an effectual precaution, and her people were satisfied that escape in that way was impossible.

On the other hand, the steamer was doing very well. Driven by the breeze, and propelled by her wheels, away she went, edging farther and farther from the island, as the person from the Custom-house succeeded, as it might be, inch by inch, in persuading the captain of the necessity of his so doing. At length a sail was dimly seen ahead, and then no doubt was entertained that the brig had got to the northward and eastward of them. Half an hour brought the steamer alongside of this sail, which turned out to be a brig that had come over the shoals, and was beating into the ocean, on her way to one of the southern ports. Her captain said there had nothing passed to the eastward.

Round went the steamer, and in went all her canvas. Ten minutes later the lookout saw a sail to the westward, standing before the wind. Odd as it might seem, the steamer's people now fancied they were sure of the Swash. There she was, coming directly for them, with squared yards! The distance was short, or a vessel could not have been seen by that light, and the two craft were soon near each other. A gun was actually cleared on board the steamer, ere it was ascertained that the stranger was the schooner! It was now midnight, and nothing was in sight but the coasting brig. Reluctantly, the revenue people gave the matter up; the Molly Swash having again eluded them, though by means unknown.

CHAPTER IV.

"Leander dived for love. Leucadia's cliff
The Lesbian Sappho leaped from in a miff,
To punish Phaon ; Icarus went dead,
Because the wax did not continue stiff ;
And, had he minded what his father said,
He had not given a name unto his watery bed."

SANDS.

WE must now advance the time several days, and change the scene to a distant part of the ocean ; within the tropics indeed. The females had suffered slight attacks of sea-sickness, and recovered from them, and the brig was safe from all her pursuers. The manner of Spike's escape was simple enough, and without any necromancy. While the steamer, on the one hand, was standing away to the northward and eastward, in order to head him off, and the schooner was edging in with the island, in order to prevent his beating up to windward of it, within its shadows, the brig had run close round the northern margin of the land, and hauled up to leeward of the island, passing between it and the steamer. All this time, her movements were concealed from the schooner by the island itself, and from the steamer, by its shadow and dark background, aided by the distance. By making short tacks, this expedient answered perfectly well ; and, at the very moment when the two revenue vessels met, at midnight, about three leagues to leeward of Block Island, the brigantine, Molly Swash, was just clearing its most weatherly point, on the larboard tack, and coming out exactly at the spot where the steamer was when first seen that afternoon. Spike stood to the westward, until he was cer-

93

tain of having the island fairly between him and his pursuers, when he went about, and filled away on his course, running out to sea again on an easy bowline. At sunrise the next day he was fifty miles to the southward and eastward of Montauk ; the schooner was going into New London, her officers and people quite chop-fallen ; and the steamer was paddling up the Sound, her captain being fully persuaded that the runaways had returned in the direction from which they had come, and might yet be picked up in that quarter.

The weather was light, just a week after the events related in the close of the last chapter. By this time the brig had got within the influence of the trades ; and, it being the intention of Spike to pass to the southward of Cuba, he had so far profited by the westerly winds, as to get well to the eastward of the Mona Passage, the strait through which he intended to shape his course on making the islands. Early on that morning Mrs. Budd had taken her seat on the trunk of the cabin, with a complacent air, and arranged her netting, some slight passages of gallantry, on the part of the captain, having induced her to propose netting him a purse. Biddy was going to and fro, in quest of silks and needles, her mistress having become slightly capricious in her tastes of late, and giving her, on all such occasions, at least a double allowance of occupation. As for Rose, she sat reading beneath the shade of the coach-house deck, while the handsome young mate was within three feet of her, working up his logarithms, but within the sanctuary of his own state-room ; the open door and window of which, however, gave him every facility he could desire to relieve his mathematics, by gazing at the sweet countenance of his charming neighbor. Jack Tier and Josh were both passing to and fro, as is the wont of stewards, between the camboose and the cabin, the breakfast table being just then in the course of preparation. In all other respects, always excepting the man at the wheel, who stood within a fathom of Rose, Spike had the quarter-deck to himself, and did not fail to pace its weather-side with an air that denoted the master and owner. After exhibiting his sturdy, but short,

person in this manner, to the admiring eyes of all beholders,
for some time, the captain suddenly took a seat at the side
of the relict, and dropped into the following discourse:

"The weather is moderate, Madam Budd; quite moderate," observed Spike, a sentimental turn coming over him
at the moment. "What I call moderate and agreeable."

"So much the better for us; the ladies are fond of
moderation, sir."

"Not in admiration, Madam Budd—ha, ha, ha! no, not in
admiration. *Immoderation* is what they like when it comes
to that. I'm a single man, but I know that the ladies
like admiration—mind where you're sheering to," the
captain said, interrupting himself a little fiercely, considering the nature of the subject, in consequence of Jack Tier's
having trodden on his toe in passing, "or I'll•teach you the
navigation of the quarter-deck, Mr. Burgoo!"

"Moderation—moderation, my good captain," said the
simpering relict. "As to admiration, I confess that it is
agreeable to us ladies; more especially when it comes from
gentlemen of sense, and intelligence, and experience."

Rose fidgeted, having heard every word that was said,
and her face flushed; for she doubted not that Harry's
ears were as good as her own. As for the man at the
wheel, he turned the tobacco over in his mouth, hitched up
his trousers, and appeared interested, though somewhat
mystified; the conversation was what he would have termed
"talking dictionary," and he had some curiosity to learn
how the captain would work his way out of it. It is probable that Spike himself had some similar gleamings of the
difficulties of his position, for he looked a little troubled,
though still resolute. It was the first time he had ever
lain yard-arm and yard-arm with a widow, and he had long
entertained a fancy that such a situation was trying to the
best of men.

"Yes, Madam Budd, yes," he said, "exper'ence and sense
carry weight with 'em, wherever they go. I'm glad to find
that you entertain these just notions of us gentlemen, and
make a difference between boys and them that's seen and
known exper'ence. For my part, I count youngsters under

forty as so much lumber about decks, as to any comfort and calculations in keepin' a family, as a family *ought* to be kept.''

Mrs. Budd looked interested, but she remained silent on hearing this remark, as became her sex.

"Every man ought to settle in life, some time or other, Madam Budd, accordin' to my notion, though no man ought to be in a boyish haste about it,'' continued the captain. "Now, in my own case, I've been so busy all my youth—not that I'm very old now, but I'm no boy—but all my younger days have been passed in trying to make things meet, in a way to put any lady who might take a fancy to me—''

"Oh, captain—that is *too* strong! The ladies do not take fancies for gentlemen, but the gentlemen take fancies for ladies!''

"Well, well, you know what I mean, Madam Budd; and so long as the parties understand each other, a word dropped, or a word put into a charter-party, makes it neither stronger nor weaker. There's a time, howsomever, in every man's life, when he begins to think of settling down, and of considerin' himself as a sort of mooring-chain, for children and the likes of them to make fast to. Such is my natur', I will own; and ever since I've got to be intimate in your family, Madam Budd, that sentiment has grown stronger and stronger in me, till it has got to be uppermost in all my idees. Bone of my bone, and flesh of my flesh, as a body might say.''

Mrs. Budd now looked more than interested, for she looked a little confused, and Rose began to tremble for her aunt. It was evident that the parties most conspicuous in this scene were not at all conscious that they were overheard, the intensity of their attention being too much concentrated on what was passing to allow of any observation without their own narrow circle. What may be thought still more extraordinary, but what in truth was the most natural of all, each of the parties was so intently bent on his, or her, own train of thought, that neither in the least suspected any mistake.

"Grown with your growth, and strengthened with your strength," rejoined the relict, smiling kindly enough on the captain to have encouraged a much more modest man than he happened to be.

"Yes, Madam Budd—very just that remark; grown with my strength, and strengthened with my growth, as one might say; though I've not done much at growing for a good many years. Your late husband, Captain Budd, often remarked how very early I got my growth; and rated me as an 'able-bodied' hand when most lads think it an honor to be placed among the 'or'naries.'"

The relict looked grave; and she wondered at any man's being so singular as to allude to a first husband, at the very moment he was thinking of offering himself for a second. As for herself, she had not uttered as many words in the last four years, as she had uttered in that very conversation, without making some allusion to her "poor dear Mr. Budd." The reader is not to do injustice to the captain's widow, however, by supposing for a moment that she was actually so weak as to feel any tenderness for a man like Spike, which would be doing a great wrong to both her taste and her judgment, as Rose well knew, even while most annoyed by the conversation she could not but overhear. All that influenced the good relict was that besetting weakness of her sex, which renders admiration so universally acceptable; and predisposes a female, as it might be, to listen to a suitor with indulgence, and some little show of kindness, even when resolute to reject him. As for Rose, to own the truth, her aunt did not give her a thought, as yet, notwithstanding Spike was getting to be so sentimental.

"Yes, your late excellent and honorable consort always said that I got my growth sooner than any youngster he ever fell in with," resumed the captain, after a short pause; exciting fresh wonder in his companion, that he would persist in lugging in the "dear departed" so very unseasonably. "I am a great admirer of all the Budd family, my good lady, and only wish my connection with it had never tarminated; if tarminated it can be called."

"It need not be terminated, Captain Spike, so long as friendship exists in the human heart."

"Ay, so it is always with you ladies; when a man is bent on suthin' closer and more interestin' like, you're for putting us off on friendship. Now friendship is good enough in its way, Madam Budd, but friendship is n't *love*."

"*Love!*" echoed the widow, fairly starting, though she looked down at her netting, and looked as confused as she knew how. "That is a very decided word, Captain Spike, and should never be mentioned to a woman's ear lightly."

So the captain now appeared to think, too, for no sooner had he delivered himself of the important monosyllable than he left the widow's side, and began to pace the deck, as it might be to moderate his own ardor. As for Rose, she blushed, if her more practised aunt did not; while Harry Mulford laughed heartily, taking good care, how-ever, not to be heard. The man at the wheel turned the tobacco again, gave his trousers another hitch, and won-dered anew whither the skipper was bound. But the droll-est manifestation of surprise came from Josh, the steward, who was passing along the lee-side of the quarter-deck, with a teapot in his hand, when the energetic manner of the captain sent the words " friendship is n't *love*" to his ears. This induced him to stop for a single instant, and to cast a wondering glance behind him ; after which he moved on toward the galley, mumbling as he went, "Lub! what *he* want of lub, or what lub want of *him!* Well, I do t'ink Captain Spike bowse his jib out pretty 'arly dis mor-nin'."

Captain Spike soon got over the effects of his effort, and the confusion of the relict did not last any material length of time. As the former had gone so far, however, he thought the present an occasion as good as another to bring matters to a crisis.

"Our sentiments sometimes get to be so strong, Madam Budd," resumed the lover, as he took his seat again on the trunk, "that they run away with us. Men are liable to be run away with as well as ladies. I once had a ship run away with me, and a pretty time we had of it. Did you ever hear of a ship's running away with her people, Madam Budd, just as your horse ran away with your buggy?"

"I suppose I must have heard of such things, sir, my education having been so maritime, though just at this moment I cannot recall an instance. When my horse ran away, the buggy was cap-asided. Did your vessel cap-aside on the occasion you mention?"

"No, Madam Budd, no. The ship was off the wind at the time I mean, and vessels do not capsize when off the wind. I'll tell you how it happened. We was a scuddin' under a goose-wing foresail—"

"Yes, yes," interrupted the relict, eagerly. "I've often heard of that sail, which is small, and used only in tempests."

"Heavy weather, Madam Budd, only in heavy weather."

"It is amazing to me, captain, how you seamen manage to weigh the weather. I have often heard of light weather and heavy weather, but never fairly understood the manner of weighing it."

"Why we *do* make out to ascertain the difference," replied the captain, a little puzzled for an answer; "and I suppose it must be by means of the barometer, which goes up and down like a pair of scales. But the time I mean, we was a scuddin' under a goose-wing foresail—"

"A sail made of goose's wings, and a beautiful object it must be; like some of the caps and cloaks that come from the islands, which are all of feathers, and charming objects are they. I beg pardon—you had your goose's wings spread—"

"Yes, Madam Budd, yes; we was steering for a Mediterranean port, intending to clear a mole-head, when a sea took us under the larboard-quarter, gave us such a sheer to port as sent our cat-head ag'in a spile, and raked away the chain-plates of the top-mast back-stays, bringing down all the forrard hamper about our ears."

This description produced such a confusion in the mind of

the widow, that she was glad when it came to an end. As for the captain, fearful that the "goose's wings" might be touched upon again, he thought it wisest to attempt another flight on those of Cupid.

"As I was sayin', Madam Budd, friendship is n't *love* ; no, not a bit of it ! Friendship is a common sort of feelin' ; but love, as you must know by exper'ence, Madam Budd, is an uncommon sort of feelin'."

"Fie, Captain Spike, gentlemen should never allude to ladies knowing anything about love. Ladies respect, and admire and esteem, and have a regard for gentlemen ; but it is almost too strong to talk about their love."

"Yes, Madam Budd, yes ; I dare say it *is* so, and *ought* to be so ; and I ask pardon for having said as much as I did. But my love for your niece is of so animated and lastin' a natur', that I scarce know what I did say."

"Captain Spike, you amaze me ! I declare I can hardly breathe for astonishment. My niece ! Surely you do not mean Rosy ! "

"Who else should I mean? My love for Miss Rose is so very decided and animated, I tell you, Madam Budd, that I will not answer for the consequences, should you not consent to her marryin' me."

" I can scarce believe my ears ! You, Stephen Spike, and an old friend of her uncle's, wishing to marry his niece ! "

"Just so, Madam Budd ; that 's it, to a shavin'. The regard I have for the whole family is so great, that nothin' less than the hand of Miss Rose in marriage can, what I call, mitigate my feelin's."

Now the relict had not one spark of tenderness herself in behalf of Spike ; while she did love Rose better than any human being, her own self excepted. But she had viewed all the sentiment of that morning, and all the fine speeches of the captain, very differently from what the present state of things told her she ought to have viewed them ; and she felt the mortification natural to her situation. The captain was so much bent on the attainment of his own object, that he saw nothing else, and was even unconscious that his extraordinary and somewhat loud discourse had been overheard. Least of all did he suspect that his admiration had been mistaken ; and that in what he called "courtin'" the niece, he had been all the while "courtin'" the aunt. But little apt as she was to discover anything, Mrs. Budd had enough of her sex's discernment in a matter of this sort, to perceive that she had fallen into an awkward mistake, and enough of her sex's pride to resent it. Taking her work in her hand, she left her seat, and descended to the cabin, with quite as much dignity in her manner as it was in the power of one of her height and "build" to express. What is the most extraordinary, neither she nor Spike ever ascertained that their whole dialogue had been overheard. Spike continued to pace the quarter-deck for several minutes, scarce knowing what to think of the relict's manner, when his attention was suddenly drawn to other matters by the familiar cry of "Sail-ho!"

This was positively the first vessel with which the Molly Swash had fallen in since she lost sight of two or three craft that had passed her in the distance, as she left the American coast. As usual, this cry brought all hands on deck, and Mulford out of his state-room.

It has been stated already that the brig was just beginning to feel the trades, and it might have been added, to see the mountains of San Domingo. The winds had been variable for the last day or two, and they still continued light, and disposed to be unsteady, ranging from northeast to southeast, with a preponderance in favor of the first point. At the cry of "Sail-ho!" everybody looked in the indicated direction, which was west, a little northerly, but for a long time without success. The cry had come from aloft, and Mulford went up as high as the fore-top before he got any glimpse of the stranger at all. He had slung a glass, and Spike was unusually anxious to know the result of his examination.

"Well, Mr. Mulford, what do you make of her?" he called out as soon as the mate announced that he saw the strange vessel.

"Wait a moment, sir, till I get a look,—she's a long way off, and hardly visible."

"Well, sir, well?"

"I can only see the heads of her topgallant-sails. She seems a ship steering to the southward, with as many kites flying as an Indiaman in the trades. She looks as if she were carrying royal stun'-sails, sir."

"The devil she does! Such a chap must not only be in a hurry, but he must be strong-handed to give himself all this trouble in such light and var'able winds. Are his yards square? Is he man-of-war-ish?"

"There's no telling, sir, at this distance; though I rather think it's stun'-sails that I see. Go down and get your breakfast, and in half an hour I'll give a better account of him."

This was done, Mrs. Budd appearing at the table with great dignity in her manner. Although she had so naturally supposed that Spike's attentions had been intended for herself, she was rather mortified than hurt on discovering her mistake. Her appetite, consequently, was not impaired, though her stomach might have been said to be very full. The meal passed off without any scene, notwithstanding, and Spike soon reappeared on deck, still masticating the last mouthful like a man in a hurry, and a good deal *à l'Américaine*. Mulford saw his arrival, and immediately levelled his glass again.

"Well, what news now, sir?" called out the captain. "You must have a better chance at him by this time, for I can see the chap from off the coach-house here."

"Ay, ay, sir; he's a bit nearer, certainly. I should say that craft is a ship under stun'-sails, looking to the eastward of south; and that there are caps with gold bands on her quarter-deck."

"How low down can you see her?" demanded Spike, in a voice of thunder.

So emphatic and remarkable was the captain's manner in putting this question, that the mate cast a look of surprise beneath him ere he answered it. A look with the glass succeeded, when the reply was given.

"Ay, ay, sir; there can be no mistake—it's a cruiser, you may depend on it. I can see the heads of her topsails now, and they are so square and symmetrical, that gold bands are below beyond all doubt."

"Perhaps he's a Frenchman; Johnny Crapaud keeps cruisers in these seas as well as the rest on 'em."

"Johnny Crapaud's craft don't spread such arms, sir. The ship is either English or American; and he's heading for the Mona Passage as well as ourselves."

"Come down, sir, come down; there's work to be done as soon as you have breakfasted."

Mulford did come down, and he was soon seated at the table, with both Josh and Jack Tier for attendants. The aunt and the niece were in their own cabin, a few yards distant, with the door open.

"What a fuss 'e cap'in make 'bout dat sail," grumbled Josh, who had been in the brig so long that he sometimes took liberties with even Spike himself. "What good he t'ink 't will do to measure him inch by inch? Bye'm by he get alongside, and den 'e ladies even can tell all about him."

"He nat'rally wishes to know who gets alongside," put in Tier, somewhat apologetically.

"What matter dat? All sort of folk get alongside of Molly Swash; and what good it do 'em? Yoh! yoh! yoh! I *do* remem'er sich times vid 'e ole hussy!"

"What old hussy do you mean?" demanded Jack Tier a little fiercely, and in a way to draw Mulford's eyes from the profile of Rose's face to the visages of his two attendants.

"Come, come, gentlemen, if you please; recollect where you are," interrupted the mate, authoritatively. "You are not now squabbling in your galley, but are in the cabin. What is it to you, Tier, if Josh does call the brig an old hussy; she is old, as we all know, and years are respectable; and as for her being a 'hussy,' that is a term of endearment sometimes. I've heard the captain himself call the Molly a 'hussy,' fifty times, and he loves her as he does the apple of his eye."

This interference put an end to the gathering storm as a matter of course, and the two disputants shortly after passed on deck. No sooner was the coast clear than Rose stood in the door of her own cabin.

"Do you think the strange vessel is an American?" she asked eagerly.

"It is impossible to say—English or American I make no doubt. But why do you enquire?"

"Both my aunt and myself desire to quit the brig, and if the stranger should prove to be an American vessel of war, might not the occasion be favorable?"

"And what reason can you give for desiring to do so?"

"What signifies a reason," answered Rose with spirit. "Spike is not our master, and we can come and go as we may see fit."

"But a reason must be given to satisfy the commander of the vessel of war. Craft of that character are very particular about the passengers they receive; nor would it be altogether wise in two unprotected females to go on board a cruiser, unless in a case of the most obvious necessity."

"Will not what has passed this morning be thought a sufficient reason?" added Rose, drawing nearer to the mate, and dropping her voice so as not to be heard by her aunt.

Mulford smiled as he gazed at the earnest but attractive countenance of his charming companion.

"And who could tell it, or how could it be told? Would the commander of a vessel of war incur the risk of receiving such a person as yourself on board his vessel, for the reason that the master of the craft she was in when he fell in with her desired to marry her?"

Rose appeared vexed, but she was at once made sensible that it was not quite as easy to change her vessel at sea, as to step into a strange door in a town. She drew slowly back into her own cabin silent and thoughtful; her aunt pursuing her netting the whole time with an air of dignified industry.

"Well, Mr. Mulford, well," called out Spike at the head of the cabin stairs, "what news from the coffee?"

"All ready, sir," answered the mate, exchanging signifi-cant glances with Rose. "I shall be up in a moment."

That moment soon came, and Mulford was ready for duty. While below, Spike had caused certain purchases to be got aloft, and the main-hatch was open and the men collected around it, in readiness to proceed with the work. Harry asked no questions, for the preparations told him what was about to be done, but passing below, he took charge of the duty there, while the captain superintended the part that was conducted on deck. In the course of the next hour eight twelve-pound carronades were sent up out of the hold, and mounted in as many of the ports which lined the bulwarks of the brigantine. The men seemed to be accustomed to the sort of work in which they were now engaged, and soon had their light batteries in order, and ready for service. In the meantime the two vessels kept on their respective courses, and by the time the guns were mounted there was a sensible difference in their relative positions. The stranger had drawn so near the brigantine as to be very obvious from the latter's deck, while the brig-antine had drawn so much nearer to the islands of San Domingo and Porto Rico, as to render the opening between them, the well-known Mona Passage, distinctly visible.

Of all this Spike appeared to be fully aware, for he quitted the work several times before it was finished, in order to take a look at the stranger, and at the land. When the batteries were arranged, he and Mulford, each provided with a glass, gave a few minutes to a more delib-erate examination of the first.

"That's the Mona ahead of us," said the captain; "of that there can be no question, and a very pretty land-fall you've made of it, Harry. I'll allow you to be as good a navigator as floats."

"Nevertheless, sir, you have not seen fit to let me know whither the brig is really bound this voyage."

"No matter for that, young man—no matter as yet. All in good time. When I tell you to lay your course for the Mona, you can lay your course for the Mona; and, as soon as we are through the passage, I'll let you know what is wanted next—if that bloody chap, who is nearing us, will let me."

"And why should any vessel wish to molest us on our passage, Captain Spike?"

"Why, sure enough! It's war-times, you know, and war-times always bring trouble to the trader—though it sometimes brings profit, too."

As Spike concluded, he gave his mate a knowing wink which the other understood to mean that he expected himself some of the unusual profit to which he alluded. Mulford did not relish this secret communication, for the past had induced him to suspect the character of the trade in which his commander was accustomed to engage. Without making any sort of reply, or encouraging the confidence by even a smile, he levelled his glass at the stranger, as did Spike, the instant he ceased to grin.

"That's one of Uncle Sam's fellows!" exclaimed the captain, dropping the glass. "I'd swear to the chap in any admiralty court on 'arth."

"'T is a vessel of war, out of all doubt," returned the mate, "and under a cloud of canvas. I can make out the heads of her courses now, and see that she is carrying hard, for a craft that is almost close-hauled."

"Ay, ay; no merchantman keeps his light stun'-sails set, as near the wind as that fellow's going. He's a big chap, too—a frigate, at least, by his canvas."

"I do not know, sir—they build such heavy corvettes nowadays, that I should rather take her for one of them. They tell me ships are now sent to sea which mount only two-and-twenty guns, but which measure quite a thousand tons."

"With thunderin' batteries, of course."

"With short thirty-twos and a few rapping sixty-eight Paixhans—or Columbiads, as they ought in justice to be called."

"And you think this chap likely to be a craft of that sort?"

"Nothing is more probable, sir. Government has several, and, since this war has commenced, it has been sending off cruiser after cruiser into the Gulf. The Mexicans dare not send a vessel of war to sea, which would be sending them to Norfolk, or New York, at once; but no one can say when they may begin to make a prey of our commerce."

"They have taken nothing as yet, Mr. Mulford, and, to tell you the truth, I'd much rather fall in with one of Don Montezuma's craft than one of Uncle Sam's."

"That is a singular taste, for an American, Captain Spike, unless you think, now our guns are mounted, we can handle a Mexican," returned Mulford, coldly. "At all events, it is some answer to those who ask 'What is the navy about?' that months of war have gone by, and not an American has been captured. Take away that navy, and the insurance offices in Wall Street would tumble like a New York party-wall in a fire."

"Nevertheless, I'd rather take my chance, just now, with Don Montezuma than with Uncle Sam."

Mulford did not reply, though the earnest manner in which Spike expressed himself, helped to increase his distrust touching the nature of the voyage. With him the captain had no further conference, but it was different as respects the boatswain. That worthy was called aft, and for half an hour he and Spike were conversing apart, keeping their eyes fastened on the strange vessel most of the time.

It was noon before all uncertainty touching the character of the stranger ceased. By that time, however, both vessels were entering the Mona Passage; the brig well to windward, on the Porto Rico side; while the ship was so far to leeward as to be compelled to keep everything close-hauled, in order to weather the island. The hull of the last could now be seen, and no doubt was entertained about her being a cruiser, and one of some size too. Spike thought she was a frigate; but Mulford still inclined to the opinion that she was one of the new ships; perhaps a real corvette, or with a light spar-deck over her batteries. Two or three of the new vessels were known to be thus fitted, and this might be one. At length all doubt on the subject ceased, the stranger setting an American ensign, and getting so near as to make it apparent that she had but a single line of guns. Still she was a large ship, and the manner that she ploughed through the brine, close-hauled as she was, extorted admiration even from Spike.

"We had better begin to shorten sail, Mr. Mulford," the captain at length most reluctantly remarked. "We might give the chap the slip, perhaps, by keeping close in under Porto Rico, but he would give us a long chase, and might drive us away to windward, when I wish to keep off between Cuba and Jamaica. He's a traveller; look, how he stands up to it under that cloud of canvas!"

Mulford was slow to commence on the studding-sails, and the cruiser was getting nearer and nearer. At length a gun was fired, and a heavy shot fell about two hundred yards short of the brig, and a little out of line with her. On this hint, Spike turned the hands up, and began to shorten sail. In ten minutes the Swash was under her topsail, mainsail, and jib, with her light sails hanging in the gear, and all the steering canvas in. In ten minutes more the cruiser was so near as to admit of the faces of the three or four men whose heads were above the hammock-cloths being visible, when she too began to fold her wings. In went her royals, topgallant-sails, and various kites, as it might be by some common muscular agency; and up went her courses. Everything was done at once. By this time she was crossing the brig's wake, looking exceedingly beautiful, with her topsails lifting, her light sails blowing out, and even her heavy courses fluttering in the breeze. There flew the glorious Stars and Stripes also; of brief existence, but full of recollections! The moment she had room, her helm went up, her bows fell off, and down she came, on the weather quarter of the Swash, so near as to render a trumpet nearly useless.

On board the brig everybody was on deck; even the relict having forgotten her mortification in curiosity. On board the cruiser no one was visible, with the exception of a few men in each top, and a group of gold-banded caps on the poop. Among these officers stood the captain, a red-faced, middle-aged man, with the usual signs of his rank

about him ; and at his side was his lynx-eyed first lieutenant. The surgeon and purser were also there, though they
stood a little apart from the more nautical dignitaries. The
hail that followed came out of a trumpet that was thrust
through the mizzen-rigging ; the officer who used it taking
his cue from the poop.

"What brig is that?" commenced the discourse.

"The Molly Swash, of New York, Stephen Spike, master."

"Where from, and whither bound?"

"From New York, and bound to Key West and a market."

A pause succeeded this answer, during which the officers
on the poop of the cruiser held some discourse with him of
the trumpet. During the interval the cruiser ranged fairly
up abeam.

"You are well to windward of your port, sir," observed
he of the trumpet significantly.

"I know it ; but it's war times, and I did n't know but
there might be piccaroons hovering about the Havana."

"The coast is clear, and our cruisers will keep it so. I
see you have a battery, sir ! "

"Ay, ay ; some old guns that I've had aboard these
ten years ; they 're useful, sometimes, in these seas."

"Very true. I 'll range ahead of you, and as soon as
you 've room, I 'll thank you to heave-to. I wish to send a
boat on board you."

Spike was sullen enough on receiving this order, but there
was no help for it. He was now in the jaws of the lion,
and his wisest course was to submit to the penalties of his
position with the best grace he could. The necessary orders
were consequently given, and the brig no sooner got room
than she came by the wind and backed her topsail. The
cruiser went about, and passing to windward, backed her
main-topsail just forward of the Swash's beam. Then the
latter lowered a boat, and sent it, with a lieutenant and
a midshipman in its stern-sheets, on board the brigantine.
As the cutter approached, Spike went to the gangway to
receive the strangers.

Although there will be frequent occasion to mention this cruiser, the circumstances are of so recent occurrence, that we do not choose to give either her name, or that of any one belonging to her. We shall, consequently, tell the curious, who may be disposed to turn to their navy-lists and blue-books, that the search will be of no use, as all the names we shall use, in reference to this cruiser, will be fictitious. As much of the rest of our story as the reader please may be taken for gospel; but we tell him frankly, that we have thought it most expedient to adopt assumed names, in connection with this vessel and all her officers. There are good reasons for so doing; and, among others, is that of abstaining from arming a *clique* to calumniate her commander (who, by the way, like another commander in the Gulf, that might be named, and who has actually been exposed to the sort of *tracasserie* to which there is allusion, is one of the very ablest men in the service), in order to put another in his place.

The officer who now came over the side of the Swash we shall call Wallace; he was the second lieutenant of the vessel of war. He was about thirty, and the midshipman who followed him was a well-grown lad of nineteen. Both had a decided man-of-war look, and both looked a little curiously at the vessel they had boarded.

"Your servant, sir," said Wallace, touching his cap in reply to Spike's somewhat awkward bow. "Your brig is the Molly Swash, Stephen Spike, bound from New York to Key West and a market."

"You 've got it all as straight, lieutenant, as if you was a readin' it from the log."

"The next thing, sir, is to know of what your cargo is composed?"

"Flour; eight hundred barrels of flour."

"Flour! Would you not do better to carry that to Liverpool? The Mississippi must be almost turned into paste by the quantity of flour it floats to market."

"Notwithstanding that, lieutenant, I know Uncle Sam's economy so well, as to believe I shall part with every barrel of my flour to his contractors, at a handsome profit."

"You read whig newspapers principally, I rather think Mr. Spike," answered Wallace, in his cool, deliberate way, smiling, however, as he spoke.

We may just as well say here, that nature intended this gentleman for a second lieutenant, the very place he filled. He was a capital second lieutenant, while he would not have earned his rations as first. So well was he assured of this peculiarity in his moral composition, that he did not wish to be the first lieutenant of anything in which he sailed. A respectable seaman, a well-read and intelligent man, a capital deck officer, or watch officer, he was too indolent to desire to be anything more, and was as happy as the day was long, in the easy berth he filled. The first lieutenant had been his messmate as a midshipman, and ranked him but two on the list in his present commission ; but he did not envy him in the least. On the contrary, one of his greatest pleasures was to get "Working Willy," as he called his senior, over a glass of wine, or a tumbler of "hot stuff," and make him recount the labors of the day. On such occasions, Wallace never failed to compare the situation of "Working Willy" with his own gentle-manlike ease and independence. As second lieutenant, his rank raised him above most of the unpleasant duty of the ship, while it did not raise him high enough to plunge him into the never-ending labors of his senior. He delighted to call himself the "ship's gentleman," a *sobriquet* he well deserved, on more accounts than one.

"You read whig newspapers principally, I rather think, Mr. Spike," answered the lieutenant, as has just been men-tioned, "while we on board the Poughkeepsie indulge in looking over the columns of the *Union*, as well as over those of the *Intelligencer*, when by good luck we can lay our hands on a stray number."

"That ship, then, is called the Poughkeepsie, is she, sir?" inquired Spike.

"Such is her name, thanks to a most beneficent and sage provision of Congress, which has extended its paren-tal care over the navy so far as to imagine that a man chosen by the people to exercise so many of the functions

of a sovereign, is not fit to name a ship. All our two and
three deckers are to be called after states : the frigates
after rivers ; and the sloops after towns. Thus it is that
our craft has the honor to be called the United States ship,
the Poughkeepsie instead of the Arrow, or the Wasp, or the
Curlew, or the Petrel, as might otherwise have been the case.
But the wisdom of Congress is manifest, for the plan teaches
us sailors geography.''

"Yes, sir, yes, one can pick up a bit of l'arnin' in that
way cheap. The Poughkeepsie, Captain——?''

"The United States ship Poughkeepsie, 20, Captain Adam
Mull, at your service. But, Mr. Spike, you will allow me to
look at your papers. It is a duty I like, for it can be performed quietly, and without any fuss.''

Spike looked distrustfully at his new acquaintance, but
went for his vessel's papers without any very apparent hesitation. Everything was *en regle*, and Wallace soon got
through with the clearance, manifest, etc. Indeed the cargo,
on paper at least, was of the simplest and least complicated
character, being composed of nothing but eight hundred
barrels of flour.

"It all looks very well on paper, Mr. Spike,'' added the
boarding officer. "With your permission, we will next see
how it looks in sober reality. I perceive your main hatch is
open, and I suppose it will be no difficult matter just to take
a glance at your hold.''

"Here is a ladder, sir, that will take us at once to the
half-deck, for I have no proper 'twixt decks in this craft ;
she's too small for that sort of outfit.''

"No matter, she has a hold, I suppose, and that can contain cargo. Take me to it by the shortest road, Mr. Spike,
for I am no great admirer of trouble.''

Spike now led the way below, Wallace following, leaving
the midshipman on deck, who had fallen into conversation
with the relict and her pretty niece. The half-deck of the brigantine contained spare sails, provisions, and water, as usual,
while quantities of old canvas lay scattered over the cargo ;
more especially in the wake of the hatches, of which there
were two besides that which led from the quarter-deck.

"Flour to the number of eight hundred barrels," said Wallace, striking his foot against a barrel that lay within his reach. " The cargo is somewhat singular to come from New York, going to Key West, my dear Spike ! "

" I suppose you know what sort of a place Key West is, sir ; a bit of an island in which there is scarce so much as a potato grows."

" Ay, ay, sir ; I know Key West very well, having been in and out a dozen times. All eatables are imported, turtle excepted. But flour can be brought down the Mississippi so much cheaper than it can be brought from New York."

" Have you any idee, lieutenant, what Uncle Sam's men are paying for it at *New Orleens*, just to keep soul and bodies together among the so'gers? "

" That may be true, sir—quite true, I dare say, Mr. Spike. Have n't you a bit of a chair that a fellow can sit down on ? this half-deck of yours is none of the most comfortable places to stand in. Thank you, sir—thank you with all my heart. What lots of old sails you have scattered about the hold, especially in the wake of the hatches ! "

" Why, the craft being little more than in good ballast trim, I keep the hatches off to air her ; and the spray might spit down upon the flour at odd times but for them 'ere sails."

" Ay, a prudent precaution. So you think Uncle Sam's people will be after this flour as soon as they learn you have got it snug in at Key West? "

" What more likely, sir ? You know how it is with our government—always wrong, whatever it does ! and I can show you paragraphs in letters written from *New Orleens*, which tell us that Uncle Sam is paying seventy-five and eighty per cent. more for flour than anybody else."

" He must be a flush old chap to be able to do that, Spike."

" Flush ! I rather think he is. Do you know that he is spendin', accordin' to approved accounts, at this blessed moment, as much as half a million a day ? I own a wish to be pickin' up some of the coppers while they are scattered about so plentifully."

8

"Half a million a day! why that is only at the rate of $187,000,000 per annum ; a mere trifle, Spike, that is scarce worth mentioning among us mariners."

" 'It's so in the newspapers, I can swear, lieutenant."

"Ay, ay, and the newspapers will swear to it, too, and they that gave the newspapers their cue. But no matter, our business is with this flour. Will you sell us a barrel or two for our mess? I heard the caterer say we should want flour in the course of a week or so."

Spike seemed embarrassed, though not to a degree to awaken suspicion in his companion.

"I never sold cargo at sea, long as I 've sailed and owned a craft," he answered, as if uncertain what to do. "If you'll pay the price I expect to get in the Gulf, and will take *ten* barrels, I don't know but we may make a trade on't. I shall only ask expected prices."

"Which will be—?"

"Ten dollars a barrel. For one hundred silver dollars I will put into your boat ten barrels of the very best brand known in the western country."

"This is dealing rather more extensively than I antici- pated, but we will reflect on it."

Wallace now indolently arose and ascended to the quarter- deck, followed by Spike, who continued to press the flour on him, as if anxious to make money. But the lieutenant hesitated about paying a price as high as ten dollars, or to take a quantity as large as ten barrels.

"Our mess is no great matter after all," he said care- lessly. "Four lieutenants, the purser, two doctors, the master, and a marine officer, and you get us all. Nine men could never eat ten barrels of flour, my dear Spike, you will see for yourself, with the quantity of excellent bread we carry. You forget the bread."

"Not a bit of it, Mr. Wallace, since that is your name. But such flour as this of mine has not been seen in the Gulf this many a day. I ought in reason to ask twelve dollars for it, and insist on such a ship as your'n's taking twenty instead of the ten barrels."

"I thank you, sir, the ten will more than suffice ; unless

indeed, the captain wants some for the cabin. How is it with your steerage messes, Mr. Archer; do *you* want any flour?''

"We draw a little from the ship, according to rule, sir, but we can't go as many puddings latterly as we could before we touched last at the Havana,'' answered the laughing midshipman. "There is n't a fellow among us, sir, that could pay a shore-boat for landing him, should we go in again before the end of another month. I never knew such a place as Havana. They say midshipmen's money melts there twice as soon as lieutenants' money.''

"It 's clear, then, *you 'll* not take any of the ten. I am afraid after all, Mr. Spike, we cannot trade, unless you will consent to let me have two barrels. I 'll venture on two at ten dollars, high as the price is.''

"I should n't forgive myself in six months for making so bad a bargain, lieutenant, so we 'll say no more about it, if you please.''

"Here is a lady that wishes to say a word to you, Mr. Wallace, before we go back to the ship, if you are at leisure to hear her, or *them*—for there are two of them,'' put in Archer.

At this moment Mrs. Budd was approaching with a dignified step, while Rose followed timidly a little in the rear. Wallace was a good deal surprised at this application, and Spike was quite as much provoked. As for Mulford, he watched the interview from a distance, a great deal more interested in its result than he cared to have known, more especially to his commanding officer. Its object was to get a passage in the vessel of war.

"You are an officer of that Uncle Sam vessel,'' commenced Mrs. Budd, who thought that she would so much the more command the respect and attention of her listener, by showing him early how familiar she was with even the slang dialect of the seas.

"I have the honor, ma'am, to belong to that Uncle Sam craft,'' answered Wallace gravely, though he bowed politely at the same time, looking intently at the beautiful girl in the background as he so did.

"So I've been told, sir. She's a beautiful vessel, lieutenant, and is full-jiggered, I perceive."

For the first time in his life, or at least for the first time since his first cruise, Wallace wore a mystified look, being absolutely at a loss to imagine what "full-jiggered" could mean. He only looked, therefore, for he did not answer.

"Mrs. Budd means that you've a full-*rigged* craft," put in Spike, anxious to have a voice in the conference, "this vessel being only a *half*-rigged brig."

"Oh! ay; yes, yes—the lady is quite right. We are full-jiggered from our dead-eyes to our eye-bolts."

"I thought as much, sir, from your ground hamper and top-tackles," added the relict, smiling. "For my part there is nothing in nature that I so much admire as a full-jiggered ship, with her canvas out of the bolt-ropes, and her clew-lines and clew-garnets braced sharp, and her yards all abroad."

"Yes, ma'am, it is just as you say, a very charming spectacle. Our baby was born full grown, and with all her hamper aloft just as you see her. Some persons refer vessels to art, but I think you are quite right in referring them to nature."

"Nothing *can* be more natural to me, lieutenant, than a fine ship standing on her canvas. It's an object to improve the heart and to soften the understanding."

"So I should think, ma'am," returned Wallace, a little quizzically, "judging from the effect on yourself."

This speech, unfortunately timed as it was, wrought a complete change in Rose's feelings, and she no longer wished to exchange the Swash for the Poughkeepsie. She saw that her aunt was laughed at in secret, and that was a circumstance that never failed to grate on every nerve in her system. She had been prepared to second and sustain the intended application; she was now determined to oppose it.

"Yes, sir," resumed the unconscious relict, "and to soften the understanding. Lieutenant, did you ever cross the Capricorn?"

"No less than six times; three going and three returning, you know."

"And did Neptune come on board you, and were you shaved?"

"Everything was done *secundem artem*, ma'am. The razor was quite an example of what are called in poetry 'thoughts too deep for tears.'"

"That must have been delightful. As for me, I'm quite a devotee of Neptune's; but I'm losing time, for no doubt your ship is all ready to pull away and carry on sail——"

"Aunt, may I say a word to you before you go any further?" put in Rose in her quiet but very controlling way.

The aunt complied, and Wallace, as soon as left alone, felt like a man who was released from a quicksand, into which every effort to extricate himself only plunged him so much the deeper. At this moment the ship hailed, and the lieutenant took a hasty leave of Spike, motioned to the midshipman to precede him, and followed the latter into his boat. Spike saw his visitor off in person, tending the side and offering the man-ropes with his own hands. For this civility Wallace thanked him, calling out as his boat pulled him from the brig's side, "If we '*pull* away,'" accenting the "pull" in secret derision of the relict's mistake, "*you* can *pull* away; our filling the topsail being a sign for you to do the same."

"There you go, and joy go with you," muttered Spike, as he descended from the gangway. "A pretty kettle of fish would there have been cooked had I let him have his two barrels of flour."

The man-of-war's cutter was soon under the lee of the ship, where it discharged its freight, when it was immediately run up. During the whole time Wallace had been absent, Captain Mull and his officers remained on the poop, principally occupied in examining and discussing the merits of the Swash. No sooner had their officer returned, however, than an order was given to fill away, it being supposed that the Poughkeepsie had no further concern with the brigantine. As for Wallace, he ascended to the poop and made the customary report.

"It's a queer cargo to be carrying to Key West from the Atlantic coast," observed the captain in a deliberating sort of manner, as if the circumstance excited suspicion. "Yet the Mexicans can hardly be in want of any such supplies."

"Did you *see* the flour, Wallace?" inquired the first lieutenant, who was well aware of his messmate's indolence.

"Yes, sir, and *felt it* too. The lower hold of the brig is full of flour, and of nothing else."

"Ware round, sir—ware round and pass athwart the brig's wake," interrupted the captain. "There's plenty of room now, and I wish to pass as near that craft as we can."

This manœuvre was executed. The sloop-of-war no sooner filled her maintop-sail than she drew ahead, leaving plenty of room for the brigantine to make sail on her course. Spike did not profit by this opening, however, but he sent several men aloft forward, where they appeared to be getting ready to send down the upper yards and the topgallant-mast. No sooner was the sloop-of-war's helm put up than that vessel passed close along the brigantine's weather side, and kept off across her stern on her course. As she did this the canvas was fluttering aboard her, in the process of making sail, and Mull held a short discourse with Spike.

"Is anything the matter aloft?" demanded the man-of-war's man.

"Ay, ay; I've sprung my topgallant-mast, and think this a good occasion to get another up in its place."

"Shall I lend you a carpenter or two, Mr. Spike?"

"Thank'ee, sir, thankee with all my heart; but we can do without them. It's an old stick, and it's high time a better stood where it does. Who knows but I may be chased and feel the want of reliable spars?"

Captain Mull smiled and raised his cap in the way of an adieu, when the conversation ended; the Poughkeepsie sliding off rapidly with a free wind, leaving the Swash nearly stationary. In ten minutes the two vessels were more than a mile apart; in twenty, beyond the reach of shot.

Notwithstanding the natural and commonplace manner in which this separation took place, there was much distrust on board each vessel, and a good deal of consummate management on the part of Spike. The latter knew that every foot the sloop-of-war went on her course, carried her just so far to leeward, placing his own brig, in so much, dead to windward of her. As the Swash's best point of sailing, relatively considered, was close-hauled, this was giving to Spike a great security against any change of purpose on the part of the vessel of war. Although his people were aloft and actually sent down the topgallant-mast, it was only to send it up again, the spar being of admirable toughness, and as sound as the day it was cut.

"I don't think, Mr. Mulford," said the captain, sarcastically, "that Uncle Sam's glasses are good enough to tell the difference in wood at two leagues' distance, so we'll trust to the old stick a little longer. Ay, ay, let 'em run off before it, we'll find another road by which to reach our port."

"The sloop-of-war is going round the south side of Cuba, Captain Spike," answered the mate, "and I have understood you to say that you intended to go by the same passage."

"A body may change his mind, and no murder. Only consider, Harry, how common it is for folks to change their minds. I *did* intend to pass between Cuba and Jamaica, but I intend it no longer. Our run from Montauk has been oncommon short, and I've time enough to spare to go to the southward of Jamaica too, if the notion takes me."

"That would greatly prolong the passage, Captain Spike; a week at least."

"What if it does? I've a week to spare; we're nine days afore our time."

"Our time for what, sir? Is there any particular time set for a vessel's going into Key West?"

"Don't be womanish and over-cur'ous, Mulford. I sail with sealed orders, and when we get well to windward of Jamaica, 'twill be time enough to open them."

Spike was as good as his word. As soon as he thought the sloop-of-war was far enough to leeward, or when she was hull down, he filled away and made sail on the wind to get nearer to Porto Rico. Long ere it was dark he had lost sight of the sloop-of-war, when he altered his course to southwesterly, which was carrying him in the direction he named, or to windward of Jamaica.

While this artifice was being practised on board the Molly Swash, the officers of the Poughkeepsie were not quite satisfied with their own mode of proceeding with the brigantine. The more they reasoned on the matter, the more unlikely it seemed to them that Spike could be really carrying a cargo of flour from New York to Key West, in the expectation of disposing of it to the United States contractors, and the more out of the way did he seem to be in running through the Mona Passage.

"His true course should have been by the Hole in the Wall, and so down along the north side of Cuba, before the wind," observed the first lieutenant. "I wonder that never struck you, Wallace; *you*, who so little like trouble."

"Certainly I knew it, but we lazy people like running off before the wind, and I did not know but such were Mr. Spike's tastes," answered the "ship's gentleman." "In my judgment, the reluctance he showed to letting us have any of his flour, is much the most suspicious circumstance in the whole affair."

These two speeches were made on the poop, in the presence of the captain, but in a sort of an aside that admitted of some of the ward-room familiarity exhibited. Captain Mull was not supposed to hear what passed, though hear it he in fact did, as was seen by his own remarks, which immediately succeeded.

"I understood you to say, Mr. Wallace," observed the captain, a little dryly, "that you *saw* the flour yourself?"

"I saw the flour-*barrels*, sir; and as regularly built were they as any barrels that ever were branded. But a flour-barrel may have contained something beside flour."

"Flour usually makes itself visible in the handling; were these barrels quite clean?"

"Far from it, sir. They showed flour on their staves, like any other cargo. After all, the man may have more sense than we give him credit for, and find a high market for his cargo."

Captain Mull seemed to muse, which was a hint for his juniors not to continue the conversation, but rather to seem to muse, too. After a short pause the captain quietly remarked, "Well, gentlemen, he will be coming down after us, I suppose, as soon as he gets his new topgallant-mast on end, and then we can keep a bright lookout for him. We shall cruise off Cape St. Antonio for a day or two, and no doubt shall get another look at him. I should like to have one baking from his flour.

But Spike had no intention to give the Poughkeepsie the desired opportunity. As has been stated, he stood off to the southward on a wind, and completely doubled the eastern end of Jamaica, when he put his helm up, and went, with favoring wind and current, toward the north-ward and westward. The consequence was, that he did not fall in with the Poughkeepsie at all, which vessel was keeping a sharp lookout for him in the neighborhood of Cape St. Antonio and the Isle of Pines, at the very mo-ment he was running down the coast of Yucatan. Of all the large maritime countries of the world, Mexico, on the Atlantic, is that which is the most easily blockaded, by a superior naval power. By maintaining a proper force between Key West and the Havana, and another squadron between Cape St. Antonio and Loggerhead Key, the whole country, the Bay of Honduras excepted, is shut up, as it might be in a band-box. It is true the Gulf would be left open to the Mexicans, were not squadrons kept nearer in; but, as for anything getting out into the broad Atlan-tic, it would be next to hopeless. The distance to be watched between the Havana and Key West is only about sixty miles, while that in the other direction is not much greater.

While the Swash was making the circuit of Jamaica, as described, her captain had little communication with his passengers. The misunderstanding with the relict em-barrassed him as much as it embarrassed her; and he was quite willing to let time mitigate her resentment. Rose would be just as much in his power a fortnight hence as she was to-day. This cessation in the captain's attentions gave the females greater liberty, and they improved it, sin-gularly enough as it seemed to Mulford, by cultivating a strange sort of intimacy with Jack Tier. The very day

that succeeded the delicate conversation with Mrs. Budd, to
a part of which Jack had been an auditor, the uncouth-
looking steward's assistant was seen in close conference with
the pretty Rose ; the subject of their conversation being,
apparently, of a most engrossing nature. From that hour,
Jack got to be not only a confidant, but a favorite, to Mulford's great surprise. A less inviting subject for *tête-à-
têtes* and confidential dialogues, thought the young man,
could not well exist ; but so it was ; woman's caprices are
inexplicable ; and not only Rose and her aunt, but even
the captious and somewhat distrustful Biddy, manifested on
all occasions not only friendship, but kindness and consideration for Jack.

"You quite put my nose out o'joint, you Jack Tier, with
'e lady," grumbled Josh, the steward *de jure*, if not now *de
facto*, of the craft, "and I neber see nuttin' like it ! I s'pose
you expect ten dollar, at least, from dem passenger, when
we gets in. But I'd have you to know, Misser Jack, if you
please, dat a steward be a steward, and he don't like to hab
trick played wid him, afore he own face."

"Poh, poh ! Joshua," answered Jack good-naturedly,
"don't distress yourself on a consait. In the first place,
you've got no nose to be put out of joint ; or, if you have
really a nose, it has no joint. It's nat'ral for folks to like
their own color, and the ladies prefar me, because I'm white."

"No so werry white as all dat, nudder," grumbled Josh.
"I see great many whiter dan you. But, if dem lady like
you so much as to gib you ten dollar, as I expects, when
we gets in, I presumes you'll hand over half, or six dollar,
of dat money to your superior officer, as is law in de case."

"Do you call six the half of ten, Joshua, my scholar,
eh ?"

"Well, den, seven, if you like dat better. I wants just
half, and just half I means to git."

"And half you shall have, maty. I only wish you would
just tell me where we shall be, when we gets in."

"How I know, white man ? Dat belong to skipper, and
better ask him. If he don't gib you lick in de chop, p'rhaps
he tell you."

As Jack Tier had no taste for "licks in the chops," he
did not follow Josh's advice. But his agreeing to give half
of the ten dollars to the steward kept peace in the cabins.
He was even so scrupulous of his word, as to hand to Josh
a half-eagle that very day ; money he had received from
Rose ; saying he would trust to Providence for his own
half of the expected *douceur*. This concession placed Jack
Tier on high grounds with his "superior officer," and
from that time the former was left to do the whole of the
customary service of the ladies' cabin.

As respects the vessel, nothing worthy of notice occurred
until she had passed Loggerhead Key, and was fairly
launched in the Gulf of Mexico. Then, indeed, Spike took
a step that greatly surprised his mate. The latter was directed to bring all his instruments, charts, etc., and place
them in the captain's state-room, where it was understood
they were to remain until the brig got into port. Spike
was but an indifferent navigator, while Mulford was one
of a higher order than common. So much had the former
been accustomed to rely on the latter, indeed, as they approached a strange coast, that he could not possibly have
taken any step, that was not positively criminal, which
would have given his mate more uneasiness than this.

At first, Mulford naturally enough suspected that Spike
intended to push for some Mexican port, by thus blinding
his eyes as to the position of the vessel. The direction
steered, however, soon relieved the mate from this apprehension. From the eastern extremity of Yucatan, the Mexican coast trends to the westward, and even to the south
of west, for a long distance, whereas the course steered by
Spike was north, easterly. This was diverging from the
enemy's coast instead of approaching it, and the circumstance greatly relieved the apprehensions of Mulford.

Nor was the sequestration of the mate's instruments the
only suspicious act of Spike. He caused the brig's paint
to be entirely altered, and even went so far toward dis-
guising her, as to make some changes aloft. All this was
done as the vessel passed swiftly on her course, and everything had been effected, apparently to the captain's satis-

faction, when the cry of "Land-ho!" was once more heard.
The land proved to be a cluster of low, small islands, part
coral, part sand, that might have been eight or ten in
number, and the largest of which did not possess a surface
of more than a very few acres. Many were the merest
islets imaginable, and on one of the largest of the cluster
rose a tall, gaunt light-house, having the customary dwelling of its keeper at its base. Nothing else was visible;
the broad expanse of the blue waters of the Gulf excepted.
All the land in sight would not probably have made one
field of twenty acres in extent, and that seemed cut off from
the rest of the world, by a broad barrier of water. It was
a spot of such singular situation and accessories, that Mulford gazed at it with a burning desire to know where he
was, as the brig steered through a channel between two of
the islets, into a capacious and perfectly safe basin, formed
by the group, and dropped her anchor in its centre.

CHAPTER V.

"He sleeps; but dreams of massy gold,
    And heaps of pearl. He stretched his hands—
He hears a voice, 'I'll man withhold!'
    A pale one near him stands."

DANA.

IT was near night-fall when the Swash anchored among
the low and small islets mentioned. Rose had been on
deck, as the vessel approached this singular and solitary haven, watching the movements of those on board,
as well as the appearance of objects on the land, with the interest her situation would be likely to awaken. She saw the
light and manageable craft glide through the narrow and
crooked passages that led into the port, the process of anchoring, and the scene of tranquil solitude that succeeded ; each
following the other as by a law of nature. The light-house
next attracted her attention, and, as soon as the sun disappeared, her eyes were fastened on the lantern, in expectation of beholding the watchful and warning fires gleaming
there, to give the mariner notice of the position of the
dangers that surrounded the place. Minute went by after
minute, however, and the customary illumination seemed to
be forgotten.

"Why is not this light shining?" Rose asked of Mulford,
as the young man came near her, after having discharged
his duty in helping to moor the vessel, and in clearing
the decks. "All the light-houses we have passed, and they
have been fifty, have shown bright lights at this hour, but
this."

"I cannot explain it ; nor have I the smallest notion
where we are. I have been aloft, and there was nothing

in sight but this cluster of low islets, far or near. I did fancy, for a moment, I saw a speck like a distant sail, off here, to the northward and eastward, but I rather think it was a gull, or some other sea-bird glancing upward on the wing. I mentioned it to the captain when I came down, and he appeared to believe it a mistake. I have watched that light-house closely, too, ever since we came in, and I have not seen the smallest sign of life about it. It is altogether an extraordinary place!"

"One suited to acts of villainy, I fear, Harry!"

"Of that we shall be better judges to-morrow. You, at least, have one vigilant friend, who will die sooner than harm shall come to you. I believe Spike to be thoroughly unprincipled; still he knows he can go so far and no further, and has a wholesome dread of the law. But the circumstance that there should be such a port as this, with a regular light-house, and no person near the last, is so much out of the common way, that I do not know what to make of it."

"Perhaps the light-house keeper is afraid to show himself, in the presence of the Swash?"

"That can hardly be, for vessels must often enter the port, if port it can be called. But Spike is as much concerned at the circumstance that the lamps are not lighted, as any of us can be. Look, he is about to visit the building in the boat, accompanied by two of his oldest sea-dogs."

"Why might we not raise the anchor, and sail out of this place, leaving Spike ashore?" suggested Rose, with more decision and spirit than discretion.

"For the simple reason that the act would be piracy, even if I could get the rest of the people to obey my orders, as certainly I could not. No, Rose; you, and your aunt, and Biddy, however, might land at these buildings, and refuse to return, Spike having no authority over his passengers."

"Still he would have the power to make us come back to his brig. Look, he has left the vessel's side, and is going directly toward the light-house."

Mulford made no immediate answer, but remained at Rose's side, watching the movements of the captain. The last pulled directly to the islet with the buildings, a distance of only a few hundred feet, the light-house being constructed on a rocky island that was nearly in the centre of the cluster, most probably to protect it from the ravages of the waves. The fact, however, proved, as Mulford did not fail to suggest to his companion, that the beacon had been erected less to guide vessels *into* the haven, than to warn mariners at a distance, of the position of the whole group.

In less than five minutes after he had landed, Spike himself was seen in the lantern, in the act of lighting its lamps. In a very short time the place was in a brilliant blaze, reflectors and all the other parts of the machinery of the place performing their duties as regularly as if tended by the usual keeper. Soon after Spike returned on board, and the anchor-watch was set. Then everybody sought the rest that it was customary to take at that hour.

Mulford was on deck with the appearance of the sun; but he found that Spike had preceded him, had gone ashore again, had extinguished the lamps, and was coming alongside of the brig on his return. A minute later the captain came over the side.

"You were right about your sail, last night, a'ter all, Mr. Mulford," said Spike, on coming aft. "There she is, sure enough; and we shall have her alongside to strike cargo out and in, by the time the people have got their breakfasts."

As Spike pointed toward the light-house while speaking, the mate changed his position a little, and saw that a schooner was coming down towards the islets before the wind. Mulford now began to understand the motives of the captain's proceedings, though a good deal yet remained veiled in mystery. He could not tell where the brig was, nor did he know precisely why so many expedients were adopted to conceal the transfer of a cargo as simple as that of flour. But he who was in the secret left but little time for reflection; for swallowing a hasty breakfast on deck, he issued orders enough to his mate to give him quite as much duty as he could perform, when he again entered the yawl, and pulled toward the stranger.

Rose soon appeared on deck, and she naturally began to question Harry concerning their position and prospects. He was confessing his ignorance, as well as lamenting it, when his companion's sweet face suddenly flushed. She advanced a step eagerly toward the open window of Spike's state-room, then compressed her full, rich under-lip with the ivory of her upper teeth, and stood a single instant, a beautiful statue of irresolution instigated by spirit. The last quality prevailed; and Mulford was really startled when he saw Rose advance quite to the window, thrust in an arm, and turn toward him with his own sextant in her hand. During the course of the passage out, the young man had taught Rose to assist him in observing the longitude; and she was now ready to repeat the practice. Not a moment was lost in executing her intention. Sights were had, and the instrument was returned to its place without attracting the attention of the men, who were all busy in getting up purchases, and in making the other necessary dispositions for discharging the flour. The observations answered the purpose, though somewhat imperfectly made. Mulford had a tolerable notion of their latitude, having kept the brig's run in his head since quitting Yucatan; and he now found that their longitude was about eighty-three degrees west from Greenwich. After ascertaining this fact, a glance at the open chart, which lay on Spike's desk, satisfied him that the vessel was anchored within the group of the Dry Tortugas, or at the western termination of the well-known, formidable, and extensive Florida Reef. He had never been in that part of the world before, but had heard enough in sea-gossip, and had read enough in books, to be at once apprised of the true character of their situation. The islets were American; the light-house was American; and the haven in which the Swash lay was the very spot in the contemplation of government for an outer man-of-war harbor, where fleets might rendezvous in the future wars of that portion of the world. He now saw plainly enough the signs of the existence of a vast reef, a short distance to the southward of the vessel, that formed a species of sea-wall, or mole, to protect the port against the waves of the

Gulf in that direction. This reef he knew to be miles in width.

There was little time for speculation, Spike soon bringing the strange schooner directly alongside of the brig. The two vessels immediately became a scene of activity, one discharging, and the other receiving the flour as fast as it could be struck out of the hold of the Swash and lowered upon the deck of the schooner. Mulford, however, had practised a little artifice, as the stranger entered the haven, which drew down upon him an anathema or two from Spike, as soon as they were alone. The mate had set the brig's ensign, and this compelled the stranger to be markedly rude, or to answer the compliment. Accordingly he had shown the ancient flag of Spain. For thus extorting a national symbol from the schooner, the mate was sharply rebuked at a suitable moment, though nothing could have been more forbearing than the deportment of his commander when they first met.

When Spike returned to his own vessel, he was accompanied by a dark-looking, well-dressed, and decidedly gentleman-like personage, whom he addressed indifferently, in his very imperfect Spanish, as Don Wan (Don Juan, or John), or Señor Montefalderon. By the latter appellation he even saw fit to introduce the very respectable-looking stranger to his mate. This stranger spoke English well, though with an accent.

"Don Wan has taken all the flour, Mr. Mulford, and intends shoving it over into Cuba, without troubling the custom-house, I believe; but that is not a matter to give *us* any concern, you know."

The wink, and the knowing look by which this speech was accompanied, seemed particularly disagreeable to Don Juan, who now paid his compliments to Rose, with no little surprise betrayed in his countenance, but with the ease and reserve of a gentleman. Mulford thought it strange that a smuggler of flour should be so polished a personage, though his duty did not admit of his bestowing much attention on the little trifling of the interview that succeeded.

For about an hour the work went steadily and rapidly

9

on. During that time Mulford was several times on board
the schooner, as, indeed, were Josh, Jack Tier, and others
belonging to the Swash. The Spanish vessel was Baltimore, or clipper built, with a trunk-cabin, and had every
appearance of sailing fast. Mulford was struck with her
model, and, while on board of her, he passed both forward
and aft to examine it. This was so natural in a seaman,
that Spike, while he noted the proceeding, took it in good
part. He even called out to his mate, from his own quarter-deck, to admire this or that point in the schooner's construction. As is customary with the vessels of southern
nations, this stranger was full of men, but they continued at
their work, some half dozen of brawny negroes among
them, shouting their songs as they swayed at the falls, no
one appearing to manifest jealousy or concern. At length
Tier came near the mate, and said,—

"Uncle Sam will not be pleased when he hears the reason
that the keeper is not in his light-house."

"And what is that reason, Jack? If you know it, tell it
to me."

"Go aft and look down the companion-way, maty, and
see it for yourself."

Mulford did go aft, and he made an occasion to look down
into the schooner's cabin, where he caught a glimpse of the
persons of a man and a boy, whom he at once supposed had
been taken from the light-house. This one fact of itself
doubled his distrust of the character of Spike's proceedings.
There was no sufficient apparent reason why a mere smuggler should care about the presence of an individual more
or less in a foreign port. Everything that had occurred,
looked like pre-concert between the brig and the schooner ;
and the mate was just beginning to entertain the strongest
distrust that their vessel was holding treasonable communication with the enemy, when an accident removed all
doubt on the subject, from his own mind at least. Spike
had, once or twice, given his opinion that the weather was
treacherous, and urged the people of both crafts to extraordinary exertions, in order that the vessels might get clear of
each other as soon as possible. This appeal had set various

expedients in motion to second the more regular work of the purchases. Among other things, planks had been laid from one vessel to the other, and barrels were rolled along them with very little attention to the speed or the direction. Several had fallen on the schooner's deck with rude shocks, but no damage was done, until one, of which the hoops had not been properly secured, met with a fall, and burst nearly at Mulford's feet. It was at the precise moment when the mate was returning, from taking his glance into the cabin, toward the side of the Swash. A white cloud arose, and half a dozen of the schooner's people sprang for buckets, kids, or dishes, in order to secure enough of the contents of the broken barrel to furnish them with a meal. At first nothing was visible but the white cloud that succeeded the fall, and the scrambling sailors in its midst. No sooner, however, had the air got to be a little clear, than Mulford saw an object lying in the centre of the wreck, that he at once recognized for a keg of the gunpowder! The captain of the schooner seized this keg, gave a knowing look at Mulford, and disappeared in the hold of his own vessel, carrying with him, what was out of all question, a most material part of the true cargo of the Swash.

At the moment when the flour-barrel burst, Spike was below, in close conference with his Spanish, or Mexican guest; and the wreck being so soon cleared away, it is probable that he never heard of the accident. As for the two crews, they laughed a little among themselves at the revelation which had been made, as well as at the manner; but to old sea-dogs like them, it was a matter of very little moment, whether the cargo was, in reality, flour or gunpowder. In a few minutes the affair seemed to be forgotten. In the course of another hour the Swash was light, having nothing in her but some pig-lead, which she used for ballast, while the schooner was loaded to her hatches, and full. Spike now sent a boat, with orders to drop a kedge about a hundred yards from the place where his own brig lay. The schooner warped up to this kedge, and dropped an anchor of her own, leaving a very short range of cable out, it being a flat calm. Ordinarily, the trades prevail at the Dry

Tortugas, and all along the Florida Reef. Sometimes, indeed, this breeze sweeps across the whole width of the Gulf of Mexico, blowing home, as it is called—reaching even to the coast of Texas. It is subject, however, to occasional interruptions everywhere, varying many points in its direction, and occasionally ceasing entirely. The latter was the condition of the weather about noon on this day, or when the schooner hauled off from the brig, and was secured at her own anchor.

"Mr. Mulford," said Spike, "I do not like the state of the atmosphere. D' ye see that fiery streak along the western horizon? well, sir, as the sun gets nearer to that streak, there'll be trouble, or I'm no judge of weather."

"You surely do not imagine, Captain Spike, that the sun will be any nearer to that fiery streak, as you call it, when he is about to set, than he is at this moment?" answered the mate, smiling.

"I'm sure of one thing, young man, and that is, that old heads are better than young ones. What a man has once seen, he may expect to see again, if the same leading signs offer. Man the boat, sir, and carry out the kedge, which is still in it, and lay it off here, about three p'ints on our larboard bow."

Mulford had a profound respect for Spike's seamanship, whatever he might think of his principles. The order was consequently obeyed. The mate was then directed to send down various articles out of the top, and to get the topgallant and royal yards on deck. Spike carried his precautions so far, as to have the mainsail lowered, it ordinarily brailing at that season of the year, with a standing gaff. With this disposition completed, the captain seemed more at his ease, and went below to join Señor Montefalderon in a *siesta*. The Mexican, for such, in truth, was the national character of the owner of the schooner, had preceded him in this indulgence ; and most of the people of the brig having laid themselves down to sleep under the heat of the hour, Mulford soon enjoyed another favorable opportunity for a private conference with Rose.

"Harry," commenced the latter, as soon as they were

alone, "I have much to tell you. While you have been absent I have overheard a conversation between this Spanish gentleman and Spike, that shows the last is in treaty with the other for the sale of the brig. Spike extolled his vessel to the skies, while Don Wan, as he calls him, complains that the brig is old, and cannot last long; to which Spike answered, 'To be sure she is old, Señor Montefalderon, but she will last as long as *your war*, and under a bold captain might be made to return her cost a hundred fold!' What war can he mean, and to what does such a discourse tend?"

"The war alludes to the war now existing between America and Mexico, and the money to be made is to be plundered at sea, from our own merchant-vessels. If Don Juan Montefalderon is really in treaty for the purchase of the brig, it is to convert her into a Mexican cruiser, either public or private."

"But this would be treason on the part of Spike!"

"Not more so than supplying the enemy with gunpowder, as he has just been doing. I have ascertained the reason he was so unwilling to be overhauled by the revenue steamer, as well as the reason why the revenue steamer wished so earnestly to overhaul us. Each barrel of flour contains another of gunpowder, and that has been sold to this Señor Montefalderon, who is doubtless an officer of the Mexican government, and no smuggler."

"He has been at New York, this very summer I know," continued Rose, "'for he spoke of his visit, and made such other remarks, as leaves no doubt that Spike expected to find him here, on this very day of the month. He also paid Spike a large sum of money in doubloons, and took back the bag to his schooner, when he had done so, after showing the captain enough was left to pay for the brig could they only agree on the terms of their bargain."

"Ay, ay; it is all plain enough now, Spike has determined on a desperate push for fortune, and foreseeing it might not soon be in his power to return to New York in safety, he has included his designs on you and your fortune, in the plot."

"My fortune! the trifle I possess can scarcely be called a fortune, Harry!"

"It would be a fortune to Spike, Rose; and I shall be honest enough to own it would be a fortune to me. I say this frankly, for I do believe you think too well of me to suppose that I seek you for any other reason than the ardent love I bear your person and character; but a fact is not to be denied because it may lead certain persons to distrust our motives. Spike is poor, like myself; and the brig is not only getting to be very old, but she has been losing money for the last twelve months."

Mulford and Rose now conversed long and confidentially on their situation and prospects. The mate neither magnified nor concealed the dangers of both; but freely pointed out the risk to himself, in being on board a vessel that was aiding and comforting the enemy. It was determined between them that both would quit the brig the moment an opportunity offered; and the mate even went so far as to propose an attempt to escape in one of the boats, although he might incur the hazards of a double accusation, those of mutiny and larceny, for making the experiment. Unfortunately, neither Rose, nor her aunt, nor Biddy, nor Jack Tier had seen the barrel of powder, and neither could testify as to the true character of Spike's connection with the schooner. It was manifestly necessary, therefore, independently of the risks that might be run by "bearding the lion in his den," to proceed with great intelligence and caution.

This dialogue between Harry and Rose occurred just after the turn of the day, and lasted fully an hour. Each had been too much interested to observe the heavens, but, as they were on the point of separating, Rose pointed out to her companion the unusual and most menacing aspect of the sky in the western horizon. It appeared as if a fiery heat was glowing there, behind a curtain of black vapor; and what rendered it more remarkable, was the circumstance that an extraordinary degree of placidity prevailed in all other parts of the heavens. Mulford scarce knew what to make of it; his experience not going so far as to enable him to explain the novel and alarming appearance. He stepped on a gun, and gazed around him for a moment. There lay the schooner, without a being visible on board of her, and there stood the light-house, gloomy in its desertion and solitude. The birds alone seemed to be alive, and conscious of what was approaching. They were all on the wing, wheeling wildly in the air, and screaming discordantly, as belonged to their habits. The young man leaped off the gun, gave a loud call to Spike, at the companion-way, and sprang forward to call all hands.

One minute only was lost, when every seaman on board the Swash, from the captain to Jack Tier, was on deck. Mulford met Spike at the cabin door, and pointed toward the fiery column, that was booming down upon the anchorage, with a velocity and direction that would now admit of no misinterpretation. For one instant that sturdy old seaman stood aghast; gazing at the enemy as one conscious of his impotency might have been supposed to quail before an assault that he foresaw must prove irresistible. Then his native spirit, and most of all the effects of training, began to show themselves in him, and he became at once, not only the man again, but the resolute, practised, and ready commander.

"Come aft to the spring, men!" he shouted; "clap on the spring, Mr. Mulford, and bring the brig head to wind."

This order was obeyed as seamen best obey, in case of sudden and extreme emergency; or with intelligence, aptitude, and power. The brig had swung nearly round, in the desired direction, when the tornado struck her. It will be difficult, we do not know but it is impossible, to give a clear and accurate account of what followed. As most of our readers have doubtless felt how great is the power of the wind, whiffling and pressing different ways, in sudden and passing gusts, they have only to imagine this power increased many, many fold, and the baffling currents made furious, as it might be, by meeting with resistance, to form some notion of the appalling strength and frightful inconstancy with which it blew for about a minute.

Notwithstanding the circumstance of Spike's precaution had greatly lessened the danger, every man on the deck of the Swash believed the brig was gone when the gust struck her. Over she went, in fact, until the water came pouring in above her half-ports, like so many little cascades, and spouting up through her scupper-holes, resembling the blowing of young whales. It was the whiffling energy of the tornado that alone saved her. As if disappointed in not destroying its intended victim at one swoop, the tornado "let up" in its pressure, like a dexterous wrestler, making a fresh and desperate effort to overturn the vessel, by a slight variation in its course. That change saved the Swash. She righted, and even rolled in the other direction, or what might be called to windward, with her decks full of water. For a minute longer these baffling, changing gusts continued, each causing the brig to bow like a reed to their power, one lifting as another pressed her down, and then the weight, or the more dangerous part of the tornado was passed, though it continued to blow heavily, always in whiffling blasts, several minutes longer.

During the weight of the gust, no one had leisure, or indeed inclination to look to aught beyond its effect on the brig. Had one been otherwise disposed, the attempt would have been useless, for the wind had filled the air with spray, and near the islets even with sand. The lurid but fiery tinge, too, interposed a veil that no human eye could penetrate. As the tornado passed onward, however, and the winds lulled, the air again became clear, and in five minutes after the moment when the Swash lay nearly on her side, with her lower yard-arm actually within a few feet of the water, all was still and placid around her, as one is accustomed to see the ocean in a calm, of a summer's afternoon. Then it was that those who had been in such extreme jeopardy could breathe freely and look about them. On board the Swash all was well—not a rope-yarn had parted, or an eye-bolt drawn. The timely precautions of Spike had saved his brig, and great was his joy thereat.

In the midst of the infernal din of the tornado, screams had ascended from the cabin, and the instant he could quit the deck with propriety, Mulford sprang below, in order to ascertain their cause. He apprehended that some of the females had been driven to leeward when the brig went over, and that part of the luggage or furniture had fallen on them. In the main cabin, the mate found Señor Monte-falderon just quitting his berth, composed, gentleman-like, and collected. Josh was braced in a corner nearly gray with fear, while Jack Tier still lay on the cabin floor, at the last point to which he had rolled. One word sufficed to let Don Juan know that the gust had passed, and the brig was safe, when Mulford tapped at the door of the inner cabin. Rose appeared, pale, but calm and unhurt.

"Is any one injured?" asked the young man, his mind relieved at once, as soon as he saw that she who most occupied his thoughts was safe; "we heard screams from this cabin."

"My aunt and Biddy have been frightened," answered Rose, "but neither has been hurt. Oh, Harry, what terrible thing has happened to us? I heard the roaring of—"

"'T was a tornado," interrupted Mulford, eagerly, "but 't is over. 'T was one of those sudden and tremendous gusts that sometimes occur within the tropics, in which the danger is usually in the first shock. If no one is injured in this cabin, no one is injured at all."

"Oh, Mr. Mulford—dear Mr. Mulford!" exclaimed the relict, from the corner into which she had been followed and jammed by Biddy, "Oh, Mr. Mulford, are we foundered or not?"

"Heaven be praised, not, my dear ma'am, though we came nearer to it than I ever was before."

"Are we cap-asided?"

"Nor that, Mrs. Budd; the brig is as upright as a church."

"Upright!" repeated Biddy, in her customary accent, "is it as a church? Sure, then, Mr. Mate, 't is a Presbyterian church that you mane, and that is always totterin'."

"Catholic, or Dutch—no church in York is more completely up and down than the brig at this moment."

"Get off of me—get off of me, Biddy, and let me rise," said the widow, with dignity. "The danger is over, I see, and, as we return our thanks for it, we have the consolation of knowing that we have done our duty. It is incumbent on all, at such moments, to be at their posts, and to set examples of decision and prudence."

As Mulford saw all was well in the cabin, he hastened on deck followed by Señor Montefalderon. Just as they emerged from the companion-way, Spike was hailing the forecastle.

"Forecastle, there," he cried, standing on the trunk himself as he did so, and moving from side to side, as if to catch a glimpse of some object ahead.

"Sir," came back from an old salt, who was coiling up rigging in that seat of seamanship.

"Whereaway is the schooner? She ought to be dead ahead of us, as we tend now—but blast me if I can see as much as her mast-heads."

At this suggestion, a dozen men sprang upon guns or other objects, to look for the vessel in question. The old salt forward, however, had much the best chance, for he stepped on the heel of the bowsprit, and walked as far out as the knight-heads, to command the whole view ahead of the brig. There he stood half a minute, looking first on one side of the head-gear, then the other, when he gave his trousers a hitch, put a fresh quid in his mouth, and called out in a voice almost as hoarse as the tempest, that had just gone by,—

"The schooner has gone down at her anchor, sir. There's her buoy watching still, as if nothing had happened: but as for the craft itself, there's not so much as a bloody yard-arm, or mast-head of her to be seen!"

This news produced a sensation in the brig at once, as may be supposed. Even Señor Montefalderon, a quiet, gentleman-like person, altogether superior in deportment to the bustle and fuss that usually marks the manners of persons in trade, was disturbed; for to him the blow was heavy indeed. Whether he were acting for himself, or was an agent of the Mexican government, the loss was much the same.

"Tom is right enough," put in Spike, rather coolly for the circumstances; "that there schooner of yourn has foundered, Don Wan, as any one can see. She must have capsized and filled, for I obsarved they had left the hatches off, meaning, no doubt, to make an end of the storage as soon as they had done sleeping."

"And what has become of all her men, Don Esteban?" for so the Mexican politely called his companion. "Have all my poor countrymen perished in this disaster?"

"I fear they have, Don Wan; for I see no head, as of any one swimming. The vessel lay so near that island next to it, that a poor swimmer would have no difficulty in reaching the place; but there is no living thing to be seen. But man the boat, men; we will go to the spot, Señor, and examine for ourselves."

There were two boats in the water, and alongside of the brig. One was the Swash's yawl, a small but convenient craft, while the other was much larger, fitted with a sail, and had all the appearance of having been built to withstand breezes and seas. Mulford felt perfectly satisfied, the moment he saw this boat, which had come into the haven in tow of the schooner, that it had been originally in the service of the light-house keeper. As there was a very general desire among those on the quarter-deck to go to the assistance of the schooner, Spike ordered both boats manned, jumping into the yawl himself, accompanied by Don Juan Montefalderon, and telling Mulford to follow with the larger craft, bringing with him as many of the females as might choose to accompany him. As Mrs. Budd thought it incumbent on her to be active in such a scene, all did go, including Biddy, though with great reluctance on the part of Rose.

With the buoy for a guide, Spike had no difficulty in finding the spot where the schooner lay. She had scarcely shifted her berth in the least, there having been no time for her even to swing to the gust, but she had probably capsized at the first blast, filled, and gone down instantly. The water was nearly as clear as the calm, mild atmosphere of the tropics; and it was almost as easy to discern the vessel, and all her hamper, as if she lay on a beach. She had sunk as she filled, or on her side, and still continued in that position. As the water was little more than three fathoms deep, the upper side was submerged but a few inches, and her yard-arms would have been out of the water, but for the circumstance that the yards had canted under the pressure.

At first, no sign was seen of any of those who had been on board this ill-fated schooner when she went down. It was known that twenty-one souls were in her, including the man and the boy who had belonged to the light-house. As the boat moved slowly over this sad ruin, however, a horrible and startling spectacle came in view. Two bodies were seen, within a few feet of the surface of the water, one grasped in the arms of the other, in the gripe of despair. The man held in the grasp was kept beneath the water solely by the death-lock of his companion, who was himself held where he floated, by the circumstance that one of his feet was entangled in a rope. The struggle could not have been long over, for the two bodies were slowly settling toward the bottom when first seen. It is probable that both these men had more than once risen to the surface in their dreadful struggle. Spike seized a boat-hook, and made an effort to catch the clothes of the nearest body, but ineffectually, both sinking to the sands beneath, lifeless, and without motion. There being no sharks in sight, Mulford volunteered to dive and fasten a line to one of these unfortunate men, whom Don Juan declared at once was the schooner's captain. Some little time was lost in procuring a lead-line from the brig, when the lead was dropped alongside of the drowned. Provided with another piece of the same sort of line, which had a small running bowline around that which was fastened to the lead, the mate made his plunge, and went down with great vigor of arm. It required resolution and steadiness to descend so far into salt water; but Harry succeeded, and rose with the bodies, which came up with the slightest impulse. All were immediately got into the boat, and away the latter went toward the light-house, which was nearer and more easy of access than the brig.

It is probable that one of these unfortunate men might have been revived under judicious treatment; but he was not fated to receive it. Spike, who knew nothing of such matters, undertook to direct everything, and, instead of having recourse to warmth and gentle treatment, he ordered the bodies to be rolled on a cask, suspended them by the heels, and resorted to a sort of practice that might have destroyed well men, instead of resuscitating those in whom the vital spark was dormant, if not actually extinct.

Two hours later, Rose, seated in her own cabin, unavoidably overheard the following dialogue, which passed in English, a language that Señor Montefalderon spoke perfectly well, as has been said.

"Well, Señor." said Spike, "I hope this little accident will not prevent our final trade. You will want the brig now, to take the schooner's place."

"And how am I to pay you for the brig, Señor Spike, even if I did buy her?"

"I'll ventur' to guess there is plenty of money in Mexico. Though they do say the government is so backward about paying, I have always found you punctual, and am not afraid to put faith in you ag'in."

"But I have no longer any money to pay you half in hand, as I did for the powder, when last in New York."

"The bag was pretty well lined with doubloons when I saw it last, Señor."

"And do you know where that bag is; and where there is another that holds the same sum?"

Spike started, and he mused in silence some little time ere he again spoke.

"I had forgotten," he at length answered. "The gold must have all gone down in the schooner, along with the powder!"

"And the poor men!"

"Why, as for the men, Señor, more may be had for the asking; but powder and doubloons will be hard to find, when most wanted. Then the men were *poor* men, accordin' to my idees of what an able seaman should be, or they never would have let their schooner turn turtle with them as she did."

"We will talk of the money, Don Esteban, if you please," said the Mexican, with reserve.

"With all my heart, Don Wan; nothing is more agreeble to me than money. How many of them doubloons shall fall to my share, if I raise the schooner and put you in possession of your craft again?"

"Can that be done, Señor?" demanded Don Juan earnestly.

"A seaman can do almost anything, in that way, Don Wan, if you will give him time and means. For one half the doubloons I can find in the wrack, the job shall be done."

"You can have them," answered Don Juan quietly, a good deal surprised that Spike should deem it necessary to offer him any part of the sum he might find. "As for the powder, I suppose that is lost to my country."

"Not at all, Don Wan. The flour is well packed around it, and I don't expect it would take any harm in a month. I shall not only turn over the flour to you, just as if nothing had happened, but I shall put four first-rate hands aboard your schooner, who will take her into port for you, with a good deal more sartainty than forty of the men you had. My mate is a prime navigator."

This concluded the bargain, every word of which was heard by Rose, and every word of which she did not fail to communicate to Mulford, the moment there was an opportunity. The young man heard it with great interest, telling Rose that he should do all he could to assist in raising the schooner, in the hope that something might turn up to enable him to escape in her, taking off Rose and her aunt. As for his carrying her into a Mexican port, let them trust him for that! Agreeably to the arrangement, orders were given that afternoon to commence the necessary preparations for the work, and considerable progress was made in them by the time the Swash's people were ordered to knock off work for that night.

After the sun had set, the reaction in the currents again commenced, and it blew for a few hours heavily, during the night. Toward morning, however, it moderated, and when the sun reappeared it scarcely ever diffused its rays over a more peaceful or quiet day. Spike caused all hands to be called, and immediately set about the important business he had before him.

In order that the vessel might be as free as possible, Jack Tier was directed to scull the females ashore, in the brig's yawl; Señor Montefalderon, a man of polished manners, as we maintain is very apt to be the case with Mexican gentlemen, whatever may be the opinion of this good Republic on the subject just at this moment, asked permission to be of the party. Mulford found an opportunity to beg Rose, if they landed at the light, to reconnoitre the place well, with a view to ascertain what facilities it could afford in an attempt to escape. They did land at the light, and glad enough were Mrs. Budd, Rose, and Biddy to place their feet on *terrâ firmâ* after so long a confinement to the narrow limits of a vessel.

"Well," said Jack Tier, as they walked up to the spot where the buildings stood, "this is a rum place for a light'us, Miss Rose, and I don't wonder the keeper and his messmates has cleared out."

"I am very sorry to say," observed Señor Montefalderon, whose countenance expressed the concern he really felt, "that the keeper and his only companion, a boy, were on board the schooner, and have perished in her, in common with so many of my poor countrymen. There are the graves of two whom we buried here last evening, after vain efforts to restore them to life!"

"What a dreadful catastrophe it has been, Señor!" said Rose, whose sweet countenance eloquently expressed the horror and regret she so naturally felt; "twenty fellow-beings hurried into eternity without even an instant for prayer!"

"You feel for them, Señorita—it is natural you should, and it is natural that I, their countryman and leader, should feel for them, also. I do not know what God has in reserve for my unfortunate country! We may have cruel and unscrupulous men among us, Señorita, but we have thousands who are just, and brave, and honorable."

"So Mr. Mulford tells me, Señor; and he has been much in your ports, on the west coast."

"I like that young man, and wonder not a little at his and your situation in this brig," rejoined the Mexican, dropping his voice so as not to be heard by their companions, as they walked a little ahead of Mrs. Budd and Biddy.

"The Señor Spike is scarcely worthy to be *his* commander or *your* guardian."

"Yet you find him worthy of your intercourse and trust, Don Juan?"

The Mexican shrugged his shoulders, and smiled equivocally; still, in a melancholy manner. It would seem he did not deem it wise to push this branch of the subject further, since he turned to another.

"I like the Señor Mulford," he resumed, "for his general deportment and principles, so far as I can judge of him on so short an acquaintance."

"Excuse me, Señor," interrupted Rose, hurriedly, "but you never saw *him* until you met him here."

"Never—I understand you, Señorita, and can do full justice to the young man's character. I am willing to think he did not know the errand of his vessel, or I should not have seen him now. But what I most like him for is this: Last night, during the gale, he and I walked the deck together, for an hour. We talked of Mexico, and of this war, so unfortunate for my country already, and which may become still more so, when he uttered this noble sentiment,—'My country is more powerful than yours, Señor Montefalderon,' he said, 'and in this it has been more favored by God. You have suffered from ambitious rulers, and from military rule, while we have been advancing under the arts of peace, favored by a most beneficent Providence. As for this war, I know but little about it, though I dare say the Mexican government may have been wrong in some things that it might have controlled and some that it might not—but let right be where it will, I am sorry to see a nation that has taken so firm a stand in favor of popular government, pressed upon so hard by another that is supposed to be the great support of such principles. America and Mexico are neighbors, and ought to be friends; and while I do not, cannot blame my own country for pursuing the war with vigor, nothing would please me more than to hear peace proclaimed.'"

"That is just like Harry Mulford," said Rose thoughtfully, as soon as her companion ceased to speak. "I do wish, Señor, that there could be no use for this powder, that is now buried in the sea."

Don Juan Montefalderon smiled, and seemed a little surprised that the fair young thing at his side should have known of the treacherous contents of the flour-barrels. No doubt he found it inexplicable, that persons like Rose and Mulford should, seemingly, be united with one like Spike ; but he was too well-bred, and, indeed, too effectually mystified, to push the subject further than might be discreet.

By this time they were near the entrance of the light-house, into which the whole party entered, in a sort of mute awe at its silence and solitude. At Señor Montefalderon's invitation, they ascended to the lantern, whence they could command a wide and fair view of the surrounding waters. The reef was much more apparent from that elevation than from below ; and Rose could see that numbers of its rocks were bare, while on other parts of it there was the appearance of many feet of water. Rose gazed at it with longing eyes, for, from a few remarks that had fallen from Mulford, she suspected he had hopes of escaping among its channels and coral.

As they descended and walked through the buildings, Rose also took good heed of the supplies the place afforded. There were flour, and beef, and pork, and many other of the common articles of food, as well as water in a cistern, that caught it as it flowed from the roof of the dwelling. Water was also to be found in casks—nothing like a spring or a well existing among those islets. All these things Rose noted, putting them aside in her memory for ready reference hereafter.

In the meantime the mariners were not idle. Spike moved his brig, and moored her, head and stern, alongside of the wreck, before the people got their breakfasts. As soon as that meal was ended, both captain and mate set about their duty in earnest. Mulford carried out an anchor on the off-side of the Swash, and dropped it at a distance of about eighty fathoms from the vessel's beam. Purchases were brought from both mast-heads of the brig to the chain of this anchor, and were hove upon until the vessel was given a heel of more than a streak, and the cable was tolerably taut. Other purchases were got up opposite, and overhauled down, in readiness to take hold of the schooner's masts. The anchor of the schooner was weighed by its buoy-rope, and the chain, after being rove through the upper or opposite hawse-hole, brought in on board the Swash. Another chain was dropped astern, in such a way, that when the schooner came upright, it would be sure to pass beneath her keel, some six or eight feet from the rudder. Slings were then sunk over the mast-heads, and the purchases were hooked on. Hours were consumed in these preliminary labors, and the people went to dinner as soon as they were completed.

When the men had dined, Spike brought one of his purchases to the windlass, and the other to the capstan, though not until each was bowsed taut by hand; a few minutes having brought the strain so far on everything, as to enable a seaman, like Spike, to form some judgment of the likelihood that his preventers and purchases would stand. Some changes were found necessary, to equalize the strain, but, on the whole, the captain was satisfied with his work, and the crew were soon ordered to " heave-away ; the windlass best."

In the course of half an hour the hull of the vessel, which lay on its bilge, began to turn on its keel, and the heads of the spars to rise above the water. This was the easiest part of the process, all that was required of the purchases being to turn over a mass which rested on the sands of the bay. Aided by the long levers afforded by the spars, the work advanced so rapidly, that, in just one hour's time after his people had begun to heave, Spike had the pleasure to see the schooner standing upright, alongside of his own brig, though still sunk to the bottom. The wreck was secured in this position, by means of guys and preventers, in order that it might not again cant, when the order was issued to hook on the slings that were to raise it to the surface. These slings were the chains of the schooner, one of which went under her keel, while for the other the captain trusted to the strength of the two hawse-holes, having passed the cable out of one and in at the other, in a way to serve his purposes, as has just been stated.

When all was ready, Spike mustered his crew, and made a speech. He told the men that he was about a job that was out of the usual line of their duty, and that he knew they had a right to expect extra pay for such extra work. The schooner contained money, and his object was to get at it. If he succeeded, their reward would be a doubloon a man, which would be earning more than a month's wages by twenty-four hours' work. This was enough. The men wanted to hear no more; but they cheered their commander, and set about their task in the happiest disposition possible.

The reader will understand that the object to be first achieved was to raise a vessel, with a hold filled with flour and gunpowder, from off the bottom of the bay to its surface. As she stood, the deck of this vessel was about six feet under water, and every one will understand that her weight, so long as it was submerged in a fluid as dense as that of the sea, would be much more manageable than if suspended in air. The barrels, for instance, were not much heavier than the water they displaced, and the woodwork of the vessel itself was, on the whole, positively lighter than the element in which it had sunk. As for the water in the hold, that was of the same weight as the water on the outside of the craft, and there had not been much to carry the schooner down, beside her iron, the spars that were out of water, and her ballast. This last, some ten or twelve tons in weight, was in fact the principal difficulty, and alone induced Spike to have any doubts about his eventual success. There was no foreseeing the result until he had made a trial, however; and the order was again given to " heave away."

To the infinite satisfaction of the Swash's crew, the weight was found quite manageable, so long as the hull remained beneath the water. Mulford, with three or four assistants, was kept on board the schooner lightening her by getting the other anchor off her bows, and throwing the different objects overboard, or on the decks of the brig. By the time the bulwarks reached the surface, as much was gained in this way, as was lost by having so much of the lighter wood-work rise above the water. As a matter of course, however, the weight increased as the vessel rose, and more especially as the lower portion of the spars, the bowsprit, boom, etc., from being buoyant assistants, became so much dead weight to be lifted.

Spike kept a watchful eye on his spars, and the extra supports he had given them. He was moving, the whole time, from point to point, feeling shrouds and back-stays and preventers, in order to ascertain the degree of strain on each, or examining how the purchases stood. As for the crew, they cheered at their toil, incessantly, passing from capstan bars to the handspikes, and *vice versâ*. They, too, felt that their task was increasing in resistance as it advanced, and now found it more difficult to gain an inch, than it had been at first to gain a foot. They seemed, indeed, to be heaving their own vessel out, instead of heaving the other craft up, and it was not long before they had the Swash heeling over toward the wreck several streaks. The strain, moreover, on everything, became not only severe, but samewhat menacing. Every shroud, back-stay, and preventer was as taut as a bar of iron, and the chain-cable that led to the anchor planted off abeam, was as straight as if the brig were riding by it in a gale of wind. One or two ominous surges aloft, too, had been heard, and, though no more than straps and slings settling into their places under hard strains, they served to remind the crew that danger might come from that quarter. Such was the state of things when Spike called out to "heave and pall," that he might take a look at the condition of the wreck.

Although a great deal remained to be done, in order to get the schooner to float, a great deal had already been done. Her precise condition was as follows: Having no cabin windows, the water had entered her, when she capsized, by the only four apertures her construction possessed. These were the companion-way, or cabin doors; the sky-light; the main-hatch, or the large inlet amid-ships, by which cargo went up and down ; and the booby-hatch, which was the counterpart of the companion-way, forward ; being intended to admit of ingress to the forecastle, the apartment of the crew. Each of these hatchways, or orifices, had the usual defences of " coamings," strong frame-work around their margins. These coamings rose six or eight inches above the deck, and answered the double purpose of strengthening the vessel, in a part, that without them would be weaker than common, and of preventing any water that might be washing about the decks from running below. As soon, therefore, as these three apertures, or their coamings, could be raised above the level of the water of the basin, all danger of the vessel's receiving any further tribute of that sort from the ocean would be over. It was to this end, consequently, that Spike's efforts had been latterly directed, though they had only in part succeeded. The schooner possessed a good deal of sheer, as it is termed ; or, her two extremities rose nearly a foot above her centre, when on an even keel. This had brought her extremities first to the surface, and it was the additional weight which had consequently been brought into the air that had so much increased the strain, and induced Spike to pause. The deck forward, as far aft as the foremast, and aft as far forward as the centre of the trunk, or to the sky-light, was above the water, or at least awash, while all the rest of it was covered. In the vicinity of the main-hatch there were several inches of water ; enough indeed to leave the upper edge of the coamings submerged by about an inch. To raise the keel that inch by means of the purchases, Spike well knew would cost him more labor, and would incur more risk than all that had been done previously, and he paused before he would attempt it.

The men were now called from the brig and ordered to come on board the schooner. Spike ascertained by actual measurement how much was wanted to bring the coamings of the main-hatch above the water, until which, he knew, pumping and bailing would be useless. He found it was quite an inch, and was at a great loss to know how that inch should be obtained. Mulford advised another trial with the handspikes and bars, but to this Spike would not consent. He believed that the masts of the brig had already as much pressure on them as they would bear. The mate next proposed getting the main boom off the vessel, and to lighten the craft by cutting away her bowsprit and masts. The captain was well enough disposed to do this, but he doubted whether it would meet with the approbation of " Don Wan," who was still ashore with Rose and her aunt, and who probably looked forward to recovering his gunpowder by means of those very spars. At length the carpenter hit upon a plan that was adopted.

This plan was very simple, though it had its own ingenuity. It will be remembered that water could now only enter the vessel's hold at the main-hatch, all the other hatchways having their coamings above the element. The carpenter proposed, therefore, that the main-hatches, which had been off when the tornado occurred, but which had been found on deck when the vessel righted, should now be put on, oakum being first laid along in their rabbetings, and that the cracks should be stuffed with additional oakum, to exclude as much water as possible. He thought that two or three men, by using caulking irons for ten minutes, would make the hatchway so tight that very little water would penetrate. While this was doing, he himself would bore as many holes forward and aft as he could, with a two-inch auger, out of which the water then in the vessel would be certain to run. Spike was delighted with this project, and gave the necessary orders on the spot.

This much must be said of the crew of the Molly Swash —whatever they did in their own profession, they did intelligently and well. On the present occasion they maintained their claim to this character, and were both active and expert. The hatches were soon on, and, in an imperfect manner, caulked. While this was doing, the carpenter got into a boat, and going under the schooner's bows, where a whole plank was out of water, he chose a spot between two of the timbers, and bored a hole as near the surface of the water as he dared to do. Not satisfied with one hole, however, he bored many, choosing both sides of the

vessel to make them, and putting some aft as well as forward. In a word, in the course of twenty minutes the
schooner was tapped in at least a dozen places, and jets of
water, two inches in diameter, were spouting from her on
each bow, and under each quarter.

Spike and Mulford noted the effect. Some water, doubtless, still worked itself into the vessel about the main-hatch,
but that more flowed from her by means of the outlets just
named, was quite apparent. After close watching at the
outlets for some time, Spike was convinced that the
schooner was slowly rising, the intense strain that still
came from the brig producing that effect as the vessel gradually became lighter. By the end of half an hour, there
could be no longer any doubt, the holes, which had been
bored within an inch of the water, being now fully two
inches above it. The auger was applied anew, still nearer
to the surface of the sea, and as fresh outlets were made,
those that began to manifest a dulness in their streams
were carefully plugged.

Spike now thought it was time to take a look at the
state of things on deck. Here, to his joy, he ascertained
that the coamings had actually risen a little above the water.
The reader is not to suppose by this rising of the vessel,
that she had become sufficiently buoyant, in consequence of
the water that had run out of her, to float of herself. This
was far from being the case; but the constant upward pressure from the brig, which, on mechanical principles, tended
constantly to bring that craft upright, had the effect to lift
the schooner as the latter was gradually relieved from the
weight that pressed her toward the bottom.

The hatches were next removed, when it was found that
the water in the schooner's hold had so far lowered, as to
leave a vacant space of quite a foot between the lowest part
of the deck and its surface. Toward the two extremities
of the vessel this space necessarily was much increased, in
consequence of the sheer. Men were now sent into the
hatchway with orders to hook on to the flour-barrels—a
whip having been rigged in readiness to hoist them on deck.
At the same time gangs were sent to the pumps, though

Spike still depended for getting rid of the water somewhat on the auger—the carpenter continuing to bore and plug his holes as new opportunities offered, and the old outlets became useless. It was true this expedient would soon cease, for the water having found its level in the vessel's hold, was very nearly on a level also with that on the outside. Bailing also was commenced, both forward and aft,

Spike's next material advantage was obtained by means of the cargo. By the time the sun had set, fully two hundred barrels had been rolled into the hatchway, and passed on deck, whence about half of them were sent in the lighthouse boat to the nearest islet, and the remainder were transferred to the deck of the brig. These last were placed on the off side of the Swash, and aided in bringing her nearer upright. A great deal was gained in getting rid of these barrels. The water in the schooner lowered just as much as the space they had occupied, and the vessel was relieved at once of twenty tons in weight.

Just after the sun had set, Señor Don Juan Montefalderon and his party returned on board. They had stayed on the island to the last moment, at Rose's request, for she had taken as close an observation of everything as possible, in order to ascertain if any means of concealment existed, in the event of her aunt, Biddy, and herself quitting the brig. The islets were all too naked and too small, however; and she was compelled to return to the Swash, without any hopes derived from this quarter.

Spike had just directed the people to get their suppers as the Mexican came on board. Together they descended to the schooner's deck, where they had a long but secret conference. Señor Montefalderon was a calm, quiet, and reasonable man, and while he felt as one would be apt to feel who had recently seen so many associates swept suddenly out of existence, the late catastrophe did not in the least unman him. It is too much the habit of the American people to receive their impressions from newspapers, which throw off their articles unreflectingly, and often ignorantly, as crones in petticoats utter their gossip. In a word, the opinions thus obtained are very much on a level, in value, with the thoughts of those who are said to think aloud, and who give utterance to all the crudities and trivial rumors that may happen to reach their ears. In this manner, we apprehend, very false notions of our neighbors of Mexico have become circulated among us. That nation is a mixed race, and has necessarily the various characteristics of such an origin, and it is unfortunately little influenced by the diffusion of intelligence which certainly exists here. Although an enemy, it ought to be acknowledged, however, that even Mexico has her redeeming points. Anglo-Saxons as we are, we have no desire unnecessarily to illustrate that very marked feature in the Anglo-Saxon character, which prompts the mother stock to calumniate all who oppose it, but would rather adopt some of that chivalrous courtesy of which so much that is lofty and commendable is to be found among the descendants of Old Spain.

The Señor Montefalderon was earnestly engaged in what he conceived to be the cause of his country. It was scarcely possible to bring together two men impelled by motives more distinct than Spike and this gentleman. The first was acting under impulses of the lowest and most grovelling nature; while the last was influenced by motives of the highest. However much Mexico may, and has, weakened her cause by her own punic faith, instability, military oppression, and political revolutions, giving to the Texans in particular ample justification for their revolt, it was not probable that Don Juan Montefalderon saw the force of all the arguments that a casuist of ordinary ingenuity could certainly adduce against his country; for it is a most unusual thing to find a man anywhere, who is willing to admit that the positions of an opponent are good. He saw in the events of the day, a province wrested from his nation; and, in his reasoning on the subject, entirely overlooking the numerous occasions on which his own fluctuating government had given sufficient justification, not to say motives, to their powerful neighbors to take the law into their own hands, and redress themselves, he fancied all that had occurred was previously planned; instead of regarding it, as it truly is, as merely the result of political events that no man could have foreseen, that no man had originally imagined, or that any man could control.

Don Juan understood Spike completely, and quite justly appreciated not only his character, but his capabilities. Their acquaintance was not of a day, though it had ever been marked by that singular combination of caution and reliance that is apt to characterize the intercourse between the knave and the honest man, when circumstances compel not only communication, but, to a certain extent, confidence. They now paced the deck of the schooner, side by side, for fully an hour, during which time the price of the vessel, the means, and the mode of payment and transfer, were fully settled between them.

"But what will you do with your passengers, Don Esteban?" asked the Mexican, pleasantly, when the more material points were adjusted. "I feel a great interest in the young lady in particular, who is a charming Señorita, and who tells me that her aunt brought her this voyage on account of her health. She looks much too blooming to be out of health, and if she were, this is a singular voyage for an invalid to make!"

"You don't understand human natur' yet, altogether, I see, Don Wan," answered Spike, chuckling and winking. "As you and I are not only good friends, but what a body may call *old* friends, I 'll let you into a secret in this affair, well knowing that you 'll not betray it. It 's quite true that the old woman thinks her niece is a pulmonary, as they call it, and that this v'y'ge is recommended for her, but the gal is as healthy as she 's handsom'."

"Her constitution, then, must be very excellent, for it is seldom I have seen so charming a young woman. But if the aunt is misled in this matter, how has it been with the niece?"

Spike did not answer in words, but he leered upon his companion, and he winked.

"You mean to be understood that you are in intelligence with each other, I suppose, Don Esteban," returned the Señor Montefalderon, who did not like the captain's manner, and was willing to drop the discourse.

Spike then informed his companion, in confidence, that he and Rose were affianced, though without the aunt's knowledge; that he intended to marry the niece the moment he reached a Mexican port with the brig, and that it was their joint intention to settle in the country. He added that the affair required management, as his intended had property, and expected more, and he begged Don Juan to aid him, as things drew near to a crisis. The Mexican evaded an answer, and the discourse dropped.

The moon was now shining, and would continue to throw its pale light over the scene for two or three hours longer. Spike profited by the circumstance to continue the work of lightening the schooner. One of the first things done next was to get up the dead, and to remove them to the boat. This melancholy office occupied an hour, the bodies being landed on the islet, near the powder, and there interred in the sands. Don Juan Montefalderon attended on this occasion, and repeated some prayers over the graves, as he had done in the morning, in the cases of the two who had been buried near the light-house.

While this melancholy duty was in the course of performance, that of pumping and bailing was continued, under the immediate personal superintendence of Mulford. It would not be easy to define, with perfect clearness, the conflicting feelings by which the mate of the Swash was now impelled. He had no longer any doubt on the subject of Spike's treason, and had it not been for Rose, he would not have hesitated a moment about making off in the light-house boat for Key West, in order to report all that had passed to the authorities. But not only Rose was there, and to be cared for, but what was far more difficult to get along with, her aunt was with her. It is true, Mrs. Budd was no longer Spike's dupe; but under any circumstances she was a difficult subject to manage, and most especially so in all matters that related to the sea. Then the young man submitted, more or less, to the strange influence which a fine craft almost invariably obtains over those that belong to her. He did not like the idea of deserting the Swash, at the very moment he would not have hesitated about punishing her owner for his many misdeeds. In a word, Harry was too much of a tar not to feel a deep reluctance to turn against his cruise, or his voyage, however much either might be condemned by his judgment, or even by his principles.

It was quite nine o'clock when the Señor Montefalderon and Spike returned from burying the dead. No sooner did the last put his foot on the deck of his own vessel, than he felt the fall of one of the purchases which had been employed in raising the schooner. It was so far slack as to satisfy him that the latter now floated by her own buoyancy though it might be well to let all stand until morning, for the purposes of security. Thus apprised of the condition of the two vessels, he gave the welcome order to " knock off for the night."

CHAPTER VI.

"At the piping of all hands,
When the judgment signal 's spread—
When the islands and the land,
And the seas give up their dead,
And the south and the north shall come;
When the sinner is dismayed,
And the just man is afraid,
Then heaven be thy aid,
Poor Tom."

BRAINARD.

THE people had now a cessation from their toil. Of
all the labor known to sea-faring men, that of
pumping is usually thought to be the most severe.
Those who work at it have to be relieved every
minute, and it is only by having gangs to succeed each
other, that the duty can be done at all with anything like
steadiness. In the present instance, it is true, that the people of the Swash were sustained by the love of gold, but
glad enough were they when Mulford called out to them to
" knock off, and turn in for the night." It was high time
this summons should be made, for not only were the people
excessively wearied, but the customary hours of labor were
so far spent, that the light of the moon had some time before
begun to blend with the little left by the parting sun. Glad
enough were all hands to quit the toil ; and two minutes
were scarcely elapsed ere most of the crew had thrown themselves down, and were buried in deep sleep. Even Spike
and Mulford took the rest they needed, the cook alone being
left to look out for the changes in the weather. In a word,
everybody but this idler was exhausted with pumping and

bailing, and even gold had lost its power to charm, until nature was recruited by rest.

The excitement produced by the scenes through which they had so lately passed, caused the females to sleep soundly too. The death-like stillness which pervaded the vessel contributed to their rest, and Rose never woke, from the first few minutes after her head was on her pillow, until near four in the morning. The deep quiet seemed ominous to one who had so lately witnessed the calm which precedes the tornado, and she arose. In that low latitude and warm season, few clothes were necessary, and our heroine was on deck in a very few minutes. Here she found the same grave-like sleep pervading everything. There was not a breath of air, and the ocean seemed to be in one of its profoundest slumbers. The hard breathing of Spike could be heard through the open windows of his state-room, and this was positively the only sound that was audible. The common men, who lay scattered about the decks, more especially from the mainmast forward, seemed to be so many logs, and from Mulford no breathing was heard.

The morning was neither very dark nor very light, it being easy to distinguish objects that were near, while those at a distance were necessarily lost in obscurity. Availing herself of the circumstance, Rose went as far as the gang-way, to ascertain if the cook were at his post. She saw him lying near his galley, in as profound a sleep as any of the crew. This she felt to be wrong, and she felt alarmed, though she knew not why. Perhaps it was the conscious-ness of being the only person up and awake at that hour of the deepest night, in a vessel so situated as the Swash, and in a climate in which hurricanes seem to be the natural off-spring of the air. Some one must be aroused, and her tastes, feelings, and judgment all pointed to Harry Mulford as the person she ought to awaken. He slept habitually in his clothes—the lightest summer dress of the tropics ; and the window of his little state-room was always open for air. Moving lightly to the place, Rose laid her own little soft hand on the arm of the young man, when the latter was on his feet in an instant. A single moment only was necessary to regain his consciousness, when Mulford left the stateroom and joined Rose on the quarter-deck.

"Why am I called, Rose," the young man asked, attempering his voice to the calm that reigned around him; "and why am I called by *you* ?"

Rose explained the state of the brig, and the feeling which induced her to awaken him. With woman's gentleness she now expressed her regret for having robbed Harry of his rest; had she reflected a moment, she might have kept watch herself, and allowed him to obtain the sleep he must surely so much require.

But Mulford laughed at this; protested he had never been awakened at a more favorable moment, and would have sworn, had it been proper, that a minute's further sleep would have been too much for him. After these first explanations, Mulford walked round the decks, carefully felt how much strain there was on the purchases, and rejoined Rose to report that all was right, and that he did not consider it necessary to call even the cook. The black was an idler in no sense but that of keeping watch, and he had toiled the past day as much as any of the men, though it was not exactly at the pumps.

A long and semi-confidential conversation now occurred between Harry and Rose. They talked of Spike, the brig, and her cargo, and of the delusion of the captain's widow. It was scarcely possible that powder should be so much wanted at the Havana as to render smuggling, at so much cost, a profitable adventure; and Mulford admitted his convictions that the pretended flour was originally intended for Mexico. Rose related the tenor of the conversation she had overheard between the two parties, Don Juan and Don Esteban, and the mate no longer doubted that it was Spike's intention to sell the brig to the enemy. She also alluded to what had passed between herself and the stranger.

Mulford took this occasion to introduce the subject of Jack Tier's intimacy and favor with Rose. He even professed to feel some jealousy on account of it, little as there might be to alarm most men in the rivalry of such a competitor. Rose laughed, as girls will laugh when there is question of their power over the other sex, and she fairly shook her rich tresses as she declared her determination to continue to smile on Jack to the close of the voyage. Then, as if she had said more than she intended, she added with woman's generosity and tenderness,—

"After all, Harry, you know how much I promised to you even before we sailed, and how much more since, and have no just cause to dread even Jack. There is another reason, however, that ought to set your mind entirely at ease on his account. Jack is married, and has a partner living at this very moment, as he does not scruple to avow himself."

A hissing noise, a bright light, and a slight explosion, interrupted the half-laughing girl, and Mulford, turning on his heel, quick as thought, saw that a rocket had shot into the air, from a point close under the bows of the brig. He was still in the act of moving toward the forecastle, when, at the distance of several leagues, he saw the explosion of another rocket high in the air. He knew enough of the practices of vessels of war, to feel certain that these were a signal and its answer from some one in the service of government. Not at all sorry to have the career of the Swash arrested, before she could pass into hostile hands, or before evil could befall Rose, Mulford reached the forecastle just in time to answer the inquiry that was immediately put to him, in the way of a hail. A gig, pulling four oars only, with two officers in its stern-sheets, was fairly under the vessel's bows, and the mate could almost distinguish the countenance of the officer who questioned him, the instant he showed his head and shoulders above the bulwarks.

"What vessels are these?" demanded the stranger, speaking in the authoritative manner of one who acted for the state, but not speaking much above the usual conversational tone.

"American and Spanish," was the answer. "This brig is American; the schooner alongside is a Spaniard, that turned turtle in a tornado, about six-and-thirty hours since, and on which we have been hard at work trying to raise her, since the gale which succeeded the tornado has blown its pipe out."

" Ay, ay, that's the story, is it? I did not know what to make of you, lying cheek by jowl, in this fashion. Was anybody lost on board the schooner?"

" All hands, including every soul aft and forward, the supercargo excepted, who happened to be aboard here. We buried seventeen bodies this afternoon on the smallest of the Keys that you see near at hand, and two this morning alongside of the light. But what boat is that, and where are *you* from, and whom are you signalling?"

" The boat is a gig," answered the stranger, deliberately, " and she belongs to a cruiser of Uncle Sam's, that is off the reef, a short bit to the eastward, and we signalled our captain. But I'll come on board you, sir, if you please."

Mulford walked aft to meet the stranger at the gangway, and was relieved, rather than otherwise, at finding that Spike was already on the quarter-deck. Should the vessel of war seize the brig, he could rejoice at it, but so strong were his professional ideas of duty to the craft he sailed in, that he did not find it in his heart to say aught against her. Were any mishap to befall it, or were justice to be done, he preferred that it might be done under Spike's own supervision, rather than under his.

" Call all hands, Mr. Mulford," said Spike, as they met. " I see a streak of day coming yonder in the east ; let all hands be called at once. What strange boat is this we have alongside?"

This question was put to the strangers, Spike standing on his gangway-ladder to ask it, while the mate was summoning up the crew. The officer saw that a new person was to be dealt with, and in his quiet, easy way, he answered, while stretching out his hands to take up the man-rope,—

" Your servant, sir ; we are man-of-war's men, belonging to one of Uncle Sam's craft, outside, and have just come in to pay you a visit of ceremony. I told one, whom I suppose was your mate, that I would just step on board of you."

" Ay, ay ; one at a time, if you please. It's war time, and I cannot suffer armed boat's crews to board me at night, without knowing something about them. Come up yourself, if you please, but order your people to stay in the boat. Here, muster about this gangway, half a dozen of you, and keep an eye on the crew of this strange boat.''

These orders had no effect on the cool and deliberate lieutenant, who ascended the brig's side, and immediately stood on her deck. No sooner had he and Spike confronted each other, than each gave a little start, like that of recognition, and the lieutenant spoke.

"Ay, ay, I believe I know this vessel now. It is the Molly Swash, of New York, bound to Key West, and a market; and I have the honor to see Captain Stephen Spike again.''

It was Mr. Wallace, the second lieutenant of the sloop-of-war that had boarded the brig in the Mona Passage, and to avoid whom Spike had gone to the southward of Jamaica. The meeting was very *mal-à-propos*, but it would not do to betray that the captain and owner of the vessel thought as much as this; on the contrary, Wallace was warmly welcomed, and received, not only as an old acquaintance, but as a very agreeable visitor. To have seen the two, as they walked aft together, one might have supposed that the meeting was conducive of nothing but a very mutual satisfaction, it was so much like that which happens between those who keep up a hearty acquaintance.

"Well, I'm glad to see you again, Captain Spike,'' cried Wallace, after the greetings were passed, "if it be only to ask where you flew to, the day we left you in the Mona Passage? We looked out for you with all our eyes, expecting you would be down between San Domingo and Jamaica, but I hardly think you got by us in the night. Our master thinks you must have dove, and gone past loon-fashion. Do you ever perform that manœuvre?''

"No, we've kept above water the whole time, lieutenant,'' answered Spike, heartily; "and that is more than can be said of the poor fellow alongside of us. I was so much afraid of the Isle of Pines, that I went round Jamaica.''

"You might have given the Isle of Pines a berth, and

still have passed to the northward of the Englishmen,"
said Wallace, a little dryly. "However, that island *is*
somewhat of a scarecrow, and we have been to take a look
at it ourselves. All's right there, just now. But you seem
light ; what have you done with your flour?"

"Parted with every barrel of it. You may remember I
was bound to Key West, and a market. Well, I found my
market here, in American waters."

"You have been lucky, sir. This 'emporium' does not
seem to be exactly a commercial emporium."

"The fact is, the flour is intended for the Havana ; and I
fancy it is to be shipped for slavers. But I am to know
nothing of all that, you'll understand, lieutenant. If I
sell my flour in American waters, at two prices, it's no concern of mine what becomes of it a'terwards."

"Unless it happens to pass into enemy's hands, certainly
not ; and you are too patriotic to deal with Mexico, just
now, I'm sure. Pray, did that flour go down when the
schooner turned turtle?"

"Every barrel of it ; but Don Wan, below there, thinks
that most of it may yet be saved, by landing it on one of
those Keys to dry. Flour, well packed, wets in slowly.
You see we have some of it on deck."

"And who may Don Wan be, sir, pray? We are sent
here to look after Dons and Doñas, you know."

Don Wan is a Cuban merchant, and deals in such articles
as he wants. I fell in with him among the reefs here,
where he was rummaging about in hopes of meeting
with a wrack, he tells me, and thinking to purchase something profitable in that way ; but finding I had flour, he
agreed to take it out of me at this anchorage, and send me
away in ballast at once. I have found Don Wan Montefalderon ready pay, and very honorable."

Wallace then requested an explanation of the disaster,
to the details of which he listened with a sailor's interest.
He asked a great many questions, all of which bore on the
more nautical features of the event ; and, day having now
fairly appeared, he examined the purchases and backings
of the Swash with professional nicety. The schooner was

no lower in the water than when the men had knocked off work the previous night; and Spike set the people at the pumps at their bailing again, as the most effectual method of preventing their making any indiscreet communications to the man-of-war's men.

About this time the relict appeared on deck, when Spike gallantly introduced the lieutenant anew to his passengers. It is true he knew no name to use, but that was of little moment, as he called the officer "the lieutenant" and nothing else.

Mrs. Budd was delighted with this occasion to show off, and she soon broke out on the easy, indolent, but waggish Wallace, in a strain to surprise him, notwithstanding the specimen of the lady's skill from which he had formerly escaped.

"Captain Spike is of opinion, lieutenant, that our cast-anchor here is excellent, and I know the value of a good cast-anchor place ; for my poor Mr. Budd was a sea-faring man, and taught me almost as much of your noble profession as he knew himself."

"And he taught you, ma'am," said Wallace, fairly opening his eyes, under the influence of astonishment, "to be very particular about cast-anchor places ! "

"Indeed he did. He used to say, that roads-instead were never as good, for such purposes, as land that's locked havens, for the anchors would return home, as he called it, in roads-instead."

"Yes, ma'am," answered Wallace, looking very queer at first, as if disposed to laugh outright, then catching a glance of Rose, and changing his mind ; "I perceive that Mr. Budd knew what he was about, and preferred an anchorage where he was well land-locked, and where there was no danger of his anchors coming home, as so often happens in your open roadsteads."

"Yes that's just it ! That was just his notion ! You cannot feel how delightful it is, Rose, to converse with one that thoroughly understands such subjects ! My poor Mr. Budd did, indeed, denounce roads-instead, at all times calling them 'savage.' "

"Savage, aunt," put in Rose, hoping to stop the good relict by her own interposition, "that is a strange word to apply to an anchorage!"

"Not at all, young lady," said Wallace gravely. "They are often *wild* berths, and wild berths are not essentially different from wild beasts. Each is savage, as a matter of course."

"I knew I was right!" exclaimed the widow. "Savage cast-anchors come of wild births, as do savage Indians. Oh! the language of the ocean, as my poor Mr. Budd used to say, is eloquence tempered by common sense!"

Wallace stared again, but his attention was called to other things just at that moment. The appearance of Don Juan Montefalderon y Castro on deck, reminded him of his duty, and approaching that gentleman he condoled with him on the grave loss he had sustained. After a few civil expressions on both sides, Wallace made a delicate allusion to the character of the schooner.

"Under other circumstances," he said, "it might be my duty to inquire a little particularly as to the nationality of your vessel, Señor, for we are at war with the Mexicans, as you doubtless know."

"Certainly," answered Don Juan, with an unmoved air and great politeness of manner, though it would be out of my power to satisfy you. Everything was lost in the schooner, and I have not a paper of any sort to show you. If it be your pleasure to make a prize of a vessel in this situation, certainly it is in your power to do it. A few barrels of wet flour are scarce worth disputing about."

Wallace now seemed a little ashamed, the *sang froid* of the other throwing dust in his eyes, and he was in a hurry to change the subject. Señor Don Juan was very civilly condoled with again, and he was made to repeat the incidents of the loss, as if his auditor took a deep interest in what he said, but no further hint was given touching the nationality of the vessel. The lieutenant's tact let him see that Señor Montefalderon was a person of a very different calibre from Spike, as well as of different habits; and he did not choose to indulge in the quiet irony that formed so large an ingredient in his own character, with this new acquaintance. He spoke Spanish himself, with tolerable fluency, and a conversation now occurred between the two, which was maintained for some time with spirit and a very manifest courtesy.

This dialogue between Wallace and the Spaniard gave Spike a little leisure for reflection. As the day advanced the cruiser came more and more plainly in view, and his first business was to take a good survey of her. She might have been three leagues distant, but approaching with a very light breeze, at the rate of something less than two knots in the hour. Unless there was some one on board her who was acquainted with the channels of the Dry Tortugas, Spike felt little apprehension of the ship's getting very near to him; but he very well understood that, with the sort of artillery that was in modern use among vessels of war, he would hardly be safe could the cruiser get within a league. That near Uncle Sam's craft might certainly come without encountering the hazards of the channels, and within that distance she would be likely to get in the course of the morning, should he have the complaisance to wait for her. He determined, therefore, not to be guilty of that act of folly.

All this time the business of lightening the schooner proceeded. Although Mulford earnestly wished that the man-of-war might get an accurate notion of the true character and objects of the brig, he could not prevail on himself to become an informer. In order to avoid the temptation so to do, he exerted himself in keeping the men at their tasks, and never before had pumping and bailing been carried on with more spirit. The schooner soon floated of herself, and the purchases which led to the Swash were removed. Near a hundred more barrels of the flour had been taken out of the hold of the Spanish craft, and had been struck on the deck of the brig, or sent to the Key by means of the boats. This made a material change in the buoyancy of the vessel, and enabled the bailing to go on with greater facility. The pumps were never idle, but two small streams of water were running the whole time toward the scuppers, and through them into the sea.

At length the men were ordered to knock off, and to get their breakfasts. This appeared to arouse Wallace, who had been chatting, quite agreeably to himself, with Rose, and seemed reluctant to depart, but who now became sensible that he was neglecting his duty. He called away his boat's crew, and took a civil leave of the passengers; after which he went over the side. The gig was some little distance from the Swash, when Wallace rose and asked to see Spike, with whom he had a word to say at parting.

"I will soon return," he said, "and bring you forty or fifty fresh men, who will make light work with your wreck. I am certain our commander will consent to my doing so, and will gladly send on board you two or three boats' crews."

"If I let him," muttered Spike between his teeth, "I shall be a poor, miserable cast-anchor devil, that's all."

To Wallace, however, he expressed his hearty acknowledgments; begged him not to be in a hurry, as the worst was now over, and the row was still a long one. If he got back toward evening it would be all in good time. Wallace waved his hand, and the gig glided away. As for Spike, he sat down on the plank-sheer where he had stood, and remained there ruminating intently for two or three minutes. When he descended to the deck his mind was fully made up. His first act was to give some private orders to the boatswain, after which he withdrew to the cabin, whither he summoned Tier, without delay.

"Jack," commenced the captain, using very little circumlocution in opening his mind, "you and I are old shipmates, and ought to be old friends, though I think your natur' has undergone some changes since we last met. Twenty years ago there was no man in the ship on whom I could so certainly depend as on Jack Tier; now, you seem given up altogether to the women. Your mind has changed even more than your body."

"Time does that for all of us, Captain Spike," returned

Tier coolly. "I am *not* what I used to be, I'll own, nor are you yourself, for that matter. When I saw you last, noble captain, you were a handsome man of forty, and could go aloft with any youngster in the brig; but, now, you're heavy, and not over-active."

"I! Not a bit of change has taken place in me for the last thirty years. I defy any man to show the contrary. But that's neither here nor there; you are no young woman, Jack, that I need be boasting of my health and beauty before you. I want a bit of real sarvice from you, and want it done in old-times fashion; and I mean to pay for it in old-times fashion, too."

As Spike concluded, he put into Tier's hand one of the doubloons that he had received from Señor Montefalderon, in payment for the powder. The doubloons, for which so much pumping and bailing were then in process, were still beneath the waters of the Gulf.

"Ay, ay, sir," returned Jack, smiling and pocketing the gold, with a wink of the eye, and a knowing look; "this does resemble old times sum'at. I now begin to know Captain Spike, my old commander again, and see that he's more like himself than I had just thought him. What am I to do for this, sir? speak plain, that I may be sartain to steer the true course."

"Oh, just a trifle, Jack—nothing that will break up the ground-tier of your wits, my old shipmate. You see the state of the brig, and know that she is in no condition for ladies.

"T would have been better all round, sir, had they never come aboard at all," answered Jack, looking dark.

Spike was surprised, but he was too much bent on his projects to heed trifles.

"You know what sort of flour they're whipping out of the schooner, and must understand that the brig will soon be in a pretty litter. I do not intend to let them send a single barrel of it beneath my hatches again, but the deck and the islands must take it all. Now I wish to relieve my passengers from the confinement this will occasion, and I have ordered the boatswain to pitch a tent for them on the largest of these here Tortugas ; and what I want of you, is to muster food and water, and other women's knick-nacks, and go ashore with them, and make them as comfortable as you can for a few days, or until we can get this schooner loaded and off.''

Jack Tier looked at his commander as if he would penetrate his most secret thoughts. A short pause succeeded, during which the steward's mate was intently musing, then his countenance suddenly brightened ; he gave the doubloon a fillip, and caught it on the palm of his hand as it descended, and he uttered the customary ''Ay, ay, sir,'' with apparent cheerfulness. Nothing more passed between these two worthies, who now parted, Jack to make his arrangements, and Spike to '' tell his yarn,'' as he termed the operation in his own mind, to Mrs. Budd, Rose, and Biddy. The widow listened complacently, though she seemed half doubting, half ready to comply. As for Rose, she received the proposal with delight, the confinement of the vessel having become irksome to her. The principal obstacle was in overcoming the difficulties made by the aunt, Biddy appearing to like the notion quite as much as '' Miss Rosy.'' As for the light-house, Mrs. Budd had declared nothing would induce her to go there ; for she did not doubt that the place would soon be, if it were not already, haunted. In this opinion she was sustained by Biddy ; and it was the knowledge of this opinion that induced Spike to propose the tent.

'' Are you sure, Captain Spike, it is not a desert island ? '' asked the widow ; '' I remember that my poor Mr. Budd always spoke of desert islands as horrid places, and spots that every one should avoid.''

'' What if it is, aunty ? '' said Rose, eagerly, '' while we have the brig here, close at hand. We shall suffer none of the wants of such a place, so long as our friends can supply us.''

'' And *such* friends, Miss Rose,'' exclaimed Spike, a little sentimentally for him, '' friends that would undergo hunger and thirst themselves, before you should want for any comforts.''

"Do, now, Madam Budd," put in Biddy in her hearty
way, "it 's an island, ye 'll remimber : and sure that 's just
what ould Ireland has ever been, God bless it ! Islands
make the pleasantest risidences."

"Well, I 'll venture to oblige you and Biddy, Rosy,
dear," returned the aunt, still half reluctant to yield ;
"but you 'll remember, that if I find it at all a desert isl-
and, I 'll not pass the night on it on any account whatever."

With this understanding the party was transferred to the
shore. The boatswain had already erected a sort of a tent,
on a favorable spot, using some of the old sails that had
covered the flour-barrels, not only for the walls, but for a
carpet of some extent also. This tent was ingeniously
enough contrived. In addition to the little room that was
entirely inclosed, there was a sort of piazza, or open veranda,
which would enable its tenants to enjoy the shade in the
open air. Beneath this veranda, a barrel of fresh water was
placed, as well as three or four ship's stools, all of which had
been sent ashore with the materials for constructing the tent.
The boat had been going and coming for some time, and the
distance being short, the "desert island" was soon a desert
no longer. It is true that the supplies necessary to support
three women for as many days, were no great matter, and
were soon landed, but Jack Tier had made a provision somewhat more ample. A capital caterer, he had forgotten nothing within the compass of his means, that could contribute
to the comfort of those who had been put especially under
his care. Long before the people "knocked off" for their
dinners, the arrangements were completed, and the boatswain
was ready to take his leave.

"Well, ladies," said that grum old salt, "I can do no
more for you, as I can see. This here island is now almost
as comfortable as a ship that has been in blue water for a
month, and I don't know how it can be made more com-
fortabler."

This was only according to the boatswain's notion of comfort ; but Rose thanked him for his care in her winning
way, while her aunt admitted that, "for a place that was

almost a desert island, things did look somewhat promising."
In a few minutes the men were all gone, and the islet was
left to the sole possession of the three females, and their constant companion, Jack Tier. Rose was pleased with the
novelty of her situation, though the islet certainly did de-
serve the opprobrium of being a "desert island." There
was no shade but that of the tent, and its veranda-like covering, though the last, in particular, was quite extensive.
There was no water, that in the barrel and that of the ocean
excepted. Of herbage there was very little on this islet, and
that was of the most meagre and coarse character, being
long wiry grass, with here and there a few stunted bushes.
The sand was reasonably firm, however, more especially
round the shore, and the walking was far from unpleasant.
Little did Rose know it, but a week earlier, the spot would
have been next to intolerable to her, on account of the
mosquitoes, gallinippers, and other similar insects of the
family of tormentors; but everything of the sort had temporarily disappeared in the currents of the tornado. To do
Spike justice, he was aware of this circumstance, or he
might have hesitated about exposing females to the ordinary
annoyances of one of these spots. Not a mosquito, or anything of the sort was left, however, all having gone to leeward, in the vortex which had come so near sweeping off
the Mexican schooner.

"This place will do very well, aunty, for a day or two,"
cried Rose cheerfully, as she returned from a short excursion, and threw aside her hat, one made to shade her face
from the sun of a warm climate, leaving the sea-breeze that
was just beginning to blow, to fan her blooming and sunny
cheek. "It is better than the brig. The worst piece of
land is better than the brig."

"Do not say that, Rose, not if it's a desert island, dear;
and this is desperately like a desert island; I am almost
sorry I ventured on it."

"It will not be deserted by us, aunty, until we shall see
occasion to do so. Why not endeavor to get on board of
yonder ship, and return to New York in *her*; or at least
induce her captain to put us ashore somewhere near this

and go home by land. Your health never seemed better than it is at this moment, and as for mine, I do assure you, aunty dear, I am as perfectly well as I ever was in my life.''

"All from this voyage. I knew it would set you up, and am delighted to hear you say as much. Biddy and I were talking of you this very morning, my child, and we both agreed that you *were* getting to be yourself again. Oh, ships, and brigs, and schooners, full-jigger or half-jigger, for pulmonary complaints, say I! My poor Mr. Budd always maintained that the ocean was the cure for all diseases, and I determined that to sea you should go, the moment I became alarmed for your health.''

The good widow loved Rose most tenderly, and she was obliged to use her handkerchief to dry the tears from her eyes as she concluded. Those tears sprung equally from a past feeling of apprehension, and a present feeling of gratitude. Rose saw this, and she took a seat at her aunt's side, touched herself, as she never failed to be on similar occasions, with this proof of her relative's affection. At that moment even Harry Mulford would have lost a good deal in her kind feelings toward him, had he so much as smiled at one of the widow's nautical absurdities. At such times, Rose seemed to be her aunt's guardian and protectress, instead of reversing the relations, and she entirely forgot herself the many reasons which existed for wishing that she had been placed in childhood under the care of one better qualified than the well-meaning relict of her uncle, for the performance of her duties.

"Thank you, aunty; thank'ee, dear aunty," said Rose, kissing the widow affectionately. "I know that you mean the best for me, though you *are* a little mistaken in supposing me ill. I do assure you, dear," patting her aunt's cheek, as if she herself had been merely a playful child, "I never was better; and if I *have* been pulmonary, I am entirely cured, and am now ready to return home.''

"God be praised for this, Rosy. Under *His* divine providence, it is all owing to the sea. If you really feel so much restored, however, I do not wish to keep you a moment longer on a ship's board than is necessary. We owe something to Captain Spike's care, and cannot quit him too unceremoniously; but as soon as he is at liberty to go into a harbor, I will engage him to do so, and we can return home by land—unless, indeed, the brig intends to make the home voyage herself."

"I do not like this brig, aunty, and now we are out of her, I wish we could keep out of her. Nor do I like your Captain Spike, who seems to me anything but an agreeable gentleman."

"That's because you are n't accustomed to the sea. My poor Mr. Budd had *his* ways, like all the rest of them; it takes time to get acquainted with them. All sailors are so."

Rose bent her face involuntarily, but so low as to conceal the increasing brightness of her native bloom, as she answered,—

"Harry Mulford is not so, aunty dear; and he is every inch a sailor."

"Well, there *is* a difference, I must acknowledge, though I dare say Harry will grow every day more and more like all the rest of them. In the end, he will resemble Captain Spike."

"Never!" said Rose, firmly.

"You can't tell, child. I never saw your uncle when he was Harry's age, for I was n't born till he was thirty; but often and often has he pointed out to me some slender, genteel youth, and said, 'just such a lad was I at twenty,' though nothing could be less alike, at the moment he was speaking, than they two. We all change with our years. Now I was once as slender, and almost—not quite, Rosy, for few there are that be—but *almost* as handsome as you yourself."

"Yes, aunty, I 've heard that before," said Rose, springing up, in order to change the discourse; "but Harry Mulford will never become like Stephen Spike. I wish we had never known the man, dearest aunty."

"It was all your own doings, child. He's a cousin of your most intimate friend, and she brought him to the house : and one could n't offend Mary Mulford, by telling her we did n't like her cousin.''

Rose seemed vexed, and she kept her little foot in motion, patting the sail that formed the carpet, as girls will pat the ground with their feet when vexed. This gleam of displeasure was soon over, however, and her countenance became as placid as the clear, blue sky that formed the vault of the heavens above her head. As if to atone for the passing rebellion of her feelings, she threw her arms around her aunt's neck ; after which she walked away, along the beach, ruminating on her present situation, and of the best means of extricating their party from the power of Spike.

It requires great familiarity with vessels and the seas, for one to think, read, and pursue the customary train of reasoning on board a ship that one has practised ashore. Rose had felt this embarrassment during the past month, for the whole of which time she had scarcely been in a condition to act up to her true character, suffering her energies, and in some measure her faculties, to be drawn into the vortex produced by the bustle, novelties, and scenes of the vessel and the ocean. But, now she was once more on the land, diminutive and naked as was the islet that composed her present world, and she found leisure and solitude for reflection and decision. She was not ignorant of the nature of a vessel of war, or of the impropriety of unprotected females placing themselves on board of one ; but gentlemen of character, like the officers of the ship in sight, could hardly be wanting in the feelings of their caste ; and anything was better than to return voluntarily within the power of Spike. She determined within her own mind that voluntarily she would not. We shall leave this young girl, slowly wandering along the beach of her islet, musing on matters like these, while we return to the vessels and the mariners.

A good breeze had come in over the reef from the Gulf, throwing the sloop-of-war dead to leeward of the brigantine's anchorage. This was the reason that the former had closed so slowly. Still the distance between the vessels was so small, that a swift cruiser, like the ship of war, would soon have been alongside of the wreckers, but for the intervening islets and the intricacies of their channels. She had made sail on the wind, however, and was evidently disposed to come as near to the danger as her lead showed would be safe, even if she did not venture among them.

Spike noted all these movements, and he took his measures accordingly. The pumping and bailing had been going on since the appearance of light, and the flour had been quite half removed from the schooner's hold. That vessel consequently floated with sufficient buoyancy, and no further anxiety was felt on account of her sinking. Still, a great deal of water remained in her, the cabin itself being nearly half full. Spike's object was to reduce this water sufficiently to enable him to descend into the state-room which Señor Montefalderon had occupied, and bring away the doubloons that alone kept him in the vicinity of so ticklish a neighbor as the Poughkeepsie. Escape was easy enough to one who knew the passages of the reef and islets; more especially since the wind had so fortunately brought the cruiser to leeward. Spike most apprehended a movement upon him in the boats, and he had almost made up his mind should such an enterprise be attempted, to try his hand in beating it off with his guns. A good deal of uncertainty on the subject of Mulford's consenting to resist the recognized authorities of the country, as well as some doubts of a similar nature in reference to two or three of the best of the foremast hands, alone left him at all in doubt as to the expediency of such a course. As no boats were lowered from the cruiser, however, the necessity of resorting to so desperate a measure did not occur, and the duty of lightening the schooner had proceeded without interruption. As soon as the boatswain came off from the islet, he and the men with him were directed to take the hands and lift the anchors, of which it will be remembered the Swash had several down. Even Mulford was shortly after set at work on the same duty, and these expert and ready seamen soon had the brig clear of

the ground. As the schooner was anchored, and floated
without assistance, the Swash rode by her.

Such was the state of things when the men turned to,
after having had their dinners. By this time the sloop-of-
war was within half a league of the bay, her progress
having been materially retarded by the set of the current,
which was directly against her. Spike saw that a collision
of some sort or other must speedily occur, and he determined to take the boatswain with him, and descend into
the cabin of the schooner in quest of the gold. The boatswain was summoned, and Señor Montefalderon repeated
in this man's presence the instructions that he thought it
necessary for the adventurers to follow, in order to secure
the prize. Knowing how little locks would avail on board
a vessel, were the men disposed to rob him, that gentleman
had trusted more to secreting his treasure, than to securing
it in the more ordinary way. When the story had again
been told, Spike and his boatswain went on board the
schooner, and, undressing, they prepared to descend into
the cabin. The captain paused a single instant to take a
look at the sloop-of-war, and to examine the state of the
weather. It is probable some new impression was made
on him by this inquiry, for, hailing Mulford, he ordered
him to loosen the sails, and to sheet home, and hoist the
fore-topsail. In a word, to "see all ready to cast off, and
make sail on the brig at the shortest notice." With this
command he disappeared by the schooner's companion-way.

Spike and his companion found the water in the cabin
very much deeper than they had supposed. With a view to
comfort, the cabin-floor had been sunk much lower than is
usual on board American vessels, and this brought the
water up nearly to the arm-pits of two men as short as our
captain and his sturdy little boatswain. The former grumbled a good deal, when he ascertained the fact, and said
something about the mate's being better fitted to make a
search in such a place, but concluding with the remark, that
" the man who wants ticklish duty well done, must see to it
himself."

The gold-hunters groped their way cautiously about the

cabin for some time, feeling for a drawer, in which they had been told they should find the key of Señor Montefalderon's state-room door. In this Spike himself finally succeeded, he being much better acquainted with cabins and their fixtures than the boatswain.

"Here it is, Ben," said the captain, "now for a dive among the Don's val'ables. Should you pick up anything worth speaking of, you can condemn it for salvage, as I mean to cast off, and quit the wrack the moment we've made sure of the doubloons."

"And what will become of all the black flour that is lying about, sir?" asked the boatswain with a grin.

"It may take care of itself. My agreement will be up as soon as the doubloons are found. If the Don will come down handsomely with his share of what will be left, I may be bought to put the kegs we have in the brig ashore for him somewhere in Mexico; but my wish is to get out of the neighborhood of that bloody sloop-of-war as soon as possible."

"She makes but slow headway ag'in the current, sir; but a body would think she might send in her boats."

"The boats might be glad to get back again," muttered Spike. "Ay, here is the door unlocked, and we can now fish for the money."

Some object had rolled against the state-room door, when the vessel was capsized, and there was a good deal of difficulty in forcing it open. They succeeded at last, and Spike led the way by wading into the small apartment. Here they began to feel about beneath the water, and by a very insufficient light, in quest of the hidden treasure. Spike and his boatswain differed as to the place which had just been described to them, as men will differ even in the account of events that pass directly before their eyes. While thus employed, the report of a heavy gun came through the doors of the cabin, penetrating to the recess in which they were thus employed.

"Ay, that's the beginning of it!" exclaimed Spike. "I wonder that the fool has put it off so long."

"That gun was a heavy fellow, Captain Spike," returned

the boatswain; "and it sounded in my ears as if 't was shotted."

"Ay, ay, I dare say you 're right enough in both opinions. They put such guns on board their sloops-of-war, nowadays, as a fellow used to find in the lower batteries of a two-decker only in old times; and as for shot, why Uncle Sam pays, and they think it cheaper to fire one out of a gun, than to take the trouble of drawing it."

"I believe here 's one of the bags, Captain Spike," said the boatswain, making a dip, and coming up with one half of the desired treasure in his fist. "By George, I 've grabbed him, sir; and the other bag can't be far off."

"Hand that over to me," said the captain, a little authoritatively, "and take a dive for the next."

As the boatswain was obeying this order, a second gun was heard, and Spike thought that the noise made by the near passage of a large shot was audible also. He called out to Ben to "bear a hand, as the ship seems in 'arnest." But the head of the boatswain being under water at the time, the admonition was thrown away. The fellow soon came up, however, puffing like a porpoise that has risen to the surface to blow.

"Hand it over to me at once," said Spike, stretching out his unoccupied hand to receive the prize; "we have little time to lose."

"That 's sooner said than done, sir," answered the boatswain; "a box has driven down upon the bag, and there 's a tight jam. I got hold of the neck of the bag, and pulled like a horse, but it would n't come no how."

"Show me the place, and let me have a drag at it. There goes another of his bloody guns!"

Down went Spike, and the length of time he was under water proved how much he was in earnest. Up he came at length, and with no better luck than his companion. He had got hold of the bag, satisfied himself by feeling its outside that it contained the doubloons, and hauled with all his strength, but it would not come. The boatswain now proposed to take a jamming hitch with a rope around the neck of the bag, which was long enough to admit of such a fastening, and then to apply their united force. Spike assented, and the boatswain rummaged about for a piece of small rope to suit his purpose. At this moment Mulford appeared at the companion-way to announce the movements on the part of the sloop-of-war. He had been purposely tardy, in order to give the ship as much time as possible; but he saw by the looks of the men that a longer delay might excite suspicion.

"Below there!" called out the mate.

"What's wanting, sir?—what's wanting, sir?" answered Spike; "let's know at once."

"Have you heard the guns, Captain Spike?"

"Ay, ay, every grumbler of them. They've done no mischief, I trust, Mr. Mulford?"

"None as yet, sir; though the last shot, and it was a heavy fellow, passed just above the schooner's deck. I've the topsail sheeted home and hoisted, and it's that which has set them at work. If I clewed up again I dare say they'd not fire another gun."

"Clew up nothing, sir, but see all clear for casting off and making sail through the South Pass. What do you say Ben, are you ready for a drag?"

"All ready, sir," answered the boatswain, once more coming up to breathe. "Now for it, sir; a steady pull, and a pull all together."

They *did* pull, but the hitch slipped, and both went down beneath the water. In a moment they were up again, puffing a little and swearing a great deal. Just then another gun, and a clatter above their heads, brought them to a stand.

"What mean's that, Mr. Mulford?" demanded Spike, a good deal startled.

It means that the sloop-of-war has shot away the head of this schooner's foremast, sir, and that the shot has chipp'd a small piece out of the heel of our maintop-mast—that's all."

Though excessively provoked at the mate's cool manner of replying, Spike saw that he might lose all by being too tenacious about securing the remainder of the doubloons. Pronouncing in very energetic terms on Uncle Sam, and all his cruisers, an anathema that we do not care to repeat, he gave a surly order to Ben to "knock-off," and abandoned his late design. In a minute he was on deck and dressed.

"Cast off, lads," cried the captain, as soon as on the deck of his own brig again, "and four of you man that boat. We have got half of your treasure, Señor Wan, but have been driven from the rest of it, as you see. There is the bag; when at leisure we'll divide it, and give the people their share. Mr. Mulford, keep the brig in motion, hauling up toward the South Pass, while I go ashore for the ladies. I'll meet you just in the throat of the passage."

This said, Spike tumbled into his boat, and was pulled ashore. As for Mulford, though he cast many an anxious glance toward the islet, he obeyed his orders, keeping the brig standing off and on, under easy canvas, but working her up toward the indicated passage.

Spike was met by Jack Tier on the beach of the little island.

"Muster the women at once," ordered the captain; "we have no time to lose, for that fellow will soon be firing broadsides, and his shot now range half a mile beyond us."

"You'll no more move the widow and her maid, than you'll move the island," answered Jack, laconically.

"Why should I not move them? Do they wish to stay here and starve?"

"It's little that they think of *that*. The sloop-of-war no sooner began to fire than down went Mrs. Budd on the canvas floor of the tent, and set up just such a screaming as you may remember she tried her hand at the night the revenue craft fired into us. Biddy lay down alongside of her mistress, and at every gun, they just scream as loud as they can, as if they fancied they might frighten off Uncle Sam's men from their duty."

"Duty! You little scamp, do you call tormenting honest traders in this fashion the duty of any man?"

"Well, captain, I'm no ways partic'lar about a word or two. Their 'ways,' if you like that better than duty, sir."

"Where's Rose? Is she down too, screaming and squalling?"

"No, Captain Spike, no. Miss Rose is endeavoring, like a handsome young Christian lady as she is, to pacify and mollify her aunt and Biddy ; and right down sensible talk does she give them."

"Then she at least can go aboard the brig," exclaimed Spike, with a sudden animation, and an expression of countenance that Jack did not at all like.

"I *ray-y-ther* think she'll wish to hold on to the old lady," observed the steward's mate, a little emphatically.

"You be d——d," cried Spike, fiercely ; "when your opinon is wanted, I'll ask for it. If I find you've been setting that young woman's mind ag'in me, I'll toss you overboard as I would the offals of a shark."

"Young women's minds, when they are only nineteen, get set ag'in boys of fifty-six without much assistance."

"Fifty-six yourself."

"I'm fifty-three—that I'll own without making faces at it," returned Jack, meekly ; "and, Stephen Spike, you logged fifty-six your last birthday, or a false entry was made."

This conversation did not take place in the presence of the boat's crew, but as the two walked together toward the tent. They were now in the veranda, as we have called the shaded opening in front, and actually within sound of the sweet voice of Rose, as she exhorted her aunt, in tones a little louder than usual for her to use, to manifest more fortitude. Under such circumstances Spike did not deem it expedient to utter that which was uppermost in his mind, but, turning short upon Tier, he directed a tremendous blow directly between his eyes. Jack saw the danger and dodged, falling backward to avoid a concussion which he knew would otherwise be fearful, coming as it would from one of the best forecastle boxers of his time. The full force of the blow was avoided, though Jack got enough of it to knock him down, and to give him a pair of black eyes. Spike did not stop to pick the assistant steward up, for another gun was fired at that very instant, and Mrs. Budd and Biddy renewed their screams. Instead of pausing to kick the prostrate Tier, as had just before been his intention, the captain entered the tent.

A scene that was sufficiently absurd met the view of Spike, when he found himself in the presence of the females. The widow had thrown herself on the ground, and was grasping the cloth of the sail, on which the tent had been erected, with both her hands, and was screaming at the top of her voice. Biddy's imitation was not exactly literal, for she had taken a comfortable seat at the side of her mistress, but in the way of cries, she rather outdid her principal.

"We must be off," cried Spike, somewhat unceremoniously. "The man-of-war is blazing away, as if she was a firin' minute-guns over our destruction, and I can wait no longer."

"I'll not stir," answered the widow; "I can't stir—I shall be shot if I go out. No, no, no,—I'll not stir an inch."

"We'll be kilt!—we'll be kilt!" echoed Biddy, "and a wicket murther 't will be in that same man, war or no war."

The captain perceived the uselessness of remonstrance at such a moment, and perhaps he was secretly rejoiced thereat; but it is certain that he whipped Rose up under his arm, and walked away with her, as if she had been a child of two or three years of age. Rose did not scream, but she struggled and protested vehemently. It was in vain. Already the captain had carried her half the distance between the tent and the boat, in the last of which a minute more would have deposited his victim, when a severe blow on the back of his head caused Spike to stumble, and he permitted Rose to escape from his grasp, in the effort to save himself from a fall. Turning fiercely toward his assailant, whom he suspected to be one of his boat's crew, he saw Tier standing within a few yards, levelling a pistol at him.

"Advance a step, and you're a dead man, villain!" screamed Jack, his voice almost cracked with rage, and the effort he made to menace.

Spike muttered an oath too revolting for our pages; but it was such a curse as none but an old salt could give vent to, and that in the bitterness of his fiercest wrath. At that critical moment, while Rose was swelling with indigna-

tion and wounded maiden pride, almost within reach of his
arms, looking more lovely than ever, as the flush of anger
deepened the color in her cheeks, a fresh and deep report
from one of the guns of the sloop-of-war drew all eyes
in her direction. The belching of that gun seemed to be
of double the power of those which had preceded it, and
jets of water, that were twenty feet in height, marked the
course of the formidable missile that was projected from
the piece. The ship had, indeed, discharged one of those
monster cannons that bear the name of a distinguished
French engineer, but which should more properly be called
by the name of the ingenious officer who is at the head of
our own ordnance, as they came originally from his inven-
tive faculties, though somewhat improved by their European adopter. Spike suspected the truth, for he had heard
of these "Pazans," as he called them, and he watched the
booming, leaping progress of the eight-inch shell that this
gun threw, with the apprehension that unknown danger is
apt to excite. As jet succeeded jet, each rising nearer and
nearer to his brig, the interval of time between them seeming fearfully to diminish, he muttered oath upon oath.
The last leap that the shell made on the water was at
about a quarter of a mile's distance of the islet on which
his people had deposited at least a hundred and fifty barrels of his spurious flour: thence it flew, as it might be
without an effort, with a grand and stately bound into the
very centre of the barrels, exploding at the moment it
struck. All saw the scattering of flour, which was instantly succeeded by the heavy though slightly straggling
explosion of all the powder on the island. A hundred kegs
were lighted, as it might be, in a common flash, and a cloud
of white smoke poured out and concealed the whole islet,
and all near it.

Rose stood confounded, nor was Jack Tier in a much better state of mind, though he still kept the pistol levelled, and
menaced Spike. But the last was no longer dangerous to
any there. He recollected that piles of the barrels encum-
bered the decks of his vessel, and he rushed to the boat,
nearly frantic with haste, ordering the men to pull for their

lives. In less than five minutes he was alongside, and on the deck of the Swash, his first order being to "Tumble every barrel of this bloody powder into the sea, men. Over with it, Mr. Mulford, clear away the midship ports, and launch as much as you can through them."

Remonstrance on the part of Señor Montefalderon would have been useless, had he been disposed to make it ; but, sooth to say, he was as ready to get rid of the powder as any there, after the specimen he had just witnessed of the power of a Paixhan gun.

Thus it is ever with men. Had two or three of those shells been first thrown without effect, as might very well have happened under the circumstances, none there would have cared for the risk they were running ; but the chance explosion which had occurred presented so vivid a picture of the danger, dormant and remote as it really was, as to throw the entire crew of the Swash into a frenzy of exertion.

Nor was the vessel at all free from danger. On the contrary, she ran very serious risk of being destroyed, and in some degree, in the very manner apprehended. Perceiving that Spike was luffing up through one of the passages nearest the reef, which would carry him clear of the group, a long distance to windward of the point where he could only effect the same object, the commander of the sloop-of-war opened his fire in good earnest, hoping to shoot away something material on board the Swash, before she could get beyond the reach of his shot. The courses steered by the two vessels, just at that moment, favored such an attempt, though they made it necessarily very short-lived. While the Swash was near the wind, the sloop-of-war was obliged to run off to avoid islets ahead of her, a circumstance which, while it brought the brig square with the ship's broadside, compelled the latter to steer on a diverging line to the course of her chase. It was in consequence of these facts, that the sloop-of-war now opened in earnest, and was soon canopied in the smoke of her own fire.

Great and important changes, as has been already mentioned, have been made in the arrangements of all the smaller cruisers within the last few years. Half a generation since, a ship of the rate—we do not say of the size—of the vessel which was in chase of Spike and his craft, would not have had it in her power to molest an enemy at the distance these two vessels were now apart. But recent improvements have made ships of this nominal force formidable at nearly a league's distance ; more especially by means of their Paixhans and their shells.

For some little time the range carried the shot directly over the islet of the tent ; Jack Tier and Rose, both of whom were watching all that passed with intense interest, standing in the open air the whole time, seemingly with no concern for themselves, so absorbed was each, notwithstanding all that had passed, in the safety of the brig. As for Rose, she thought only of Harry Mulford, and of the danger he was in by those fearful explosions of the shells. Her quick intellect comprehended the peculiar nature of the risk that was incurred by having the flour-barrels on deck, and she could not but see the manner in which Spike and his men were tumbling them into the water, as the quickest manner of getting rid of them. After what had just passed between Jack Tier and his commander, it might not be so easy to account for his manifest, nay, intense interest in the escape of the Swash. This was apparent by his troubled countenance, by his exclamations, and occasionally by his openly expressed wishes for her safety. Perhaps it was no more than the interest the seaman is apt to feel in the craft in which he has so long sailed, and which to him has been a home, and of which Mulford exhibited so much, in his struggles between feeling and conscience, between a true and a false duty.

As for Spike and his people, we have already mentioned their efforts to get rid of the powder. Shell after shell exploded, though none very near the brig, the ship working her guns as if in action. At length the officers of the sloop-of-war detected a source of error in their aim, that is of very common occurrence in sea-gunnery. Their shot had been thrown to *ricochet*, quartering a low, but very regular succession of little waves. Each shot striking the water at an acute angle to its agitated surface, was deflected from a straight line, and described a regular curve toward the end of its career ; or, it might be truer to say, an irregular curvature, for the deflection increased as the momentum of the missile diminished.

No sooner did the commanding officer of the sloop-of-war discover this fact, and it was easy to trace the course of the shots by the jets of water they cast into the air, and to see as well as to hear the explosions of the shells, then he ordered the guns pointed more to windward, as a means of counteracting the departure from the straight lines. This expedient succeeded in part, the solid shot falling much nearer to the brig the moment the practice was resorted to. No shell was fired for some little time after the new order was issued, and Spike and his people began to hope these terrific missiles had ceased their annoyance. The men cheered, finding their voices for the first time since the danger had seemed so imminent, and Spike was heard animating them to their duty. As for Mulford, he was on the coach-house deck, working the brig, the captain having confided to him that delicate duty, the highest proof he could furnish of confidence in his seamanship. The handsome young mate had just made a half-board, in the neatest manner, shoving the brig by its means through a most difficult part of the passage, and had got her handsomely filled again on the same tack, looking right out into open water, by a channel through which she could now stand on a very easy bowline. Everything seemed propitious, and the sloop-of-war's solid shot began to drop into the water, a hundred yards short of the brig. In this state of things one of the Paixhans belched forth its angry flame and sullen roar again. There was no mistaking the gun. Then came its mass of iron, a globe that would have weighed just sixty-eight pounds, had not sufficient metal been left out of its interior to leave a cavity to contain a single pound of powder. Its course, as usual, was to be marked by its path along the sea, as it bounded, half a mile at a time, from wave to wave. Spike saw by its undeviating course that this shell was booming terrifically toward his brig, and a cry to "look out

for the shell," caused the work to be suspended. That shell
struck the water for the last time, within two hundred yards
of the brig, rose dark and menacing in its furious leap, but
exploded at the next instant. The fragments of the iron
were scattered on each side, and ahead. Of the last, three
or four fell into the water so near the vessel as to cast their
spray on her decks.

"Overboard with the rest of the powder!" shouted Spike.
"Keep the brig off a little, Mr. Mulford—keep her off, sir;
you luff too much, sir."

"Ay, ay, sir," answered the mate. "Keep her off, it is."

"There comes the other shell!" cried Ben, but the men
did not quit their toil to gaze this time. Each seaman
worked as if life and death depended on his single exertions. Spike alone watched the course of the missile.
On it came, booming and hurtling through the air, tossing
high the jets, at each leap it made from the surface, striking the water for its last bound, seemingly in a line with
the shell that had just preceded it. From that spot it
made its final leap. Every hand in the brig was stayed
and every eye was raised as the rushing tempest was heard
advancing. The mass went muttering directly between
the masts of the Swash. It had scarcely seemed to go by
when the fierce flash of fire and the sharp explosion followed. Happily for those in the brig, the projectile force
given by the gun carried the fragments from them, as in the
other instance it had brought them forward; else would
few have escaped mutilation or death, among their crew.

The flashing of fire so near the barrels of powder that
still remained on their deck, caused the frantic efforts to be
renewed, and barrel after barrel was tumbled overboard,
amid the shouts that were now raised to animate the people
to their duty.

"Luff, Mr. Mulford—luff you may, sir," cried Spike.

No answer was given.

"D' ye hear there, Mr. Mulford?—it is luff you may,
sir."

"Mr. Mulford is not aft, sir," called out the man at the
helm, "but luff it is, sir."

" Mr. Mulford not aft ! Where's the mate, man ? Tell him he is wanted.''

No Mulford was to be found ! A call passed round the decks, was sent below, and echoed through the entire brig, but no sign or tidings could be had of the handsome mate. At that exciting moment the sloop-of-war seemed to cease her firing, and appeared to be securing her guns.

CHAPTER VII.

"Thou art the same, eternal sea!
 The earth has many shapes and forms,
 Of hill and valley, flower and tree;
 Fields that the fervid noontide warms,
 Or winter's rugged grasp deforms,
 Or bright with autumn's golden store;
 Thou coverest up thy face with storms,
 Or smilest serene—but still thy roar
And dashing foam go up to vex the sea-beat shore."

LUNT.

WE shall now advance the time eight-and-forty hours. The baffling winds and calms that succeeded the tornado had gone, and the trades blew in their stead. Both vessels had disappeared, the brig leading, doubling the western extremity of the reef, and going off before both wind and current, with flowing sheets, fully three hours before the sloop-of-war could beat up against the latter, to a point that enabled her to do the same thing. By that time, the Swash was five-and-twenty miles to the eastward, and consequently but just discernible in her loftiest sails, from the ship's royal yards. Still, the latter continued the chase; and that evening both vessels were beating down along the southern margin of the Florida Reef, against the trades, but favored by a three or four knot current, the brig out of sight to windward. Our narrative leads us to lose sight of both these vessels, for a time, in order to return to the islets of the Gulf. Eight-and-forty hours had made some changes in and around the haven of the Dry Tortugas. The tent still stood, and a small fire that was boiling its pot and its

kettle, at no great distance from it, proved that the tent
was still inhabited. The schooner also rode at her anchors, very much as she had been abandoned by Spike.
The bag of doubloons, however, had been found and there
it lay, tied but totally unguarded, in the canvas veranda
of Rose Budd's habitation. Jack Tier passed and repassed
it with apparent indifference, as he went to and fro, between his pantry and kitchen, busy as a bee in preparing
his noontide meal for the day. This man seemed to have
the islet all to himself, however, no one else being visible
on any part of it. He sang his song, in a cracked *contre
alto* voice, and appeared to be happy in his solitude. Occasionally he talked to himself aloud, most probably because he had no one else to speak to. We shall record
one of his recitatives, which came in between the strains
of a very inharmonious air, the words of which treated of
the seas, while the steward's assistant was stirring an exceedingly savory mess that he had concocted of the ingredients to be found in the united larders of the Swash and
the Mexican schooner.

"Stephen Spike is a capital willain!" exclaimed Jack,
smelling at a ladle filled with his soup, "a capital willain,
I call him. To think, at his time of life, of such a handsome and pleasant young thing as this Rose Budd; and
then to try to get her by underhand means, and by making
a fool of her silly old aunt. It's wonderful what fools
some old aunts be! Quite wonderful! If I was as great
a simpleton as this Mrs. Budd, I'd never cross my threshold. Yes, Stephen Spike is a prodigious willain, as his
best friend must own! Well, I gave him a thump on the
head that he'll not forget this v'y'ge. To think of carryin'
off that pretty Rose Budd in his very arms, in so indecent
a manner! Yet, the man has his good p'ints, if a body
could only forget his bad ones. He's a first-rate seaman.
How he worked the brig till he doubled the reef, a'ter she
got into open water; and how he made her walk off afore
the wind, with stun'sails alow and aloft, as soon as ever he
could make 'em draw! My life for it, he'll tire the legs
of Uncle Sam's man, afore he can fetch up with him.

For running away, when hard chased, Stephen Spike has n't his equal on 'arth. But he 's a great willain—a prodigious willain! I cannot say I actually wish him hanged; but I would rather have him hanged than see him get pretty Rose in his power. What has he to do with girls of nineteen? If the rascal is one year old, he 's fifty-six. I hope the sloop-of-war will find her match, and I think she will. The Molly 's a great traveller, and not to be outdone easily. 'T would be a thousand pities so lovely a craft should be cut off in the flower of her days, as it might be, and I *do* hope she 'll lead that bloody sloop on some sunken rock.

"Well, there's the other bag of doubloons. It seems Stephen could not get it. That's odd, too, for he 's great at grabbin' gold. The man bears his age well; but he 's a willain! I wonder whether he or Mulford made that half-board in the narrow channel. It was well done, and Stephen is a perfect sailor; but he says Mulford is the same. Nice young man, that Mulford; just fit for Rose, and Rose for him. Pity to part them. Can find no great fault with him, except that he has too much conscience. There 's such a thing as having too much, as well as too little conscience. Mulford has too much, and Spike has too little. For him to think of carryin' off a gal of nineteen! I say he 's fifty-six, if he 's a day. How fond he used to be of this very soup! If I 've seen him eat a quart of it, I 've seen him eat a puncheon full of it, in my time. What an appetite the man has when he 's had a hard day's duty on 't. There 's a great deal to admire, and a great deal to like in Stephen Spike, but he 's a reg'lar willain. I dare say he fancies himself a smart, jaunty youth ag'n, as I can remember him; a lad of twenty, which was about his years when I first saw him, by the sign that I was very little turned of fifteen myself. Spike *was* comely then, though I acknowledge he 's a willain. I can see him now, with his deep blue roundabout, his bell-mouthed trousers, both of fine cloth—too fine for such a willain—but fine it was, and much did it become him."

Here Jack made a long pause, during which, though he may have thought much, he said nothing. Nevertheless, he wasn't idle the while. On the contrary, he passed no less than three several times from the fire to the tent, and returned. Each time in going and coming, he looked intently at the bag of doubloons, though he did not stop at it or touch it. Some associations connected with Spike's fruitless attempts to obtain it must have formed its principal interest with this singular being, as he muttered his captain's name each time in passing, though he said no more audibly. The concerns of the dinner carried him back and forth; and in his last visit to the tent, he began to set a small table—one that had been brought for the convenience of Mrs. Budd and her niece, from the brig, and which of course still remained on the islet. It was while thus occupied, that Jack Tier recommenced his soliloquy.

"I hope that money may do some worthy fellow good yet. It's Mexican gold, and that's inemy's gold, and might be condemned by law, I do suppose. Stephen had a hankerin' a'ter it, but he did not get it. It come easy enough to the next man that tried. That Spike's a willain, and the gold was too good for him. He has no conscience at all to think of a gal of nineteen! And one fit for his betters, in the bargain. The time has been when Stephen Spike might have pretended to be Rose Budd's equal. That much I'll ever maintain, but that time's gone; and, what is more, it will never come again. I should like Mulford better if he had a little less conscience. Conscience may do for Uncle Sam's ships, but it is sometimes in the way aboard a trading craft. What can a fellow do with a conscience when dollars is to be smuggled off, or tobacco smuggled ashore? I do suppose I've about as much conscience as it is useful to have, and I've got ashore in my day twenty thousand dollars' worth of stuff, of one sort or another, if I've got ashore the valie of ten dollars. But Spike carries on business on too large a scale, and many's the time I've told him so. I could have forgiven him anything but this attempt on Rose Budd; and he's altogether too old for that, to say nothing of other people's rights. He's an up-and-down willain, and a body can make no more, nor any less of him. That soup must be near done, and I 'll hoist the signal for grub.''

This signal was a blue-peter of which one had been brought ashore to signal the brig ; and with which Jack now signalled the schooner. If the reader will turn his eyes toward the last-named vessel, he will find the guests whom Tier expected to surround his table. Rose, her aunt, and Biddy were all seated, under an awning made by a sail, on the deck of the schooner, which now floated so buoyantly as to show that she had materially lightened since last seen. Such indeed was the fact, and he who had been the instrument of producing this change appeared on deck, in the person of Mulford, as soon as he was told that the blue-peter of Jack Tier was flying.

The boat of the light-house, that in which Spike had landed in quest of Rose, was lying alongside of the schooner, and sufficiently explained the manner in which the mate had left the brig. This boat, in fact, had been fastened astern, in the hurry of getting from under the sloop-of-war's fire, and Mulford had taken the opportunity of the consternation and frantic efforts produced by the explosion of the last shell thrown, to descend from his station on the coach-house into this boat, to cut the painter, and to let the Swash glide away from him. This the vessel had done with great rapidity, leaving him unseen under the cover of her stern. As soon as in the boat, the mate had seized an oar, and sculled to an islet that was within fifty yards, concealing the boat behind a low hummock that formed a tiny bay. All this was done so rapidly, that united to the confusion on board the Swash, no one discovered the mate or the boat. Had he been seen, however, it is very little probable that Spike would have lost a moment of time in the attempt to recover either. But he was not seen, and it was the general opinion on board the Swash, for quite an hour, that her handsome mate had been knocked overboard and killed, by a fragment of the shell that had seemed to explode almost in the ears of her people. When the reef was doubled, however, and Spike made his preparations for meeting the rough weather, he hove to, and ordered his own yawl, which was also towing astern, to be hauled up along side, in order to be hoisted in. Then, indeed, some glimmerings of the truth were shed on the crew, who missed the light-house boat. Though many contended that its painter must also have been cut by a fragment of the shell, and that the mate had died loyal to roguery and treason. Mulford was much liked by the crew, and he was highly valued by Spike, on account of his seamanship and integrity, this latter being a quality that is just as necessary for one of the captain's character to meet with in those he trusts as to any other man. But Spike thought differently of the cause of Mulford's disappearance, from his crew. He ascribed it altogether to love for Rose, when, in truth, it ought in justice to have been quite as much imputed to a determination to sail no longer with a man who was clearly guilty of treason. Of smuggling, Mulford had long suspected Spike, though he had no direct proof of the fact; but now he could not doubt that he was not only engaged in supplying the enemy with the munitions of war, but was actually bargaining to sell his brig for a hostile cruiser, and possibly to transfer himself and crew along with her.

It is scarcely necessary to speak of the welcome Mulford received when he reached the islet of the tent. He and Rose had a long private conference, the result of which was to let the handsome mate into the secret of his pretty companion's true feelings toward himself. She had received him with tears, and a betrayal of emotion that gave him every encouragement, and now she did not deny her preference. In that interview the young people plighted to each other their troth. Rose never doubted of obtaining her aunt's consent in due time, all her prejudices being in favor of the sea and sailors; and should she not, she would soon be her own mistress, and at liberty to dispose of herself and her pretty little fortune as she might choose. But a cipher as she was, in all questions of real moment, Mrs. Budd was not a person likely to throw any real obstacle in the way of the young people's wishes; the true grounds of whose present apprehensions were all to be referred to Spike, his intentions, and his well-known perseverance. Mulford was convinced that the brig would be back in quest of the remaining doubloons, as soon as she could get clear of the sloop-of-war, though he was not altogether without a hope that the latter, when she found it impossible to over-haul her chase, might also return in order to ascertain what discoveries could be made in and about the schooner. The explosion of the powder, on the islet, must have put the man-of-war's men in possession of the secret of the real quality of the flour that had composed her cargo, and it doubtless had awakened all their distrust on the subject of the Swash's real business in the Gulf. Under all the cir-cumstances, therefore, it did appear quite as probable that one of the parties should reappear at the scene of their re-cent interview as the other.

Bearing all these things in mind, Mulford had lost no time in completing his own arrangements. He felt that he had some atonement to make to the country, for the part he had seemingly taken in the late events, and it oc-curred to him could he put the schooner in a state to be moved, then place her in the hands of the authorities, his own peace would be made, and his character cleared. Rose no sooner understood his plans and motives than she en-tered into them with all the ardor and self-devotion of her sex; for the single hour of confidential and frank com-munication which had just passed, doubled the interest she felt in Mulford and in all that belonged to him. Jack Tier was useful on board a vessel, though his want of stature and force rendered him less so than was common with sea-faring men. His proper sphere certainly had been the cabins, where his usefulness had been beyond all cavil; but he was now very serviceable to Mulford on the deck of the schooner. The first two days, Mrs. Budd had been left on the islet, to look to the concerns of the kitchen, while Mul-ford, accompanied by Rose, Biddy, and Jack Tier, had gone off to the schooner, and set her pumps in motion again. It was little that Rose could do, or indeed attempt to do, at this toil, but the pumps being small and easily worked, Biddy and Jack were of great service. By the end of the second day the pumps sucked; the cargo that remained in the schooner, as well as the form of her bottom, contributing greatly to lessen the quantity of the water that was to be got out of her.

Then it was that the doubloons fell into Mulford's hands, along with everything else that remained below decks. It was perhaps fortunate that the vessel was thoroughly purified by her immersion, and the articles that were brought on deck to be dried were found in a condition to give no great offence to those who removed them. By leaving the hatches off, and the cabin doors open, the warm winds of the trades effectually dried the interior of the schooner in the course of a single night, and when Mulford repaired on board of her, on the morning of the third day, he found her in a condition to be fitted for his purposes. On this occasion Mrs. Budd had expressed a wish to go off to look at her future accommodations, and Jack was left on the islet to cook the dinner, which will explain the actual state of things as described in the opening of this chapter.

As those who toil usually have a relish for their food, the appearance of the blue-peter was far from being unwelcome to those on board of the schooner. They got into the boat, and were sculled ashore by Mulford, who, seaman-like, used only one hand in performing this service. In a very few minutes they were all seated at the little table, which was brought out into the tent-veranda for the enjoyment of the breeze.

"So far, well," said Mulford, after his appetite was mainly appeased; Rose picking crumbs, and affecting to eat, merely to have the air of keeping him company; one of the minor proofs of the little attentions that spring from the affections. "So far, well. The sails are bent, and though they might be newer and better, they can be made to answer. It was fortunate to find anything like a second suit on board a Mexican craft of that size at all. As it is, we have foresail, mainsail, and jib, and with that canvas I think we might beat the schooner down to Key West in the course of a day and a night. If I dared to venture outside of the reef, it might be done sooner even, for they tell me there is a four-knot current sometimes in that track; but I do not like to venture outside, so short-handed. The current inside must serve our turn, and we shall get smooth water by keeping under the lee of the rocks. I only hope we shall not get into an eddy as we go farther from the end of the reef, and into the bight of the coast.''

"Is there danger of that?" demanded Rose, whose quick intellect had taught her many of these things, since her acquaintance with vessels.

"There may be, looking at the formation of the reef and islands, though I know nothing of the fact by actual observation. This is my first visit in this quarter.''

"Eddies are serious matters," put in Mrs. Budd, "and my poor husband could not abide them. Tides are good things ; but eddies are very disagreeable.''

"Well, aunty, I should think eddies might sometimes be as welcome as tides. It must depend, however, very much on the way one wishes to go.''

"Rose, you surprise me ! All that you have read, and all that you have heard, must have shown you the difference. Do they not say 'a man is floating with the tide,' when things are prosperous with him—and don't ships drop down with the tide, and beat the wind with the tide? And don't vessels sometimes 'tide it up to town,' as it is called, and isn't it thought an advantage to have the tide with you?''

"All very true, aunty ; but I do not see how that makes eddies any the worse.''

"Because eddies are the opposite of tides, child. When the tide goes one way, the eddy goes another—isn't it so, Harry Mulford? You never heard of one's floating in an eddy.''

"That's what we mean by an eddy, Mrs. Budd," answered the handsome mate, delighted to hear Rose's aunt call him by an appellation so kind and familiar,—a thing she had never done previously to the intercourse which had been the consequence of their present situation. "Though I agree with Rose in thinking an eddy may be a good or a bad thing, and very much like a tide, as one wishes to steer.''

"You amaze me, both of you ! Tides are always spoken of favorably, but eddies never. If a ship gets ashore, the tide can float her off; *that* I 've heard a thousand times. Then, what do the newspapers say of President ——, and Governor ——, and Congressman ——?[1] Why, that they all ' float in the tide of public opinion,' and that must mean something particularly good, as they are always in office. No, no, Harry; I 'll acknowledge that you do know something about ships ; a good deal, considering how young you are ; but you have something to learn about eddies. Never trust one as long as you live."

Mulford was silent, and Rosa took the occasion to change the discourse.

"I hope we shall soon be able to quit this place," she said ; "for I confess to some dread of Captain Spike's return."

"Captain Stephen Spike has greatly disappointed me," observed the aunt, gravely. "I do not know that I was ever before deceived in judging a person. I could have sworn he was an honest, frank, well-meaning sailor—a character, of all others, that I love ; but it has turned out otherwise."

"He 's a willain !" muttered Jack Tier.

Mulford smiled ; at which speech we must leave to conjecture ; but he answered Rose, as he ever did, promptly and with pleasure.

"The schooner is ready, and this must be our last meal ashore," he said. "Our outfit will be no great matter ; but if it will carry us down to Key West, I shall ask no more of it. As for the return of the Swash, I look upon it as certain. She could easily get clear of the sloop-of-war, with the start she had, and Spike is a man that never yet abandoned a doubloon, when he knew where one was to be found."

"Stephen Spike is like all his fellow-creatures," put in Jack Tier, pointedly. "He has his faults, and he has his virtues."

[1] We suppress the names used by Mrs. Budd, out of delicacy to the individuals mentioned, who are still living.

"Virtue is a term I should never think of applying to such a man," returned Mulford, a little surprised at the fellow's earnestness. "The word is a big one, and belongs to quite another class of persons." Jack muttered a few syllables that were unintelligible, when again the conversation changed.

Rose now inquired of Mulford as to their prospects of getting to Key West. He told her that the distance was about sixty miles; their route lying along the north or inner side of the Florida Reef. The whole distance was to be made against the trade-wind, which was then blowing about an eight-knot breeze, though, bating eddies, they might expect to be favored with the current, which was less strong inside than outside of the reef. As for handling the schooner, Mulford saw no great difficulty in that. She was not large, and was both lightly sparred and lightly rigged. All her top-hamper had been taken down by Spike, and nothing remained but the plainest and most readily-managed gear. A fore-and-aft vessel, sailing close by the wind, is not difficult to steer; will almost steer herself, indeed, in smooth water. Jack Tier could take his trick at the helm, in any weather, even in running before the wind, the time when it is most difficult to guide a craft, and Rose might be made to understand the use of the tiller, and taught to govern the motions of a vessel so small and so simply rigged, when on a wind and in smooth water. On the score of managing the schooner, therefore, Mulford thought there would be little cause for apprehension. Should the weather continue settled, he had little doubt of safely landing the whole party at Key West, in the course of the next four-and-twenty hours. Short sail he should be obliged to carry, as well on account of the greater facility of managing it, as on account of the circumstance that the schooner was now in light ballast trim, and would not bear much canvas. He thought that the sooner they left the islets the better, as it could not be long ere the brig would be seen hovering around the spot. All these matters were discussed as the party still sat at table; and when they left it, which was a few minutes later, it was to remove the effects they intended to carry away to the boat. This was soon done, both Jack Tier and Biddy proving very serviceable, while Rose tripped backward and forward, with a step elastic as a gazelle's, carrying light burdens. In half an hour the boat was ready. " Here lies the bag of doubloons still," said Mulford, smiling. " Is it to be left, or shall we give it up to the admiralty court at Key West, and put in a claim for salvage ? "

" Better leave it for Spike," said Jack unexpectedly. "Should he come back and find the doubloons, he may be satisfied and not look for the schooner. On the other hand, when the vessel is missing, he will think that the money is in her. Better leave it for old Stephen."

" I do not agree with you, Tier," said Rose, though she looked as amicably at the steward's assistant, as she thus opposed his opinion, as if anxious to persuade rather than coerce. "I do not quite agree with you. This money belongs to the Spanish merchant ; and, as we take away with us his vessel, to give it up to the authorities at Key West, I do not think we have a right to put his gold on the shore and abandon it."

This disposed of the question. Mulford took the bag, and carried it to the boat, without waiting to ascertain if Jack had any objection ; while the whole party followed. In a few minutes everybody and everything in the boat were transferred to the deck of the schooner. As for the tent, the old sails of which it was made, the furniture it contained, and such articles of provisions as were not wanted, they were left on the islet without regret. The schooner had several casks of fresh water, which were found in her hold, and she had also a cask or two of salted meats, besides several articles of food more delicate, that had been provided by Señor Montefalderon for his own use, and which had not been damaged by the water. A keg of Boston crackers were among these eatables, quite half of which were still in a state to be eaten. They were Biddy's delight ; and it was seldom that she could be seen when not nibbling at one of them. The bread of the crew was hopelessly damaged. But Jack had made an ample provision of bread when sent ashore, and there were still a hundred barrels of the flour in the schooner's hold. One of these had been hoisted on deck by Mulford, and opened. The injured flour was easily removed, leaving a considerable quantity fit for the uses of the kitchen. As for the keg of gunpowder, it was incontinently committed to the deep.

Thus provided for, Mulford decided that the time had arrived when he ought to quit his anchorage. He had been employed most of that morning in getting the schooner's anchor, a work of great toil to him, though everybody had assisted. He had succeeded, and the vessel now rode by a kedge, that he could easily weigh by means of a deck tackle. It remained now, therefore, to lift this kedge, and to stand out of the bay of the islets. No sooner was the boat secured astern, and its freight disposed of, than the mate began to make sail. In order to hoist the mainsail well up, he was obliged to carry the halyards to the windlass. Thus aided, he succeeded without much difficulty. He and Jack Tier and Biddy got the jib hoisted by hand ; and as for the foresail, that would almost set itself. Of course it was not touched until the kedge was aweigh. Mulford found little difficulty in lifting the last, and he soon had the satisfaction of finding his craft clear of the ground. As Jack Tier was every way competent to take charge of the forecastle, Mulford now sprang aft, and took his own station at the helm, Rose acting as his pretty assistant on the quarter-deck.

There is little mystery in getting a fore-and-aft vessel under way. Her sails fill almost as a matter of course, and motion follows as a necessary law. Thus did it prove with the Mexican schooner, which turned out to be a fast-sailing and an easily worked craft. She was, indeed, an American bottom, as it is termed, having been originally built for the Chesapeake ; and, though not absolutely what is understood by a Baltimore clipper, so nearly of that mould and nature as to possess some of the more essential qualities. As usually happens, however, when a foreigner gets hold of an American schooner, the Mexican had shortened her masts and lessened her canvas. This circumstance was rather an advantage to Mulford, who would probably have had more to attend to than he wished under the original rig of the craft,

Everybody, even to the fastidious Mrs. Budd, was delighted with the easy and swift movement of the schooner. Mulford, now he had got her under canvas, handled her without any difficulty, letting her stand toward the channel through which he intended to pass, with her sheets just taken in, though compelled to keep a little off, in order to enter between the islets. No difficulty occurred, however, and in less than ten minutes the vessel was clear of the channels, and in open water. The sheets were now flattened in, and the schooner brought close by the wind. A trial of the vessel on this mode of sailing was no sooner made, than Mulford was induced to regret he had taken so many precautions against any increasing power of the wind. To meet emergencies, and under the notion he should have his craft more under command, the young man had reefed his mainsail, and taken the bonnets off of the foresail and jib. As the schooner stood up better than he had anticipated, the mate felt as all seamen are so apt to feel, when they see that their vessel might be made to perform more than is actually got out of them. As the breeze was fresh, however, he determined not to let out the reef; and the labor of lacing on the bonnets again was too great to be thought of just at that moment.

We all find relief on getting in motion, when pressed by circumstances. Mulford had been in great apprehension of the reappearance of the Swash all that day ; for it was about the time when Spike would be apt to return, in the event of his escaping from the sloop-of-war, and he dreaded Rose's again falling into the hands of a man so desperate. Nor is it imputing more than a very natural care to the young man, to say that he had some misgivings concerning himself. Spike by this time, must be convinced that his business in the Gulf was known ; and one who had openly thrown off his service, as his mate had done, would unquestionably be regarded as a traitor to *his* interests, whatever might be the relation in which he would stand to the laws of the country. It was probable such an alleged offender would not be allowed to appear before the tribunals of the land, to justify himself and to accuse the truly guilty, if it were in the power of the last to prevent it. Great, therefore, was the satisfaction of our handsome young mate when he found himself again fairly in motion, with a craft under him, that glided ahead in a way to prove that she might give even the Swash some trouble to catch her, in the event of a trial of speed.

Everybody entered into the feelings of Mulford, as the schooner passed gallantly out from between the islets, and entered the open water. Fathom by fathom did her wake rapidly increase, until it could no longer be traced back as far as the sandy beaches that had just been left. In a quarter of an hour more, the vessel had drawn so far from the land, that some of the smallest and lowest of the islets were getting to be indistinct. At that instant everybody had come aft, the females taking their seats on the trunk, which, in this vessel as in the Swash herself, gave space and height to the cabin.

"Well," exclaimed Mrs. Budd, who found the freshness of the sea air invigorating, as well as their speed exciting, "this is what I call maritime, Rosy, dear. This is what is meant by the Maritime States, about which we read so much, and which are commonly thought to be so important. We are now in a Maritime State, and I feel perfectly happy after all our dangers and adventures!"

"Yes, aunty, and I am delighted that you are happy," answered Rose, with frank affection. "We are now rid of that infamous Spike, and may hope never to see his face more."

"Stephen Spike has his good p'ints as well as another," said Jack Tier abruptly.

"I know that he is an old shipmate of yours, Tier, and that you cannot forget how he once stood connected with you, and am sorry I have said so much against him," answered Rose, expressing her concern even more by her looks and tones, than by her words.

Jack was mollified by this, and he let his feeling be seen, though he said no more than to mutter, "He's a willain!" words that had frequently issued from him within the last day or two.

"Stephen Spike is a capital seaman, and that is something in any man," observed the relict of Captain Budd. "He learned his trade from one who was every way qualified to teach him, and it's no wonder he should be expert. Do you expect, Mr. Mulford, to beat the wind the whole distance to Key West?"

It was not possible for any one to look more grave than the mate did habitually, while the widow was floundering through her sea-terms. Rose had taught him that respect for her aunt was to be one of the conditions of her own regard, though Rose had never opened her lips to him on the subject.

"Yes, ma'am," answered the mate, respectfully, "we are in the trades, and shall have to turn to windward, every inch of the way to Key West."

"Of what lock is this place the key, Rosy?" asked the aunt, innocently enough. "I know that forts and towns are sometimes called keys, but they always have locks of some sort or other. Now, Gibraltar is the key of the Mediterranean, as your uncle has told me fifty times; and I have been there, and can understand why it should be; but I do not know of what lock this West is the key."

"It is not that sort of key which is meant, aunty, at all, but quite a different thing. The key meant is an island."

"And why should any one be so silly as to call an island a key?"

"The place where vessels unload is sometimes called a key," answered Mulford; "the French calling it a *quai*, and the Dutch *kaye*. I suppose our English word is derived from these. Now, a low, sandy island, looking somewhat like keys, or wharves, seamen have given them this name. Key West is merely a low island."

"Then there is no lock to it, or anything to be unfastened," said the widow, in her most simple manner.

"It may turn out to be the key to the Gulf of Mexico, one of these days, ma'am. Uncle Sam is surveying the reef, and intends to do something here, I believe. When Uncle Sam is really in earnest, he is capable of performing great things."

Mrs. Budd was satisfied with this explanation, though she told Biddy that evening, that "locks and keys go together, and that the person who christened the island to which they were going, must have been very weak in his upper story." But these reflections on the intellects of her fellow-creatures were by no means uncommon with the worthy relict; and we cannot say that her remarks made any particular impression on her Irish maid.

In the meantime, the Mexican schooner behaved quite to Mulford's satisfaction. He thought her a little tender in the squalls, of which they had several that afternoon; but he remarked to Rose, who expressed her uneasiness at the manner in which the vessel lay over in one of them, that "she comes down quite easy to her bearings, but it is hard forcing her beyond them. The vessel needs more cargo to ballast her, though, on the whole, I find her as stiff as one could expect. I am now glad that I reefed, and reduced the head sails, though I was sorry at having done so when we first came out. At this rate of sailing, we ought to be up with Key West by morning."

But that rate of sailing did not continue. Toward evening, the breeze lessened almost to a calm again, the late tornado appearing to have quite deranged the ordinary stability of the trades. When the sun set, and it went down into the broad waters of the Gulf a flood of flame, there was barely a two-knot breeze, and Mulford had no longer any anxiety on the subject of keeping his vessel on her legs. His solicitude, now, was confined to the probability of falling in with the Swash. As yet, nothing was visible, either in the shape of land or in that of a sail. Between the islets of the Dry Tortugas and the next nearest visible keys, there is a space of open water, of some forty miles in width. The reef extends across it, of course; but nowhere does the rock protrude itself above the surface of the sea. The depth of water on this reef varies essentially. In some places, a ship of size might pass on to it, if not across it; while in others a man could wade for miles. There is one deep and safe channel—safe to those who are acquainted with it—through the centre of this open space, and which is sometimes used by vessels that wish to pass from one side to the other ; but it is ever better for those whose business does not call them in that direction to give the rocks a good berth, more especially in the night.

Mulford had gleaned many of the leading facts connected with the channels, and the navigation of those waters, from Spike and the older seamen of the brig, during the time they had been lying at the Tortugas. Such questions and answers are common enough on board ships, and, as they are usually put and given with intelligence, one of our mate's general knowledge of his profession was likely to carry away much useful information. By conversations of this nature, and by consulting the charts, which Spike did not affect to conceal after the name of his port became known, the young man, in fact, had so far made himself master of the subject, as to have tolerably accurate notions of the courses, distances, and general peculiarities of the reef. When the sun went down, he supposed himself to be about half way across the space of open water, and some five-and-twenty miles dead to windward of his port of departure. This was doing very well for the circumstances, and Mulford believed himself and his companions clear of Spike, when, as night drew its veil over the tranquil sea, nothing was in sight.

A very judicious arrangement was made for the watches on board the Mexican schooner, on this important night. Mrs. Budd had a great fancy to keep a watch, for once in her life, and after the party had supped, and the subject came up in the natural course of things, a dialogue like this occurred :

"Harry must be fatigued," said Rose, kindly, "and must want sleep. The wind is so light, and the weather appears to be so settled, that I think it would be better for him to 'turn in,' as he calls it,"—here Rose laughed so prettily that the handsome mate wished she would repeat the words —"better that he should 'turn in' now, and we can call him, should there be need of his advice or assistance. I dare say Jack Tier and I can take very good care of the schooner until daylight."

Mrs. Budd thought it would be no more than proper for one of her experience and years to rebuke this levity, as well as to enlighten the ignorance her niece had betrayed.

"You should be cautious, my child, how you propose anything to be done on a ship's board," observed the aunt. "It requires great experience and a suitable knowledge of rigging to give maritime advice. Now, as might have been expected, considering your years, and the short time you have been at sea, you have made several serious mistakes in what you have proposed. In the first place, there should always be a mate on the deck, as I have heard your dear departed uncle say, again and again; and how can there be a mate on the deck if Mr. Mulford 'turns in,' as you propose, seeing that he's the only mate we have. Then you should never laugh at any maritime expression, for each and all are, as a body might say, solemnized by storms and dangers. That Harry is fatigued I think is very probable; and he must set our watches, as they call it, when he can make his arrangements for the night, and take his rest as is usual. Here is my watch to begin with; and I'll engage he does not find it two minutes out of the way, though yours, Rosy dear, like most girl's time-pieces, is, I'll venture to say, dreadfully wrong. Where is your chronometer, Mr. Mulford? let us see how this excellent watch of mine, which was once my poor departed Mr. Budd's, will agree with that piece of yours, which I have heard you say is excellent."

Here was a flight in science and nautical language that poor Mulford could not have anticipated, even in the captain's relict! That Mrs. Budd should mistake "setting the watch" for "setting our watches," was not so very violent a blunder that one ought to be much astonished at it in *her*; but that she should expect to find a chronometer that was intended to keep the time of Greenwich agreeing with a watch that was set for the time of New York, betrayed a degree of ignorance that the handsome mate was afraid Rose would resent on him, when the mistake was made to appear. As the widow held out her own watch for the comparison, however, he could not refuse to produce his

own. By Mrs. Budd's watch it was past seven o'clock, while
by his own, or the Greenwich-set chronometer, it was a little
past twelve.

"How very wrong your watch is, Mr. Mulford," cried the
good lady, "notwithstanding all you have said in its favor.
It's quite five hours too fast, I do declare; and now, Rosy
dear, you see the importance of setting watches on a ship's
board, as is done every evening, my departed husband has
often told me."

"Harry's must be what he calls a dog-watch, aunty," said
Rose, laughing, though she scarce knew at what.

"The watch goes, too," added the widow, raising the
chronometer to her ear, "though it is so very wrong. Well,
set it, Mr. Mulford; then we will set Rose's, which I'll engage is half an hour out of the way, though it can never be
as wrong as yours."

Mulford was a good deal embarrassed, but he gained
courage by looking at Rose, who appeared to him to be
quite as much mystified as her aunt. For once he hoped
Rose was ignorant; for nothing would be so likely to diminish the feeling produced by the exposure of the aunt's mistake, as to include the niece in the same category.

"My watch is a chronometer, you will recollect, Mrs.
Budd," said the young man.

"I know it; and they ought to keep the very best time—
that I've always heard. My poor Mr. Budd had two, and
they were as large as compasses, and sold for hundreds after
his lamented decease."

"They were ship's chronometers, but mine was made for
the pocket. It is true, chronometers are intended to keep
the most accurate time, and usually they do; this of mine,
in particular, would not lose ten seconds in a twelvemonth,
did I not carry it on my person."

"No, no, it does not seem to lose any, Harry; it only
gains," cried Rose, laughing.

Mulford was now satisfied, notwithstanding all that had
passed on a previous occasion, that the laughing, bright-
eyed, and quick-witted girl at his elbow knew no more of
the uses of a chronometer than her usually dull and igno-

rant aunt ; and he felt himself relieved from all embarrassment at once. Though he dared not even seem to distrust Mrs. Budd's intellect or knowledge before Rose, he did not scruple to laugh at Rose herself, to Rose. With her there was no jealousy on the score of capacity, her quickness being almost as obvious to all who approached her as her beauty.

"Rose Budd, you do not understand the use of a chronometer, I see," said the mate, firmly, "notwithstanding all I have told you concerning them."

"It is to keep time, Harry Mulford, is it not?"

"True, to keep time—but to keep the time of a particular meridian ; you know what a meridian means, I hope?"

Rose looked intently at her lover, and she looked singularly lovely, for she blushed slightly, though her smile was as open and amicable as ingenuousness and affection could make it.

"A meridian means a point over our heads, the spot where the sun is at noon," said Rose, doubtingly.

"Quite right ; but it also means longitude, in one sense. If you draw a line from one pole to the other, all the places it crosses are on the same meridian. As the sun first appears in the east, it follows that it rises sooner in places that are east, than in places that are farther west. Thus it is, that at Greenwich, in England, where there is an observatory made for nautical purposes, the sun rises about five hours sooner than it does here. All this difference is subject to rules, and we know exactly how to measure it."

"How can that be, Harry? You told me this but the other day, yet have I forgotten it."

"Quite easily. As the earth turns round in just twenty-four hours, and its circumference is divided into three hundred and sixty equal parts, called degrees, we have only to divide 360 by 24, to know how many of these degrees are included in the difference produced by one hour of time. There are just fifteen of them, as you will find by multiplying 24 by 15. It follows that the sun rises just one hour later, each fifteen degrees of longitude, as you go west, or one hour earlier each fifteen degrees as you go east.

Having ascertained the difference by the hour, it is easy
enough to calculate for the minutes and seconds."

"Yes, yes," said Rose, eagerly, "I see all that—go on."

"Now a chronometer is nothing but a watch, made with
great care, so as not to lose or gain more than a few seconds in a twelvemonth. Its whole merit is in keeping time
accurately."

"Still I do not see how that can be anything more than a
very good watch."

"You will see in a minute, Rose. For purposes that you
will presently understand, books are calculated for certain
meridians, or longitudes, as at Greenwich and Paris, and
those who use the books calculated for Greenwich get their
chronometers set at Greenwich, and those who use the Paris
get their chronometers set to Paris time. When I was last
in England, I took this watch to Greenwich, and had it set
at the Observatory by the true solar time. Ever since it has
been running by that time, and what you see here is the
true Greenwich time, after allowing for a second or two that
it may have lost or gained."

"All that is plain enough," said the much interested
Rose, "but of what use is it all?"

"To help mariners to find their longitude at sea, and
thus know where they are. As the sun passes so far north,
and so far south of the equator each year, it is easy enough
to find the latitude, by observing his position at noonday ;
but for a long time seamen had great difficulty in ascertaining their longitudes. That, too, is done by observing the
different heavenly bodies, and with greater accuracy than by
any other process ; but this thought of measuring the time
is very simple, and so easily put in practice, that we all run
by it now."

"Still I cannot understand it," said Rose, looking so intently, so eagerly, and so intelligently into the handsome
mate's eyes, that he found it was pleasant to teach her other
things besides how to love.

"I will explain it. Having the Greenwich time in the
watch, we observe the sun, in order to ascertain the true
time, wherever we may happen to be. It is a simple thing

to ascertain the true time of day by an observation of the sun, which marks the hours in his track ; and when we get our observation, we have some one to note the time at a particular instant on the chronometer. By noting the hour, minutes, and seconds, at Greenwich, at the very instant we observe here, when we have calculated from that observation the time here, we have only to add, or substract, the time here from that of Greenwich, to know precisely how far east or west we are from Greenwich, which gives us our longitude.''

"I begin to comprehend it again," exclaimed Rose, delighted at the acquisition in knowledge she had just made. "How beautiful it is, yet how simple, but why do I forget it ?"

"Perfectly simple, and perfectly sure, too, when the chronometer is accurate, and the observations are nicely made. It is seldom we are more than eight or ten miles out of the way, and for them we keep a lookout. . It is only to ascertain the time where you are, by means that are easily used, then look at your watch to learn the time of day at Greenwich, or any other meridian you may have selected, and to calculate your distance, east or west, from that meridian, by the difference in the two times.''

Rose could have listened all night, for her quick mind readily comprehended the principle which lies at the bottom of this useful process, though still ignorant of some of the details. This time she was determined to secure her acquisition, though it is quite probable that, woman-like, they were once more lost, almost as easily as made. Mulford, however, was obliged to leave her, to look at the vessel, before he stretched himself on the deck, in an old sail ; it having been previously determined that he should sleep first, while the wind was light, and that Jack Tier, assisted by the females, should keep the first watch. Rose would not detain the mate, therefore, but let him go his way, in order to see that all was right before he took his rest.

Mrs. Budd had listened to Mulford's second explanation of the common mode of ascertaining the longitude, with all the attention of which she was capable ; but it far ex-

ceeded the powers of her mind to comprehend it. There
are persons who accustom themselves to think so superficially, that it becomes a painful process to attempt to
dive into any of the *arcana* of nature, and who ever turn
from such investigations wearied and disgusted. Many of
these persons, perhaps most of them, need only a little
patience and perseverance to comprehend all the more
familiar phenomena, but they cannot command even that
much of the two qualities named to obtain the knowledge
they would fain wish to possess. Mrs. Budd did not belong to a division as high in the intellectual scale as even
this vapid class. Her intellect was unequal to embracing
anything of an abstracted character, and only received the
most obvious impressions, and those quite half the time it
received wrong. The mate's reasoning, therefore, was not
only inexplicable to her, but it sounded absurd and impossible.

"Rosy, dear," said the worthy relict as soon as she saw
Mulford stretch his fine frame on his bed of canvas, speaking at the same time in a low, confidential tone to her niece,
"what was it that Harry was telling you a little while ago?
It sounded to me like rank nonsense; and men will talk
nonsense to young girls, as I have so often warned you,
child. You must never listen to their nonsense, Rosy; but
remember your catechism and confirmation vow, and be a
good girl."

To how many of the feeble-minded and erring do those
offices of the church prove a stay and support, when their
own ordinary powers of resistance would fail them! Rose,
however, viewed the matter just as it was, and answered
accordingly.

"But this was nothing of that nature, aunty," she said,
"and only an account of the mode of finding out where a
ship is, when out of sight of land, in the middle of the
ocean. We had the same subject up the other day."

"And how did Harry tell you, this time, that was done,
my dear?"

"By finding the difference in the time of day between
two places—just as he did before."

"But there *is* no difference in the time of day, child, when the clocks go well."

"Yes, there is, aunty dear, as the sun rises in one place before it does in another."

"Rose, you've been listening to nonsense now! Remember what I have so often told you about young men, and their way of talking. I admit Harry Mulford is a respectable youth, and has respectable connections, and since you like one another you may have him, with all my heart, as soon as he gets a full-jiggered ship, for I am resolved no niece of my poor dear husband's shall ever marry a mate, or a captain even, unless he has a full-jiggered ship under his feet. But do not talk nonsense with him. Nonsense is nonsense, though a sensible man talks it. As for all this stuff about the time of day, you can see it is nonsense, as the sun rises but once in twenty-four hours, and of course there cannot be two times, as you call it."

"But, aunty dear, it is not always noon at London when it is noon at New York."

"Fiddle-faddle, child; noon is noon, and there are no more two noons than two suns, or two times. Distrust what young men tell you, Rosy, if you would be safe, though they should tell you you are handsome."

Poor Rose sighed, and gave up the explanation in despair. Then a smile played around her pretty mouth. It was not at her aunt that she smiled; this she never permitted herself to do, weak as was that person, and weak as she saw her to be; she smiled at the recollection how often Mulford had hinted at her good looks—for Rose was a female, and had her own weaknesses, as well as another. But the necessity of acting soon drove these thoughts from her mind, and Rose sought Jack Tier, to confer with him on the subject of their new duties.

As for Harry Mulford, his head was no sooner laid on its bunch of sail than he fell into a profound sleep. There he lay, slumbering as the seaman slumbers, with no sense of surrounding things. The immense fatigues of that and of the two preceding days—for he had toiled at the pumps even long after night had come, until the vessel was clear—

weighed him down, and nature was now claiming her influence, and taking a respite from exertion. Had he been left to himself, it is probable the mate would not have arisen until the sun had reappeared some hours.

It is now necessary to explain more minutely the precise condition, as well as the situation of the schooner. On quitting his port, Mulford had made a stretch of some two leagues in length, toward the northward and eastward, when he tacked, and stood to the southward. There was enough of southing in the wind, to make his last course nearly due south. As he neared the reef, he found that he fell in some miles to the eastward of the islets,—proof that he was doing very well, and that there was no current to do him any material harm, if, indeed, there were not actually a current in his favor. He next tacked to the northward again, and stood in that direction until near night, when he once more went about. The wind was now so light that he saw little prospect of getting in with the reef again, until the return of day ; but as he had left orders with Jack Tier to be called at twelve o'clock, at all events, this gave him no uneasiness. At the time when the mate lay down to take his rest, therefore, the schooner was quite five-and-twenty miles to windward of the Dry Tortugas, and some twenty miles to the northward of the Florida Reef, with the wind quite light at east-southeast. Such, then, was the position or situation of the schooner.

As respects her condition, it is easily described. She had but the three sails bent,—mainsail, foresail, and jib. Her topmasts had been struck, and all the hamper that belonged to them was below. The mainsail was single reefed, and the foresail and jib were without their bonnets, as has already been mentioned. This was somewhat short canvas, but Mulford knew that it would render his craft more manageable in the event of a blow. Usually, at that season, and in that region, the east trades prevailed with great steadiness, sometimes diverging a little south of east, as at present, and generally blowing fresh. But, for a short time previously to, and ever since the tornado, the wind had been unsettled, the old currents appearing to regain their ascendency by fits, and then losing it, in squalls, contrary currents, and even by short calms.

The conference between Jack Tier and Rose was frank and confidential.

"We must depend mainly on you," said the latter, turning to look toward the spot where Mulford lay, buried in the deepest sleep that had ever gained power over him. "Harry is *so* fatigued! It would be shameful to awaken him a moment sooner than is necessary."

"Ay, ay; so it is always with young women, when they lets a young man gain their ears," answered Jack, without the least circumlocution; "so it is, and so it always will be, I 'm afeard. Nevertheless, men is willains."

Rose was not affronted at this plain allusion to the power that Mulford had obtained over her feelings. It would seem that Jack had got to be so intimate in the cabins, that his sex was, in a measure, forgotten; and it is certain that his recent services were not. Without a question, but for his interference, the pretty Rose Budd would, at that moment, have been the prisoner of Spike, and most probably the victim of his design to compel her to marry him.

"All men are not Stephen Spikes," said Rose, earnestly, "and least of all is Harry Mulford to be reckoned as one of his sort. But, we must manage to take care of the schooner the whole night, and let Harry get his rest. He wished to be called at twelve, but we can easily let the hour go by, and not awaken him."

"The commanding officer ought not to be sarved so, Miss Rose. What he says is to be done."

"I know it, Jack, as to ordinary matters; but Harry left these orders that we might have our share of rest, and for no other reason at all. And what is to prevent our having it? We are four, and can divide ourselves into two watches; one watch can sleep while the other keeps a lookout."

"Ay, ay, and pretty watches they would be! There 's Madam Budd, now; why, she 's quite a navigator, and knows all about weerin' and haulin', and I dares to say could put the schooner about, to keep her off the reef, on a pinch; though which way the craft would come round, could best be told a'ter it has been done. It's as much as I 'd undertake myself, Miss Rose, to take care of the schooner, should it come on to blow; and as for you, Madam Budd, and that squalling Irishwoman, you 'd be no better than so many housewives ashore.''

"We have strength, and we have courage, and we can pull, as you have seen. I know very well which way to put the helm now, and Biddy is as strong as you are yourself, and could help me all I wished. Then we could always call you, at need, and have your assistance. Nay, Harry himself can be called, if there should be a real necessity for it, and I do wish he may not be disturbed until there is that necessity.''

It was with a good deal of reluctance that Jack allowed himself to be persuaded into this scheme. He insisted, for a long time, that an officer should be called at the hour mentioned by himself, and declared he had never known such an order neglected, '' marchant-man, privateer, or man-of-war.'' Rose prevailed over his scruples, however, and there was a meeting of the three females to make the final arrangements. Mrs. Budd, a kind-hearted woman, at the worst, gave her assent most cheerfully, though Rose was a little startled with the nature of the reasoning with which it was accompanied.

"You are quite right, Rosy dear,'' said the aunt, "and the thing is very easily done. I 've long wanted to keep one watch, at sea; just one watch; to complete my maritime education. Your poor uncle used to say, 'Give my wife but one night-watch, and you 'd have as good a seaman in her as heart could wish.' I 'm sure I 've had nightwatches enough with him and his ailings; but it seems that they were not the sort of watches he meant. Indeed, I did n't know till this evening there were so many watches in the world, at all. But this is just what I want, and, just what I 'm resolved to have. Tier shall command one watch and I 'll command the other. Jack's shall be the 'dog-watch,' as they call it, and mine shall be the 'middle-watch,' and last till morning. You shall be in Jack's watch, Rose, and Biddy shall be in mine. You know a good deal that Jack don't know, and Biddy can do a good deal I'm rather too stout to do. I don't like pulling ropes, but as for ordering, I'll turn my back on no captain's widow out of York.''

Rose had her own misgivings on the subject of her aunt's issuing orders on such a subject to any one, but she made the best of necessity and completed the arrangements without further discussion. Her great anxiety was to secure a good night's rest for Harry, already feeling a woman's care in the comfort and ease of the man she loved. And Rose did love Harry Mulford warmly and sincerely. If the very decided preference with which she regarded him before they sailed had not absolutely amounted to passion, it had come so very near it as to render that excess of feeling certain, under the influence of the association and events which succeeded. We have not thought it necessary to relate a tithe of the interviews and intercourse that had taken place between the handsome mate and the pretty Rose Budd, during the month they had now been shipmates, having left the reader to imagine the natural course of things, under such circumstances. Nevertheless, the plighted troth had not been actually given until Harry joined her on the islet, at a moment when she fancied herself abandoned to a fate almost as serious as death. Rose had seen Mulford quit the brig, and had watched the mode and manner of his escape in almost breathless amazement, and felt how dear to her he had become, by the glow of delight which warmed her heart, when assured that he could not, would not, forsake her, even though he remained at the risk of life. She was now, true to the instinct of her sex, mostly occupied in making such a return for an attachment so devoted as became her tenderness and the habits of her mind.

As Mrs. Budd chose what she was pleased to term the '' middle-watch,'' giving to Jack Tier and Rose her '' dog-watch,'' the two last were first on duty. It is scarcely necessary to say, the captain's widow got the names of the watches all wrong, as she got the names of everything else about a vessel; but the plan was to divide the night equally between these *quasi* mariners, giving the first half

to those who were first on the lookout, and the remainder
to their successors. It soon became so calm that Jack left
the helm, and came and sat by Rose, on the trunk, where
they conversed confidentially for a long time. Although
the reader will, hereafter, be enabled to form some plau-
sible conjectures on the subject of this dialogue, we shall
give him no part of it here. All that need now be said
is to add, that Jack did most of the talking, that his past
life was the principal theme, and that the terrible Stephen
Spike, he from whom they were now so desirous of escaping, was largely mixed up with the adventures recounted.
Jack found in his companion a deeply interested listener,
although this was by no means the first time they had
gone over together the same story and discussed the same
events. The conversation lasted until Tier who watched
the glass, seeing that its sands had run out for the last
time, announced the hour of midnight. This was the
moment when Mulford should have been called but when
Mrs. Budd and Biddy Noon were actually awakened in
his stead.

"Now, dear aunty," said Rose as she parted from the
new watch to go and catch a little sleep herself, "remember
you are not to awaken Harry first, but to call Tier and myself. It would have done your heart good to have seen how
sweetly he has been sleeping all this time. I do not think
he has stirred once since his head was laid on that bunch of
sails, and there he is, at this moment, sleeping like an
infant!"

"Yes," returned the relict, "it is always so with your
true maritime people. I have been sleeping a great deal
more soundly, the whole of the dog-watch, than I ever
slept at home, in my own excellent bed. But it's your
watch below, Rosy, and contrary to rule for you to stay on
the deck, after you've been relieved. I've heard this a
thousand times."

Rose was not sorry to lie down; and her head was
scarcely on its pillow, in the cabin, before she was fast
asleep. As for Jack, he found a place among Mulford's
sails, and was quickly in the same state.

To own the truth, Mrs. Budd was not quite as much at ease, in her new station, for the first half hour, as she had fancied to herself might prove to be the case. It was a flat calm, it is true; but the widow felt oppressed with responsibility and the novelty of her situation. Time and again had she said, and even imagined, she should be delighted to fill the very station she then occupied, or to be in charge of a deck, in a "middle watch." In this instance, however, as in so many others, reality did not equal anticipation. She wished to be doing everything, but did not know how to do anything. As for Biddy, she was even worse off than her mistress. A month's experience, or for that matter a twelvemonth's, could not unravel to her the mysteries of even a schooner's rigging. Mrs. Budd had placed her "at the wheel," as she called it, though the vessel had no wheel, being steered by a tiller on deck, in the 'long-shore fashion. In stationing Biddy, the widow told her that she was to play "tricks at the wheel," leaving it to the astounded Irishwoman's imagination to discover what those tricks were. Failing in ascertaining what might be the nature of her " tricks at the wheel," Biddy was content to do nothing, and nothing, under the circumstances, was perhaps the very best thing she could have done.

Little was required to be done for the first four hours of Mrs. Budd's watch. All that time, Rose slept in her berth, and Mulford and Jack Tier on their sail, while Biddy had played the wheel a "trick," indeed, by lying down on deck, and sleeping, too, as soundly as if she were in the county Down itself. But there was to be an end of this tranquillity. Suddenly the wind began to blow. At first, the breeze came in fitful puffs, which were neither very strong nor very lasting. This induced Mrs. Budd to awaken Biddy. Luckily, a schooner without a topsail could not very well be taken aback, especially as the head-sheets worked on travellers, and Mrs. Budd and her assistant contrived to manage the tiller very well for the first hour that these varying puffs of wind lasted. It is true, the tiller was lashed, and it is also true, the schooner ran in all

directions, having actually headed to all the cardinal points
of the compass, under her present management. At length,
Mrs. Budd became alarmed. A puff of wind came so
strong, as to cause the vessel to lie over so far as to bring
the water into the lee scuppers. She called Jack Tier
herself, therefore, and sent Biddy down to awaken Rose.
In a minute, both these auxiliaries appeared on deck. The
wind just then lulled, and Rose, supposing her aunt was
frightened at trifles, insisted on it that Harry should be
permitted to sleep on. He had turned over once, in the
course of the night, but not once had he raised his head
from his pillow.

As soon as reinforced, Mrs. Budd began to bustle about,
and to give commands, such as they were, in order to prove
that she was unterrified. Jack Tier gaped at her elbow,
and by way of something to do, he laid his hand on the
painter of the Swash's boat, which boat was towing astern,
and remarked that "some know-nothing had belayed it
with three half-hitches." This was enough for the relict.
She had often heard the saying that "*three* half-hitches
lost the king's long-boat," and she busied herself, at once,
in repairing so imminent an evil. It was far easier for the
good woman to talk than to act ; she became what is called
"all fingers and thumbs," and in loosening the third half-
hitch, she cast off the two others. At that instant, a puff
of wind struck the schooner again, and the end of the
painter got away from the widow, who had a last glimpse
at the boat, as the vessel darted ahead, leaving its little
tender to vanish in the gloom of the night.

Jack was excessively provoked at this accident, for he
had foreseen the possibility of having recourse to that boat
yet, in order to escape from Spike. By abandoning the
schooner, and pulling on to the reef, it might have been
possible to get out of their pursuer's hands, when all other
means should fail them. As he was at the tiller, he put
his helm up, and ran off, until far enough to leeward to be
to the westward of the boat, when he might tack, fetch, and
recover it. Nevertheless, it now blew much harder than
he liked, for the schooner seemed to be unusually tender.

Had he had the force to do it, he would have brailed the foresail. He desired Rose to call Mulford, but she hesitated about complying.

"Call him—call the mate, I say," cried out Jack, in a voice that proved how much he was in earnest. "These puffs come heavy, I can tell you, and they come often, too. Call him—call him, at once, Miss Rose, for it is time to tack if we wish to recover the boat. Tell him, too, to brail the foresail, while we are in stays—that's right; another call will start him up."

The other call was given, aided by a gentle shake from Rose's hand. Harry was on his feet in a moment. A passing instant was necessary to clear his faculties, and to recover the tenor of his thoughts. During that instant, the mate heard Jack Tier's shrill cry of "Hard a-lee—get in that foresail; bear a-hand—in with it, I say!"

The wind came rushing and roaring, and the flaps of the canvas were violent and heavy.

"In with the foresail, I say," shouted Jack Tier. "She flies round like a top, and will be off the wind on the other tack presently. Bear a-hand!—bear a-hand! It looks black as night to windward."

Mulford then regained all his powers. He sprang to the fore-sheet, calling on the others for aid. The violent surges produced by the wind prevented his grasping the sheet as soon as he could wish, and the vessel whirled round on her heel, like a steed that is frightened. At that critical and dangerous instant, when the schooner was nearly without motion through the water, a squall struck the flattened sails, and bowed her down as the willow bends to the gale. Mrs. Budd and Biddy screamed as usual, and Jack shouted until his voice seemed cracked, to "let go the head-sheets." Mulford did make one leap forward, to execute this necessary office, when the inclining plane of the deck told him it was too late. The wind fairly howled for a minute, and over went the schooner, the remains of her cargo shifting as she capsized, in a way to bring her very nearly bottom upward.

CHAPTER VIII.

"Ay, fare you well, fair gentleman."

As You Like It.

WHILE the tyro believes the vessel is about to capsize at every puff of wind, the practised seaman alone knows when danger truly besets him in this particular form. Thus it was with Harry Mulford, when the Mexican schooner went over, as related in the close of the preceding chapter. He felt no alarm until the danger actually came. Then, indeed, no one there was so quickly, or so thoroughly apprised of what the result would be, and he directed all his exertions to meet the exigency. While there was the smallest hope of success, he did not lessen, in the least, his endeavors to save the vessel ; making almost superhuman efforts to cast off the fore-sheet, so as to relieve the schooner from the pressure of one of her sails. But no sooner did he hear the barrels in the hold surging to leeward, and feel by the inclination of the deck beneath his feet, that nothing could save the craft, than he abandoned the sheet, and sprang to the assistance of Rose. It was time he did ; for having followed him into the vessel's lee-waste, she was the first to be submerged in the sea, and would have been hopelessly drowned, but for Mulford's timely succor. Women might swim more readily than men, and do so swim, in those portions of the world where the laws of nature are not counteracted by human conventions. Rose Budd, however, had received the vicious education which civilized society inflicts on her sex, and, as a matter of course, was totally helpless in an element in which it was the design of Divine Providence she

222

should possess the common means of sustaining herself, like every other being endued with animal life. Not so with Mulford; he swam with ease and force, and had no difficulty in sustaining Rose until the schooner had settled into her new berth, or in hauling her on the vessel's bottom immediately after.

Luckily, there was no swell, or so little as not to endanger those who were on the schooner's bilge; and Mulford had no sooner placed her in momentary safety at least, whom he prized far higher than his own life, than he bethought him of his other companions. Jack Tier had hauled himself up to windward by the rope that steadied the tiller, and he had called on Mrs. Budd to imitate his example. It was so natural for even a woman to grasp anything like a rope at such a moment, that the widow instinctively obeyed, while Biddy seized, at random, the first thing of the sort that offered. Owing to these fortunate chances, Jack and Mrs. Budd succeeded in reaching the quarter of the schooner, the former actually getting up on the bottom of the wreck, onto which he was enabled to float the widow, who was almost as buoyant as cork, as indeed was the case with Jack himself. All the stern and bows of the vessel were under water, in consequence of her leanness forward and aft; but though submerged, she offered a precarious footing, even in these extremities, to such as could reach them. On the other hand, the place where Rose stood, or the bilge of the vessel, was two or three feet above the surface of the sea, though slippery and inclining in shape.

It was not half a minute from the time that Mulford sprang to Rose's succor, ere he had her on the vessel's bottom. In another half minute, he had waded down on the schooner's counter, where Jack Tier was lustily calling to him for " help ! " and assisted the widow to her feet, and supported her until she stood at Rose's side. Leaving the last in her aunt's arms, half distracted between dread and joy, he turned to the assistance of Biddy. The rope at which the Irishwoman had caught was a straggling end that had been made fast to the main channels of the schooner, for the support of a fender, and had been

hauled partly in-board to keep it out of the water. Biddy
had found no difficulty in dragging herself up to the chains,
therefore ; and had she been content to sustain herself by
the rope, leaving as much of her body submerged as comported with breathing, her task would have been easy. But,
like most persons who do not know how to swim, the good
woman was fast exhausting her strength, by vain efforts to
walk on the surface of an element that was never made to
sustain her. Unpractised persons, in such situations, cannot be taught to believe that their greatest safety is in leaving as much of their bodies as possible beneath the water,
keeping the mouth and nose alone free for breath. But we
have seen even instances in which men, who were in danger
of drowning, seemed to believe it might be possible for them
to crawl over the waves on their hands and knees. The
philosophy of the contrary course is so very simple, that
one would fancy a very child might be made to comprehend
it ; yet, it is rare to find one unaccustomed to the water, and
who is suddenly exposed to its dangers, that does not resort,
under the pressure of present alarm, to the very reverse of
the true means to save his or her life.

Mulford had no difficulty in finding Bridget, whose
exclamations of "murther!" "help!" "he-l-lup!"
"Jasus!" and other similar cries, led him directly to the
spot, where she was fast drowning herself by her own senseless struggles. Seizing her by the arm, the active young
mate soon placed her on her feet, though her cries did not
cease until she was ordered by her mistress to keep silence.

Having thus rescued the whole of his companions from
immediate danger, Mulford began to think of the future.
He was seized with sudden surprise that the vessel did not
sink, and for a minute he was unable to account for the unusual fact. On the former occasion, the schooner had gone
down almost as soon as she fell over ; but now she floated
with so much buoyancy as to leave most of her keel and all
of her bilge on one side quite clear of the water. As one
of the main hatches was off, and the cabin-doors, and booby-
hatch doors forward were open, and all were under water,
it required a little reflection on the part of Mulford to un-

derstand on what circumstance all their lives now depended. The mate soon ascertained the truth, however, and we may as well explain it to the reader in our own fashion, in order to put him on a level with the young seaman.

The puff of wind, or little squall, had struck the schooner at the most unfavorable moment for her safety. She had just lost her way in tacking, and the hull not moving ahead, as happens when a craft is thus assailed with the motion on her, all the power of the wind was expended in the direction necessary to capsize her. Another disadvantage arose from the want of motion. The rudder, which acts solely by pressing against the water as the vessel meets it, was useless, and it was not possible to luff, and throw the wind from the sails, as is usually practised by fore-and-aft rigged craft, in moments of such peril. In consequence of these united difficulties, the shifting of the cargo in the hold, the tenderness of the craft itself, and the force of the squall, the schooner had gone so far over as to carry all three of the openings to her interior suddenly under water, where they remained, held by the pressure of the cargo that had rolled to leeward. Had not the water completely covered these openings, or hatches, the schooner must have sunk in a minute or two, or by the time Mulford had got all his companions safe on her bilge. But they were completely submerged, and so continued to be, which circumstance alone prevented the vessel from sinking, as the following simple explanation will show.

Any person who will put an empty tumbler, bottom upwards, into a bucket of water, will find that the water will not rise within the tumbler more than an inch at most. At that point it is arrested by the resistance of the air, which, unable to escape, and compressed into a narrow compass, forms a body that the other fluid cannot penetrate. It is on this simple and familiar principle, that the chemist keeps his gases, in inverted glasses, placing them on shelves, slightly submerged in water. Thus it was, then, that the schooner continued to float, though nearly bottom upward, and with three inlets open, by which the water could and did penetrate. A considerable quantity of the element had rushed in at the instant of capsizing, but meeting with resistance from the compressed and pent air, its progress had been arrested, and the wreck continued to float, sustained by the buoyancy that was imparted to it, in containing so large a body of a substance no heavier than atmospheric air. After displacing its weight of water, enough of buoyancy remained to raise the keel a few feet above the level of the sea.

As soon as Mulford had ascertained the facts of their situation, he communicated them to his companions, encouraging them to hope for eventual safety. It was true, their situation was nearly desperate, admitting that the wreck should continue to float forever, since they were almost without food, or anything to drink, and had no means of urging the hull through the water. They must float, too, at the mercy of the winds and waves, and should a sea get up, it might soon be impossible for Mulford himself to maintain his footing on the bottom of the wreck. All this the young man had dimly shadowed forth to him, through his professional experience; but the certainty of the vessel's not sinking immediately had so far revived his spirits, as to cause him to look on the bright side of the future, pale as that glimmering of hope was made to appear whenever reason cast one of its severe glances athwart it.

Harry had no difficulty in making Rose comprehend their precise situation. Her active and clear mind understood at once the causes of their present preservation, and most of the hazards of the future. It was not so with Jack Tier. He was composed, even resigned; but he could not see the reason why the schooner still floated.

"I know that the cabin doors were open," he said, "and if they was n't, of no great matter would it be, since the joints are n't caulked, and the water would run through them as through a sieve. I 'm afeard, Mr. Mulford, we shall find the wreck going from under our feet afore long, and when we least wish it, perhaps."

"I tell you the wreck will float so long as the air remains in its hold," returned the mate, cheerfully. "Do you not see how buoyant it is?—the certain proof that there is plenty of air within. So long as that remains, the hull must float."

"I've always understood," said Jack, sticking to his opinion, "that wessels float by vartue of water, and not by vartue of air; and, that when the water gets on the wrong side of 'em there's little hope left of keepin' 'em up."

"What has become of the boat?" suddenly cried the mate. "I have been so much occupied as to have forgotten the boat. In that boat we might all of us still reach Key West. I see nothing of the boat!"

A profound silence succeeded this sudden and unexpected question. All knew that the boat was gone, and all knew that it had been lost by the widow's pertinacity and clumsiness; but no one felt disposed to betray her at that grave moment. Mulford left the bilge, and waded as far aft as it was at all prudent for him to proceed, in the vain hope that the boat might be there, fastened by its painter to the schooner's tafferel, as he had left it, but concealed from view by the darkness of the night. Not finding what he was after, he returned to his companions, still uttering exclamations of surprise at the unaccountable loss of the boat. Rose now told him that the boat had got adrift some ten or fifteen minutes before the accident befell them, and that they were actually endeavoring to recover it when the squall which capsized the schooner struck them.

"And why did you not call me, Rose?" asked Harry, with a little of gentle reproach in his manner. "It must have soon been my watch on deck, and it would have been better that I should lose half an hour of my watch below, than that we should lose the boat."

Rose was now obliged to confess that the time for calling him had long been past, and that the faint streak of light, which was just appearing in the east, was the near approach of day. This explanation was made gently, but frankly; and Mulford experienced a glow of pleasure at his heart, even in that moment of jeopardy, when he understood Rose's motive for not having him disturbed. As the boat was gone, with little or no prospect of its being recovered again, no more was said about it; and the widow, who had stood on thorns the while, had the relief of believing that her awkwardness was forgotten.

It was such a relief from an imminent danger to have escaped from drowning when the schooner capsized, that those on her bottom did not, for some little time, realize all the terrors of their actual situation. The inconvenience of being wet was a trifle not to be thought of, and, in fact, the light summer dresses worn by all, linen or cotton as they were entirely, were soon effectually dried in the wind. The keel made a tolerably convenient seat, and the whole party placed themselves on it to await the return of day, in order to obtain a view of all that their situation offered in the way of a prospect. While thus awaiting, a broken and short dialogue occurred.

"Had you stood to the northward the whole night?" asked Mulford, gloomily, of Jack Tier; for gloomily he began to feel, as all the facts of their case began to press more closely on his mind. "If so, we must be well off the reef, and out of the track of wreckers and turtlers. How had you the wind, and how did you head before the accident happened?"

"The wind was light the whole time, and for some hours it was nearly calm," answered Jack, in the same vein; "I kept the schooner's head to the nor'ard, until I thought we were getting too far off our course, and then I put her about. I do not think we could have been any great distance from the reef when the boat got away from us, and I suppose we are in its neighborhood now, for I was tacking to fall in with the boat when the craft went over."

"To fall in with the boat! Did you keep off to leeward of it, then, that you expected to fetch it by tacking?"

"Ay, a good bit; and I think the boat is now away here to windward of us, drifting athwart our bows."

This was important news to Mulford. Could he only get that boat, the chances of being saved would be increased a hundred fold, nay, would almost amount to a certainty; whereas, so long as the wind held to the southward and eastward, the drift of the wreck must be toward the open water, and consequently so much the further removed from the means of succor. The general direction of the trades, in that quarter of the world, is east, and should they get round into their old and proper quarter, it would not benefit them much ; for the reef running southwest, they could scarcely hope to hit the Dry Tortugas again, in their drift, were life even spared them sufficiently long to float the distance. Then there might be currents, about which Mulford knew nothing with certainty ; they might set them in any direction ; and did they exist, as was almost sure to be the case, were much more powerful than the wind in controlling the movements of a wreck.

The mate strained his eyes in the direction pointed out by Jack Tier, in the hope of discovering the boat through the haze of the morning, and he actually did discern something that, it appeared to him, might be the much desired little craft. If he were right, there was every reason to think the boat would drift down so near them as to enable him to recover it by swimming. This cheering intelligence was communicated to his companions, who received it with gratitude and delight. But the approach of day gradually dispelled that hope, the object which Mulford had mistaken for the boat, within two hundred yards of the wreck, turning out to be a small, low, but bare hummock of the reef, at a distance of more than two miles.

"That is a proof that we are not far from the reef, at least," cried Mulford, willing to encourage those around him all he could, and really much relieved at finding himself so near even this isolated fragment of *terra firma*. "This fact is the next encouraging thing to finding ourselves near the boat, or to falling in with a sail."

"Ay, ay," said Jack gloomily ; "boat or no boat, 't will make no great matter of difference now. *There's* customers that 'll be sartain to take all the grists you can send to their mill."

"What things are those glancing about the vessel?" cried Rose, almost in the same breath ; "those dark, sharp-looking sticks—see, there are five or six of them ! and they move as if fastened to something under the water that pulls them about."

"'Them's the customers I mean, Miss Rose," answered Jack, in the same strain as that in which he had first spoken; "they're the same thing at sea as lawyers be ashore, and seem made to live on other folks. Them's sharks.''

"And yonder is truly the boat!" added Mulford, with a sigh that almost amounted to a groan. The light had, by this time, so far returned as to enable the party not only to see the fins of half a dozen sharks, which were already prowling about the wreck, the almost necessary consequence of their proximity to a reef in that latitude, but actually to discern the boat drifting down toward them at a distance that promised to carry it past, within the reach of Mulford's powers of swimming, though not as near as he could have wished, even under more favorable circumstances. Had their extremity been greater, or had Rose begun to suffer from hunger or thirst, Mulford might have attempted the experiment of endeavoring to regain the boat, though the chances of death by means of the sharks would be more than equal to those of escape; but still fresh, and not yet feeling even the heat of the sun of that low latitude, he was not quite goaded into such an act of desperation. All that remained for the party, therefore, was to sit on the keel of the wreck, and gaze with longing eyes at a little object floating past, which, once at their command, might so readily be made to save them from a fate that already began to appear terrible in the perspective. Near an hour was thus consumed, ere the boat was about half a mile to leeward; during which scarcely an eye was turned from it for one instant, or a word was spoken.

"It is beyond my reach now," Mulford at length exclaimed, sighing heavily, like one who became conscious of some great and irretrievable loss. "Were there no sharks, I could hardly venture to attempt swimming so far, with the boat drifting from me at the same time."

"I should never consent to let you make the trial, Harry," murmured Rose, "though it were only half as far.''

Another pause succeeded.

"We have now the light of day," resumed the mate a minute or two later, "and may see our true situation. No sail is in sight, and the wind stands steadily in its old quarter. Still I do not think we leave the reef. There, you may see the breakers off here at the southward, and it seems as if more rocks rise above the sea, in that direction. I do not know that our situation would be any the better, however, were we actually on them, instead of being on this floating wreck."

"The rocks will never sink," said Jack Tier, with so much emphasis as to startle the listeners.

"I do not think this hull will sink until we are taken off it, or are beyond caring whether it sink or swim," returned Mulford.

"I do not know that, Mr. Mulford. Nothing keeps us up but the air in the hold, you say."

"Certainly not; but that air will suffice as long as it remains there."

"And what do you call these things?" rejoined the assistant steward, pointing at the water near him, in or on which no one else saw anything worthy of attention.

Mulford, however, was not satisfied with a cursory glance, but went nearer to the spot where Tier was standing. Then, indeed, he saw to what the steward alluded, and was impressed by it, though he said nothing. Hundreds of little bubbles rose to the surface of the water, much as one sees them rising in springs. These bubbles are often met with in lakes and other comparatively shallow waters, but they are rarely seen in those of the ocean. The mate understood, at a glance, that those he now beheld were produced by the air which escaped from the hold of the wreck; in small quantities at a time, it was true, but by a constant and increasing process. The great pressure of the water forced this air through crevices so minute that, under ordinary circumstances, they would have proved impenetrable to this, as they were still to the other fluid, though they now permitted the passage of the former. It might take a long time to force the air from the interior of the vessel by such means, but the result was as certain as it might be slow. As constant dropping will wear a stone, so might the power that kept the wreck afloat be exhausted by the ceaseless rising of these minute air-bubbles.

Although Mulford was entirely sensible of the nature of this new source of danger, we cannot say he was much affected by it at the moment. It seemed to him far more probable that they must die of exhaustion, long before the wreck would lose all of its buoyancy by this slow process, than that even the strongest of their number could survive for such a period. The new danger, therefore, lost most of its terrors under this view of the subject, though it certainly did not add to the small sense of security that remained, to know that inevitably their fate must be sealed through its agency, should they be able to hold out for a sufficient time against hunger and thirst. It caused Mulford to muse in silence for many more minutes.

"I hope we are not altogether without food," the mate at length said. "It sometimes happens that persons at sea carry pieces of biscuit in their pockets, especially those who keep watch at night. The smallest morsel is now of the last importance."

At this suggestion, every one set about an examination. The result was, that neither Mrs. Budd nor Rose had a particle of food of any sort about their persons. Biddy produced from her pockets, however, a whole biscuit, a large bunch of excellent raisins that she had filched from the steward's stores, and two apples,—the last being the remains of some fruit that Spike had procured a month earlier in New York. Mulford had half a biscuit, at which he had been accustomed to nibble in his watches; and Jack lugged out, along with a small plug of tobacco, a couple of sweet oranges. Here, then, was everything in the shape of victuals or drink, that could be found for the use of five persons, in all probability for many days. The importance of securing it for equal distribution was so obvious, that Mulford's proposal to do so met with a common assent. The whole was put in Mrs. Budd's bag, and she was intrusted with the keeping of this precious store.

"It may be harder to abstain from food at first, when

we have not suffered from its want, than it will become after a little endurance,'' said the mate. '' We are now strong, and it will be wiser to fast as long as we conveniently can, to-day, and relieve our hunger by a moderate allowance toward evening, than to waste our means by too much indulgence at a time when we are strong. Weakness will be sure to come if we remain long on the wreck.''

'' Have you ever suffered in this way, Harry ?'' demanded Rose, with interest.

'' I have, and that dreadfully. But a merciful Providence came to my rescue then, and it may not fail me now. The seaman is accustomed to carry his life in his hand, and to live on the edge of eternity.''

The truth of this was so apparent as to produce a thoughtful silence. Anxious glances were cast around the horizon from time to time, in quest of any sail that might come in sight, but uselessly. None appeared, and the day advanced without bringing the slightest prospect of relief. Mulford could see, by the now almost sunken hummocks, that they were slowly drifting along the reef, toward the southward and eastward, a current no doubt acting slightly from the northwest. Their proximity to the reef, however, was of no advantage, as the distance was still so great as to render any attempt to reach it, even on the part of the mate, unavailable. Nor would he have been any better off could he have gained a spot on the rocks that was shallow enough to admit of his walking, since wading about in such a place would have been less desirable than to be floating where he was.

The want of water to drink threatened to be the great evil. Of this, the party on the wreck had not a single drop ! As the warmth of the day was added to the feverish feeling produced by excitement, they all experienced thirst, though no one murmured. So utterly without means of relieving this necessity did each person know them all to be, that no one spoke on the subject at all. In fact, shipwreck never produced a more complete destitution of all the ordinary agents of helping themselves, in any form or manner, than was the case here. So sudden and complete had been the disaster, that not a single article, beyond those on the persons of the sufferers, came even in view. The mast's sails, rigging, spare spars, in a word, everything belonging to the vessel was submerged and hidden from their sight, with the exception of a portion of the vessel's bottom, which might be forty feet in length, and some ten or fifteen in width, including that which was above water on both sides of the keel, though one only of these sides was available to the females, as a place to move about on. Had Mulford only a boat-hook, he would have felt it a relief; for not only did the sharks increase in number, but they grew more audacious, swimming so near the wreck that, more than once, Mulford apprehended that some one of the boldest of them might make an effort literally to board them. It is true, he had never known of one of these fishes attempting to quit his own element in pursuit of his prey; but such things were reported, and those around the wreck swam so close, and seemed so eager to get at those who were on it, that there really might be some excuse for fancying they might resort to unusual means of effecting their object. It is probable that, like all other animals, they were emboldened by their own numbers, and were acting in a sort of concert, that was governed by some of the many mysterious laws of nature that have still escaped human observation.

Thus passed the earlier hours of that appalling day. Toward noon, Mulford had insisted on the females dividing one of the oranges between them, and extracting its juice by way of assuaging their thirst. The effect was most grateful, as all admitted, and even Mrs. Budd urged Harry and Tier to take a portion of the remaining orange; but this both steadily refused. Mulford did consent to receive a small portion of one of the apples, more with a view of moistening his throat than to appease his hunger, though it had, in a slight degree, the latter effect also. As for Jack Tier, he declined even the morsel of apple, saying that tobacco answered his purpose, as indeed it temporarily might.

It was near sunset, when the steward's assistant called

Mulford aside, and whispered to him that he had something private to communicate. The mate bade him say on, as they were out of ear-shot of their companions.

"I've been in situations like this afore," said Jack, "and one l'arns exper'ence by exper'ence. I know how cruel it is on the feelin's to have the hopes disapp'inted in these cases, and therefore shall proceed with caution. But, Mr. Mulford, there's a sail in sight, if there is a drop of water in the Gulf!"

"A sail, Jack! I trust in Heaven you are not deceived!"

"Old eyes are true eyes in such matters, sir. Be careful not to start the women. They go off like gunpowder, and, Lord help 'em! have no more command over themselves, when you loosen 'em once, than so many flying-fish with a dozen dolphins a'ter them. Look hereaway, sir, just clear of the Irishwoman's bonnet, a little broad off the spot where the reef was last seen—if that an't a sail, my name is not Jack Tier."

A sail there was, sure enough! It was so very distant, however, as to render its character still uncertain, though Mulford fancied it was a square-rigged vessel heading to the northward. By its position, it must be in one of the channels of the reef, and by its course, if he were not deceived it was standing through, from the main passage along the southern side of the rocks, to come out on the northern. All this was favorable, and at first the young mate felt such a throbbing of the heart as we all experience when great and unexpected good intelligence is received. A moment's reflection, however, made him aware how little was to be hoped for from this vessel. In the first place, her distance was so great as to render it uncertain even which way she was steering. Then, there was the probability that she would pass at so great a distance as to render it impossible to perceive an object as low as the wreck, and the additional chance of her passing in the night. Under all the circumstances, therefore, Mulford felt convinced that there was very little probability of their receiving any succor from the strange sail; and he fully appreciated Jack Tier's motive in forbearing to give the usual call of "Sail ho!'' when he made this discovery. Still, he could not deny himself the pleasure of communicating to Rose the cheering fact that a vessel was actually in sight. She could not reason on the circumstances as he had done, and might at least pass several hours of comparative happiness by believing that there was some visible chance of delivery.

The females received the intelligence with very different degrees of hope. Rose was delighted. To her their rescue appeared an event so very probable now, that Harry Mulford almost regretted he had given rise to an expectation which he himself feared was to be disappointed. The feelings of Mrs. Budd were more suppressed. The wreck and her present situation were so completely at variance with all her former notions of the sea and its incidents, that she was almost dumfounded, and feared either to speak or to think. Biddy differed from either of her mistresses—the young or the old ; she appeared to have lost all hope, and her physical energy was fast giving way under her profound moral debility.

From the return of light that day, Mulford had thought, if it were to prove that Providence had withdrawn its protecting hand from them, Biddy, who to all appearance ought to be the longest liver among the females at least, would be the first to sink under her sufferings. Such is the influence of moral causes on the mere animal.

Rose saw the night shut in around them, amid the solemn solitude of the ocean, with a mingled sensation of awe and hope. She had prayed devoutly, and often, in the course of the preceding day, and her devotions had contributed to calm her spirits. Once or twice, while kneeling with her head bowed to the keel, she had raised her eyes toward Harry with a look of entreaty, as if she would implore him to humble his proud spirit and place himself at her side, and ask that succor from God which was so much needed, and which indeed it began most seriously to appear that God alone could yield. The young mate did not comply, for his pride of profession and of manhood offered themselves as stumbling-blocks to prevent submission to his secret wishes. Though he rarely prayed, Harry

Mulford was far from being an unbeliever, or one altogether regardless of his duties and obligations to his Divine
Creator. On the contrary, his heart was more disposed to
resort to such means of self-abasement and submission than
he put in practice, and this because he had been taught to
believe that the Anglo-Saxon mariner did not call on
Hercules on every occasion of difficulty and distress that
occurred, as was the fashion with the Italian and Romish
seamen, but he put his own shoulder to the wheel, confident
that Hercules would not forget to help him who knew how
to help himself. But Harry had great difficulty in with-
standing Rose's silent appeal that evening, as she knelt at
the keel for the last time, and turned her gentle eyes upward
at him, as if to ask him once more to take his place at her
side. Withstand the appeal he did, however, though in his
inward spirit he prayed fervently to God to put away this
dreadful affliction from the young and innocent creature
before him. When these evening devotions were ended, the
whole party became thoughtful and silent.

It was necessary to sleep, and arrangements were made
to do so, if possible, with a proper regard for their security.
Mulford and Tier were to have the lookout, watch and
watch. This was done that no vessel might pass near
them unseen, and that any change in the weather might be
noted and looked to. As it was, the wind had fallen, and
seemed about to vary, though it yet stood in its old quarter, or a little more easterly, perhaps. As a consequence,
the drift of the wreck, insomuch as it depended on the
currents of the air, was more nearly in a line with the
direction of the reef, and there was little ground for appre-
hending that they might be driven farther from it in the
night. Although that reef offered in reality no place of
safety, that was available to his party, Mulford felt it as a
sort of relief, to be certain that it was not distant, possibly
influenced by a vague hope that some passing wrecker or
turtler might yet pick them up.

The bottom of the schooner and the destitute condition
of the party admitted of only very simple arrangements for
the night. The females placed themselves against the

keel in the best manner they could, and thus endeavored to get a little of the rest they so much needed. The day had been warm, as a matter of course, and the contrast produced by the setting of the sun was at first rather agreeable than otherwise. Luckily Rose had thrown a shawl over her shoulders, not long before the vessel capsized, and in this shawl she had been saved. It had been dried, and it now served for a light covering to herself and her aunt, and added essentially to their comfort. As for Biddy, she was too hardy to need a shawl, and she protested that she should not think of using one, had she been better provided. The patient, meek manner in which that humble, but generous-hearted creature submitted to her fate, and the earnestness with which she had begged that "Miss Rosy" might have her morsel of the portion of biscuit each received for a supper, had sensibly impressed Mulford in her favor; and knowing how much more necessary food was to sustain one of her robust frame and sturdy habits than to Rose, he had contrived to give the woman, unknown to herself, a double allowance. Nor was it surprising that Biddy did not detect this little act of fraud in her favor, for this double allowance was merely a single mouthful. The want of water had made itself much more keenly felt than the want of food, for as yet anxiety, excitement, and apprehension prevented the appetite from being much awakened, while the claims of thirst were increased rather than the reverse, by these very causes. Still, no one had complained, on this or on any other account, throughout the whole of the long and weary day which had passed.

Mulford took the first lookout, with the intention of catching a little sleep, if possible, during the middle hours of the night, and of returning to his duty as morning approached. For the first hour nothing occurred to divert his attention from brooding on the melancholy circumstances of their situation. It seemed as if all around him had actually lost the sense of their cares in sleep, and no sound was audible amid that ocean waste, but the light washing of the water, as the gentle waves rolled at intervals against the weather side of the wreck. It was now that Mulford found a moment for prayer; and, seated on the keel, he called on the Divine aid, in a fervent but silent petition to God, to put away this trial from the youthful and beautiful Rose, at least, though he himself perished. It was the first prayer that Mulford had made in many months, or since he had joined the Swash—a craft in which that duty was very seldom thought of.

A few minutes succeeded this petition, when Biddy spoke.

"Missus—Madam Budd—dear missus!" half whispered the Irishwoman, anxious not to disturb Rose, who lay farthest from her; "missus, bees ye asleep at sich a time as this?"

"No, Biddy; sleep and I are strangers to each other, and are likely to be till morning. What do you wish to say?"

"Anything is betther than my own t'oughts, missus dear, and I wants to talk to ye. Is it no wather at all they 'll give us so long as we stay in this place?"

"There is no one to give it to us but God, poor Biddy, and he alone can say what, in his gracious mercy, it may please him to do. Ah! Biddy, I fear me that I did an unwise and thoughtless thing, to bring my poor Rose to such a place as this. Were it to be done over again, the riches of Wall Street would not tempt me to be guilty of so wrong a thing!"

The arm of Rose was thrown around her aunt's neck, and its gentle pressure announced how completely the offender was forgiven.

"I's very sorry for Miss Rose," rejoined Biddy, "and I suffers so much the more meself in thinking how hard it must be for the like of her to be wantin' in a swallow of fresh wather."

"It is no harder for me to bear it, poor Biddy," answered the gentle voice of our heroine, "than it is for yourself."

"Is it meself, then? Sure am I, that if I had a quar-r-t of good, swate wather from our own pump, and that 's far betther is it than the Crothon the best day the Crothon ever seed—but had I quar-r-t of it, every dhrap would I give to you, Miss Rose, to app'ase your thirst, I would."

"Water would be a great relief to us all, just now, my excellent Biddy," answered Rose, "and I wish we had but a tumblerful of that you name, to divide equally among the whole five of us."

"Is it divide? Then it would be ag'in dividin' that my voice would be raised, for that same ra'son that the tumbler would never hold as much as you could dhrink yourself, Miss Rose."

"Yet the tumblerful would be a great blessing for us all, just now," murmured Mrs. Budd.

"And is n't mutthon good 'atin', ladies! Och! if I had but a good swate pratie, now, from my own native Ireland, and a dhrap of milk to help wash it down! It's mighty little that a body thinks of sich trifles when there's abundance of them; but when there's none at all, they get to be stronger in the mind than riches and honors."

"You say the truth, Biddy," rejoined the mistress, "and there is a pleasure in talking of them, if one can't enjoy them. I've been thinking all the afternoon, Rose, what a delicious food is a good roast turkey, with cranberry sauce; and I wonder, now, that I have not been more grateful for the very many that Providence has bestowed on me in my time. My poor Mr. Budd was passionately fond of mutton, and I used wickedly to laugh at his fondness for it, sometimes, when he always had his answer ready, and that was that there are no sheep at sea. How true that is, Rosy dear! there are indeed no sheep at sea!"

"No, aunty," answered Rose's gentle voice from beneath the shawl; "there are no such animals on the ocean, but God is with us here as much as he would be in New York."

A long silence succeeded this simple remark of his well beloved, and the young mate hoped that there would be no more of a dialogue, every syllable of which was a dagger to his feelings. But nature was stronger than reflection in Mrs. Budd and Biddy, and the latter spoke again, after a pause of near a quarter of an hour.

"Pray for me, missus," she said moaningly, "that I may

sleep. A bit of sleep would do a body almost as much good as a bit of bread—I won't say as much as a dhrap of wather.''

''Be quiet, Biddy, and we will pray for you,'' answered Rose, who fancied by her breathing that her aunt was about to forget her sufferings for a brief space, in broken slumbers.

''Is it for you I'll do *that*—and sure will I, Miss Rose. Niver would I have quitted Ireland, could I have thought there was sich a spot on this earth as a place where no wather was to be had.''

This was the last of Biddy's audible complaints, for the remainder of this long and anxious watch of Mulford. He then set himself about an arrangement which shall be mentioned in its proper place. At twelve o'clock, or when he thought it was twelve, he called Jack Tier, who in turn called the mate again at four.

''It looks dark and threatening,'' said Mulford, as he rose to his feet and began to look about him once more, ''though there does not appear to be any wind.''

''It's a flat calm, Mr. Mate, and the darkness comes from yonder cloud, which seems likely to bring a little rain.''

''Rain ! Then God is indeed with us here. You are right, Jack ; rain must fall from that cloud. We must catch some of it, if it be only a drop to cool Rose's parched tongue.''

''In what?'' answered Tier, gloomily. ''She may wring her clothes when the shower is over, and in that way get a drop. I see no other method.''

''I have bethought me of all that, and passed most of my watch in making the preparations.''

Mulford then showed Tier what he had been about, in the long and solitary hours of the first watch. It would seem that the young man had dug a little trench with his knife, along the schooner's bottom, commencing two or three feet from the keel, and near the spot where Rose was lying, and carrying it as far as was convenient toward the run, until he reached a point where he had dug out a sort of reservoir to

16

contain the precious fluid, should any be sent them by Prov·
idence. While doing this, there were no signs of rain ; but
the young man knew that a shower alone could save them
from insanity, if not from death ; and in speculating on the
means of profiting by one, should it come, he had bethought
him of this expedient. The large knife of a seaman had
served him a good turn, in carrying on his work, to complete which there remained now very little to do, and that
was in enlarging the receptacle for the water. The hole was
already big enough to contain a pint, and it might easily be
sufficiently enlarged to hold double that quantity.

Jack was no sooner made acquainted with what had been
done, than he out knife and commenced tearing splinter after
splinter from the planks, to help enlarge the reservoir. This
could only be done by cutting on the surface, for the wood
was not three inches in thickness, and the smallest hole
through the plank, would have led to the rapid escape of
the air and to the certain sinking of the wreck. It required
a good deal of judgment to preserve the necessary level also,
and Mulford was obliged to interfere more than once to prevent his companion from doing more harm than good. He
succeeded, however, and had actually made a cavity that
might contain more than a quart of water, when the first
large drop fell from the heavens. This cavity was not a
hole, but a long, deep trench,—deep for the circumstances,—
so nicely cut on the proper level, as to admit of its holding
a fluid in the quantity mentioned.

"Rose—dearest—rise, and be ready to drink," said Mulford, tenderly disturbing the uneasy slumbers of his beloved.
"It is about to rain, and God is with us here, as he might
be on the land."

"Wather !" exclaimed Biddy, who was awoke with the
same call. "What a blessed thing is good, swate wather,
and sure am I we ought all to be thankful that there is such
a precious gift in the wor-r-ld."

"Come, then," said Mulford, hurriedly, "it will soon
rain—I hear it pattering on the sea. Come hither, all of
you, and drink, as a merciful God furnishes the means."

This summons was not likely to be neglected. All arose

in haste, and the word "water" was murmured from every
lip. Biddy had less self-command than the others, and she
was heard saying aloud, "Och! and did n't I dhrame of the
blessed springs and wells of Ireland the night, and have n't
I dhrunk at 'em all? but now it's over, and I am awake, no
good has't done me, and I'm ready to die for one dhrap of
wather."

That drop soon came, however, and with it the blessed
relief which such a boon bestows. Mulford had barely time
to explain his arrangements, and to place the party on their
knees, along his little reservoir and the gutter which led to
it, when the pattering of the rain advanced along the sea,
with a deep, rushing sound. Presently, the uplifted faces
and open mouths caught a few heavy straggling drops, to
cool the parched tongues, when the water came tumbling
down upon them in a thousand little streams. There was
scarcely any wind, and merely the skirt of a large black
cloud floated over the wreck, on which the rain fell barely
one minute. But it fell as rain comes down within the
tropics, and in sufficient quantities for all present purposes.
Everybody drank, and found relief, and, when all was over,
Mulford ascertained by examination that his receptacle for
the fluid was still full to overflowing. The abstinence had
not been of sufficient length, nor the quantity taken of large
enough amount, to produce injury, though the thirst was
generally and temporarily appeased. It is probable that
the coolness of the hour, day dawning as the cloud moved
past, and the circumstance that the sufferers were wetted to
their skins, contributed to the change.

"Oh, blessed, blessed wather!" exclaimed Biddy, as she
rose from her knees; "America, afther all, is n't as dhry a
country as some say. I niver tasted swater wather in Ireland itself!"

Rose murmured her thanksgiving in more appropriate
language. A few exclamations also escaped Mrs. Budd, and
Jack Tier had his sententious eulogy on the precious qualities of sweet water.

The wind rose as the day advanced, and a swell began to
heave the wreck with a power that had hitherto been dor-

mant. Mulford understood this to be a sign that there had
been a blow at some distance from them, that had thrown
the sea into a state of agitation, which extended itself beyond the influence of the wind. Eagerly did the young
mate examine the horizon, as the curtain of night arose,
inch by inch, as it might be, on the watery panorama, in
the hope that a vessel of some sort or other might be brought
within the view. Nor was he wholly disappointed. The
strange sail seen the previous evening was actually there;
and what was more, so near as to allow her hull to be distinctly visible. It was a ship, under her square canvas,
standing from between divided portions of the reef, as if
getting to the northward, in order to avoid the opposite current of the Gulf Stream. Vessels bound to Mobile, New Orleans, and other ports along the coast of the Republic, in
that quarter of the ocean, often did this; and when the
young mate first caught glimpses of the shadowy outline of
this ship, he supposed it to be some packet, or cotton-droger,
standing for her port on the northern shore. But a few minutes removed the veil, and with it the error of this notion.
A seaman could no longer mistake the craft. Her length,
her square and massive hamper, with the symmetry of her
spars, and the long, straight outline of the hull, left no doubt
that it was a cruiser, with her hammocks unstowed. Mulford now cheerfully announced to his companions, that the
ship they so plainly saw, scarcely a gun-shot distance from
them, was the sloop-of-war which had already become a sort
of an acquaintance.

"If we can succeed in making them see our signal,"
cried Mulford, "all will yet be well. Come, Jack, and
help me to put abroad this shawl, the only ensign we can
show."

The shawl of Rose was the signal spread. Tier and Mulford stood on the keel, and holding opposite corners, let the
rest of the cloth blow out with the wind. For near an hour
did these two extend their arms, and try all possible expedients to make their signal conspicuous. But, unfortunately,
the wind blew directly toward the cruiser, and instead of exposing a surface of any breadth to the vision of those on

board her, it must, at most, have offered little more than a flitting, waving line.

As the day advanced, sail was made on the cruiser. She had stood through the passage, in which she had been becalmed most of the night, under short canvas; but now she threw out fold after fold of her studding-sails, and moved away to the westward, with the stately motion of a ship before the wind. No sooner had she got far enough to the northward of the reef, than she made a deviation from her course as first seen, turning her stern entirely to the wreck, and rapidly becoming less and less distinct to the eyes of those who floated on it.

Mulford saw the hopelessness of their case, as it respected relief from this vessel; still, he persevered in maintaining his position on the keel, tossing and waving the shawl, in all the variations that his ingenuity could devise. He well knew, however, that their chances of being seen would have been trebled could they have been ahead instead of astern of the ship. Mariners have few occasions to look behind them, while a hundred watchful eyes are usually turned ahead, more especially when running near rocks and shoals. Mrs. Budd wept like an infant when she saw the sloop-of-war gliding away, reaching a distance that rendered sight useless, in detecting an object that floated as low on the water as the wreck. As for Biddy, unable to control her feelings, the poor creature actually called to the crew of the departing vessel, as if her voice had the power to make itself heard, at a distance which already exceeded two leagues. It was only by means of the earnest remonstrances of Rose, that the faithful creature could be quieted. "Why will ye not come to our relief?" she cried at the top of her voice. "Here are we, helpless as new-born babies, and ye sailing away from us in a con*thra*ry way. D'ye not bethink you of the missus, who is much of a sailor, but not sich a one as to sail on a wrack; and poor Miss Rose, who is the char-rin and delight of all eyes. Only come and take off Miss Rose, and leave the rest of us, if ye so likes; for it's a sin and a shame to lave the likes of her to die in the midst of the ocean, as if she was no betther nor a

fish. Then it will be soon that we shall ag'in feel the want
of wather, and that, too, with nothing but wather to be seen
on all sides of us.''

''It is of no use,'' said Harry, mournfully, stepping down
from the keel, and laying aside the shawl. ''They cannot
see us, and the distance is now so great as to render it
certain they never will. There is only one hope left. We
are evidently set to and fro by the tides, and it is possible
that by keeping in or near this passage, some other craft
may appear, and we be more fortunate. The relief of the
rain is a sign that we are not forgotten by Divine Providence,
and with such a protector we ought not to despair.''

A gloomy and scanty breaking of the fast succeeded.
Each person had one large mouthful of bread, which was
all that prudence would authorize Mulford to distribute.
He attempted a pious fraud, however, by placing his own
allowance along with that of Rose's under the impression
that her strength might not endure privation as well as his
own. But the tender solicitude of Rose was not to be thus
deceived. Judging of his wishes and motives by her own,
she at once detected the deception, and insisted on retaining no more than her proper share. When this distribution
was completed, and the meagre allowance taken, only
sufficient bread remained to make one more similar scanty
meal, if meal a single mouthful could be termed. As for
the water, a want of which would be certain to be felt as
soon as the sun obtained its noonday power, the shawl was
extended over it, in a way to prevent evaporation as much
as possible, and at the same time to offer some resistance
to the fluid's being washed from its shallow receptacle by
the motion of the wreck, which was sensibly increasing with
the increase of the wind and waves.

Mulford had next an anxious duty to perform. Throughout the whole of the preceding day he had seen the air escaping from the hull, in an incessant succession of small
bubbles, which were formidable through their numbers, if
not through their size. The mate was aware that this unceasing loss of the buoyant property of the wreck must
eventually lead to their destruction, should no assistance

come, and he had marked the floating line, on the bottom
of the vessel with his knife, ere darkness set in, on the previous evening. No sooner did his thoughts recur to this
fact, after the excitement of the first hour of daylight was
over, than he stepped to the different places thus marked,
and saw, with an alarm that it would be difficult to describe,
that the wreck had actually sunk into the water several
inches within the last few hours. This was, indeed menacing their security in a most serious manner, setting a
limit to their existence, which rendered all precaution on
the subject of food and water useless. By the calculations
of the mate, the wreck could not float more than eight-and-
forty hours, should it continue to lose the air at the rate at
which it had been hitherto lost. Bad as all this appeared,
things were fated to become much more serious. The motion of the water quite sensibly increased, lifting the wreck
at times in a way greatly to increase the danger of their
situation. The reader will understand this movement did
not proceed from the waves of the existing wind, but from
what is technically called a ground-swell, or the long, heavy
undulations that are left by the tempest that is past, or by
some distant gale. The waves of the present breeze were
not very formidable, the reef making a lee; though they
might possibly become inconvenient from breaking on the
weather side of the wreck, as soon as the drift carried the
latter fairly abreast of the passage already mentioned. But
the dangers that proceeded from the heavy ground-swell,
which now began to give a considerable motion to the wreck,
will best explain itself by narrating the incidents as they
occurred.

Harry had left his marks, and had taken his seat on the
keel at Rose's side, impatiently waiting for any turn that
Providence might next give to their situation, when a heavy
roll of the wreck first attracted his attention to this new
circumstance.

"If any one is thirsty," he observed quietly, "he or she
had better drink now, while it may be done. Two or three
more such rolls as this last will wash all the water from our
gutters."

"Wather is a blessed thing," said Biddy, with a longing expression of the eyes, "and it would be betther to swallow it than to let it be lost."

"Then drink, for Heaven's sake, good woman; it may be the last occasion that will offer."

"Sure am I that I would not touch a dhrap, while the missus and Miss Rosy was sufferin'."

"I have no thirst at all," answered Rose, sweetly, "and have already taken more water than was good for me, with so little food on my stomach."

"Eat another morsel of the bread, beloved," whispered Harry, in a manner so urgent that Rose gratefully complied. Drink, Biddy, and we will come and share with you before the water is wasted by this increasing motion."

Biddy did as desired, and each knelt in turn and took a little of the grateful fluid, leaving about a gill in the gutters for the use of those whose lips might again become parched.

"Wather is a blessed thing," repeated Biddy, for the twentieth time, "a blessed, blessed thing is wather?"

A little scream from Mrs. Budd, which was dutifully taken up by the maid, interrupted the speech of the latter, and every eye was turned on Mulford, as if to ask an explanation of the groaning sound that had been heard within the wreck. The young mate comprehended only too well. The rolling of the wreck had lifted a portion of the open hatchway above the undulating surface of the sea, and a large quantity of the pent air within the hold had escaped in a body. The entrance of water to supply the vacuum had produced the groan. Mulford had made new marks on the vessel's bottom with his knife, and he stepped down to them, anxious and nearly heart-broken, to note the effect. That one surging of the wreck had permitted air enough to escape to lower it in the water several inches. As yet, however, the visible limits of their floating foundation had not been sufficiently reduced to attract the attention of the females; and the young man said nothing on the subject. He thought that Jack Tier was sensible of the existence of this new source of danger, but if he were, that experienced mariner imitated his own reserve and made no allusion to it. Thus passed the day. Occasionally the wreck rolled heavily, when more air escaped, the hull settling lower and lower in the water as a necessary consequence. The little bubbles continued incessantly to rise, and Mulford became satisfied that another day must decide their fate. Taking this view of their situation, he saw no use in reserving their food, but encouraged his companions to share the whole of what remained at sunset. Little persuasion was necessary, and when night once more came to envelop them in darkness, not a mouthful of food or a drop of water remained to meet the necessities of the coming morn. It had rained again for a short time, in the course of the afternoon, when enough water had been caught to allay their thirst, and what was almost of as much importance to the females now, a sufficiency of sun had succeeded to dry their clothes, thus enabling them to sleep without enduring the chilling damps that might otherwise have prevented it. The wind had sensibly fallen, and the ground-swell was altogether gone, but Mulford was certain that the relief had come too late. So much air had escaped while it lasted as scarce to leave him the hope that the wreck could float until morning. The rising of the bubbles was now incessant, the crevices by which they escaped having most probably opened a little, in consequence of the pressure and the unceasing action of the currents, small as the latter were.

Just as darkness was shutting in around them for the second time, Rose remarked to Mulford that it seemed to her that they had not as large a space for their little world as when they were first placed on it. The mate, however, successfully avoided an explanation ; and when the watch was again set for the night, the females lay down to seek their repose, more troubled with apprehensions for a morrow of hunger and thirst, than by any just fears that might so well have arisen from the physical certainty that the body which alone kept them from being engulfed in the sea could float but a few hours longer. This night Tier kept the lookout until Jupiter reached the zenith, when Mulford was called to hold the watch until light returned,

It may seem singular that any could sleep at all in such
a situation. But we get accustomed, in an incredibly short
time, to the most violent changes; and calamities that seem
insupportable, when looked at from a distance, lose half
their power if met and resisted with fortitude. The last
may, indeed, be too insignificant a word to be applied to
all the party on the wreck, on the occasion of which we
are writing, though no one of them all betrayed fears
that were troublesome. Of Mulford it is unnecessary to
speak. His deportment had been quiet, thoughtful, and
full of manly interest in the comfort of others, from the
first moment of the calamity. That Rose should share the
largest in his attentions was natural enough, but he neglected no essential duty to her companions. Rose, herself, had little hope of being rescued. Her naturally
courageous character, however, prevented any undue exhibitions of despair, and now it was that the niece became
the principal support of the aunt, completely changing the
relations that had formerly existed between them. Mrs.
Budd had lost all the little buoyancy of her mind. Not a
syllable did she now utter concerning ships and their
manœuvres. She had been, at first, a little disposed to be
querulous and despairing, but the soothing and pious conversation of Rose awakened a certain degree of resolution
in her, and habit soon exercised its influence over even her
inactive mind. Biddy was a strange mixture of courage,
despair, humility, and consideration for others. Not once
had she taken her small allowance of food without first
offering it, and that, too, in perfect good faith, to her
"missus and Miss Rosy"; yet her moanings for this sort
of support, and her complaints of bodily suffering, much
exceeded that of all the rest of the party put together.
As for Jack Tier, his conduct singularly belied his appearance. No one would have expected any great show of
manly resolution from the little rotund, lymphatic figure of
Tier; but he had manifested a calmness that denoted either
great natural courage, or a resolution derived from familiarity
with danger. In this particular, even Mulford regarded his
deportment with surprise, not unmingled with respect.

"You have had a tranquil watch, Jack," said Harry, when he was called by the person named, and had fairly aroused himself from his slumbers. "Has the wind stood as it is since sunset?"

"No change whatever, sir. It has blown a good working breeze the whole watch, and what is surprising not as much lipper has got up as would frighten a colt on a sea-beach."

"We must be near the reef, by that. I think the only currents we feel come from the tide, and they seem to be setting us back and forth, instead of carrying us in any one settled direction."

"Quite likely, sir; and this makes my opinion of what I saw an hour since all the more probable."

"What you saw! In the name of a Merciful Providence, Tier, do not trifle with me! Has anything been seen near by?"

"Don't talk to me of your liquors and other dhrinks," murmured Biddy in her sleep. "It's wather that is a blessed thing; and I wish I lived, the night and the day, by the swate pump that's in our own yard, I do."

"The woman has been talking in her sleep, in this fashion, most of the watch," observed Jack, coolly, and perhaps a little contemptuously. "But, Mr. Mulford, unless my eyes have cheated me, we are near that boat again. The passage through the reef is close aboard us, here, on our larboard bow, as it might be, and the current has sucked us in it in a fashion to bring it in a sort of athwart-hawse direction to us."

"If that boat, after all, should be sent by Providence to our relief! How long is it since you saw it Jack?"

"But a bit since, sir; or, for that matter, I think I see it now. Look hereaway, sir, just where the dead-eyes of the fore-rigging would bear from us, if the craft stood upon her legs, as she ought to do. If that is n't a boat, it's a rock out of water."

Mulford gazed through the gloom of midnight, and saw, or fancied he saw, an object that really might be the boat. It could not be very distant either; and his mind was instantly made up as to the course he would pursue. Should

it actually turn out to be that which he now so much
hoped for, and its distance in the morning did not prove
too great for human powers, he was resolved to swim for it
at the hazard of his life.   In the meantime, or until light
should return, there remained nothing to do but to exercise
as much patience as could be summoned, and to confide in
God, soliciting his powerful succor by secret prayer.

Mulford was no sooner left alone, as it might be, by
Tier's seeking a place in which to take his rest, than he
again examined the state of the wreck.   Little as he had
hoped from its long continued buoyancy, he found matters
even worse than he apprehended they would be.   The hull
had lost much air, and had consequently sunk in the water
in an exact proportion to this loss.   The space that was
actually above the water was reduced to an area not more
than six or seven feet in one direction, by some ten or
twelve in the other.   This was reducing its extent, since
the evening previous, by fully one half; and there could
be no doubt that the air was escaping, in consequence of
the additional pressure, in a ratio that increased by a sort
of arithmetical progression.   The young man knew that
the whole wreck under its peculiar circumstances, might
sink entirely beneath the surface, and yet possess sufficient
buoyancy to sustain those that were on it for a time longer,
but this involved the terrible necessity of leaving the females partly submerged themselves.

Our mate heard his own heart beat, as he became satisfied of the actual condition of the wreck, and of the
physical certainty that existed of its sinking, at least to the
point last mentioned, ere the sun came to throw his glories
over the last view that the sufferers would be permitted to
take of the face of day.   It appeared to him that no time
was to be lost.   There lay the dim and shapeless object
that seemed to be the boat, distant, as he thought, about a
mile.   It would not have been visible at all but for the
perfect smoothness of the sea, and the low position occupied by the observer.   At times it did disappear altogether,
when it would rise again, as if undulating in the ground-
swell.   This last circumstance, more than any other, per-

suaded Harry that it was not a rock, but some floating object that he beheld. Thus encouraged, he delayed no longer. Every moment was precious, and all might be lost by indecision. He did not like the appearance of deserting his companions, but, should he fail, the motive would appear in the act. Should he fail, every one would alike soon be beyond the reach of censure, and in a state of being that would do full justice to all.

Harry threw off most of his clothes, reserving only his shirt and a pair of light summer trousers. He could not quit the wreck, however, without taking a sort of leave of Rose. On no account would he awake her, for he appreciated the agony she would feel during the period of his struggles. Kneeling at her side, he made a short prayer, then pressed his lips to her warm cheek, and left her, Rose murmured his name at that instant, but it was as the innocent and young betray their secrets in their slumbers. Neither of the party awoke.

It was a moment to prove the heart of man, that in which Harry Mulford, in the darkness of midnight, alone, unsustained by any encouraging eye, or approving voice, with no other aid than his own stout arm, and the unknown designs of a mysterious Providence, committed his form to the sea. For an instant he paused, after he had waded down on the wreck to a spot where the water already mounted to his breast, but it was not in misgivings. He calculated the chances, and made an intelligent use of such assistance as could be had. There had been no sharks near the wreck that day, but a splash in the water might bring them back again in a crowd. They were probably prowling over the reef, near at hand. The mate used great care, therefore, to make no noise. There was the distant object, and he set it by a bright star, that wanted about an hour before it would sink beneath the horizon. That star was his beacon, and muttering a few words in earnest prayer, the young man threw his body forward, and left the wreck swimming lightly but with vigor.

CHAPTER IX.

"The night has been unruly: where we lay,
Our chimneys were blown down: and, as they say,
Lamentings heard i' the air; strange screams of death;
And prophesying, with accents terrible,
Of dire combustion, and confused events,
New hatched to the woful time."

Macbeth.

IT is seldom that man is required to make an exertion as desperate and appalling, in all its circumstances, as that on which Harry Mulford was now bent. The night was starlight, it was true, and it was possible to see objects near by with tolerable distinctness; still, it was midnight, and the gloom of that hour rested on the face of the sea, lending its solemn mystery and obscurity to the other trying features of the undertaking. Then there was the uncertainty whether it was the boat at all, of which he was in pursuit; and, if the boat, it might drift away from him as fast as he could follow it. Nevertheless, the perfect conviction that, without some early succor, the party on the wreck, including Rose Budd, must inevitably perish, stimulated him to proceed, and a passing feeling of doubt, touching the prudence of his course that came over the young mate, when he was a few yards from the wreck, vanished under a vivid renewal of this last conviction. On he swam, therefore, riveting his eye on the "thoughtful star" that guided his course, and keeping his mind as tranquil as possible, in order that the exertions of his body might be the easier.

Mulford was an excellent swimmer. The want of food was a serious obstacle to his making one of his best efforts, but, as yet, he was not very sensible of any great loss of strength. Understanding fully the necessity of swimming easily, if he would swim long, he did not throw out all his energy at first, but made the movements of his limbs as regular, continued, and skilful as possible. No strength was thrown away, and his progress was in proportion to the prudence of this manner of proceeding. For some twenty minutes he held on his course, in this way, when he began to experience a little of that weariness which is apt to accompany an unremitted use of the same set of muscles, in a monotonous and undeviating mode. Accustomed to all the resources of his art, he turned on his back, for the double purpose of relieving his arms for a minute, and of getting a glimpse of the wreck, if possible, in order to ascertain the distance he had overcome. Swim long in this new manner, however, he could not with prudence, as the star was necessary in order to keep the direct line of his course. It may be well to explain to some of our readers, that, though the surface of the ocean may be like glass, as sometimes really happens, it is never absolutely free from the long, undulating motion that is known by the name of a "ground-swell." This swell on the present occasion, was not very heavy, but it was sufficient to place our young mate, at moments, between two dark mounds of water, that limited his view in either direction to some eighty or a hundred yards; then it raised him on the summit of a rounded wave, that enabled him to see, far as his eye could reach under that obscure light. Profiting by this advantage, Mulford now looked behind him, in quest of the wreck, but uselessly. It might have been in the trough, while he was thus on the summit of the waves, or it might be that it floated so low as to be totally lost to the view of one whose head was scarcely above the surface of the water. For a single instant, the young man felt a chill at his heart, as he fancied that the wreck had already sunk; but it passed away when he recalled the slow progress by which the air escaped, and he saw the certainty that the catastrophe, however inevitable, could not yet have really arrived. He waited for another swell to lift him on its summit, when, by "treading water," he raised his head and shoulders fairly above the surface of the sea, and strained his eyes in another vain effort to catch a glimpse of the wreck. He could not see it. In point of fact, the mate had swum much farther than he had supposed, and was already so distant as to render any such attempt hopeless. He was fully a third of a mile distant from the point of his departure.

Disappointed, and in a slight degree disheartened, Mulford turned, and swam in the direction of the sinking star. He now looked anxiously for the boat. It was time that it came more plainly into view, and a new source of anxiety beset him, as he could discover no signs of its vicinity. Certain that he was on the course, after making a due allowance for the direction of the wind, the stout-hearted young man swam on. He next determined not to annoy himself by fruitless searches, or vain regrets, but to swim steadily for a certain time, a period long enough to carry him a material distance, ere he again looked for the object of his search.

For twenty minutes longer did that courageous and active youth struggle with the waste of waters, amid the obscurity and solitude of midnight. He now believed himself near a mile from the wreck, and the star which had so long served him for a beacon was getting near to the horizon. He took a new observation of another of the heavenly bodies nigh it, to serve him in its stead when it should disappear altogether, and then he raised himself in the water, and looked about again for the boat. The search was in vain. No boat was very near him, of a certainty, and the dreadful apprehension began to possess his mind, of perishing uselessly in that waste of gloomy waters. While thus gazing about him, turning his eyes in every quarter, hoping intently to catch some glimpse of the much-desired object in the gloom, he saw two dark, pointed objects, that resembled small stakes, in the water, within twenty feet of him. Mulford knew them at a glance, and a cold shudder passed through his frame, as he recognized them. They were, out of all question, the fins of an enormous shark ; an animal that could not measure less than eighteen or twenty feet in length.

It is scarcely necessary to say, that when our young mate discovered the proximity of this dangerous animal, situated as he was, he gave himself up for lost. He possessed his knife, however, and had heard of the manner in which even sharks were overcome, and that too in their own element, by the skilful and resolute. At first, he was resolved to make one desperate effort for life, before he submitted to a fate as horrible as that which now menaced him; but the movements of his dangerous neighbor induced him to wait. It did not approach any nearer, but continued swimming back and fro, on the surface of the water, according to the known habits of the fish, as if watching his own movements. There being no time to be wasted, our young mate turned on his face, and began again to swim in the direction of the setting star, though nearly chilled by despair. For ten minutes longer did he struggle on, beginning to feel exhaustion, however, and always accompanied by those two dark, sharp, and gliding fins. There was no difficulty in knowing the position of the animal, and Mulford's eyes were oftener on those fins than on the beacon before him. Strange as it may appear, he actually became accustomed to the vicinity of this formidable creature, and soon felt his presence a sort of relief against the dreadful solitude of his situation. He had been told by seamen of instances, and had once witnessed a case himself, in which a shark had attended a swimming man for a long distance, either forbearing to do him harm, from repletion, or influenced by that awe which nature has instilled into all of the inferior, for the highest animal of the creation. He began to think that he was thus favored, and really regarded the shark as a friendly neighbor, rather than as a voracious foe. In this manner did the two proceed, nearly another third of a mile, the fins sometimes in sight ahead, gliding hither and thither, and sometimes out of view behind the swimmer, leaving him in dreadful doubts as to the movements of the fish, when Mulford suddenly felt something hard hit his foot. Believing it to be the shark, dipping for his prey, a slight exclamation escaped him. At the next instant both feet hit the unknown substance again, and he stood erect,

the water no higher than his waist! Quick, and comprehending everything connected with the sea, the young man
at once understood that he was on a part of the reef where
the water was so shallow as to admit of his wading.

Mulford felt that he had been providentially rescued
from death. His strength had been about to fail him, when
he was thus led, unknown to himself, to a spot where his
life might yet be possibly prolonged for a few more hours,
or days. He had leisure to look about him, and to reflect
on what was next to be done. Almost unwittingly, he
turned in quest of his terrible companion, in whose voracious mouth he had actually believed himself about to be
immolated, a few seconds before. There the two horn-like
fins still were, gliding about above the water, and indicating
the smallest movement of their formidable owner. The
mate observed that they went a short distance ahead of him,
describing nearly a semicircle, and then returned, doing the
same thing in his rear, repeating the movements incessantly,
keeping always on his right. This convinced him that
shoaler water existed on his left hand, and he waded in that
direction, until he reached a small spot of naked rock.

For a time, at least, he was safe! The fragment of coral
on which the mate now stood was irregular in shape, but
might have contained a hundred feet square in superficial
measurement, and was so little raised above the level of the
water as not to be visible, even by daylight, at the distance
of a hundred yards. Mulford found it was perfectly dry,
however, an important discovery to him, as by a close calculation he had made of the tides, since quitting the Dry
Tortugas, he knew it must be near high water. Could he
have even this small portion of bare rock secure, it made
him, for the moment, rich as the most extensive landholder
living. A considerable quantity of sea-weed had lodged on
the rock, and, as most of this was also quite dry, it convinced the young sailor that the place was usually bare.
But, though most of this sea-weed was dry, there were portions of the more recent accessions there that still lay in,
or quite near to the water, which formed exceptions. In
handling these weeds, in order to ascertain the facts, Mul-

ford caught a small shell-fish, and finding it fresh and easy
to open, he swallowed it with the eagerness of a famishing
man. Never had food proved half so grateful to him as
that single swallow of a very palatable testaceous animal.
By feeling further, he found several others of the same
family, and made quite as large a meal, as, under the circumstances, was probably good for him. Then, grateful for
his escape, but overcome by fatigue, he hastily arranged a
bed of sea-weed, drew a portion of the plant over his body,
to keep him warm, and fell into a deep sleep that lasted for
hours.

Mulford did not regain his consciousness until the rays
of the rising sun fell upon his eyelids, and the genial
warmth of the great luminary shed its benign influence over
his frame. At first his mind was confused, and it required
a few seconds to bring a perfect recollection of the past,
and a true understanding of his real situation. They came,
however, and the young man moved to the highest part of
his little domain, and cast an anxious, hurried look around
in quest of the wreck. A knowledge of the course in which
he had swum, aided by the position of the sun, told him on
what part of the naked waste to look for the object he
sought. God had not yet forsaken them! There was the
wreck; or it might be more exact to say, there were those
whom the remaining buoyancy of the wreck still upheld
from sinking into the depths of the Gulf. In point of fact,
but a very little of the bottom of the vessel actually remained above water, some two or three yards square at
most, and that little was what seamen term nearly awash.
Two or three hours must bury that small portion of the
still naked wood beneath the surface of the sea, though
sufficient buoyancy might possibly remain for the entire day
still to keep the living from death.

There the wreck was, however, yet floating; and, though
not visible to Mulford, with a small portion of it above
water. He saw the four persons only; and what was more,
they saw him. This was evident by Jack Tier's waving
his hat like a man cheering. When Mulford, returned this
signal, the shawl of Rose was tossed into the air, in a way

to leave no doubt that he was seen and known. The explanation of this early recognition and discovery of the young mate was very simple. Tier was not asleep when Harry left the wreck, though, seeing the importance of the step the other was taking, he had feigned to be so. When Rose awoke, missed her lover, and was told what had happened, her heart was kept from sinking by his encouraging tale and hopes. An hour of agony had succeeded, nevertheless, when light returned and no Mulford was to be seen. The despair that burst upon the heart of our heroine was followed by the joy of discovering him on the rock.

It is scarcely necessary to say how much the parties were relieved on ascertaining their prospective positions. Faint as were the hopes of each of eventual delivery, the two or three minutes that succeeded seemed to be minutes of perfect happiness. After this rush of unlooked-for joy, Mulford continued his intelligent examination of surrounding objects.

The wreck was fully half a mile from the rock of the mate, but much nearer to the reef than it had been the previous night. "Could it but ground on the rocks," thought the young man, "it would be a most blessed event." The thing was possible, though the first half hour of his observations told him that its drift was in the direction of the open passage so often named, rather than toward the nearest rocks. Still, that drift brought Rose each minute nearer and nearer to himself again. In looking round, however, the young man saw the boat. It was a quarter of a mile distant, with open water between them, apparently grounded on a rock for it was more within the reef than he was himself. He must have passed it in the dark, and the boat had been left to obey the wind and currents, and to drift to the spot where it then lay.

Mulford shouted aloud when he saw the boat, and at once determined to swim in quest of it, as soon as he had collected a little refreshment from among the sea-weed. On taking a look at his rock by daylight, he saw that its size was quadrupled to the eye by the falling of the tide, and that water was lying in several of the cavities of its uneven surface. At first he supposed this to be sea-water left by the flood; but, reflecting a moment, he remembered the rain, and he hoped it might be possible that one little cavity, containing two or three gallons of the fluid, would turn out to be fresh. Kneeling beside it, he applied his lips in feverish haste, and drank the sweetest draught that had ever passed his lips. Slaking his thirst, which had begun again to be painfully severe, he arose with a heart overflowing with gratitude—could he only get Rose to that narrow and barren rock, it would seem to be an earthly paradise. Mulford next made his scanty, but all things considered, sufficient meal, drank moderately afterward, and then turned his attention and energies toward the boat, which, though now aground and fast, might soon float on the rising tide, and drift once more beyond his reach. It was his first intention to swim directly for his object; but, just when about to enter the water, he saw with horror the fins of at least a dozen sharks, which were prowling about in the deeper water of the reef, and almost encircling his hold. To throw himself in the midst of such enemies would be madness, and he stopped to reflect, and again to look about him. For the first time that morning, he took a survey of the entire horizon, to see if anything were in sight; for, hitherto, his thoughts had been too much occupied with Rose and her companions, to remember anything else. To the northward and westward he distinctly saw the upper sails of a large ship, that was standing on a wind to the northward and eastward. As there was no port to which a vessel of that character would be likely to be bound in that quarter of the Gulf to which such a course would lead, Mulford at once inferred it was the sloop-of-war, which, after having examined the islets, at the Dry Tortugas, and finding them deserted, was beating up, either to go into Key West, or to pass to the southward of the reef again, by the passage through which she had come as lately as the previous day. This was highly encouraging; and could he only get to the boat, and remove the party from the wreck before it sunk, there was now every prospect of a final escape.

To the southward, also, the mate fancied he saw a sail.
It was probably a much smaller vessel than the ship in
the northwest, and at a greater distance. It might, however, be the lofty sails of some large craft standing along
the reef, going westward, bound to New Orleans, or to that
new and important port, Point Isabel: or it might be some
wrecker, or other craft, edging away into the passage. As
it was, it appeared only as a speck in the horizon, and was
too far off to offer much prospect of succor.

Thus acquainted with the state of things around him,
Mulford gave his attention seriously to his duties. He was
chiefly afraid that the returning tide might lift the boat from
the rock on which it had grounded, and that it would float
beyond his reach. Then there was the frightful and ever-
increasing peril of the wreck, and the dreadful fate that so
inevitably menaced those that it held, were not relief prompt.
This thought goaded him nearly to desperation, and he felt
at moments almost ready to plunge into the midst of the
sharks, and fight his way to his object.

But reflection showed him a less hazardous way of making
an effort to reach the boat. The shark's fins described a
semicircle only, as had been the case of his single attendant
during the night, and he thought that the shoalness of the
water prevented their going farther than they did, in a south-
easterly direction, which was that of the boat. He well knew
that a shark required sufficient water to sink beneath its
prey, ere it made its swoop, and that it uniformly turned on
its back, and struck upward whenever it gave one of its voracious bites. This was owing to the greater length of its
upper than of its lower jaw, and Mulford had heard it was
a physical necessity of its formation. Right or wrong, he
determined to act on this theory, and began at once to wade
along the part of the reef that his enemies seemed unwilling
to approach.

Had our young mate a weapon of any sort larger than his
knife, he would have felt greater confidence in his success.
As it was, however, he drew that knife, and was prepared to
sell his life dearly should a foe assail him. No sooner was
his step heard in the water, than the whole group of sharks

were set in violent motion, glancing past, and frequently quite near him, as if aware their intended prey was about to escape. Had the water deepened much, Harry would have returned at once, for a conflict with such numbers would have been hopeless; but it did not; on the contrary, it shoaled again, after a very short distance, at which it had been waist-deep; and Mulford found himself wading over a long, broad surface of rock, and that directly toward the boat, through water that seldom rose above his knees, and which, occasionally, scarcely covered his feet. There was no absolutely naked rock near him, but there seemed to be acres of that which might be almost said to be awash. Amid the greedy throng that endeavored to accompany him, the mate even fancied he recognized the enormous fins of his old companion, who sailed to and fro in the crowd in a stately manner, as if merely a curious looker-on of his own movements. It was the smaller, and probably the younger sharks, that betrayed the greatest hardihood and voracity. One or two of these made fierce swoops toward Harry, as if bent on having him at every hazard; but they invariably glided off when they found their customary mode of attack resisted by the shoalness of the water.

Our young mate got ahead but slowly, being obliged to pay a cautious attention to the movements of his escort. Sometimes he was compelled to wade up to his arms in order to cross narrow places, that he might get on portions of the rock that were nearly bare; and once he was actually compelled to swim eight or ten yards. Nevertheless, he did get on, and after an hour of this sort of work, he found himself within a hundred yards of the boat, which lay grounded near a low piece of naked rock, but separated from it by a channel of deep water, into which all the sharks rushed in a body, as if expressly to cut off his escape. Mulford now paused to take breath, and to consider what ought to be done. On the spot where he stood he was quite safe, though ankle-deep in the sea, the shallow water extending to a considerable distance on all sides of him, with the single exception of the channel in his front. He stood on the very verge of that channel, and could see in the pellucid element before him, that it was deep enough to float a vessel of some size.

To venture into the midst of twenty sharks required desperation, and Harry was not yet reduced to that. He had been so busy in making his way to the point where he stood as to have no leisure to look for the wreck; but he now turned his eyes in quest of that all-interesting object. He saw the shawl fluttering in the breeze, and that was all he could see. Tier had contrived to keep it flying as a signal where he was to be found, but the hull of the schooner had sunk so low in the water that they who were seated on its keel were not visible even at the short distance which now separated them from Mulford. Encouraged by this signal, and animated by the revived hope of still saving his companions, Harry turned toward the channel, half inclined to face every danger rather than to wait any longer. At that moment the fins were all gliding along the channel from him, and in the same direction. Some object drew the sharks away in a body, and the young mate let himself easily into the water, and swam as noiselessly as he could toward the boat.

It was a fearful trial, but Mulford felt that everything depended on his success. Stimulated by his motive, and strengthened by the food and water taken an hour before, never had he shown so much skill and power in the water. In an incredibly short period he was half-way across the channel, still swimming strong and unharmed. A few strokes more sent him so near the boat that hope took full possession of his soul, and he shouted in exultation. That indiscreet but natural cry, uttered so near the surface of the sea, turned every shark upon him, as the pack springs at the fox in view. Mulford was conscious of the folly of his cry the instant it escaped him, and involuntarily he turned his head to note the effect on his enemies. Every fin was gliding toward him—a dark array of swift and furious foes. Ten thousand bayonets, levelled in their line, could not have been one half as terrible, and the efforts of the young man became nearly frantic. But strong as he was, and ready in the element, what is the movement of a man in the water compared to that of a vigorous and voracious fish? Mulford could see those fins coming on like a tempest, and he had just given up all hope, and was feeling his flesh creep with terror, when his foot hit the rock. Giving himself an onward plunge, he threw his body upward toward the boat, and into so much shoaler water, at least a dozen feet by that single effort. Recovering his legs as soon as possible, he turned to look behind him. The water seemed alive with fins, each pair gliding back and forth, as the bull-dog bounds in front of the ox's muzzle. Just then a light-colored object glanced past the young man, so near as almost to touch him. It was a shark that had actually turned on its back to seize its prey, and was only prevented from succeeding by being driven from the line of its course by hitting the slimy rock, over which it was compelled to make its plunge. The momentum with which it came on, added to the inclination of the rock, forced the head and half of the body of this terrible assailant into the air, giving the intended victim an opportunity of seeing from what a fate he had escaped. Mulford avoided this fish without much trouble, however, and the next instant he threw himself into the boat, on the bottom of which he lay panting with the violence of his exertions, and unable to move under the reaction which now came over his system.

The mate lay in the bottom of the boat, exhausted and unable to rise, for several minutes; during that space he devoutly returned thanks to God for his escape, and bethought him of the course he was next to pursue, in order to effect the rescue of his companions. The boat was larger than common. It was also well equipped—a mast and sail lying along with the oars on its thwarts. The rock placed Harry to windward of the wreck, and by the time he felt sufficiently revived to rise and look about him, his plan of proceeding was fully arranged in his own mind. Among other things that he saw, as he still lay in the bottom of the boat, was a breaker which he knew contained fresh water, and a bread-bag. These were provisions that it was customary for the men to make when employed on boat duty;

and the articles had been left where he now saw them, in the hurry of the movements, as the brig quitted the islet.

Harry rose the instant he felt his strength returning. Striking the breaker with his foot, and feeling the basket with a hand, he ascertained that the one held its water, and the other its bread. This was immense relief, for by this time the sufferings of the party on the wreck must be returning with redoubled force. The mate then stepped to the mast, and fitted the sprit to the sail, knowing that the latter would be seen fluttering in the wind by those on the wreck, and carry joy to their hearts. After this considerate act, he began to examine into the position of the boat. It was still aground, having been left by the tide; but the water had already risen several inches, and by placing himself on a gunwale, so as to bring the boat on its bilge, and pushing with an oar, he soon got it into deep water. It only remained to haul aft the sheet, and right the helm, to be standing through the channel, at a rate that promised a speedy deliverance to his friends, and, most of all, to Rose.

Mulford glanced past the rocks and shoals, attended by the whole company of the sharks. They moved before, behind and on each side of him, as if unwilling to abandon their prey, even after he had got beyond the limits of their power to do him harm. It was not an easy thing to manage the boat in that narrow and crooked channel, with no other guide for the courses than the eye, and it required so much of the mate's vigilance to keep clear of the sharp angles of the rocks, that he could not once cast his eyes aside, to look for the fluttering shawl, which now composed the standing signal of the wreck. At length the boat shot through the last passage of the reef, and issued into open water. Mulford knew that he must come out half a mile at least to leeward of his object, and, without even raising his head, he flattened in the sheet, put his helm down, and luffed close to the wind. Then, and then only, did he venture to look around him.

Our mate felt his heart leap towards his mouth, as he observed the present state of the wreck. It was dead to windward of him, in the first place, and it seemed to be entirely

submerged. He saw the shawl fluttering as before ; for Tier
had fastened one corner to a button-hole of his own jacket,
and another to the dress of Biddy, leaving the part which
might be called the fly to rise at moments almost perpendicularly in the air, in a way to render it visible at some distance. He saw also the heads and the bodies of those on
the schooner's bottom, but to him they appeared to be standing in, or on, the water. The distance may have contributed
a little to this appearance, but no doubt remained that so
much air had escaped from the hold of the vessel, as to
permit it to sink altogether beneath the surface of the
sea. It was time, indeed, to proceed to the relief of the
sufferers.

Notwithstanding the boat sailed particularly fast, and
worked beautifully, it could not equal the impatience of
Mulford to get on. Passing away to the northeast a sufficient distance, as he thought, to weather on the wreck, the
young man tacked at last, and had the happiness to see that
every foot he proceeded was now in a direct line toward
Rose. It was only while tacking he perceived that all the
fins had disappeared. He felt little doubt that they had deserted him, in order to push for the wreck, which offered so
much larger, and so much more attainable prey. This increased his feverish desire to get on, the boat seeming to
drag, in his eyes, at the very moment it was leaving a wake
full of eddies and little whirlpools. The wind was steady,
but it seemed to Mulford that the boat was set to leeward
of her course by a current, though this could hardly have
been the case, as the wreck, the sole mark of his progress,
would have had at least as great a drift as the boat. At
length Mulford—to him it appeared to be an age ; in truth
it was after a run of about twenty minutes—came near the
goal he so earnestly sought, and got an accurate view of
the state of the wreck and of those on it. The hull of the
schooner had, in truth, sunk entirely beneath the surface of
the sea ; and the party it sustained stood already knee-deep
in the water. This was sufficiently appalling ; but the presence of the sharks, who were crowding around the spot,
rendered the whole scene frightful. To the young mate it

seemed as if he must still be too late to save Rose from a
fate more terrible than drowning, for his boat fell so far to
leeward as to compel him to tack once more. As he swept
past the wreck, he called out to encourage his friends, beg-
ging them to be of good heart for five minutes longer, when
he should be able to reach them. Rose held out her arms
entreatingly, and the screams of Mrs. Budd and Biddy,
which were extorted by the closer and closer approach of
the sharks, proclaimed the imminency of the danger they
ran, and the importance of not losing a moment of time.

Mulford took his distance with a seaman's eye, and the
boat went about like a top. The latter fell off, and the sail
filled on the other tack. Then the young mariner saw, with
a joy no description can portray, that he looked to windward of the fluttering shawl, toward which his little craft
was already flying. He afterward believed that shawl alone
prevented the voracious party of fish from assailing those
on the wreck, for, though there might not yet be sufficient
depth of water to allow of their customary mode of attack,
creatures of their voracity did not always wait for such con-
veniences. But the boat was soon in the midst of the fins,
scattering them in all directions; and Mulford let go his
sheet, put his helm down, and sprang forward to catch the
extended arms of Rose.

It might have been accident, or it might have been the
result of skill and interest in our heroine, but certain it is,
that the bows of the boat came on the wreck precisely at
the place where Rose stood, and her hand was the first object that the young man touched.

"Take my aunt first," cried Rose, resisting Mulford's
efforts to lift her into the boat; "she is dreadfully alarmed,
and can stand with difficulty."

Although two of Rose's activity and lightness might
have been drawn into the boat, while the process was going on in behalf of the widow, Mulford lost no time in
discussion, but did as he was desired. First directing Tier
to hold on to the painter, he applied his strength to the
arms of Mrs. Budd, and, assisted by Rose and Biddy, got
her safely into the boat, over its bows. Rose now waited

not for assistance, but followed her aunt with a haste that
proved fear lent her strength in despite her long fast.
Biddy came next, though clumsily, and not without trouble,
and Jack Tier followed the instant he was permitted so to
do. Of course, the boat, no longer held by its painter,
drifted away from the spot, and the hull of the schooner,
relieved from the weight of four human beings, rose so
near the surface again as to bring a small line of its keel
out of water. No better evidence could have been given
of the trifling power which sustained it, and of the timely
nature of the succor brought by Mulford. Had the boat
remained near the schooner, it would have been found half
an hour later that the hull had sunk slowly out of sight,
finding its way, doubtless, inch by inch, toward the bottom
of the Gulf.

By this time the sun was well up, and the warmth of
the hour, season, and latitude was shed on the sufferers.
There was an old sail in the boat, and in this the party
dried their limbs and feet, which were getting to be numb
by their long immersion. Then the mate produced the
bag and opened it, in quest of bread. A small portion
was given to each, and, on looking further, the mate discovered that a piece of boiled ship's beef had been secreted
in this receptacle. Of this also he gave each a moderate
slice, taking a larger portion for himself, as requiring less
precaution. The suffering of the party from hunger was
far less than that they endured from thirst. Neither had
been endured long enough seriously to enfeeble them or
render a full meal very dangerous, but the thirst had been
much the hardest to be borne. Of this fact Biddy soon
gave audible evidence.

"The mate is good," she said, "and the bread tastes
swate and refreshing, but wather is a blessed thing. Can
you no give us one dhrap of the wather that falls from heaven,
Mr. Mulford; for this wather of the sea is of no use but to
drown Christians in?"

In an instant the mate had opened a breaker, and filled
the tin pot which is almost always to be found in a boat.
Biddy said no more, but her eyes pleaded so eloquently,

that Rose begged the faithful creature might have the first drink. One eager swallow went down, and then a cry of disappointment succeeded. The water was salt, and had been put in the breaker for ballast. The other breaker was tried with the same success.

"It is terrible to be without one drop of water," murmured Rose, "and this food makes it more necessary than ever."

"Patience, patience, dearest Rose,—patience for ten minutes, and you shall all drink," answered the mate filling the sail and keeping the boat away while speaking. "There is water, God be praised, on the rock to which I first swam, and we will secure it before another day's sun help to make it evaporate."

This announcement quieted the longings of those who endured a thirst which disappointment rendered doubly hard to bear; and away the boat glided toward the rock. As he now flew over the distance, lessened more than one half by the drift of the wreck, Mulford recalled the scene through which he had so painfully passed the previous night. As often happens, he shuddered at the recollection of things which, at the moment, a desperate resolution had enabled him to encounter with firmness. Still, he thought nothing less than the ardent desire to save Rose could have carried him through the trial with the success which attended his struggles. The dear being at his side asked a few explanations of what had passed; and she bowed her head and wept, equally with pain and delight, as imagination pictured to her the situation of her betrothed, amid that waste of water, with his fearful companions, and all in the hours of deep night.

But that was over now. There was the rock—the blessed rock on which Mulford had so accidentally struck, close before them—and presently they were all on it. The mate took the pot and ran to the little reservoir, returning with a sweet draught for each of the party.

"A blessed, blessed thing is wather!" exclaimed Biddy, this time finding the relief she sought, "and a thousand blessings on you, Mr. Mulford, who have niver done us anything but good."

Rose looked a still higher eulogy on the young man, and even Mrs. Budd had something commendatory and grateful to say. Jack Tier was silent, but he had all his eyes about him, as he now proved.

"We 've all on us been so much taken up with our own affairs," remarked the steward's assistant, "that we 've taken but little notice of the neighborhood. If that is n't the brig, Mr. Mulford, running through this very passage, with stun'sails set alow and aloft, I don't know the Molly Swash when I see her!"

"The brig!" exclaimed the mate, recollecting the vessels he had seen at the break of day, for the first time in hours. "Can it be possible that the craft I made out to the southward, is the brig?"

"Look, and judge for yourself, sir. There she comes, like a race-horse, and if she holds her present course, she must pass somewhere within a mile or so of us, if we stay where we are."

Mulford did look, as did all with him. There was the Swash, sure enough, coming down before the wind, and under a cloud of canvas. She might be still a league, or a league and a half distant, but, at the rate at which she was travelling, that distance would soon be past. She was running through the passage, no doubt with a view to proceed to the Dry Tortugas, to look after the schooner, Spike having the hope that he had dodged his pursuers on the coast of Cuba. The mate now looked for the ship, in the northwestern board, believing, as he did, that she was the sloop-of-war. That vessel had gone about, and was standing to the southward, on a taut bowline. She was still a long way off, three or four leagues at least, but the change she had made in her position, since last seen, proved that she was a great sailer. Then she was more than hull down, whereas, now, she was near enough to let the outline of a long, straight fabric be discovered beneath her canvas.

"It is hardly possible that Spike should not see the vessel here in the northern board," Mulford observed to Tier, who had been examining the ship with him. "The lookout is usually good on board the Swash, and, just now, should certainly be as good as common. Spike is no dawdler with serious business before him.''

'' He 's a willain ! '' muttered Jack Tier.

The mate regarded his companion with some surprise. Jack was a very insignificant-looking personage in common, and one would scarcely pause to give him a second look, unless it might be to laugh at his rotundity and little waddling legs. But, now, the mate fancied he was swelling with feelings that actually imparted somewhat more than usual stature and dignity to his appearance. His face was full of indignation, and there was something about the eye, that to Mulford was inexplicable. As Rose, however, had related to him the scene that took place on the islet, at the moment when Spike was departing, the mate supposed that Jack still felt a portion of the resentment that such a collision would be apt to create. From the expression of Jack's countenance at that instant, it struck him Spike might not be exactly safe, should accident put it in the power of the former to do him an injury.

It was now necessary to decide on the course that ought to be pursued. The bag contained sufficient food to last the party several days, and a gallon of water still remained in the cavity of the rock. This last was collected and put in one of the breakers, which was emptied of the salt water in order to receive it. As water, however, was the great necessity in that latitude, Mulford did not deem it prudent to set sail with so small a supply, and he accordingly commenced a search on some of the adjacent rocks, Jack Tier accompanying him. They succeeded in doubling their stock of water, and collected several shell-fish, that the females found exceedingly grateful and refreshing. On the score of hunger and thirst, indeed, no one was now suffering. By judiciously sipping a little water at a time, and retaining it in the mouth before swallowing, the latter painful feeling had been gotten rid of; and as for food, there was even more than was actually needed, and that of a very good quality. It is probable that standing in the water for hours, as Rose, and her aunt, and Biddy had been obliged to do, had contributed to lessen the pain endured from thirst, though they had all suffered a good deal from that cause, especially while the sun shone.

Mulford and Tier were half an hour in obtaining the water. By the end of that period the brigantine was so near as to render her hull distinctly visible. It was high time to decide on their future course. The sail had been brailed when the boat reached the rock, and the boat itself lay on the side of the latter opposite to the brig, and where no part of it could be seen by those on board the Swash, with the exception of the mast. Under the circumstances, therefore, Mulford thought it wisest to remain where they were, and let the vessel pass, before they attempted to proceed toward Key West, their intended place of refuge. In order to do this, however, it was necessary to cause the whole party to lie down, in such a way as to be hid by the inequalities in the rock, as it was now very evident the brig would pass within half a mile of them. Hitherto, it was not probable that they had been seen, and by using due caution, the chances of Spike's overlooking them altogether amounted nearly to certainty.

The necessary arrangements were soon made, the boat's masts unstepped, the party placed behind their covers, and the females comfortably bestowed in the spare sail, where they might get a little undisturbed sleep after the dreadful night, or morning, they had passed. Even Jack Tier lay down to catch his nap, as the most useful manner of bestowing himself for a couple of hours; the time Mulford had mentioned as the period of their stay where they were.

As for the mate, vigilance was his portion, and he took his position, hid like all the rest, where he could watch the movements of his old craft. In about twenty minutes, the brig was quite near; so near that Mulford not only saw the people on board her, who showed themselves in the rigging, but fancied he could recognize their persons. As yet, nothing had occurred in the way of change, but, just as the Swash got abreast of the rock, she began to take in her studding-sails, and that hurriedly, as is apt to occur on board a vessel in sudden emergencies. Our young man was a little alarmed at first, believing that they might have been

discovered, but he was soon induced to think that the crew
of the brigantine had just then begun to suspect the character of the ship to the northward. That vessel had been
drawing near all this time, and was now only some three
leagues distant. Owing to the manner in which she headed,
or bows on, it was not a very easy matter to tell the character of this stranger, though the symmetry and squareness
of his yards rendered it nearly certain he was a cruiser.
Though Spike could not expect to meet his old acquaintance
here, after the chase he had so lately led her, down on the
opposite coast, he might and would have his misgivings, and
Mulford thought it was his intention to haul up close round
the northern angle of the reef, and maintain his advantage
of the wind, over the stranger. If this were actually done,
it might expose the boat to view, for the brig would pass
within a quarter of a mile of it, and on the side of the rock
on which it lay. It was too late, however, to attempt a
change, since the appearance of human beings in such a
place would be certain to draw the brig's glasses on them,
and the glasses must at once let Spike know who they were.
It remained, therefore, only to await the result as patiently
as possible.

A very few minutes removed all doubt. The brig hauled
as close round the reef as she dared to venture, and in a
very short time the boat lay exposed to view to all on board
her. The vessel was now so near that Mulford plainly saw
the boatswain get upon the coach-house, or little hurricane-
house deck, where Spike stood examining the ship with his
glass, and point out the boat, where it lay at the side of the
rock. In an instant, the glass was levelled at the spot, and
the movements on board the brig immediately betrayed to
Mulford that the boat was recognized. Sail was shortened
on board the Swash, and men were seen preparing to lower
her stern boat, while everything indicated that the vessel
was about to be hove-to. There was no time now to be lost,
but the young man immediately gave the alarm.

No sooner did the party arise and show themselves, than
the crew of the Swash gave three cheers. By the aid of the
glass, Spike doubtless recognized their persons, and the fact

was announced to the men, by way of stimulating their exertions. This gave an additional spur to the movements of those on the rock, who hastened into their own boat, and made sail as soon as possible.

It was far easier to do all that has been described, than to determine on the future course. Capture was certain if the fugitives ventured into the open water, and their only hope was to remain on the reef. If channels for the passage of the boat could be found, escape was highly probable, as the schooner's boat could sail much faster than the brig's boat could row, fast as Mulford knew the last to be. But the experience of the morning had told the mate that the rock rose too near the surface, in many places, for the boat, small as it was, to pass over it; and he must trust a great deal to chance. Away he went, however, standing along a narrow channel, through which the wind just permitted him to lay, with the sail occasionally shaking.

By this time the Swash had her boat in the water, manned with four powerful oars, Spike steering it in his own person. Our young mate placed Tier in the bows, to point out the deepest water, and kept his sail a rap full, in order to get ahead as fast as possible. Ahead he did get, but it was on a course that soon brought him out in the open water of the main passage through the reef, leaving Spike materially astern. The latter now rose in his boat, and made a signal with his hat, which the boatswain perfectly understood. The latter caused the brig to ware short round on her heel, and boarded his foretack in chase, hauling up into the passage as soon as he could again round the reef. Mulford soon saw that it would never do for him to venture far from the rocks, the brig going two feet to his one, though not looking quite as high as he did in the boat. But the Swash had her guns, and it was probable they would be used rather than he should escape. When distant two hundred yards from the reef, therefore, he tacked. The new course brought the fugitives nearly at right angles to that steered by Spike, who stood directly on, as if conscious that, sooner or later, such a rencounter must occur. It would seem that the tide was setting through the passage for when the boat of Mulford again reached the reef, it was considerably to windward of the channel out of which she had issued, and opposite to another which offered very opportunely for her entrance. Into this new channel, then, the mate somewhat blindly ran, feeling the necessity of getting out of gun-shot of the brig at every hazard. She at least could not follow him among the rocks, let Spike, in his boat, proceed as he might.

According to appearances, Spike was not likely to be very successful. He was obliged to diverge from his course, in order to go into the main passage at the very point where Mulford had just before done the same thing, and pull along the reef to windward, in order to get into the new channel, into which the boat he was pursuing had just entered. This brought him not only astern again, but a long bit astern, inasmuch as he was compelled to make the circuit described. On he went, however, as eager in the chase as the hound with his game in view.

Mulford's boat seemed to fly, and glided ahead at least three feet to that of Spike's two. The direction of the channel it was in brought it pretty close to the wind, but the water was quite smooth, and our mate managed to keep the sail full, and his little craft at the same time quite near the weatherly side of the rocks. In the course of ten minutes the fugitives were fully a mile from the brig, which was unable to follow them, but kept standing off and on, in the main passage, waiting the result. At one time Mulford thought the channel would bring him out into open water again, on the northern side of the reef, and more than a mile to the eastward of the point where the ship-channel in which the Swash was plying commenced ; but an accidental circumstance prevented his standing in far enough to ascertain the fact. That circumstance was as follows :

In running a mile and a half over the reef, in the manner described, Mulford had left the boat of Spike quite half a mile astern. He was now out of gun-shot from the brig, or at least beyond the range of her grape, the only missile he feared, and so far to windward that he kept his eye on every opening to the southward, which he fancied might allow of his making a stretch deeper into the mazes of the reef, among which he believed it easiest for him to escape, and to weary the oarsmen of his pursuers. Two or three of these openings offered as he glided along, but it struck him that they all looked so high that the boat would not lay through them—an opinion in which he was right. At length he came abreast of one that seemed straight and clear of obstacles, as far as he could see, and through which he might run with a flowing sheet. Down went his helm, and about went his boat, running away to the southward as fast as ever.

Had Spike followed, doubled the same shoal, and kept away again in the same channel as had been done by the boat he chased, all his hopes of success must have vanished at once. This he did not attempt, therefore; but sheering into one of the openings which the mate had rejected, he cut off quite half a mile in his distance. This was easy enough for him to accomplish, as a row-boat would pull even easier, near to the wind, than with the wind broad on its bow. In consequence of this short cut, therefore, Spike was actually crossing out into Mulford's new channel, just as the latter had handsomely cleared the mouth of the opening through which he effected his purpose.

It is scarcely necessary to say that the two boats must have been for a few minutes quite near to each other; so near, indeed, did the fugitives now pass to their pursuers, that it would have been easy for them to have conversed, had they been so disposed. Not a word was spoken, however, but Mulford went by, leaving Spike about a hundred yards astern. This was a trying moment to the latter, and the devil tempted him to seek his revenge. He had not come unarmed on his enterprise, but three or four loaded muskets lay in the stern-sheets of his yawl. He looked at his men, and saw that they could not hold out much longer to pull as they had been pulling. Then he looked at Mulford's boat, and saw it gliding away from him at a rate that would shortly place it another half mile in advance. He seized a musket, and raised it to his shoulder, nay, was in the act of taking aim at his mate, when Rose, who watched his movements, threw herself before Harry, and if she did not actually save his life, at least prevented Spike's attempt on it for that occasion. In the course of the next ten minutes the fugitives had again so far gained on their pursuers, that the latter began to see that their efforts were useless. Spike muttered a few bitter curses, and told his men to lay on their oars.

"It 's well for the runaway," he added, "that the gal put herself between us, else would his grog have been stopped forever. I 've long suspected this; but had I been sure of it, the Gulf Stream would have had the keeping of his body, the first dark night we were in it together. Lay on your oars, men, lay on your oars; I 'm afeared the villain will get through our fingers, a'ter all."

The men obeyed, and then, for the first time, did they turn their heads, to look at those they had been so vehemently pursuing. The other boat was quite half a mile from them, and it had again tacked. This last occurrence induced Spike to pull slowly ahead, in quest of another short passage to cut the fugitives off; but no such opening offered.

"There he goes about again, by George!" exclaimed Spike. "Give way, lads—give way; an easy stroke, for if he is embayed, he can't escape us!"

Sure enough, poor Mulford *was* embayed, and could see no outlet by which to pass ahead. He tacked his boat two or three times, and he wore round as often; but on every side shoals, or rocks that actually rose above the surface of the water, impeded his course. The fact was not to be concealed; after all his efforts, and so many promises of success, not only was his further progress ahead cut off, but equally so was retreat. The passage was not wide enough to admit the hope of getting by his pursuers, and the young man came to the conclusion that his better course was to submit with dignity to his fate. For himself he had no hope—he knew Spike's character too well for that; but he did not apprehend any great immediate danger to his companions. Spike had a coarse, brutal admiration for Rose! but her expected fortune, which was believed to be of more amount

than was actually the case, was a sort of pledge that he
would not willingly put himself in a situation that would
prevent the possibility of enjoying it. Strange, hurried, and
somewhat confused thoughts passed through Harry Mulford's mind, as he brailed his sail, and waited for his captors
to approach and take possession of his boat and himself.
This was done quietly, and with very few words on the part
of Spike.

Mulford would have liked the appearance of things
better had his old commander cursed him, and betrayed
other signs of the fury that was boiling in his very soul.
On the contrary, never had Stephen Spike seemed more
calm, or under better self-command. He smiled, and
saluted Mrs. Budd, just as if nothing unpleasant had
occurred, and alluded to the sharpness of the chase with
facetiousness and seeming good-humor. The females
were deceived by this manner, and hoped, after all, that the
worst that would happen would be a return to their old
position on board the Swash. This was being so much
better off than their horrible situation on the wreck, that
the change was not frightful to them.

"What has become of the schooner, Mr. Mulford?"
asked Spike, as the boats began to pass down the channel
to return to the brig—two of the Swash's men taking
their seats in that which had been captured, along with
their commander, while the other two got a tow from the
use of the sail. "I see you have the boat here that we
used alongside of her, and suppose you know something of
the craft itself."

"She capsized with us in a squall," answered the mate,
"and we only left the wreck this morning."

"Capsized?—hum—that was a hard fate, to be sure,
and denotes bad seamanship. Now I 've sailed all sorts
of craft these forty years, or five-and-thirty at least, and
never capsized anything in my life. Stand by there for'ard
to hold on by that rock."

A solitary cap of the coral rose above the water two or
three feet, close to the channel, and was the rock to which
Spike alluded. It was only some fifty feet in diameter,

and of an oval form, rising quite above the ordinary tides, as was apparent by its appearance. It is scarcely necessary to say it had no other fresh water than that which occasionally fell on its surface, which surface being quite smooth, retained very little of the rain it received. The boat was soon alongside of this rock, where it was held broadside-to by the two seamen.

"Mr. Mulford, do me the favor to step up here," said Spike, leading the way on to the rock himself. "I have a word to say to you before we get on board the old Molly once more."

Mulford silently complied, fully expecting that Spike intended to blow his brains out, and willing the bloody deed should be done in a way to be as little shocking to Rose as circumstances would allow. But Spike manifested no such intention. A more refined cruelty was uppermost in his mind; and his revenge was calculated, and took care to fortify itself with some of the quibbles and artifices of the law. He might not be exactly right in his legal reservations, but he did not the less rely on their virtue.

"Hark 'ee, Mr. Mulford," said Spike, sharply, as soon as both were on the rock, "you have run from my brig, thereby showing your distaste for her; and I 've no disposition to keep a man who wishes to quit me. Here you are, sir, on *terrum firm*, as the scholars call it; and here you have my full permission to remain. I wish you a good morning, sir; and will not fail to report, when we get in, that you left the brig of your own pleasure."

"You will not have the cruelty to abandon me on this naked rock, Captain Spike, and that without a morsel of food, or a drop of water."

"Wather is a blessed thing!" exclaimed Biddy. "Do not think of lavin' the gentleman widout wather."

"You left *me*, sir, without food or water, and you can fit out your own rock; yes, d——e, sir, you left me *under fire*, and that is a thing no true-hearted man would have thought of. Stand by to make sail, boys; and if he offer to enter the boat, pitch him out with the boat-hooks."

Spike was getting angry, and he entered the boat again without perceiving that Rose had left it. Light of foot, and resolute of spirit, the beautiful girl, handsomer than ever perhaps, by her excited feelings and dishevelled hair, had sprung on the rock, as Spike stepped into the boat forward, and when the latter turned round, after loosening the sail, he found he was drifting away from the very being who was the object of all his efforts. Mulford, believing that Rose was to be abandoned as well as himself, received the noble girl in his arms, though ready to implore Spike, on his knees, to return and at least to take her off. But Spike wanted no solicitation on that point. He returned of his own accord, and had just reached the rock again when a report of a gun drew all eyes toward the brig.

The Swash had again run out of the passage, and was beating up, close to the reef as she dared to go, with a signal flying. All the seamen at once understood the cause of this hint. The strange sail was getting too near, and everybody could see that it was the sloop-of-war. Spike looked at Rose, a moment in doubt. But Mulford raised his beloved in his arms, and carried her to the side of the rock, stepping on board the boat.

Spike watched the movements of the young man with jealous vigilance, and no sooner was Rose placed on her seat, than he motioned significantly to the mate to quit the boat.

"I cannot and will not voluntarily, Captain Spike," answered Harry, calmly. "It would be committing a sort of suicide."

A sign brought two of the men to the captain's assistance. While the latter held Rose in her place, the sailors shoved Harry on the rock again. Had Mulford been disposed to resist, these two men could not very easily have ejected him from the boat, if they could have done it at all ; but he knew there were others in reserve, and feared that blood might be shed, in the irritated state of Spike, in the presence of Rose. While, therefore, he would not be accessary to his own destruction, he would not engage in what he knew would prove not only a most harassing, but a bootless resistance. The consequence was that the boats proceeded, leaving him alone on the rock.

It was perhaps fortunate for Rose that she fainted. Her condition occupied her aunt and Biddy, and Spike was enabled to reach his brig without any further interruption. Rose was taken on board still nearly insensible, while her two female companions were so much confused and distressed, that neither could have given a reasonably clear account of what had just occurred. Not so with Jack Tier, however. That singular being noted all that passed seated in the eyes of the boat, away from the confusion that prevailed in its stern-sheets, and apparently undisturbed by it.

As the party was sailing back toward the brig, the lighthouse boat towing the Swash's yawl, Jack took as good an observation of the channels of that part of the reef as his low position would allow. He tried to form in his mind a sort of chart of the spot, for, from the instant Mulford was thus deserted, the little fellow had formed a stern resolution to attempt his rescue. How that was to be done, however, was more than he yet knew ; and when they reached the brig's side, Tier may be said to have been filled with good intentions, rather than with any very available knowledge to enable him to put them in execution.

As respects the two vessels, the arrival of Spike on board his own was not a moment too soon. The Poughkeepsie, for the stranger to the northward was now ascertained to be that sloop-of-war, was within long gun-shot by this time, and near enough to make certain, by means of her glasses, of the character of the craft with which she was closing. Luckily for the brig she lay in the channel so often mentioned, and through which both she and her present pursuer had so lately come, on their way to the northward. This brought her to windward, as the wind then stood, with a clear passage before her. Not a moment was lost. No sooner were the females sent below, than sail was made on the brig, and she began to beat through the passage, making long legs and short ones. She was chased, as a matter of course, and that hard, the difference in sailing between the two crafts not being sufficiently great to render the brigantine's escape by any means certain, while absolutely within the range of those terrible missiles that were used by the man-of-war's men.

But Spike soon determined not to leave a point so delicate as that of his own and his vessel's security to be decided by a mere superiority in the way of heels. The Florida Reef, with all its dangers, windings, and rocks, was as well known to him as the entrances to the port of New York. In addition to its larger channels, of which there are three or four, through which ships of size can pass, it had many others that would admit only vessels of a lighter draught of water. The brig was not flying light, it is true, but she was merely in good ballast trim, and passages would be available to her, into which the Poughkeepsie would not dare to venture. One of these lesser channels was favorably placed to further the escape of Spike, and he shoved the brig into it after the struggle had lasted less than an hour. This passage offered a shorter cut to the south side of the reef than the main channel, and the sloop-of-war, doubtless perceiving the uselessness of pursuit, under such circumstances, wore round on her heel, and came down through the main channel again, just entering the open water, near the spot where the schooner had sunk, as the sun was setting.

CHAPTER X.

"*Shallow.* Did her grandsire leave her seven hundred pound?
Evans. Aye, and her father is make her a petter penny.
Shallow. I know the young gentlewoman; she has good gifts.
Evans. Seven hundred pounds, and possibilities, is good gifts."
SHAKESPEARE.

AS for Spike, he had no intention of going to the southward of the Florida Reef again until his business called him there. The lost bag of doubloons was still gleaming before his imagination, and no sooner did the Poughkeepsie bear up, than he shortened sail, standing back and forth in his narrow and crooked channel, rather losing ground than gaining, though he took great pains not to let his artifice be seen. When the Poughkeepsie was so far to the northward as to render it safe, he took in everything but one or two of his lowest sails, and followed easily in the same direction. As the sloop-of-war carried her light and loftier sails, she remained visible to the people of the Swash long after the Swash had ceased to be visible to her. Profiting by this circumstance, Spike entered the main channel again some time before it was dark, and selected a safe anchorage there that was well known to him; a spot where sufficient sand had collected on the coral to make good holding ground, and where a vessel would be nearly embayed, though always to windward of her channel going out, by the formation of the reef. Here he anchored, in order to wait until morning ere he ventured farther north. During the whole of that dreadful day, Rose had remained in her cabin, disconsolate, nearly unable, as she was absolutely unwilling, to converse. Now it was that she felt the total insufficiency of a mind feeble as that of her aunt's to administer consolation to misery like her own. Nevertheless, the affectionate solicitude of Mrs. Budd, as well as that of the faithful creature, Biddy, brought some relief, and reason and resignation began slowly to resume their influence. Yet was the horrible picture of Harry, dying by inches, deserted in the midst of the waters on his solitary rock, ever present to her thoughts, until, once or twice, her feelings verged on madness. Prayer brought its customary relief, however; and we do not think that we much exaggerate the fact, when we say that Rose passed fully one half of that terrible afternoon on her knees.

As for Jack Tier, he was received on board the brig much as if nothing had happened. Spike passed and repassed him fifty times, without even an angry look, or a word of abuse; and the deputy-steward dropped quietly into the duties of his office, without meeting with either reproach or hindrance. The only allusion, indeed, that was made to his recent adventures, took place in a conversation that was held on the subject in the galley, the interlocutors being Jack himself, Josh, the steward, and Simon, the cook.

"Where you been scullin' to, 'bout on dat reef, Jack, wid dem 'ere women, I won'er now?" demanded Josh, after tasting the cabin soup, in order to ascertain how near it was to being done. "I t'ink it no great fun to dodge 'bout among dem rock in a boat, for anudder hurricane might come when a body least expeck him."

"Oh," said Jack, cavalierly, "two hurricanes no more come in one month, than two shot in the same hole. We've been turtlin', that's all. I wish we had in your coppers, cook, some of the critturs that we fell in with in our cruise."

"Wish 'e had, Master Steward, wid all my heart," answered the fat, glistening potentate of the galley. "But, hark'ee, Jack; what became of your young mate, can 'e tell? Some say he get kill at 'e Dry Tortugas, and some say he war' scullin' round in dat boat you hab, wid 'e young woman, eh?"

"Ah, boys," answered Jack, mournfully, "sure enough, what has become of him?"

"You know, why can't you tell? What good to hab secret among friend?"

"Are ye his friends, lads? Do you really feel as if you could give a poor soul in its agony a helpin' hand?"

"Why not?" said Josh, in a reproachful way. "Misser Mulford 'e bess mate dis brig ebber get; and I don't see why Cap'in Spike want to be rid of him."

"Because he's a willain!" returned Jack between his grated teeth. "D'ye know what that means in English, Master Josh; and can you and cook here, both of whom have sailed with the man years in and years out, say whether my words be true or not?"

"Dat as a body understand 'em. Accordin' to some rule, Stephen Spike not a werry honest man; but accordin' to 'nudder some, he as good as any body else."

"Yes, dat just be upshot of de matter," put in Simon, approvingly. "De whole case lie in dat meanin'."

"D'ye call it right to leave a human being to starve, or to suffer for water, on a naked rock, in the midst of the ocean?"

"Who do dat?"

"The willain who is captain of this brig; and all because he thinks young eyes and bloomin' cheeks prefer young eyes and bloomin' cheeks to his own grizzly beard and old look-outs."

"Dat bad; dat werry bad," said Josh, shaking his head, a way of denoting dissatisfaction in which Simon joined him; for no crime appeared sufficiently grave in the eyes of these two sleek and well-fed officials to justify such a punishment. "Dat mons'ous bad, and cap'in ought to know better dan do *dat*. I nebber starves a mouse, if I catches him in de bread-locker. Now, dat a sort of reason'ble punishment, too; but I nebber does it. If a mouse eat my bread, it do seem right to tell mouse dat he hab enough, and dat he must not eat any more for a week, or a mont', but it too cruel for me, and I nebber does it; no, I t'rows de little debil overboard, and lets him drown like a gentle'em."

"Y-e-s," drawled out Simon, in a philanthropical tone of voice, "dat 'e best way. What good it do to torment a fellow critter? If Misser Mulford run, why put him down run, and let him go, I say, only mulk his wages; but what good it do anybody to starve him? Now dis is my opinion, gentle'em, and dat is, dat starwation be wuss dan choleric. Choleric kill, I knows, and so does starwation kill; but of de two, gib me de choleric fuss; if I gets well of dat, den try starwation if you can."

"I'm glad to hear you talk in this manner, my hearties," put in Jack; "and I hope I may find you accommodatin' in a plan I've got to help the maty out of this difficulty. As a friend of Stephen Spike's I would do it; for it must be a terrible thing to die with such a murder on one's soul. Here's the boat that we pick'd up at the light-house, yonder, in tow of the brig at this minute; and there's everything in her comfortable for a good long run, as I know from having sailed in her; and what I mean is this: as we left Mr. Mulford, I took the bearings and distance of the rock he was on, d' ye understand, and think I could find my way back to it. You see the brig is travellin' slowly north ag'in, and afore long we shall be in the neighborhood of that very rock. We, cook and stewards, will be called on to keep an anchor-watch, if the brig fetches up, as I heard the captain tell the Spanish gentleman he thought she would; and then we can take the boat that's in the water and go and have a hunt for the maty."

The two blacks looked at Tier earnestly; then they turned their heads to look at each other. The idea struck each as bold and novel, but each saw serious difficulties in it. At length Josh, as became his superior station, took on himself the office of expressing the objections that occurred to his mind.

"Dat nebber do!" exclaimed the steward. "We be's quite willin' to sarve 'e mate, who's a good gentle'em, and as nice a young man as ever sung out, 'hard a-lee,' but we must t'ink little bit of number one; or, for dat matter, of number two, as Simon would be implercated as well as myself. If Cap'in Spike once knew we've lent a hand in sich a job, he'd never overlook it. I knows him well; and that is sayin' as much as need be said of any man's character.

You nebber catch *me* runnin' myself into his jaws; would rather fight a shark widout any knife. No, no—I knows him well. Den comes anudder werry unanswerable objecsh'un, and dat is, dat 'e brig owe bot' Simon and I money. Fifty dollars, each on us, if she owe one cent. Now, do you t'ink in cander, Jack, dat two color' gentle'em, like us, can t'row away our fortins like two sons of a York merchant dat has inherited a hundred t'ousand dollar tudder day?"

"There is no occasion for running at all, or for losing your wages."

"How you get 'e mate off, den? Can he walk away on de water? If so, let him go widout us. A werry good gentle'em is Misser Mulford, but not good enough to mulk Simon and me out of fifty dollar each."

"You will not hear my project, Josh, and so will never know what I would be at."

"Well, come, tell him jest as you surposes him. Now listen, Simon, so dat not a word be loss."

"My plan is to take the boat, if we anchor, as anchor I know we shall, and go and find the rock and bring Mr. Mulford off; then we can come back to the brig, and get on board ourselves, and let the mate sail away in the boat by himself. On this plan nobody will run, and no wages be mulcted."

"But dat take time and an anchor-watch last but two hour, surposin' even dat 'ey puts all t'ree of us in the same watch."

"Spike usually does that, you know. 'Let the cook and the stewards keep the midnight watch,' he commonly says, ' and that will give the foremost hands a better snooze.' "

"Yes, he do say dat, Josh," put in Simon, "most ebbery time we comes-to."

"I know he does, and surposes he will say it to-night, if he comes-to to-night. But a two-hour watch may not be long enough to do all you wants; and den, jest t'ink for a moment, should 'e cap'in come on deck and hail 'e forecastle, and find us all gone, I would n't be in your skin, Jack, for dis brig, in sich a kerlamity. I knows Cap'in Spike well; t'ree time I endebber to run myself, and each time he bring me up wid a round turn; so, nowadays, I nebber t'inks of sich a projeck any longer."

"But I do not intend to leave the forecastle without some one on it to answer a hail. No, all I want is a companion; for I do not like to go out on the reef at midnight, all alone. If one of you will go with me, the other can stay and answer the captain's hail, should he really come on deck in our watch—a thing very little likely to happen. When once his head is on his pillow, a'ter a hard day's work, it 's not very apt to be lifted ag'in without a call, or a squall. If you do know Stephen Spike well, Josh, I know him better."

"Well, Jack, dis here is a new idee, d' ye see, and a body must take time to consider on it. If Simon and I do ship for dis v'y'ge, 't will be for lub of Mr. Mulford, and not for his money or your'n."

This was all the encouragement of his project Jack Tier could obtain, on that occasion, from either his brother steward, or from the cook. These blacks were well enough disposed to rescue an innocent and unoffending man from the atrocious death to which Spike had condemned his mate, but neither lost sight of his own security and interest. They promised Tier not to betray him, however; and he had the fullest confidence in their pledges. They who live together in common, usually understand the feeling that prevails, on any given point, in their own set; and Jack felt pretty certain that Harry was a greater favorite in and about the camboose than the captain. On that feeling he relied, and he was fain to wait the course of events, ere he came to any absolute conclusion as to his own course.

The interview in the galley took place about half an hour before the brig anchored for the night. Tier, who often assisted on such occasions, went aloft to help secure the royal, one of the gaskets of which had got loose, and from the yard he had an excellent opportunity to take a look at the reef, the situation of the vessel, and the probable bearings of the rock on which poor Mulford had been devoted to a miserable death. This opportunity was much increased by Spike's hailing him, while on the yard, and ordering him to take a good look at the sloop-of-war, and at the same time to ascertain if any boats were " prowlin' about, in order to make a set upon us in the night." On receiving this welcome order, Jack answered with a cheerful " Ay, ay, sir," and standing up on the yard, he placed an arm around the mast, and remained for a long time making his observations. The command to look cut for boats would have been a sufficient excuse had he continued on the yard as long as it was light.

Jack had no difficulty in finding the Poughkeepsie, which was already through the passage, and no longer visible from the deck. She appeared to be standing to the northward and westward, under easy canvas, like a craft that was in no hurry. This fact was communicated to Spike in the usual way. The latter seemed pleased, and he answered in a hearty manner, just as if no difficulty had ever occurred between him and the steward's assistant.

" Very well, Jack ! bravo, Jack !—now take a good look for boats ; you 'll have light enough for that this half hour," cried the captain. " If any are out, you 'll find them pulling down the channel, or may be they 'll try to shorten the cut, by attempting to pull athwart the reef. Take a good and steady look for them, my man."

" Ay, ay, sir ; I 'll do all I can with naked eyes," answered Jack, " but I could do better, sir, if they would only send me up a glass by these here signal-halyards. With a glass, a fellow might speak with some sartainty."

Spike seemed struck with the truth of this suggestion : and he soon sent a glass aloft by the signal-halyards. Thus provided, Jack descended as low as the cross-trees, where he took his seat, and began a survey at his leisure. While thus employed, the brig was secured for the night, her decks were cleared, and the people were ordered to get their suppers, previously to setting an anchor-watch, and turning-in for the night. No one heeded the movements of Tier,—for Spike had gone into his own state-room,—with the exception of Josh and Simon. Those two worthies were still in the galley, conversing on the subject of Jack's recent communications ; and ever and anon one of them would stick his head out of the door and look aloft, withdrawing it, and shaking it significantly, as soon as his observations were ended.

As for Tier, he was seated quite at his ease; and having slung his glass to one of the shrouds, in a way to admit of its being turned as on a pivot, he had every opportunity for observing accurately, and at his leisure. The first thing Jack did, was to examine the channel very closely, in order to make sure that no boats were in it, after which he turned the glass with great eagerness toward the reef, in the almost hopeless office of ascertaining something concerning Mulford. In point of fact, the brig had anchored quite three leagues from the solitary rock of the deserted mate, and, favored as he was by his elevation, Jack could hardly expect to discern so small and low an object as that rock at so great a distance. Nevertheless, the glass was much better than common. It had been a present to Spike from one who was careful in his selections of such objects, and who had accidentally been under a serious obligation to the captain. Knowing the importance of a good look, as regards the boats, Spike had brought this particular instrument, of which, in common, he was very chary, from his own state-room, and sent it aloft, in order that Jack might have every available opportunity of ascertaining his facts. It was this glass, then, which was the means of the important discoveries the little fellow, who was thus perched on the fore-topmast crosstrees of the Swash, did actually succeed in making.

Jack actually started, when he first ascertained how distinctly and near the glass he was using brought distant objects. The gulls that sailed across its disk, though a league off, appeared as if near enough to be touched by the hand, and even their feathers gave out not only their hues, but their forms. Thus, too, was it with the surface of the ocean, of which the little waves that agitated the water of the reef might be seen tossing up and down, at more than twice the range of the Poughkeepsie's heaviest gun. Naked rocks, low and subdued, as they were in color, too, were to be noted, scattered up and down in the

panorama. At length Tier fancied his glass covered a
field that he recognized. It was distant, but might be
seen from his present elevation. A second look satisfied
him he was right; and he next clearly traced the last
channel in which they had endeavored to escape from
Spike, or that in which the boat had been taken. Following it along, by slowly moving the glass, he actually hit
the rock on which Mulford had been deserted. It was
peculiar in shape, size, and elevation above the water, and
connected with the circumstance of the channel, which
was easily enough seen by the color of the water, and
more easily from his height than if he had been in it, he
could not be mistaken. The little fellow's heart beat
quick as he made the glass move slowly over its surface,
anxiously searching for the form of the mate. It was not
to be seen. A second, and a more careful sweep of the
glass made it certain that the rock was deserted.

Although a little reflection might have satisfied any one,
Mulford was not to be sought in that particular spot, so
long after he had been left there, Jack Tier felt grievously
disappointed when he was first made certain of the accuracy of his observations. A minute later he began to reason
on the matter, and he felt more encouraged. The rock on
which the mate had been abandoned was smooth, and
could not hold any fresh water that might have been left
by the late showers. Jack also remembered that it had
neither sea-weed or shell-fish. In short, the utmost malice of Spike could not have selected, for the immolation
of his victim, a more suitable place. Now Tier had heard
Harry's explanation to Rose, touching the manner in which
he had waded and swum about the reef that very morning,
and it at once occurred to him that the young man had
too much energy and spirit to remain helpless and inactive
to perish on a naked rock, when there might be a possibility
of at least prolonging existence, if not of saving it. This
induced the steward to turn the glass slowly over the water,
and along all the ranges of visible rock that he could find
in that vicinity. For a long time the search was useless,
the distance rendering such an examination not only diffi-

cult, but painful. At length Jack, about to give up the
matter in despair, took one sweep with the glass nearer to
the brig, as much to obtain a general idea of the boat-
channels of the reef, as in any hope of finding Mulford,
when an object moving in the water came within the field
of the glass. He saw it but for an instant, as the glass
swept slowly past, but it struck him it was something that
had life, and was in motion. Carefully going over the same
ground again, after a long search, he again found what he
so anxiously sought. A good look satisfied him that he
was right. It was certainly a man wading along the shallow water of the reef, immersed to his waist—and it must
be Mulford.

So excited was Jack Tier by the discovery that he trembled like a leaf. A minute or two elapsed before he could
again use the glass; and when he did, a long and anxious
search was necessary before so small an object could be once
more found. Find it he did, however, and then he got its
range by the vessel, in a way to make sure of it. Yes, it
was a man, and it was Mulford.

Circumstances conspired to aid Jack in the investiga-
tion that succeeded. The sun was near setting, but a
stream of golden light gleamed over the waters, particularly illuminating the portion which came within the field
of the glass. It appeared then that Harry, in his efforts to
escape from the rock, and to get nearer to the edge of the
main channel, where his chances of being seen and rescued
would be tenfold what they were on his rock, had moved
south, by following the naked reef and the shallow places,
and was actually more than a league nearer to the brig
than he would have been had he remained stationary.
There had been hours in which to make this change,
and the young man had probably improved them to the
utmost.

Jack watched the form that was wading slowly along
with an interest he had never before felt in the movements
of any human being. Whether Mulford saw the brig or
not, it was difficult to say. She was quite two leagues
from him, and now that her sails were furled she offered

but little for the eye to rest on at that distance. At first, Jack thought the young man was actually endeavoring to get nearer to her, though it must have been a forlorn hope that should again place him in the hands of Spike. It was, however, a more probable conjecture that the young man was endeavoring to reach the margin of the passage, where a good deal of rock was above water, and near to which he had already managed to reach. At one time Jack saw that the mate was obliged to swim, and he actually lost sight of him for a time. His form, however, reappeared, and then it slowly emerged from the water, and stood erect on a bare rock of some extent. Jack breathed freer at this; for Mulford was now on the very margin of the channel, and might be easily reached by the boat, should he prevail on Josh or Simon to attempt the rescue.

At first, Jack Tier fancied that Mulford had knelt to return thanks on his arrival at a place of comparative safety; but a second look satisfied him that Harry was drinking from one of the little pools of fresh water left by the late shower. When he rose from drinking, the young man walked about the place, occasionally stooping, signs that he was picking up shell-fish for his supper. Suddenly Mulford darted forward, and passed beyond the field of the glass. When Jack found him again, he was in the act of turning a small turtle, using his knife on the animal immediately after. Had Jack been in danger of starvation himself, and found a source of food as ample and as grateful as this, he could scarcely have been more delighted. The light now began to wane perceptibly, still Harry's movements could be discerned. The turtle was killed and dressed, sufficiently at least for the mate's purposes, and the latter was seen collecting sea-weed, and bits of plank, boards, and sticks of wood, of which more or less, in drifting past, had lodged upon the rocks. "Is it possible," thought Jack, "that he is so werry partic'lar he can't eat his turtle raw! Will he, indeed, venture to light a fire, or has he the means?" Mulford was so particular, however, he did venture to light a fire, and he had the means. This may be said to be the age of matches—not in a connubial, though in an inflammatory sense—and the mate had a small stock in a tight box that he habitually carried on his person. Tier saw him at work over a little pile he had made for a long time, the beams of day departing now so fast as to make him fearful he should soon lose his object in the increasing obscurity of twilight. Suddenly a light gleamed, and the pile sent forth a clear flame. Mulford went to and fro, collecting materials to feed his fire, and was soon busied in cooking his turtle. All this Tier saw and understood, the light of the flames coming in proper time to supply the vacuum left by the departure of that of day.

In a minute Tier had no difficulty in seeing the fire that Mulford had lighted on his low and insulated domains with the naked eye. It gleamed brightly in that solitary place; and the steward was much afraid it would be seen by some one on deck, get to be reported to Spike, and lead to Harry's destruction after all. The mate appeared to be insensible to his danger, however, occasionally casting piles of dry sea-weed on his fire, in a way to cause the flames to flash up, as if kindled anew by gunpowder. It now occurred to Tier that the young man had a double object in lighting this fire, which would answer not only the purposes of his cookery, but as a signal of distress to anything passing near. The sloop-of-war, though more distant than the brig, was in his neighborhood; and she might possibly yet send relief. Such was the state of things when Jack was startled by a sudden hail from below. It was Spike's voice and came up to him short and quick.

" Fore-topmast cross-trees, there ! What are ye about all this time, Master Jack Tier, in them fore-topmast cross-trees, I say ? " demanded Spike.

" Keeping a lookout for boats from the sloop-of-war, as you bade me, sir," answered Jack, coolly.

" D' ye see any, my man? Is the water clear ahead of us, or not ? "

" It 's getting to be so dark, sir, I can see no longer. While there was daylight, no boat was to be seen."

"Come down, man—come down; I've business for you below. The sloop is far enough to the nor'ard, and we shall neither see nor hear from her to-night. Come down, I say, Jack—come down."

Jack obeyed, and securing the glass, he began to descend the rigging. He was soon as low as the top, when he paused a moment to take another look. The fire was still visible, shining like a torch on the surface of the water, casting its beams abroad like "a good deed in a naughty world." Jack was sorry to see it, though he once more took its bearing from the brig, in order that he might know where to find the spot, in the event of a search for it. When on the stretcher of the fore-rigging, Jack stopped and again looked for his beacon. It had disappeared, having sunk below the circular formation of the earth. By ascending two or three ratlins, it came into view, and by going down as low as the stretcher again, it disappeared. Trusting that no one, at that hour, would have occasion to go aloft, Jack now descended to the deck, and went aft with the spy-glass.

Spike and the Señor Montefalderon were under the coach-house, no one else appearing on any part of the quarter-deck. The people were eating their suppers, and Josh and Simon were busy in the galley. As for the females, they chose to remain in their own cabin, where Spike was well pleased to leave them.

"Come this way, Jack," said the captain, in his best-humored tone of voice, "I've a word to say to you. Put the glass in at my state-room window, and come hither."

Tier did as ordered.

"So you can make out no boats to the nor'ard, ha, Jack! nothing to be seen thereaway?"

"Nothing in the way of a boat, sir."

"Ay, ay, I dare say there's plenty of water, and some rock. The Florida Reef has no scarcity of either, to them that knows where to look for one, and to steer clear of the other. Hark'ee, Jack; so you got the schooner under way from the Dry Tortugas, and undertook to beat her up to Key West, when she fancied herself a turtle, and over she went with you—is that it, my man?"

"The schooner turned turtle with us, sure enough, sir; and we all came near drowning on her bottom."

"No sharks in that latitude and longitude, eh, Jack?"

"Plenty on 'em, sir; and I thought they would have got us all, at one time. More than twenty set of fins were in sight at once, for several hours."

"You could hardly have supplied the gentlemen with a leg, or an arm, each. But where was the boat all this time —you had the light-house boat in tow, I suppose?"

"She had been in tow, sir; but Madam Budd talked so much dictionary to the painter that it got adrift."

"Yet I found you all in it."

"Very true, sir. Mr. Mulford swam quite a mile to reach the rocks, and found the boat aground on one on 'em. As soon as he got the boat, he made sail, and came and took us off. We had reason to thank God he could do so."

Spike looked dark and thoughtful. He muttered the words "swam," and "rocks," but was too cautious to allow any expressions to escape him, that might betray to the Mexican officer that which was uppermost in his mind. He was silent, however, for quite a minute, and Jack saw that he had awakened a dangerous source of distrust in the captain's breast.

"Well, Jack," resumed Spike, after the pause, "can you tell us anything of the doubloons? I nat'rally expected to find them in the boat, but there were none to be seen. You scarcely pumped the schooner out, without overhauling her lockers, and falling in with them doubloons."

"We found them, sure enough, and had them ashore with us, in the tent, down to the moment when we sailed."

"When you took them off to the schooner, eh? My life for it, the gold was not forgotten."

"It was not, sure enough, sir; but we took it off with us to the schooner, and it went down in her when she finally sunk."

Another pause, during which Señor Montefalderon and Captain Spike looked significantly at each other.

"Do you think, Jack, you could find the spot where the schooner went down?"

"I could come pretty near it, sir, though not on the very spot itself. Water leaves no mark over the grave of a sunken ship."

"If you can take us within a reasonable distance, we might find it by sweeping for it. Them doubloons are worth some trouble; and their recovery would be better than a long v'y'ge to us, any day."

"They would, indeed, Don Esteban," observed the Mexican; "and my poor country is not in a condition to bear heavy losses. It Señor Jack Tier can find the wreck, and we regain the money, ten of those doubloons shall be his reward, though I take them from my own share, much diminished as it will be."

"You hear, Jack—here is a chance to make your fortune! You say you sailed with me in old times—and old times were good times with this brig, though times has changed; but if you sailed with me, in *old* times, you must remember that whatever the Swash touched she turned to gold."

"I hope you don't doubt, Captain Spike, my having sailed in the brig, not only in old times, but in her best times."

Jack seemed hurt as he put this question, and Spike appeared in doubt. The latter gazed at the little rotund, queer-looking figure before him, as if endeavoring to recognize him; and when he had done, he passed his hand over his brow, like one who endeavored to recall past objects by excluding those that are present.

"You will then show us the spot where my unfortunate schooner did sink, Señor Jack Tier?" put in the Mexican.

"With all my heart, Señor, if it is to be found. I think I could take you within a cable's length of the place, though hunger, and thirst, and sharks, and the fear of drowning, will keep a fellow from having a very bright lookout for such a matter."

"In what water do you suppose the craft to lie, Jack?" demanded the captain.

"You know as much of that as I do myself, sir. She went down about a cable's length from the reef, toward which she was a settin' at the time; and had she kept aloft an hour longer, she might have grounded on the rocks.''

''She's better where she is, if we can only find her by sweeping. On the rocks we could do nothing with her but break her up, and ten to one the doubloons would be lost. By the way, Jack, do you happen to know where that scoundrel of a mate of mine stowed the money?''

''When we left the island, I carried it down to the boat myself—and a good lift I had of it. As sure as you are there, Señor, I was obliged to take it on a shoulder. When it came out of the boat, Mr. Mulford carried it below; and I heard him tell Miss Rose a'terwards that he had thrown it into a bread-locker.

''Where we shall find it, Don Wan, notwithstanding all this veering and hauling. The old brig has luck when doubloons are in question, and ever has had since I've commanded her. Jack, we shall have to call on the cook and stewards for an anchor-watch to-night. The people are a good deal fagged with boxing about this reef so much, and I shall want 'em all as fresh to-morrow as they can be got. You idlers had better take the middle watches, which will give the forecastle chaps longer naps.''

''Ay, ay, sir; we'll manage that for 'em. Josh and Simon can go on at twelve, and I will take the watch at two, which will give the men all the rest they want, as I can hold out for four hours full. I'm as good for an anchor watch as any man in the brig, Captain Spike.''

''That you are, Jack, and better than some on 'em. Take you all round, and round it is, you're a rum 'un, my lad; the queerest little jigger that ever lay out on a royal-yard.''

Jack might have been a little offended at Spike's compliments, but he was certainly not sorry to find him so good-natured, after all that had passed. He now left the captain, and his Mexican companion, seemingly in close conference together, while he went below himself, and dropped as naturally into the routine of his duty as if he had never left the brig. In the cabin he found the females, of course,—Rose scarce raising her face from the shawl which lay on the bed of her own berth. Jack busied himself in a locker near this berth, until an opportunity occurred to touch Rose, unseen by her aunt or Biddy. The poor heart-stricken girl raised her face, from which all the color had departed, and looked almost vacantly at Jack, as if to ask an explanation. Hope is truly, by a most benevolent provision of Providence, one of the very last blessings to abandon us. It is probable that we are thus gifted, in order to encourage us to rely on the great atonement to the last moment, since, without this natural endowment to cling to hope, despair might well be the fate of millions, who, there is a reason to think, reap the benefit of that act of divine mercy. It would hardly do to say that anything like hope was blended with the look Rose now cast on Jack, but it was anxious and inquiring.

The steward bent his head to the locker, bringing his face quite near to that of Rose, and whispered, "There is hope, Miss Rose; but do not betray me."

These were blessed words for our heroine to hear, and they produced an immediate and great revolution in her feelings. Commanding herself, however, she looked her questions, instead of trusting even to a whisper. Jack did not say any more, just then; but, shortly after, he called Rose, whose eyes were now never off him, into the main cabin, which was empty. It was so much pleasanter to sleep in an airy state-room on deck, that Señor Montefalderon, indeed, had given up the use of this cabin, in great measure, seldom appearing in it, except at meals, having taken possession of the deserted apartment of Mulford. Josh was in the galley, where he spent most of his time, and Rose and Jack had no one to disturb their conference.

"He is safe, Miss Rose—God be praised!" whispered Jack. "Safe for the present, at least; with food, and water, and fire to keep him warm at night."

It was impossible for Rose not to understand to whom there was allusion, though her head became dizzy under the painful confusion that prevailed in it. She pressed her temples with both hands, and asked a thousand questions with her eyes. Jack considerately handed her a glass of water before he proceeded. As soon as he found her a little more composed, he related the facts connected with his discovery of Mulford, precisely as they had occurred.

"He is now on a large rock—a little island, indeed—where he is safe from the ocean unless it comes on to blow a hurricane," concluded Jack, "has fresh water and fresh turtle in the bargain. A man might live a month on one such turtle as I saw Mr. Mulford cutting up this evening."

"Is there no way of rescuing him from the situation you have mentioned, Jack? In a year or two I shall be my own mistress, and have money to do as I please with; put me only in the way of taking Mr. Mulford from that rock, and I will share all I am worth on earth with you, dear Jack."

"Ay, so it is with the whole sex," muttered Tier; "let them only once give up their affections to a man, and he becomes dearer to them than pearls and rubies! But you know me, Miss Rose, and know why and how well I would sarve you. My story and my feelin's are as much your secret, as your story and your feelin's is mine. We shall pull together, if we don't pull so very strong. Now, hearken to me, Miss Rose, and I will let you into the secret of my plan to help Mr. Mulford make a launch."

Jack then communicated to his companion his whole project for the night. Spike had, of his own accord, given to him and his two associates Simon and Josh, the care of the brig between midnight and morning. If he could prevail on either of these men to accompany him, it was his intention to take the light-house boat, which was riding by its painter astern of the brig, and proceed as fast as they could to the spot whither Mulford had found his way. By his calculations, if the wind stood as it then was, little more than an hour would be necessary to reach the rock, and about as much more to return. Should the breeze lull, of which there was no great danger, since the easterly trades were again blowing, Jack thought he and Josh might go over the distance with the oars in about double the time. Should both Josh and Simon refuse to accom-

pany him, he thought he should attempt the rescue of the
mate alone, did the wind stand, trusting to Mulford's assistance, should he need it, in getting back to the brig.

"You surely would not come back here with Harry,
did you once get him safe from off that rock!" exclaimed
Rose.

"Why, you know how it is with me, Miss Rose," answered Jack. "My business is here, on board the Swash
and I must attend to it. Nothing shall tempt me to give
up the brig so long as she floats, and sartain folk float in
her, unless it might be some such matter as that which
happened on the bit of an island at the Dry Tortugas.
Ah! he's a willain! But if I do come back, it will be
only to get into my own proper berth ag'in, and not to
bring Mr. Mulford into the lion's jaws. He will only have
to put me back on board the Molly here, when he can
make the best of his own way to Key West. Half an
hour would place him out of harm's way; especially as I
happen to know the course Spike means to steer in the
morning."

"I will go with you, Jack," said Rose, mildly, but with
great firmness.

"You, Miss Rose! But why should I show surprise?
It's like all the sex, when they have given away their
affections. Yes, woman will be woman, put her on a
naked rock, or put her in silks and satins in her parlor at
home. How different is it with men! They dote for a
little while, and turn to a new face. It must be said, men's
willains!"

"Not Mulford, Jack—no, not Harry Mulford! A truer
or a nobler heart never beat in a human breast; and you
and I will drown together, rather than he should not be
taken from that rock."

"It shall be as you say," answered Jack, a little thoughtfully. "Perhaps it would be best that you should quit the
brig altogether. Spike is getting desperate, and you will
be safer with the young mate than with so great an old
willain. Yes, you shall go with me, Miss Rose; and if
Josh and Simon both refuse, we will go alone."

"With you, Jack, but not with Mr. Mulford. I cannot desert my aunt, nor can I quit the Swash alone in company with her mate. As for Spike, I despise him too much to fear him. He must soon go into port somewhere, and at the first place where he touches we shall quit him. He dare not detain us—nay, he cannot—and I do not fear him. We will save Harry, but I shall remain with my aunt."

"We'll see, Miss Rose, we'll see," said Tier, smiling. "Perhaps a handsome young man, like Mr. Mulford, will have better luck in persuading you than an old fellow like me. If he should fail, 't will be his own fault."

So thought Jack Tier, judging of women as he had found them, but so did not think Rose Budd. The conversation ended here, however, each keeping in view its purport, and the serious business that was before them.

The duty on the vessel went on as usual. The night promised to be clouded, but not very dark, as there was a moon. When Spike ordered the anchor-watches, he had great care to spare his crew as much as possible, for the next day was likely to be one of great toil to them. He intended to get the schooner up again, if possible ; and though he might not actually pump her out so as to cause her to float, enough water was to be removed to enable him to get at the doubloons. The situation of the bread-locker was known, and as soon as the cabin was sufficiently freed from water to enable one to move about in it, Spike did not doubt his being able to get at the gold. With his resources and ingenuity, the matter in his own mind was reduced to one of toil and time. Eight-and-forty hours, and some hard labor, he doubted not would effect all he cared for.

In setting the anchor-watches for the night, therefore Stephen Spike bethought him as much of the morrow as of the present moment. Don Juan offered to remain on deck until midnight, and as he was as capable of giving an alarm as any one else, the offer was accepted. Josh and Simon were to succeed the Mexican, and to hold the lookout for two hours, when Jack was to relieve them, and to continue on deck until light returned, when he was to give the captain a call. This arrangement made, Tier turned in at once, desiring the cook to call him half an hour before the proper period of his watch commenced. That half hour Jack intended to employ in exercising his eloquence in endeavoring to persuade either Josh or Simon to be of his party. By eight o'clock the vessel lay in a profound quiet, Señor Montefalderon pacing the quarter-deck alone, while the deep breathing of Spike was to be heard issuing through the open window of his state-room; a window which it may be well to say to the uninitiated, opened in-board, or toward the deck, and not outboard, or toward the sea.

For four solitary hours did the Mexican pace the deck of the stranger, resting himself for a few minutes at a time only, when wearied with walking. Does the reader fancy that a man so situated had not plenty of occupation for his thoughts? Don Juan Montefalderon was a soldier and a gallant cavalier; and love of country had alone induced him to engage in his present duties. Not that patriotism which looks to political preferment through a popularity purchased by the vulgar acclamation which attends success in arms, even when undeserved, or that patriotism which induces men of fallen characters to endeavor to retrieve former offences by the shortest and most reckless mode, or that patriotism which shouts "Our country right or wrong," regardless alike of God and his eternal laws, that are never to be forgotten with impunity; but the patriotism which would defend his home and fire-side, his altars and the graves of his fathers, from the ruthless steps of the invader. We shall not pretend to say how far this gentleman entered into the merits of the quarrel between the two republics, which no arts of European jealousy can ever conceal from the judgment of truth, for, with him, matters had gone beyond the point when men feel the necessity of reasoning, and when, perhaps, if such a condition of the mind is ever to be defended, he found his perfect justification in feeling. He had travelled, and knew life by observation, and not through traditions and books. He had never believed, therefore, that his countrymen could march to Washington, or even to the Sabine ; but he had hoped for better things than had since occurred. The warlike qualities of the Americans of the North, as he was accustomed to call those who term themselves, *par excellence*, Americans, a name they are fated to retain, and to raise high on the scale of national power and national pre-eminence, unless they fall by their own hands, had taken him by surprise, as they have taken all but those who knew the country well, and who understood its people. Little had he imagined that the small, widely-spread body of regulars, that figured in the blue books, almanacs, and army-registers of America, as some six or seven thousand men, scattered along frontiers of a thousand leagues in extent, could, at the beck of the government, swell into legions of invaders, men able to carry war to the capitals of his own states, thousands of miles from their doors, and formidable alike for their energy, their bravery, their readiness in the use of arms, and their numbers. He saw what is perhaps justly called the boasting of the American character, vindicated by their exploits ; and marches, conquests, and victories that, if sober truth were alone to cover the pages of history, would far outdo in real labor and danger the boasted passage of the Alps under Napoleon, and the exploits that succeeded it.

Don Juan Montefalderon was a grave and thoughtful man, of pure Iberian blood. He might have had about him a little of the exaltation of the Spanish character ; the overflowings of a generous chivalry at the bottom ; and, under its influence, he may have set too high an estimate on Mexico and her sons, but he was not one to shut his eyes to the truth. He saw plainly that the northern neighbors of his country were a race formidable and enterprising, and that of all the calumnies that had been heaped upon them by rivalries and European superciliousness, that of their not being military by temperament was, perhaps, the most absurd of all. On the contrary, he had himself, though anticipating evil, been astounded by the suddenness and magnitude of their conquests, which in a few short months after the breaking out of hostilities had overrun

20

regions larger in extent than many ancient empires. All this had been done, too, not by disorderly and barbarous hordes, seeking in other lands the abundance that was wanting at home; but with system and regularity, by men who had turned the plowshare into the sword for the occasion, quitting abundance to encounter fatigue, famine, and danger. In a word, the Señor Montefalderon saw all the evils that environed his own land, and foresaw others, of a still graver character, that menaced the future. On matters such as these did he brood in his walk, and bitter did he find the minutes of that sad and lonely watch. Although a Mexican, he could feel; although an avowed foe of this good republic of ours, he had his principles, his affections, and his sense of right. Whatever may be the merits of the quarrel, and we are not disposed to deny that our provocation has been great, a sense of right should teach every man that what may be patriotic in an American would not be exactly the same thing in a Mexican, and that we ought to respect in others sentiments that are so much vaunted among ourselves. Midnight at length arrived, and, calling the cook and steward, the unhappy gentleman was relieved, and went to his berth to dream, in sorrow, over the same pictures of national misfortunes, on which, while waking, he had brooded in such deep melancholy.

The watch of Josh and Simon was tranquil, meeting with no interruption until it was time to summon Jack. One thing these men had done, however, that was of some moment to Tier, under a pledge given by Josh, and which had been taken in return for a dollar in hand. They had managed to haul the light-house boat alongside from its position astern, and this so noiselessly as not to give the alarm to any one. There it lay, when Jack appeared, ready at the main-rigging, to receive him at any moment he might choose to enter it.

A few minutes after Jack appeared on deck, Rose and Biddy came stealthily out of the cabin, the latter carrying a basket filled with bread and broken meat, and not wanting in sundry little delicacies, such as woman's hands prepare, and, in this instance, woman's tenderness had provided. The whole party met at the galley, a place so far removed from the state-rooms aft as to be out of ear-shot. Here Jack renewed his endeavors to persuade either Josh or Simon to go in the boat, but without success. The negroes had talked the matter over in their watch, and had come to the conclusion the enterprise was too hazardous.

"I tell you, Jack, you does n't know Cap'in Spike as well as I does," Josh said, in continuance of the discourse. "No, you does n't know him at all as well as I does. If he finds out that anybody has quit dis brig dis werry night, woful will come! It no good to try to run; I run t'ree time, an' Simon here run twice. What good it all do? We got cotched, and here we is, just as fast as ever. I knows Cap'in Spike, and does n't want to fall in athwart his hawse any more."

"Y-e-s, dat my judgment too," put in the cook. "We wishes you well, Jack, and we wishes Miss Rose well, and Mr. Mulford well, but we can't, no how, run ath'art-hawse, as Josh says. Dat is my judgment, too."

"Well, if your minds are made up to this, my darkies, I s'pose there 'll be no changing them," said Jack. "At all ewents you 'll lend us a hand, by answering any hail that may come from aft, in my watch, and keepin' our secret. There's another thing you can do for us, which may be of sarvice. Should Captain Spike miss the boat, and lay any trap to catch us, you can just light this here bit of lantern and hang it over the brig's bows, where he 'll not be likely to see it, that we may know matters are going wrong, and give the craft a wide berth."

"Sartain," said Josh, who entered heartily into the affair, so far as good wishes for its success were concerned, at the very moment when he had a most salutary care of his own back. "Sartain; we do all dat, and no t'ank asked. It no great matter to answer a hail, or to light a lantern and sling him over de bows; and if Captain Spike want to know who did it, let him find out."

Here both negroes laughed heartily, manifesting so little care to suppress their mirth, that Rose trembled lest their noise should awaken Spike. Accustomed sounds, however, seldom produce this effect on the ears of the sleeper, and the heavy breathing from the state-room succeeded the merriment of the blacks, as soon as the latter ceased. Jack now announced his readiness to depart. Some little care and management were necessary to get into the boat noiselessly more especially with Biddy. It was done, however, with the assistance of the blacks, who cast off the painter, when Jack gave the boat a shove to clear the brig, and suffered it to drift astern for a considerable distance before he ventured to cast loose the sail.

"I know Spike well," said Jack, in answer to a remonstrance from the impatient Rose concerning his delay; "a single flap of that canvas would wake him up, with the brig anchored, while he would sleep through a salute of heavy guns if it came in regular course. Quick ears has old Stephen, and it's best to humor them. In a minute more we'll set our canvas and be off."

All was done as Jack desired, and the boat got away from the brig unheard and undetected. It was blowing a good breeze, and Jack Tier had no sooner got the sail on the boat, than away it started at a speed that would have soon distanced Spike in his yawl, and with his best oarsmen. The main point was to keep the course, though the direction of the wind was a great assistant. By keeping the wind abeam Jack thought he should be going toward the rock of Mulford. In one hour, or even in less time, he expected to reach it, and he was guided by time in his calculations as much as by any other criterion. Previously to quitting the brig, he had gone up a few ratlins of the fore-rigging to take the bearings of the fire on Mulford's rock, but the light was no longer visible. As no star was to be seen, the course was a little vague, but Jack was navigator enough to understand that by keeping on the weather side of the channel he was in the right road, and that his great danger of missing his object was in overrunning it.

So much of the reef was above water, that it was not difficult to steer a boat along its margin. The darkness, to be sure, rendered it a little uncertain how near they were running to the rocks, but, on the whole, Jack assured Rose he had no great difficulty in getting along.

"These trades are almost as good as compasses," he said, "and the rocks are better, if we can keep close aboard them without going on to them. I do not know the exact distance of the spot we seek from the brig, but I judged it to be about two leagues, as I looked at it from aloft. Now, this boat will travel them two leagues in an hour, with this breeze and in smooth water."

"I wish you had seen the fire again before we left the brig," said Rose, too anxious for the result not to feel uneasiness on some account or other.

"The mate is asleep, and the fire has burned down; that's the explanation. Besides, fuel is not too plenty on a place like that Mr. Mulford inhabits just now. As we get near the spot, I shall look out for embers, which may sarve as a light-house, or beacon, to guide us into port."

"Mr. Mulford will be charmed to see us, now that we take him wather!" exclaimed Biddy. "Wather is a blessed thing, and it's hard will be the heart that does not fale gratitude for a plenty of swate wather."

"The maty has plenty of food and water where he is," said Jack. "I'll answer for both them sarcumstances. I saw him turn a turtle as plain as if I had been at his elbow, and I saw him drinking at a hole in the rock, as heartily as a boy ever pulled at a gimlet-hole in a molasses hogshead."

"But the distance was so great, Jack, I should hardly think you could have distinguished objects so small."

"I went by the motions altogether. I saw the man, and I saw the movements, and I knowed what the last meant. It's true I could n't swear to the turtle, though I saw something on the rock that I knowed, by the way in which it was handled, *must* be a turtle. Then I saw the mate kneel, and put his head low, and then I knowed he was drinking."

"Perhaps he prayed," said Rose, solemnly.

"Not he. Sailors isn't so apt to pray, Miss Rose; not as apt as they ought to be. Women for prayers, and men for work. Mr. Mulford is no worse than many others, but I doubt if he be much given to that."

To this Rose made no answer, but Biddy took the matter up, and, as the boat went briskly ahead, she pursued the subject.

"Then more is the shame for him," said the Irishwoman, "and Miss Rose, and missus, and even I prayin' *for* him, all as if he was our own brudder. It's seldom I ask anything for a heretic, but I could not forget a fine young man like Mr. Mulford, and Miss Rose so partial to him, and he in so bad a way. He ought to be ashamed to make his brags that he is too proud to pray."

"Harry has made no such wicked boast," put in Rose, mildly; "nor do we know that he has not prayed for us, as well as for himself. It may all be a mistake of Jack's, you know."

"Yes," added Jack, coolly, "it *may* be a mistake, a'ter all, for I was lookin' at the maty six miles off, and through a spy-glass. No one can be sure of anything at such a distance. So overlook the matter, my good Biddy, and carry Mr. Mulford the nice things you've mustered in that basket, all the same as if he was pope."

"This is a subject we had better drop," Rose quietly observed.

"Anything to oblige you, Miss Rose, though religion is a matter it would do me no harm to talk about once and awhile. It's many a long year since I've had time and opportunity to bring my thoughts to dwell on holy things. Ever since I left my mother's side, I've been a wanderer in my mind, as much as in my body."

"Poor Jack! I understand and feel for your sufferings; but a better time will come, when you may return to the habits of your youth, and to the observances of your church."

"I don't know that, Miss Rose; I don't know that," answered Tier, placing the elbow of his short arm on the seemingly shorter leg, and bending his head so low as to

lean his face on the palm of the hand, an attitude in which
he appeared to be suffering keenly through his recollections.
"Childhood and innocence never come back to us in
this world. What the grave may do, we shall all learn in
time."

"Innocence can return to all with repentance, Jack, and
the heart that prompts you to do acts as generous as
this you are now engaged in, must contain some good seed
yet."

"If Jack will go to a praste and just confess, when he can
find a father, it will do his sowl good," said Biddy, who was
touched by the mental suffering of the strange little being at
her side.

But the necessity of managing the boat soon compelled
its coxswain to raise his head, and to attend to his duty.
The wind sometimes came in puffs, and at such moments
Jack saw that the large sail of the light-house boat required watching, a circumstance that induced him to shake
off his melancholy, and give his mind more exclusively to
the business before him. As for Rose, she sympathized
deeply with Jack Tier, for she knew his history, his origin,
the story of his youth, and the well-grounded causes of his
contrition and regrets. From her, Jack had concealed nothing,—the gentle commiseration of one like Rose being a
balm to wounds that had bled for long and bitter years.
The great poet of our language, and the greatest that ever
lived, perhaps, short of the inspired writers of the Old
Testament, and old Homer and Dante, has well reminded
us that the "little beetle," in yielding its breath, can "feel
a pang as great as when a giant dies." Thus is it, too, in
morals. Abasement, and misery, and poverty, and sin, may,
and all do, contribute to lower the tone of our moral existence; but the principle that has been planted by nature, can
be eradicated by nature only. It exists as long as we exist;
and if dormant for a time, under the pressure of circumstances, it merely lies in the moral system, like the acorn or the
chestnut in the ground, waiting its time and season to sprout,
and bud, and blossom. Should that time never arrive, it is
not because the seed is not there, but because it is neglected.

Thus was it with the singular being of whose feelings we have just spoken. The germ of goodness had been implanted early in him, and was nursed with tenderness and care, until, self-willed, and governed by passion, he had thrown off the connections of youth and childhood, to connect himself with Spike—a connection that had left him what he was. Before closing our legend, we shall have occasion to explain it.

"We have run our hour, Miss Rose," resumed Jack, breaking a continued silence, during which the boat had passed through a long line of water; "we have run our hour, and ought to be near the rock we are in search of. But the morning is so dark that I fear we shall have difficulty in finding it. It will never do to run past it, and we must haul closer into the reef, and shorten sail, that we may be sartain to make no such mistake."

Rose begged her companion to omit no precaution, as it would be dreadful to fail in their search, after incurring so much risk in their own persons.

"Harry may be sleeping on the sea-weed of which you spoke," she added, "and the danger of passing him will be much increased in such a case. What a gloomy and frightful spot is this, in which to abandon a human being ! I fear, Jack, that we have come faster than we have supposed, and may already have passed the rock."

"I hope not, Miss Rose—it seems to me a good two leagues to the place where I saw him, and the boat is fast that will run two leagues in an hour."

"We do not know the time, Jack, and are obliged to guess at that as well as at the distance. How very dark it is ! "

Dark, in one sense, it was not, though Rose's apprehensions, doubtless, induced her to magnify every evil. The clouds certainly lessened the light of the moon ; but there was still enough of the last to enable one to see surrounding objects ; and most especially to render distinct the character of the solitude that reigned over the place.

The proximity of the reef, which formed a weather shore to the boat, prevented anything like a swell on the water, notwithstanding the steadiness and strength of the breeze, which had now blown for near twenty-four hours. The same wind, in open water, would have raised sea enough to cause a ship to pitch, or roll ; whereas, the light-house boat, placed where she was, scarce rose and fell under the undulations of the channel through which she was glancing.

"This is a good boat, and a fast boat too," observed Jack Tier, after he had luffed up several minutes, in order to make sure of his proximity to the reef; "and it might carry us all safe enough to Key West, or certainly back to the Dry Tortugas, was we inclined to try our hands at either."

"I cannot quit my aunt," said Rose, quickly, "so we will not even think of any such thing."

"No, 't would never do to abandon the missus," said Biddy, "and she on the wrack wid us, and falin' the want of wather as much as ourselves."

"We three have sartainly gone through much in company," returned Jack, "and it ought to make us friends for life."

"I trust it will, Jack ; I hope, when we return to New York, to see you among us, anchored, as you would call it, for the rest of your days under my aunt's roof, or under my own, should I ever have one."

"No, Miss Rose, my business is with the Swash and her captain. I shall stick by both, now I 've found 'em again, until they once more desart me. A man's duty is his duty, and a woman's duty is her duty."

"You same to like the brig and her captain, Jack Tier," observed Biddy, "and there's no use in gainsaying such a likin'. What *will* come to pass, must come to pass. Captain Spike is a mighty great sailor, anyway."

"He 's a willain !" muttered Jack.

"There !" cried Rose, almost breathless, "there is a rock above the water, surely. Do not fly by it so swiftly Jack, but let us stop and examine it."

"There is a rock, sure enough, and a large piece it is," answered Tier. "We will go alongside of it, and see what it is made of. Biddy shall be boat-keeper, while you and I, Miss Rose, explore."

"Jack had thrown the boat into the wind, and was shooting close alongside of the reef, even while speaking. The party found no difficulty in landing; the margin of the rock admitting the boat to lie close alongside of it, and its surface being even and dry. Jack had brailed the sail, and he brought the painter ashore, and fastened it securely to a fragment of stone, that made a very sufficient anchor. In addition to this precaution, a lazy painter was put into Biddy's hands, and she was directed not to let go of it while her companions were absent. These arrangements concluded, Rose and Jack commenced a hurried examination of the spot.

A few minutes sufficed to give our adventurers a tolerably accurate notion of the general features of the place on which they had landed. It was a considerable portion of the reef that was usually above water, and which had even some fragments of soil, or sand, on which was a stinted growth of bushes. Of these last, however, there were very few, nor were there many spots of the sand. Drift-wood and sea-weed were lodged in considerable quantities about its margin, and, in places, piles of both had been tossed upon the rock itself, by the billows of former gales of wind. Nor was it long before Jack discovered a turtle that had been up to a hillock of sand, probably to deposit its eggs. There was enough of the sportsman in Jack, notwithstanding the business he was on, to turn this animal; though with what object, he might have been puzzled himself to say. This exploit effected, Jack followed Rose as fast as his short legs would permit, our heroine pressing forward eagerly, though almost without hope, in order to ascertain if Mulford were there.

"I am afraid this is not the rock," said Rose, nearly breathless with her own haste, when Jack had overtaken her. "I see nothing of him, and we have passed over most of the place."

"Very true, Miss Rose," answered her companion, who was in a good humor on account of his capture of the turtle; "but there are other rocks besides this. Ha! what was that, yonder?" pointing with a finger; "here, more toward the brig. As I 'm a sinner, there was a flashing, as of fire."

"If a fire, it must be that made by Harry. Let us go to the spot at once."

Jack led the way, and, sure enough, he soon reached a place where the embers of what had been a considerable body of fire, were smouldering on the rock. The wind had probably caused some brand to kindle momentarily, which was the object that had caught Tier's eye. No doubt any longer remained of their having found the very place where the mate had cooked his supper, and lighted his beacon, though he himself was not near it. Around these embers were all the signs of Mulford's having made the meal, of which Jack had seen the preparations. A portion of the turtle, much the greater part of it, indeed, lay in its shell; and piles of wood and sea-weed, both dry, had been placed at hand, ready for use. A ship's topgallant-yard, with most of its rope attached, lay with a charred end near the fire, or where the fire had been, the wood having burned until the flames went out for the want of contact with other fuel. There were many pieces of boards of pitch-pine in the adjacent heap, and two or three beautiful planks of the same wood entire. In short, from the character and quantity of the materials of this nature that had thus been heaped together, Jack gave it as his opinion that some vessel, freighted with lumber, had been wrecked to windward, and that the adjacent rocks had been receiving the tribute of her cargo. Wrecks are of very, very frequent occurrence on the Florida Reef; and there are always moments when such gleanings are to be made in some part of it or other.

"I see no better way to give a call to the mate, Miss Rose, than to throw some of this dry weed, and some of this lumber on the fire," said Jack, after he had rummaged about the place sufficiently to become master of its condition. "There is plenty of ammunition, and here goes for a broadside."

Jack had no great difficulty in effecting his object. In a few minutes he succeeded in obtaining a flame, and then he fed it with such fragments of the brands and boards as were best adapted to his purpose. The flames extended gradually, and by the time Tier had dragged the topgallant-yard over the pile, and placed several planks, on their edges, alongside of it, the whole was ready to burst into a blaze. The light was shed athwart the rock for a long distance, and the whole place, which was lately so gloomy and ob-scure, now became gay, under the bright radiance of a blaz-ing fire.

"There is a beacon-light that might almost be seen on board!" said Jack, exulting in his success. "If the mate is anywhere in this latitude, he will soon turn up."

"I see nothing of him," answered Rose, in a melancholy voice. "Surely, surely, Jack, he cannot have left the rock just as we have come to rescue him!"

Rose and her companion had turned their faces from the fire to look in an opposite direction in quest of him they sought. Unseen by them, a human form advanced swiftly toward the fire, from a point on its other side. It advanced nearer, then hesitated, afterward rushed forward with a tread that caused the two to turn, and at the next moment, Rose was clasped to the heart of Mulford.

CHAPTER XI.

" I might have pass'd that lovely cheek,
    Nor, perchance, my heart have left me ;
But the sensitive blush that came trembling there,
    Of my heart it forever bereft me.
Who could blame had I loved that face,
    Ere my eyes could twice explore her ;
Yet it is for the fairy intelligence there,
    And her warm, warm heart I adore her."

WOLFE.

THE stories of the respective parties who had thus
    so strangely met on that barren and isolated rock
    were soon told. Harry confirmed all of Jack's
    statements as to his own proceedings, and Rose
had little more to say than to add how much her own
affections had led her to risk in his behalf. In a word, ten
minutes made each fully acquainted with the other's
movements. Then Tier considerately retired to the boat,
under the pretence of minding it, and seeing everything
ready for a departure, but as much to allow the lovers the
ten or fifteen minutes of uninterrupted discourse that they
now enjoyed, as for any other reason.

It was a strange scene that now offered on the rock. By
this time the fire was burning not only brightly, but fiercely,
shedding its bright light far and near. Under its most brilliant rays stood Harry and Rose, both smiling and happy,
delighted in their meeting, and, for the moment, forgetful
of all but their present felicity. Never, indeed, had Rose
appeared more lovely than under these circumstances. Her
face was radiant with those feelings which had so recently
changed from despair to delight,—a condition that is ever
most propitious to beauty ; and charms that always ap-

pear feminine and soft, now seemed elevated to a bright benignancy that might best be likened to our fancied images of angels. The mild, beaming, serene, and intelligent blue eyes, the cheeks flushed with happiness, the smiles that came so easily, and were so replete with tenderness, and the rich hair, deranged by the breeze, and moistened by the air of the sea, each and all, perhaps, borrowed some additional lustre from the peculiar light under which they were exhibited. As for Harry, happiness had thrown all the disadvantages of exposure, want of dress, and a face that had not felt the razor for six-and-thirty hours, into the background. When he left the wreck, he had cast aside his cap and his light summer jacket, in order that they might not encumber him in swimming, but both had been recovered when he returned with the boat to take off his friends. In his ordinary sea attire, then, he now stood, holding Rose's two hands in front of the fire, every garment clean and white as the waters of the ocean could make them, but all betraying some of the signs of his recent trials. His fine countenance was full of the love he bore for the intrepid and devoted girl who had risked so much in his behalf ; and a painter might have wished to preserve the expression of ardent, manly admiration which glowed in his face, answering to the gentle sympathy and womanly tenderness it met in that of Rose.

The background of this picture was the wide, even surface of the coral reef, with its exterior setting of the dark and gloomy sea. On the side of the channel, however, appeared the boat, already winded, with Biddy still on the rock, looking kindly at the lovers by the fire, while Jack was holding the painter, beginning to manifest a little impatience at the delay.

"They'll stay there an hour, holding each other's hands, and looking into each other's faces," half grumbled the little, rotund assistant steward, anxious to be on his way back to the brig, "unless a body gives 'em a call. Captain Spike will be in no very good humor to receive you and me on board ag'in, if he should find out what sort of a trip we've been making hereaway."

"Let 'em alone—let 'em alone, Jacky," answered the good-natured and kind-hearted Irishwoman. "It's happy they bees, jist now, and it does my eyes good to look at 'em."

"Ay, they're happy enough, *now*; I only hope it may last."

"Last! what should help its lasting? Miss Rose is so good, and so handsome—and she's a fortin', too; and the mate so nice a young man. Think of the likes of them, Jack, wantin' the blessed gift of wather, and all within one day and two nights. Sure it's Providence that takes care of us, and not we ourselves! Kings on their thrones isn't as happy as *them* at this moment."

"Men's willains!" growled Jack; "and more fools women for trustin' em."

"Not sich a nice young man as our mate, Jacky; no, not he. Now the mate of the ship I came from Liverpool in, this time ten years agone, he was a villain. He grudged us our potaties, and our own bread; and he grudged us every dhrap of swate wather that went into our mouths. Call him a villain, if you will, Jack; but niver call the likes of Mr. Mulford by so hard a name."

"I wish him well, and nothing else; and for that very reason must put a stop to his looking so fondly into that young woman's face. Time won't stand still, Biddy, to suit the wishes of lovers; and Stephen Spike is a man not to be trifled with. Halloo, there, maty! It's high time to think of getting under way."

At this summons both Harry and Rose started, becoming aware of the precious moments they were losing. Carrying a large portion of the turtle, the former moved toward the craft, in which all were seated in less than three minutes, with the sail loose, and the boat in motion. For a few moments the mate was so much occupied with Rose, that he did not advert to the course; but one of his experience could not long be misled on such a point, and he turned suddenly to Tier, who was steering, to remonstrate.

"How's this, Jack!" cried Mulford; "you've got the boat's head the wrong way."

"Not I, sir. She's headlong for the brig as straight as

she can go. This wind favors us on both legs; and its
lucky it does, for 't will be hard on upon daylight afore we
are alongside of her. You'll want half an hour of dark, at
the very least, to get a good start of the Swash, in case she
makes sail a'ter you.''

"Straight for the brig!—what have we to do with the
brig? Our course is for Key West, unless it might be better
to run down before the wind to the Dry Tortugas again, and
look for the sloop-of-war. Duty, and perhaps my own
safety, tells me to let Captain Mull know what Spike is
about with the Swash; and I shall not hesitate a moment
about doing it, after all that has passed. Give me the
helm, Jack, and let us ware short round on our heel.''

"Never, master maty—never. I must go back to the
brig. Miss Rose, there, knows that my business is with
Stephen Spike, and with him only.''

"And I must return to my aunt, Harry,'' put in Rose,
herself. "It would never do for me to desert my aunt, you
know.''

"And I have been taken from that rock, to be given up
to the tender mercies of Spike again?''

This was said rather in surprise, than in a complaining
way; and it at once induced Rose to tell the young man
the whole of their project.

"Never, Harry, never,'' she said firmly. "It is our intention to return to the brig ourselves, and let you escape
in the boat afterwards. Jack Tier is of opinion this can be
done without much risk, if we use proper caution and do not
lose too much time. On no account would I consent to
place you in the hands of Spike again—death would be
preferable to that, Harry!''

"And on no account can or will I consent to place you
again in the hands of Spike, Rose,'' answered the young
man. "Now that we know his intentions, such an act
would be almost impious.''

"Remember my aunt, dear Harry. What would be her
situation in the morning, when she found herself deserted
by her niece and Biddy—by me, whom she has nursed and
watched from childhood. and whom she loves so well.''

"I shall not deny your obligations to your aunt, Rose, and your duty to her under ordinary circumstances. But these are not ordinary circumstances; and it would be courting the direst misfortunes, nay, almost braving Providence, to place yourself in the hands of that scoundrel again, now that you are clear of them."

"Spike's a willain!" muttered Jack.

"And my desartin' the missus would be a sin that no praste would overlook aisily," put in Biddy. "When Miss Rose told me of this v'y'ge that she meant to make in the boat wid Jack Tier, I asked to come along, that I might take care of her, and see that there was plenty of wather; but ill-luck befall me if I would have t'ought of sich a thing, and the missus desarted."

"We can then run alongside of the brig, and put Biddy and Jack on board of her," said Mulford, reflecting a moment on what had just been said, "when you and I can make the best of our way to Key West, where the means of sending government vessels out after the Swash will soon offer. In this way we can not only get our friends out of the lion's jaws, but keep out of them ourselves."

"Reflect a moment, Harry," said Rose, in a low voice, but not without tenderness in its tones; "it would not do for me to go off alone with you in this boat."

"Not when you have confessed your willingness to go over the wide world with me, Rose—with me, and with me only?"

"Not even then, Harry. I know you will think better of this, when your generous nature has time to reason with your heart, on my account."

"I can only answer in your own words, Rose—never. If you return to the Swash, I shall go on board with you, and throw defiance into the very teeth of Spike. I know the men do not dislike me, and perhaps, assisted by Señor Montefalderon, and a few friends among the people, I can muster a force that will prevent my being thrown into the sea."

Rose burst into tears, and then succeeded many minutes, during which Mulford was endeavoring, with manly tender-

ness, to soothe her. As soon as our heroine recovered her
self-command, she began to discuss the matter at issue between them more coolly. For half an hour everything was
urged by each that feeling, affection, delicacy, or distrust
of Spike could well urge, and Mulford was slowly getting
the best of the argument, as well he might, the truth
being mostly of his side. Rose was bewildered, really
feeling a strong reluctance to quit her aunt, even with so
justifiable a motive, but principally shrinking from the appearance of going off alone in a boat, and almost in the
open sea, with Mulford. Had she loved Harry less, her
scruples might not have been so active, but the consciousness of the strength of her attachment, as well as her fixed
intention to become his wife the moment it was in her
power to give him her hand with the decencies of her sex,
contributed strangely to prevent her yielding to the young
man's reasoning. On the subject of the aunt, the mate
made out so good a case, that it was apparent to all in the
boat Rose would have to abandon that ground of refusal.
Spike had no object to gain by ill-treating Mrs. Budd ; and
the probability certainly was that he would get rid of her
as soon as he could, and in the most easy manner. This
was so apparent to all, that Harry had little difficulty in
getting Rose to assent to its probability. But there remained the reluctance to go alone with the mate in a
boat. This part of the subject was more difficult to manage than the other ; and Mulford betrayed as much by the
awkwardness with which he managed it. At length the
discussion was brought to a close by Jack Tier suddenly
saying,—

"Yonder is the brig ; and we are heading for her as
straight as if she was the pole, and the keel of this boat
was a compass. I see how it is, Miss Rose, and a'ter all,
I must give in. I suppose some other opportunity will
offer for me to get on board of the brig ag'n, and I'll
trust to that. If you won't go off with the mate alone, I
suppose you'll not refuse to go off in my company."

"Will you accompany us, Jack? This is more than I
had hoped for! Yes, Harry, if Jack Tier will be of the

party, I will trust my aunt to Biddy, and go with you to Key West, in order to escape from Spike.''

This was said so rapidly, and so unexpectedly, as to take Mulford completely by surprise. Scarce believing what he heard, the young man was disposed, at first, to feel hurt, though a moment's reflection showed him that he ought to rejoice in the result let the cause be what it might.

" More than I had hoped for ! " he could not refrain from repeating a little bitterly ; " is Jack Tier, then, of so much importance, that his company is thought preferable to mine ?"

"Hush, Harry !" said Rose, laying her hand on Mulford's arm, by way of strengthening her appeal. " Do not say that. You are ignorant of circumstances ; at another time you shall know them, but not now. Let it be enough for the present, that I promise to accompany you if Jack will be of our party.''

" Ay, ay, Miss Rose, I will be of the party, seeing there is no other way of getting the lamb out of the jaws of the wolf. A'ter all, it may be the wisest thing I can do, though back to the Swash I must and will come, powder or no powder, treason or no treason, at the first opportunity. Yes, my business is with the Molly, and to the Molly I shall return. It 's lucky, Miss Rose, since you have made up your mind to ship for this new cruise, that I bethought me of telling Biddy to make up a bundle of duds for you. This carpet-bag has a change or two in it, and all owing to my forethought. Your woman said, ' Miss Rose will come back wid us, Jack, and what 's the use of rumplin' the clothes for a few hours' sail in the boat ; ' but I knew womankind better, and foreseed that if master mate fell in alongside of you a'gin, you would not be apt to part company very soon.''

" I thank you, Jack, for the provision made for my comfort ; though some money would have added to it materially. My purse has a little gold in it, but a very little, and I fear you are not much better off, Harry. It will be awkward to find ourselves in Key West penniless.''

" We shall not be quite that. I left the brig absolutely

without a cent, but foreseeing that necessity might make them of use, I borrowed half a dozen of the doubloons from the bag of Señor Montefalderon, and, fortunately, they are still in my pocket. All I am worth in the world is in a bag of half eagles, rather more than a hundred altogether, which I left in my chest, in my own state-room aboard the brig.''

"You'll find that in the carpet-bag too, master mate," said Jack, coolly.

"Find what, man—not my money, surely?"

"Ay, every piece of it. Spike broke into your chest this a'ternoon, and made me hold the tools while he was doing it. He found the bag, and overhauled it—a hundred and seven half, eleven quarter, and one full-grown eagle, was the count. When he had done the job, he put all back ag'in, a'ter giving me the full-grown eagle for my share of the plunder, and told me to say nothing of what I had seen. I did say nothing, but I did a good bit of work, for, while he was at supper, I confiserated that bag, as they call it—and you will find it there among Miss Rose's clothes, with the full-grown gentleman back in his nest ag'in.''

"This is being not only honest, Tier," cried Mulford, heartily, "but thoughtful. One half that money shall be yours for this act."

"I thank'ee, sir; but I'll not touch a cent of it. It came hard, I know, Mr. Mulford; for my own hands have smarted too much with tar, not to know that the seaman ' earns his money like the horse.' "

"Still it would not be ' spending it like an ass,' Jack, to give you a portion of mine. But there will be other opportunities to talk of this. It is a sign of returning to the concerns of life, Rose, that money begins to be of interest to us. How little did we think of the doubloons, or half eagles, a few hours since, when on the wreck!"

"It was wather that we t'ought of then," put in Biddy. "Goold is good in a market, or in a town, or to send back to Ireland, to help a body's aged fader or mudder in comfort wid; but wather is the blessed thing on a wrack!"

"The brig is coming quite plainly into view, and you

had better give me the helm, Jack. It is time to bethink us of the manner of approaching her, and how we are to proceed when alongside."

This was so obviously true, that everybody felt disposed to forget all other matters, in order to conduct the proceedings of the next twenty minutes, with the necessary prudence and caution. When Mulford first took the helm, the brig was just coming clearly into view, though still looking a little misty and distant. She might then have been half a league distant, and would not have been visible at all by that light, but for the circumstance that she had no background to swallow up her outlines. Drawn against clouds, above which the rays of the moon were shed, her tracery was to be discerned, however, and minute by minute, it was getting to be more and more distinct, until it was now so plainly to be seen as to admonish the mate of the necessity of preparation in the manner mentioned.

Tier now communicated to the mate his own proposed manner of proceeding. The brig tended to the trades, the tides having very little influence on her, in the bight of the reef where she lay. As the wind stood at about east southeast, the brig's stern pointed to about west northwest, while the boat was coming down the passage from a direction nearly north from her, having, as a matter of course, the wind just free enough to lay her course. Jack's plan was to pass the brig to windward, and having got well on her bow, to brail the sail, and drift down upon her, expecting to fall in alongside, abreast of the fore-chains, into which he had intended to help Biddy, and to ascend himself, when he supposed that Mulford would again make sail, and carry off his mistress. To this scheme the mate objected that it was awkward, and a little lubberly. He substituted one in its place that differed in seamanship, and which was altogether better. Instead of passing to windward, Mulford suggested the expediency of approaching to leeward, and of coming alongside under the open bow-port, letting the sheet fly and brailing the sail, when the boat should be near enough to carry her to the point of destination without further assistance from her canvas.

Jack Tier took his officer's improvement on his own plan in perfect good part, readily and cheerfully expressing his willingness to aid the execution of it all that lay in his power. As the boat sailed unusually well, there was barely time to explain to each individual his or her part in the approaching critical movements, ere the crisis itself drew near; then each of the party became silent and anxious, and events were regarded rather than words.

It is scarcely necessary to say that Mulford sailed a boat well. He held the sheet in his hand, as the little craft came up under the lee-quarter of the brig, while Jack stood by the brail. The eyes of the mate glanced over the hull of the vessel to ascertain, if possible, who might be stirring; but not a sign of life could he detect on board her. This very silence made Mulford more distrustful and anxious, for he feared a trap was set for him. He expected to see the head of one of the blacks at least peering over the bulwarks, but nothing like a man was visible. It was too late to pause, however, and the sheet was slowly eased off, Jack hauling on the brail at the same time; the object being to prevent the sail's flapping, and the sound reaching the ears of Spike. As Mulford used great caution, and had previously schooled Jack on the subject, this important point was successfully achieved. Then the mate put his helm down, and the boat shot up under the brig's lee-bow. Jack was ready to lay hold of one of the bowsprit shrouds, and presently the boat was breasted up under the desired port, and secured in that position. Mulford quitted the stern-sheets, and cast a look in upon deck. Nothing was to be seen, though he heard the heavy breathing of the blacks, both of whom were sound asleep on a sail that they had spread on the forecastle.

The mate whispered for Biddy to come to the port. This the Irishwoman did at once, having kissed Rose, and taken her leave of her previously. Tier also came to the port, through which he passed, getting on deck with a view to assist Biddy, who was awkward, almost as a matter of course, to pass through the same opening. He had just succeeded, when the whole party was startled, some of them almost petrified, indeed, by a hail from the quarter-deck in the well-known, deep tones of Spike.

"For'ard, there!" hailed the captain. Receiving no answer, he immediately repeated, in a shorter, quicker call, "Forecastle, there!"

"Sir," answered Jack Tier, who by this time had come to his senses.

"Who has the lookout on that forecastle?"

"I have it, sir—I, Jack Tier. You know, sir, I was to have it from two till daylight."

"Ay, ay, I remember now. How does the brig ride to her anchor?"

"As steady as a church, sir. She's had no more sheer the whole watch than if she was moored head and starn."

"Does the wind stand as it did?"

"No change, sir. As dead a trade-wind as ever blowed."

"What hard breathing is that I hear for'ard?"

"'T is the two niggers, sir. They've turned in on deck, and are napping it off at the rate of six knots. There's no keepin' way with a nigger in snorin'."

"I thought I heard loud whispering, too, but I suppose it was a sort of half-dream. I'm often in that way nowadays. Jack!"

"Sir."

"Go to the scuttle-butt and get me a pot of fresh water; my coppers are hot with hard thinking."

Jack did as ordered, and soon stood beneath the coach-house deck with Spike, who had come out of his state-room, heated and uneasy at he knew not what. The captain drank a full pint of water at a single draught.

"That's refreshing." he said, returning Jack the tin-pot, "and I feel the cooler for it. How much does it want of daylight, Jack?"

"Two hours, I think, sir. The order was passed to me to have all hands called as soon as it was broad day."

"Ay, that is right. We must get our anchor and be off as soon as there is light to do it in. Doubloons may melt as well as flour, and are best cared for soon when cared for at all."

"I shall see and give the call as soon as it is day. I hope, Captain Spike, I can take the liberty of an old shipmate, however, and say one thing to you, which is this—look out for the Poughkeepsie, which is very likely to be on your heels when you least expect her."

"That's your way of thinking, is it, Jack? Well, I thank you, old one, for the hint, but have little fear of that craft. We've had our legs together, and I think the brig has the longest."

As the captain said this, he gaped like a hound, and went into his state-room. Jack lingered on the quarter-deck, waiting to hear him fairly in his berth, when he made a sign to Biddy, who had got as far aft as the galley, where she was secreted, to pass down into the cabin, as silently as possible. In a minute or two more, he moved forward, singing in a low, cracked voice, as was often his practice, slowly made his way to the forecastle. Mulford was just beginning to think the fellow had changed his mind, and meant to stick by the brig, when the little, rotund figure of the assistant-steward was seen passing through the port, and to drop noiselessly on a thwart. Jack then moved to the bow, and cast off the painter, the head of the boat slowly falling off under the pressure of the breeze on that part of her mast and sail which rose above the hull of the Swash. Almost at the same moment, the mate let go the stern-fast, and the boat was free.

It required some care to set the sail without the canvas flapping. It was done, however, before the boat fairly took the breeze, when all was safe. In half a minute the wind struck the sail, and away the little craft started, passing swiftly ahead of the brig. Soon as far enough off, Mulford put up his helm and wore short round, bringing the boat's head to the northward, or in its proper direction; after which they flew along before the wind, which seemed to be increasing in force, with a velocity that really appeared to defy pursuit. All this time the brig lay in its silence and solitude, no one stirring on board her, and all, in fact, Biddy alone excepted, profoundly ignorant of what had just been passing alongside of her. Ten minutes of running off with a flowing sheet, caused the Swash to look indistinct and hazy again; in ten minutes more she was swallowed up, hull, spars, and all, in the gloom of night.

Mulford and Rose now felt something like that security, without the sense of which happiness itself is but an uneasy feeling, rendering the anticipations of evil the more painful by the magnitude of the stake. There they sat, now in the stern-sheets by themselves, Jack Tier having placed himself near the bows of the boat, to look out for rocks, as well as to trim the craft. It was not long before Rose was leaning on Harry's shoulder, and ere an hour was past, she had fallen into a sweet sleep in that attitude, the young man having carefully covered her person with a capacious shawl, the same that had been used on the wreck. As for Jack, he maintained his post in silence, sitting with his arms crossed, and the hands thrust into the breast of his jacket, sailor fashion, a picture of nautical vigilance. It was some time after Rose had fallen asleep, that this singular being spoke for the first time.

"Keep her away a bit, maty," he said, "keep her away, half a point or so. She's been travellin' like a racer since we left the brig; and yonder's the first streak of day."

"By the time we have been running," observed Mulford, "I should think we must be getting near the northern side of the reef."

"All of that, sir, depend on it. Here's a rock close aboard on us, to which we're comin' fast—just off here, on our weather-bow, that looks to me like the place where you landed a'ter that swim, and where we had stowed ourselves when Stephen Spike made us out, and gave chase."

"It is surprising to me, Jack, that you should have any fancy to stick by a man of Spike's character. He is a precious rascal, as we all can see, now, and you are rather an honest sort of fellow."

"Do you love the young woman there that's lying in your arms, as it might be, and whom you say you wish to marry?"

"The question is a queer one, but it is easily answered. More than my life, Jack."

"Well, how happens it that you succeed, when the world has so many other young men who might please her as well as yourself?"

"It may be that no other loves her as well, and she has had the sagacity to discover it."

"Quite likely. So it is with me and Stephen Spike. I fancy a man whom other folk despise and condemn. Why I stand by him is my own secret; but stand by him I do and will."

"This is all very strange, after your conduct on the island, and your conduct to-night. I shall not disturb your secret, however, Jack, but leave you to enjoy it by yourself. Is this the rock of which you spoke, that we are now passing?"

"The same; and there's the spot in which we was stowed when they made us out from the brig; and hereaway, a cable's length, more or less, the wreck of that Mexican craft must lie."

"What is that rising above the water, thereaway, Jack; more in our weather-beam?"

"I see what you mean, sir; it looks like a spar. By George! there's two on e'm; and they *do* seem to be the schooner's masts."

Sure enough! a second look satisfied Mulford that two mast-heads were out of water, and within a hundred yards of the place the boat was running past. Standing on a short distance, or far enough to give himself room, the mate put his helm down, and tacked the boat. The flapping of the sail, and the little movement of shifting over the sheet, awoke Rose, who was immediately apprised of the discovery. As soon as round, the boat went glancing up to the spars, and presently was riding by one, Jack Tier having caught hold of a topmast-shroud, when Mulford let fly his sheet again, and luffed short up to the spot. By this time the increasing light was sufficiently strong to render objects distinct, when near by, and no doubt remained any longer in the mind of Mulford about the two mast-heads being those of the unfortunate Mexican schooner.

"Well, of all I have ever seen I 've never see'd the like of this afore ! " exclaimed Jack. "When we left this here craft, sir, you 'll remember, she had almost turned turtle, laying over so far as to bring her upper coamings under water ; now she stands right side up, as erect as if docked ! My navigation can't get along with this, Mr. Mulford, and it does seem like witchcraft."

"It is certainly a very singular incident, Jack, and I have been trying to come at its causes."

"Have you succeeded, Harry ? " asked Rose, by this time wide awake, and wondering like the others.

"It must have happened in this wise. The wreck was abandoned by us some little distance out here, to windward. The schooner's masts, of course, pointed to leeward, and when she drifted in here, they have first touched on a shelving rock, and as they have been shoved up, little by little, they have acted as levers to right the hull, until the cargo has shifted back into its proper berth, which has suddenly set the vessel up again."

"Ay, ay, sir," answered Jack, "all that might have happened had she been above water, or any part of her above water; but you 'll remember, maty, that soon after we left her she went down."

"Not entirely. The wreck settled in the water no faster after we had left it, than it had done before. It continued to sink, inch by inch, as the air escaped, and no faster after it had gone entirely out of sight than before ; not as fast, indeed, as the water became denser the lower it got. The great argument against my theory is the fact, that after the hull got beneath the surface, the wind could not act on it. This is true in one sense, however, and not in another. The waves, or the pressure of the water produced by the wind, might act on the hull some time after we ceased to see it. But the currents have set the craft in here, and the hull floating always, very little force would cant the craft. If the rock were shelving and slippery, I see no great difficulty in the way ; and the barrels may have been so lodged, that a trifle would set them rolling back again, each one helping to produce a change that would move another. As for the ballast, that, I am certain, could not shift, for it was stowed with great care. As the vessel righted, the air still in her moved, and as soon as the water permitted, it escaped by the hatches, when the craft went down, as a matter of course. The air may have aided in bringing the hull upright by its movements in the water."

This was the only explanation to which the ingenuity of Mulford could help him, under the circumstances, and it may have been the right one, or not. There lay the schooner, however, in some five or six fathoms of water, with her two topmasts and lower mast-heads out of the element, as upright as if docked! It may all have occurred as the mate fancied, or the unusual incident may have been owing to some of the many mysterious causes which baffle inquiry, when the agents are necessarily hidden from examination.

"Spike intends to come and look out for this wreck, you tell me, Jack; in the hope of getting at the doubloons it contains?" said Mulford, when the boat had lain a minute or two longer, riding by the mast-head.

"Ay, ay, sir; that's his notion, sir; and he'll be in a great stew, as soon as he turns out, which must be about this time, and finds me missing; for I was to pilot him to the spot."

"He'll want no pilot, now. It will be scarcely possible to pass anywhere near this, and not see these spars. But the discovery almost induces me to change my own plans. What say you, Rose? We have now reached the northern side of the reef, when it is time to haul close by the wind, if we wish to beat up to Key West. There is a moral certainty, however, that the sloop-of-war is somewhere in the neighborhood of the Dry Tortugas, which are much the most easily reached, being to leeward. We might run down to the light-house by mid-day, while it is doubtful if we could reach the town until to-morrow morning. I should like exceedingly to have five minutes' conversation with the commander of the Poughkeepsie."

"Ay, to let him know where he will be likely to fall in with the Molly Swash and her traitor master, Stephen

Spike," cried Jack Tier. "Never mind, maty; let 'em come on; both the Molly and her master have got long legs and clean heels. Stephen Spike will show 'em how to thread the channels of a reef."

"It is amazing to me, Jack, that you should stand by your old captain in feeling, while you are helping to thwart him, all you can, in his warmest wishes."

"He's a willain!" muttered Jack, "a reg'lar willain is Stephen Spike!"

"If a villain, why do you so evidently wish to keep him out of the hands of the law? Let him be captured and punished, as his crimes require."

"Men's willains, all round," still muttered Jack. "Hark'ee, Mr. Mulford, I've sailed in the brig longer than you, and know'd her in her comeliest and best days—when she was young, and blooming, and lovely to the eye, as the young creature at your side—and it would go to my heart to have anything happen to her. Then, I've know'd Stephen a long time, too, and old shipmates get a feelin' for each other, sooner or later. I tell you now, honestly, Mr. Mulford, Captain Adam Mull shall never make a prisoner of Stephen Spike, if I can prevent it."

The mate laughed at this sally, but Rose appeared anxious to change the conversation, and she managed to open a discussion on the subject of the course it might be best to steer. Mulford had several excellent reasons to urge for wishing to run down to the islets, all of which, with a single exception, he laid before his betrothed. The concealed reason was one of the strongest of them all, as usually happens when there is a reason to conceal, but of that he took care to say nothing. The result was an acquiescence on the part of Rose, whose consent was yielded more to the influence of one particular consideration than to all the rest united. That one was this: Harry had pointed out to her the importance to himself of his appearing early to denounce the character and movements of the brig, lest, through his former situation in her, his own conduct might be seriously called in question.

As soon as the matter was determined, Jack was told to let go his hold, the sheet was drawn aft, and away sped the boat. No sooner did Mulford cause the little craft to keep away than it almost flew, as if conscious it were bound to its proper home, skimming swiftly over the waves, like a bird returning eagerly to its nest. An hour later the party breakfasted. While at this meal, Jack Tier pointed out to the mate a white speck, in the southeastern board, which he took to be the brig coming through the passage, on her way to the wreck.

"No matter," returned the mate. "Though we can see her, she cannot see us. There is that much advantage in our being small, Rose, if it do prevent our taking exercise by walking the deck."

Soon after, Mulford made a very distant sail in the northwestern board, which he hoped might turn out to be the Poughkeepsie. It was but another speck, but its position was somewhat like that in which he had expected to meet the sloop-of-war. The two vessels were so far apart that one could not be seen from the other, and there was little hope that the Poughkeepsie would detect Spike at his toil on the wreck; but the mate fully expected that the ship would go into the anchorage, among the islets, in order to ascertain what had become of the schooner. If she did not go in herself, she would be almost certain to send in a boat.

The party from the brigantine had run down before the wind more than two hours before the light-house began to show itself, just rising out of the waves. This gave them the advantage of a beacon, Mulford having steered hitherto altogether by the sun, the direction of the wind, and the trending of the reef. Now he had his port in sight, it being his intention to take possession of the dwelling of the light-house keeper, and to remain in it, until a favorable opportunity occurred to remove Rose to Key West. The young man had also another important project in view, which it will be in season to mention as it reaches the moment of its fulfilment.

The rate of sailing of the light-house boat, running before a brisk trade-wind, could not be much less than nine miles in the hour. About eleven o'clock, therefore, the lively craft shot through one of the narrow channels of the islets, and entered the haven. In a few minutes all three of the adventurers were on the little wharf where the light-house people were in the habit of landing. Rose proceeded to the house, while Harry and Jack remained to secure the boat. For the latter purpose a sort of slip, or little dock, had been made, and when the boat was hauled into it, it lay so snug that not only was the craft secure from injury, but it was actually hid from the view of all but those who stood directly above it.

"This is a snug berth for the boat, Jack," observed the mate, when he had hauled it into the place mentioned, "and by unstepping the mast, a passer-by would not suspect such a craft of lying in it. Who knows what occasion there may be for concealment, and I 'll e'en do that thing."

To a casual listener, Harry, in unstepping the mast, might have seemed influenced merely by a motiveless impulse ; but, in truth, a latent suspicion of Jack's intentions instigated him, and as he laid the mast, sprit, and sail on the thwarts, he determined, in his own mind, to remove them all to some other place, as soon as an opportunity for doing so unobserved should occur. He and Jack now followed Rose to the house.

The islets were found deserted and tenantless. Not a human being had entered the house since Rose left it, the evening she had remained so long ashore, in company with her aunt and the Señor Montefalderon. This our heroine knew from the circumstance of finding a slight fastening of the outer door in the precise situation in which she had left it with her own hands. At first a feeling of oppression and awe prevailed with both Harry and Rose, when they recollected the fate of those who had so lately been tenants of the place ; but this gradually wore off, and each soon got to be more at home. As for Jack, he very coolly rummaged the lockers, as he called the drawers and closets of the place, and made his preparations for cooking a very delicious repast, in which calipash and calipee were to be material ingredients. The necessary condiments were easily enough found in that place, turtle being a common dish there, and it was not long before steams that might have quickened the appetite of an alderman filled the kitchen. Rose rummaged, too, and found a clean table-cloth, plates, glasses, bowls, spoons, and knives; in a word, all that was necessary to spread a plain but plentiful board. While all this was doing, Harry took some fishing-tackle, and proceeded to a favorable spot among the rocks. In twenty minutes he returned with a fine mess of that most delicious little fish that goes by the very unpoetical name of "hog-fish," from the circumstance of its giving a grunt not unlike that of a living porker, when rudely drawn from its proper element. Nothing was now wanting to not only a comfortable, but to what was really a most epicurean meal, and Jack just begged the lovers to have patience for an hour or so, when he promised them dishes that even New York could not furnish.

Harry and Rose first retired to pay a little attention to their dress, and then they joined each other in a walk. The mate had found some razors, and was clean shaved. He had also sequestered a shirt, and made some other little additions to his attire, that contributed to give him the ap-pearance of being, that which he really was, a very gentle-man-like looking young sailor. Rose had felt no necessity for taking liberties with the effects of others, though a good deal of female attire was found in the dwelling. As was afterward ascertained, a family ordinarily dwelt there, but most of it had gone to Key West, on a visit, at the moment when the man and boy left in charge had fallen into the hands of the Mexicans, losing their lives in the manner mentioned.

While walking together, Harry opened his mind to Rose, on the subject which lay nearest to his heart, and which had been at the bottom of this second visit to the islets of the Dry Tortugas. During the different visits of Wallace to the brig, the boat's crew of the Poughkeepsie had held more or less discourse with the people of the Swash. This usually happens on such occasions, and although Spike had endeavored to prevent it, when his brig lay in this bay, he had not been entirely successful. Such discourse is commonly jocular, and sometimes witty; every speech, coming from which side it may, ordinarily commencing with "shipmate," though the interlocutors never saw each other before that interview. In one of the visits an allusion was made to cargo, when "the pretty girl aft" was mentioned as being a part of the cargo of the Swash. In answer to this remark, the wit of the Poughkeepsie had told the brig's man, "You had better send her on board us, *for we carry a chaplain, a regular-built one, that will be a bishop some day or other, perhaps,* and we can get her spliced to one of our young officers." This remark had induced the sailor of the Molly to ask if a sloop-of-war really carried such a piece of marine luxury as a chaplain, and the explanation given went to say that the clergyman in question did not properly belong to the Poughkeepsie, but was to be put on board a frigate, as soon as they fell in with one that he named. Now, all this Mulford overheard, and he remembered it at a moment when it might be of use. Situated as he and Rose were, he felt the wisdom and propriety of their being united, and his present object was to persuade his companion to be of the same way of thinking. He doubted not that the sloop-of-war would come in, ere long, perhaps that very day, and he believed it would be an easy matter to induce her chaplain to perform the ceremony. America is a country in which every facility exists, with the fewest possible impediments, to getting married; and, we regret to be compelled to add, to getting unmarried also. There are no banns, no licenses, no consent of parents even, usually necessary, and persons who are of the age of discretion, which, as respects females and matrimony, is a very tender age indeed, may be married, if they see fit, almost without form or ceremony. There existed, therefore, no legal impediment to the course Mulford desired to take; and his principal, if not his only difficulty, would be with Rose. Over her scruples he hoped to prevail, and not without reason, as the case he could and did present was certainly one of a character that entitled him to be heard with great attention.

In the first place, Mrs. Budd had approved of the connection, and it was understood between them, that the young people were to be united at the first port in which a clergyman of their own persuasion could be found, and previously to reaching home. This had been the aunt's own project, for, weak and silly as she was, the relict had a woman's sense of the proprieties. It had occurred to her that it would be more respectable to make the long journey which lay before them, escorted by a nephew and husband, than escorted by even an accepted lover. It is true that she had never anticipated a marriage in a lighthouse, and under the circumstances in which Rose was now placed, though it might be more reputable that her niece should quit the islets as the wife of Harry than as his betrothed. Then Mulford still apprehended Spike. In that remote part of the world, almost beyond the confines of society, it was not easy to foretell what claims he might set up, in the event of his meeting them there. Armed with the authority of a husband, Mulford could resist him, in any such case, with far better prospects of success than if he should appear only in the character of a suitor.

Rose listened to these arguments, ardently and somewhat eloquently put, as a girl of her years and habits would be apt to listen to a favored lover. She was much too sincere to deny her own attachment, which the events of the last few days had increased almost to intenseness, so apt is our tenderness to augment in behalf of those for whom we feel solicitude; and her judgment told her that the more sober part of Harry's reasoning was entitled to consideration. As his wife, her situation would certainly be much less equivocal and awkward, than while she bore a different name, and was admitted to be a single woman, and it might yet be weeks before the duty she owed her aunt would allow her to proceed to the north. But, after all, Harry prevailed more through the influence of his hold on Rose's affections, as would have been the case with almost every other woman, than through any force of reasoning. He truly loved, and that made him eloquent when he spoke of love; sympathy in all he uttered being his great ally. When summoned to the house, by the call of Jack, who announced that the turtle-soup was ready, they returned with the understanding that the chaplain of the Poughkeepsie should unite them, did the vessel come in, and would the functionary mentioned consent to perform the ceremony.

"It would be awkward—nay, it would be distressing, Harry, to have him refuse," said the blushing Rose, as they walked slowly back to the house, more desirous to prolong their conversation than to partake of the bountiful provision of Jack Tier. The latter could not but be acceptable, nevertheless, to a young man like Mulford, who was in robust health, and who had fared so badly for the last eight-and-forty hours. When he sat down to the table, therefore, which was covered by a snow-white cloth, with smoking and most savory viands on it, it will not be surprising if we say it was with a pleasure that was derived from one of the great necessities of our nature.

Sancho calls for benediction "on the man who invented sleep." It would have been more just to have asked this boon in behalf of him who invented eating and turtle-soup. The wearied fall into sleep, as it might be unwittingly; sometimes against their will, and often against their interests; while many a man is hungry without possessing the means of appeasing his appetite. Still more daily feel hunger without possessing turtle-soup. Certain persons impute this delicious compound to the genius of some London alderman, but we rather think unjustly. Aldermanic genius is easily excited and rendered active, no doubt, by strong appeals on such a theme, but our own experience inclines us to believe that the tropics usually send their inventions to the less fruitful regions of the earth along with their products. We have little doubt, could the fact be now ascertained, that it would be found turtle-soup was originally invented by just some such worthy as Jack Tier, who, in filling his coppers to tickle the captain's appetite, had used all the condiments within his reach; ventured on a sort of Regent's punch; and, as the consequence, had brought forth the dish so often eulogized, and so well be-

loved. It is a little extraordinary that in Paris, the seat of
gastronomy, one rarely, if ever, hears of or sees this dish ;
while in London it is to be met in almost as great abundance as in one of our larger commercial towns. But so it
is, and we cannot say we much envy a *cuisine* its *patés*, and
soufflets, and its *à la* this and *à la* thats, but which was never
redolent with the odors of turtle-soup.

"Upon my word, Jack, you have made out famously
with your dinner, or supper, whichever you may please to
call it," cried Mulford, gayly, as he took his seat at table,
after having furnished Rose with a chair. "Nothing appears to be wanting ; but here is a good pilot bread, potatoes
even, and other little niceties, in addition to the turtle and
the fish. These good people of the light seem to have lived
comfortably, at any rate."

"Why should they not, maty?" answered Jack, beginning to help to soup. "Living on one of these islets is like
living afloat. Everything is laid in, as for an outward bound
craft ; then the reef must always furnish fish and turtle.
I 've overhauled the lockers pretty thoroughly, and find a
plenty of stores to last *us* a month. Tea, sugar, coffee,
bread, pickles, potatoes, onions, and all other nicknacks."

"The poor people who own these stores will be heavy-
hearted enough when they come to learn the reason why
we have been put in undisturbed possession of their property," said Rose. "We must contrive some means of re-
paying them for such articles as we may use, Harry."

"That's easily enough done, Miss Rose. Drop one of
the half-eagles in a tea-pot, or a mug, and they 'll be certain to fall in with it when they come back. Nothin' is
easier than to pay a body's debts, when a body has the
will and the means. Now, the worst enemy of Stephen
Spike must own that his brig never quits port with unsettled bills. Stephen has his faults, like other mortals ;
but he has his good p'ints, too."

"Still praising Spike, my good Jack," cried the mate,
a little provoked at this pertinacity in the deputy-steward,
in sticking to his ship and his shipmate. "I should have
thought that you had sailed with him long enough to have

found him out, and to wish never to put your foot in his cabin again."

"Why, no, maty, a craft is a craft, and a body gets to like even the faults of one in which a body has gone through gales, and squalls, with a whole skin. I like the Swash, and for sartain things I like her captain."

"Meaning by that, it is your intention to get on board of the one, and to sail with the other, again, as soon as you can."

"I do, Mr. Mulford, and make no bones in telling on 't. You know that I came here without wishing it."

"Well, Jack, no one will attempt to control your movements, but you shall be left your own master. I feel it to be a duty, however, as one who may know more of the law than yourself, as well as more of Stephen Spike, to tell you that he is engaged in a treasonable commerce with the enemy, and that he, and all who voluntarily remain with him, knowing this fact, may be made to swing for it."

"Then I'll swing for it," returned Jack, sullenly.

"There is a little obstinacy in this, my good fellow, and you must be reasoned out of it. I am under infinite obligations to you, Jack, and shall ever be ready to own them. Without you to sail the boat, I might have been left to perish on that rock—for God only knows whether any vessel would have seen me in passing. Most of those who go through that passage keep the western side of the reef aboard, they tell me, on account of there being better water on that side of the channel, and the chance of a man's being seen on a rock, by ships a league or two off, would be small indeed. Yes, Jack, I owe my life to you, and am proud to own it."

"You owe it to Miss Rose, maty, who put me up to the enterprise, and who shared it with me."

"To her I owe more than life," answered Harry, looking at his beloved as she delighted in being regarded by him, "but even she, with all her wishes to serve me, would have been helpless without your skill in managing a boat. I owe also to your good-nature the happiness of having Rose with me at this moment; for without you she would not have come."

"I'll not deny it, maty—take another ladle-full of the soup, Miss Rosy: a quart of it would n't hurt an infant—I'll not deny it, Mr. Mulford—I know by the way you 've got rid of the first bowlful that *you* are ready for another and there it is—I'll not deny it, and all I can say is that you are heartily welcome to my sarvices."

"I thank you, Jack; but all this only makes me more desirous of being of use to you, now, when it 's in my power. I wish you to stick by me, and not to return to the Swash. As soon as I get to New York I shall build or buy a ship, and the berth of steward in her shall always be open to you."

"Thankee, maty; thankee, with all my heart. It 's something to know that a port is open to leeward, and, though I cannot *now* accept your offer, the day *may* come when I shall be glad to do so."

"If you like living ashore better, our house will always be ready to receive you. I should be glad to leave as handy a little fellow as yourself behind me whenever I went to sea. There are a hundred things in which you might be useful, and fully earn your biscuit, so as to have no qualms about eating the bread of idleness."

"Thankee, thankee, maty," cried Jack, dashing a tear out of his eye with the back of his hand, "thankee, sir, from the bottom of my heart. The time *may* come, but not now. My papers is signed for this v'y'ge. Stephen Spike has a halter round his neck, as you say yourself, and it 's necessary for me to be there to look to 't. We all have our callin's and duties, and this is mine. I stick by the Molly and her captain until both are out of this scrape, or both are condemned. I know nothin' of treason; but if the law wants another victim, I must take my chance."

Mulford was surprised at this steadiness of Jack's, in what he thought a very bad cause, and was quite as much surprised that Rose did not join him, in his endeavors to persuade the steward not to be so foolhardy, as to endeavor to go back to the brig. Rose did not, however; sitting silently eating her dinner the whole time, though she occasionally cast glances of interest at both the speakers the while. In this state of things the mate abandoned the attempt, for the moment, intending to return to the subject, after having had a private conference with his betrothed.

Notwithstanding the little drawback just related, that was a happy as well as a delicious repast. The mate did full justice to the soup, and afterward to the fish with the unpoetical name; and Rose ate more than she had done in the last three days. The habits of discipline prevented Jack from taking his seat at the table, though pressed by both Rose and Harry to do so, but he helped himself to the contents of a bowl, and did full justice to his own art, on one aside. The little fellow was delighted with the praises that were bestowed on his dishes; and for the moment, the sea, its dangers, its tornadoes, wrecks, and races, were all forgotten in the security and pleasures of so savory a repast.

"Folks ashore don't know how sailors sometimes live," said Jack, holding a large spoon filled with the soup ready to plunge into a tolerably capacious mouth.

"Or how they sometimes starve," answered Rose. "Remember our own situation, less than forty-eight hours since!"

"All very true, Miss Rose; yet, you see, turtle-soup brings us up, a'ter all. Would you like a glass of wine, maty?"

"Very much indeed, Jack, after so luscious a soup; but wishing for it will not bring it here."

"That remains to be seen, sir. I call this a bottle of something that looks very much like a wine."

"Claret, as I live! Why, where should light-house keepers get the taste for claret?"

"I've thought of that myself, Mr. Mulford, and have supposed that some of Uncle Sam's officers have brought the liquor to this part of the world. I understand a party of 'em was here surveyin' all last winter. It seems they come in the cool weather, and get their sights and measure their distances, and go home in the warm weather, and work out their traverses, in the shade, as it might be."

"This seems likely, Jack; but, come whence it may it is welcome, and we will taste it."

Mulford then drew the cork of this mild and grateful liquor, and helped his companions and himself. In this age of moral *tours de force*, one scarcely dare say anything favorable of a liquid that even bears the name of wine, or extol the shape of a bottle. It is truly the era of exaggeration. Nothing is treated in the old-fashioned, natural, common-sense way. Virtue is no longer virtue, unless it get upon stilts ; and as for sin's being confined to "transgression against the law of God," audacious would be the wretch who should presume to limit the sway of the societies by any dogma so narrow ! A man may be as abstemious as an anchorite and get no credit for it, unless "he sign the pledge" ; or, signing the pledge, he may get fuddled in corners, and be cited as a miracle of sobriety. The test of morals is no longer in the abuse of the gifts of Providence, but in their use ; prayers are deserting the closet for the corners of streets, and charity (not the giving of alms) has got to be so earnest in the demonstration of its nature, as to be pretty certain to "begin at home," and to end where it begins. Even the art of mendacity has been aroused by the great progress which is making by all around it, and many manifest the strength of their ambition by telling ten lies while their fathers would have been satisfied with telling only one. This art has made an extraordinary progress within the last quarter of a century, aspiring to an ascendency that was formerly conceded only to truth, until he who gains his daily bread by it has some such contempt for the sneaking wretch who does business on the small scale, as the slayer of his thousands in the field is known to entertain for him who kills only a single man in the course of a long life.

At the risk of damaging the reputations of our hero and heroine, we shall frankly aver the fact that both Harry and Rose partook of the *vin de Bordeaux*, a very respectable bottle of Medoc, by the way, which had been forgotten by Uncle Sam's people, in the course of the preceding winter, agreeably to Jack Tier's conjecture. One glass sufficed for Rose, and, contrary as it may be to all modern theory, she was somewhat the better for it ; while the mate and Jack

Tier quite half emptied the bottle, being none the worse. There they sat, enjoying the security and abundance which had succeeded to their late danger, happy in that security, happy in themselves, and happy in the prospects of a bright future. It was just as practicable for them to remain at the Dry Tortugas, as it was for the family which ordinarily dwelt at the light. The place was amply supplied with everything that would be necessary for their wants, for months to come, and Harry caused his betrothed to blush, as he whispered to her, should the chaplain arrive, he should delight in passing the honey-moon where they then were.

"I could tend the light," he added, smiling, "which would be not only an occupation, but a useful occupation; you could read all those books from beginning to end, and Jack could keep us supplied with fish. By the way, master steward, are you in the humor for motion, so soon after your hearty meal?"

"Anything to be useful," answered Jack, cheerfully.

"Then do me the favor to go up into the lantern of the light-house, and take a look for the sloop-of-war. If she's in sight at all, you'll find her off here to the northward; and while you are aloft you may as well make a sweep of the whole horizon. There hangs the light-house keeper's glass, which may help your eyes, by stepping into the gallery outside of the lantern."

Jack willingly complied, taking the glass and proceeding forthwith to the other building. Mulford had two objects in view in giving this commission to the steward. He really wished to ascertain what was the chance of seeing the Poughkeepsie, in the neighborhood of the islets, and felt just that indisposition to move himself, that is apt to come over one who has recently made a very bountiful meal, while he also desired to have another private conversation with Rose.

A good portion of the time that Jack was gone, and he stayed quite an hour in the lantern, our lovers conversed as lovers are much inclined to converse; that is to say, of themselves, their feelings, and their prospects. Mulford told

Rose of his hopes and fears, while he visited at the house of her aunt, previously to sailing, and the manner in which his suspicions had been first awakened in reference to the intentions of Spike—intentions, so far as they were connected with an admiration of his old commander's niece and possibly in connection also with the little fortune she was known to possess, but not in reference to the bold project to which he had, in fact, resorted. No distrust of the scheme finally put in practice had ever crossed the mind of the young mate, until he received the unexpected order, mentioned in our opening chapter, to prepare the brig for the reception of Mrs. Budd and her party. Harry confessed his jealousy of one youth whom he dreaded far more even than he had ever dreaded Spike, and whose apparent favor with Rose, and actual favor with her aunt, had given him many a sleepless night.

They next conversed of the future, which to them seemed full of flowers. Various were the projects started, discussed and dismissed, between them, the last almost as soon as proposed. On one thing they were of a mind, as soon as proposed. Harry was to have a ship as quick as one could be purchased by Rose's means, and the promised bride laughingly consented to make one voyage to Europe along with her husband.

"I wonder, dear Rose, my poverty has never presented any difficulties in the way of our union," said Harry, sensibly touched with the free way his betrothed disposed of her own money in his behalf; "but neither you nor Mrs. Budd has ever seemed to think of the difference there is between us in this respect."

"What is the trifle I possess, Harry, set in the balance against your worth? My aunt, as you say, has thought I might even be the gainer by the exchange."

"I am sure I feel a thousand times indebted to Mrs. Budd—"

"*Aunt* Budd. You must learn to say, '*my* Aunt Budd,' Mr. Henry Mulford, if you mean to live in peace with her unworthy niece."

"*Aunt* Budd, then," returned Harry, laughing, for the

laugh came easily that evening ; "Aunt Budd, if you wish it, Rose. I can have no objection to call any relative of yours uncle or aunt."

"I think we are intimate enough, now, to ask you a question or two, Harry, touching my aunt," continued Rose, looking stealthily over her shoulder, as if apprehensive of being overheard. "You know how fond she is of speaking of the sea, and of indulging in nautical phrases?"

"Any one must have observed that, Rose," answered the young man, gazing up at the wall, in order not to be compelled to look the beautiful creature before him in the eyes ; "Mrs. Budd has very strong tastes that way."

"Now tell me, Harry—that is, answer me frankly, I mean—she is not always right, is she?"

"Why, no ; not absolutely so—that is, not absolutely always so ; few persons are always right, you know."

Rose remained silent and embarrassed for a moment, after which she pursued the discourse.

"But aunty does not know as much of the sea and of ships as she thinks she does?"

"Perhaps not. We all overrate our own acquirements. I dare say that even I am not as good a seaman as I fancy myself to be."

"Even Spike admits that you are what he calls ' a prime seaman.' But it is not easy for a woman to get a correct knowledge of the use of all the strange and sometimes uncouth terms that you sailors use."

"Certainly not, and for that reason I would rather you should never attempt it, Rose. We rough sons of the ocean would prefer to hear our wives make divers pretty blunders, rather than to be swaggering about like so many ' old salts.' "

"Mr. Mulford ! Does Aunt Budd swagger like an old salt ?"

"Dearest Rose, I was not thinking of your aunt, but of *you*. Of you, as you are, feminine, spirited, lovely alike in form and character, and of you a graduate of the ocean and full of its language and ideas."

It was probable Rose was not displeased at this allusion

to herself, for a smile struggled around her pretty mouth, and she did not look at all angry. After another short pause, she resumed the discourse.

"My aunt did not very clearly comprehend those explanations of yours about the time of day, and the longitude," she said, "nor am I quite certain that I did myself."

"You understood them far better than Mrs. Budd, Rose. Women are so little accustomed to think on such subjects at all, that it is not surprising they sometimes get confused. I do wish, however, that your aunt could be persuaded to be more cautious, in the presence of strangers, on the subject of terms she does not understand."

"I feared it might be so, Harry," answered Rose, in a low voice, as if unwilling even he should know the full extent of her thoughts on this subject; "but my aunt's heart is most excellent, though she may make mistakes occasionally. I owe her a great deal, if not absolutely my education, certainly my health and comfort through childhood, and more prudent, womanly advice than you may suppose, perhaps, since I have left school. How she became the dupe of Spike, indeed, is to me unaccountable; for in all that relates to health, she is, in general, both acute and skilful."

"Spike is a man of more art than he appears to be to superficial observers. On my first acquaintance with him, I mistook him for a frank, fearless, but well-meaning sailor, who loved hazardous voyages and desperate speculation— a sort of innocent gambler; but I have learned to know better. His means are pretty much reduced to his brig, and she is getting old, and can do but little more service. His projects are plain enough, now. By getting you into his power, he hoped to compel a marriage, in which case both your fortune and your aunt's would contribute to repair his."

"He might have killed me, but I never would have married him," rejoined Rose, firmly. "Is not that Jack coming down the steps of the light-house?"

"It is. I find that fellow's attachment to Spike very

extraordinary, Rose. Can you, in any manner, account for it?"

Rose at first seemed disposed to reply. Her lips parted, as if about to speak, and closed again, as glancing her eyes toward the open door, she seemed to expect the appearance of the steward's little, rotund form on the threshold, which held her tongue-tied. A brief interval elapsed, however, ere Jack actually arrived, and Rose, perceiving that Harry was curiously expecting her answer, said hurriedly, "It may be hatred, not attachment."

The next moment Jack Tier entered the room. He had been gone rather more than an hour, not returning until just as the sun was about to set in a flame of fire.

"Well, Jack, what news from the Poughkeepsie?" demanded the mate. "You have been gone long enough to make sure of your errand. Is it certain that we are not to see the man-of-war's men to-night?"

"Whatever you see, my advice to you is to keep close, and to be on your guard," answered Jack, evasively.

"I have little fear of any of Uncle Sam's craft. A plain story, and an honest heart, will make all clear to a well-disposed listener. We have not been accomplices in Spike's treasons, and cannot be made to answer for them."

"Take my advice, maty, and be in no hurry to hail every vessel you see. Uncle Sam's fellows may not always be at hand to help you. Do you not know that this island will be tabooed to seamen for some time to come?"

"Why so, Jack? The islet has done no harm, though others may have performed wicked deeds near it."

"Two of the drowned men lie within a hundred yards of this spot, and sailors never go near new-made graves, if they can find any other place to resort to."

"You deal in enigmas, Jack; and did I not know that you are very temperate, I might suspect that the time you have been gone has been passed in the company of a bottle of brandy."

"That will explain my meanin'," said Jack, laconically,

pointing as he spoke, seemingly at some object that was to be seen without.

The door of the house was wide open, for the admission of air. It faced the haven of the islets, and just as the mate's eyes were turned to it, the end of a flying-jib-boom, with the sail down, and fluttering beneath it, was coming into the view. "The Poughkeepsie!" exclaimed Mulford, in delight, seeing all his hopes realized, while Rose blushed to the eyes. A pause succeeded, during which Mulford drew aside, keeping his betrothed in the background, and as much out of sight as possible. The vessel was shooting swiftly into view, and presently all there could see it was the Swash.

CHAPTER XII.

"But no—he surely is not dreaming,
Another minute makes it clear,
A scream, a rush, a burning tear,
From Inez' cheek, dispel the fear
That bliss like his is only seeming."

WASHINGTON ALLSTON.

A MOMENT of appalled surprise succeeded the instant when Harry and Rose first ascertained the real character of the vessel that had entered the haven of the Dry Tortugas. Then the first turned toward Jack Tier, and sternly demanded an explanation of his apparent faithlessness.

"Rascal," he cried, "has this treachery been intended? Did you not see the brig and know her?"

"Hush, Harry—*dear* Harry," exclaimed Rose, entreatingly. "My life for it, Jack has *not* been faithless."

"Why, then, has he not let us know that the brig was coming? For more than an hour has he been aloft, on the lookout, and here are we taken quite by surprise. Rely on it, Rose, he has seen the approach of the brig, and might have sooner put us on our guard."

"Ay, ay, lay it on, maty," said Jack, coolly, neither angry nor mortified, so far as appearances went, at these expressions of dissatisfaction; "my back is used to it. If I didn't know what it is to get hard raps on the knuckles, I should be but a young steward. But, as for this business, a little reflection will tell you I am not to blame."

"Give us your own explanations, for without them I shall trust you no longer."

"Well, sir, what good would it have done, *had* I told you

the brig was standing for this place? There she came down, like a race-horse, and escape for you was impossible. As the wind is now blowin', the Molly would go two feet to the boat's one, and a chase would have been madness.''

"I don't know that, sirrah," answered the mate. "The boat might have got into the smaller passages of the reef, where the brig could not enter, or she might have dodged about among these islets, until it was night, and then escaped in the darkness."

"I thought of all that, Mr. Mulford, but it came too late. When I first went aloft, I came out on the northwest side of the lantern, and took my seat, to look out for the sloop-of-war, as you bade me, sir. Well, there I was sweepin' the horizon with the glass for the better part of an hour, sometimes fancyin' I saw her, and then givin' it up; for to this moment I am not sartain there is n't a sail off here to the westward, turning up toward the light on a bowline; but if there be, she 's too far off to know anything partic'-lar about her. Well, sir, there I sat, looking for the Poughkeepsie, for the better part of an hour, when I thought I would go round on t'other side of the lantern and take a look to windward. My heart was in my mouth, I can tell you, Miss Rose, when I saw the brig; and I felt both glad and sorry. Glad on my own account, and sorry on your'n. There she was, however, and no help for it, within two miles of this very spot, and coming down as if she despised touching the water at all. Now, what could I do? There was n't time, Mr. Mulford, to get the boat out, and the mast stepped, afore we should have been within reach of canister, and Stephen Spike would not have spared *that*, in order to get you again within his power."

"Depend on it, Harry, this is all true," said Rose, earnestly. "I know Jack well, and can answer for his fidelity. He wishes to, and if he can he *will* return to the brig, whither he thinks his duty calls him, but he will never willingly betray *us*—least of all, *me*. Do I speak as I ought, Jack?"

"Gospel truth, Miss Rose, and Mr. Mulford will get over this squall, as soon as he comes to think of matters as he ought. There 's my hand, maty, to show I bear no malice."

"I take it, Jack, for I must believe you honest, after all you have done for us. Excuse my warmth, which, if a little unreasonable, was somewhat natural under the circumstances. I suppose our case is now hopeless, and that we shall all be soon on board the brig again; for Spike will hardly think of abandoning me again on an island provisioned and fitted as is this!"

"It's not so sartain, sir, that you fall into his hands at all," put in Jack. "The men of the brig will never come here of their own accord, depend on that, for sailors don't like graves. Spike has come in here a'ter the schooner's chain, that he dropped into the water when he made sail from the sloop-of-war, at the time he was here afore, and is not expectin' to find us here. No—no—he thinks we are beatin' up toward Key West this very minute, if, indeed, he has missed us at all. 'T is possible he believes the boat has got adrift by accident, and has no thought of our bein' out of the brig."

"That is impossible, Jack. Do you suppose he is ignorant that Rose is missing?"

"Sartain of it, maty, if Mrs. Budd has read the letter well that Miss Rose left for her, and Biddy has obeyed orders. If they've followed instructions, Miss Rose is thought to be in her state-room, mournin' for a young man who was abandoned on a naked rock, and Jack Tier, havin' eat somethin' that has disagreed with him, is in his berth. Recollect, Spike will not be apt to look into Miss Rose's state-room or my berth, to see if all this is true. The cook and Josh are both in my secret, and know I mean to come back, and when the fit is over I have only to return to duty, like any other hand. It is my calculation that Spike believes both Miss Rose and myself on board the Molly at this very moment."

"And the boat—what can he suppose has become of the boat?"

"Sartainly, the boat makes the only chance ag'in us. But the boat was ridin' by its painter astern, and accidents sometimes happen to such craft. Then we two are the wery last he will suspect of havin' made off in the boat by

23

ourselves. There'll be Mrs. Budd and Biddy as a sort of
pledge that Miss Rose is aboard, and as for Jack Tier, he
is too insignificant to occupy the captain's thoughts just
now. He will probably muster the people for'ard, when he
finds the boat is gone, but I do not think he'll trouble the
cabins or state-rooms."

Mulford admitted that this was possible, though it scarcely
seemed probable to him. There was no help, however, for
the actual state of things, and they all now turned their attention to the brig, and to the movements of those on board
her. Jack Tier had swung-to the outer-door of the house,
as soon as the Swash came in view through it, and fortunately none of the windows on that side of the building had
been opened at all. The air entered to windward, which was
on the rear of the dwelling, so that it was possible to be
comfortable and yet leave the front, in view from the vessel,
with its deserted air. As for the brig, she had already anchored, and got both her boats into the water. The yawl
was hauled alongside, in readiness for any service that might
be required of it, while the launch had been manned at
once, and was already weighing the anchor, and securing
the chain to which Tier had alluded. All this served very
much to lessen the uneasiness of Mulford and Rose, as it
went far to prove that Spike had not come to the Dry Tortugas in quest of them, as, at first, both had very naturally
supposed. It might, indeed, turn out that his sole object
was to obtain this anchor and chain, with a view to use
them in raising the ill-fated vessel that had now twice gone
to the bottom.

"I wish an explanation with you, Jack, on one other
point," said the mate, after all three had been for some time
observing the movements on board and around the Swash.
"Do you actually intend to get on board the brig?"

"If it's to be done, maty. My v'y'ge is up with you
and Miss Rose. I may be said to have shipped for Key
West and a market, and the market's found at this port."

"You will hardly leave us _yet_, Jack," said Rose, with a
manner and emphasis that did not fail to strike her betrothed lover, though he could in no way account for either.

That Rose should not wish to be left alone with him in that solitary place was natural enough ; or, might rather be referred to education and the peculiar notions of her sex ; but he could not understand why so much importance should be attached to the presence of a being of Jack Tier's mould and character. It was true, that there was little choice, under present circumstances ; but it occurred to Mulford that Rose had manifested the same strange predilection when there might have been something nearer to a selection. The moment, however, was not one for much reflection on the subject.

"You will hardly leave us yet, Jack ?" said Rose, in the manner related.

"It 's now or never, Miss Rose. If the brig once gets away from this anchorage without me, I may never lay eyes on her ag'in. Her time is nearly up, for wood and iron won't hold together always, any more than flesh and blood. Consider how many years I 've been busy in huntin' her up, and how hard 't will be to lose that which has given me so many weary days and sleepless nights to find."

Rose said no more. If not convinced, she was evidently silenced, while Harry was left to wonder and surmise, as best he might. Both quitted the subject, to watch the people of the brig. By this time the anchor had been lifted, and the chain was heaving in on board the vessel, by means of a line that had been got around its bight. The work went on rapidly, and Mulford observed to Rose that he did not think it was the intention of Spike to remain long at the Tortugas, inasmuch as his brig was riding by a very short range of cable. This opinion was confirmed half an hour later, when it was seen that the launch was hooked on and hoisted in again, as soon as the chain and anchor of the schooner were secured.

Jack Tier watched every movement with palpable uneasiness. His apprehensions that Spike would obtain all he wanted, and be off before he could rejoin him, increased at each instant, and he did not scruple to announce an intention to take the boat and go alongside of the Swash at every hazard, rather than be left.

"You do not reflect on what you say, Jack," answered Harry; "unless, indeed, it be your intention to betray us. How could you appear in the boat, at this place, without letting it be known that we must be hard by?"

"That don't follow at all, maty," answered Jack. "Suppose I go alongside the brig and own to the captain that I took the boat last night, with the hope of findin' you, and that failin' to succeed, I bore up for this port, to look for provisions and water. Miss Rose he thinks on board at this moment, and in my judgment he would take me at my word, give me a good cursing, and think no more about it."

"It would never do, Jack," interposed Rose, instantly. "It would cause the destruction of Harry, as Spike would not believe you had not found him, without an examination of this house."

"What are they about with the yawl, Mr. Mulford?" asked Jack, whose eye was never off the vessel for a single moment. "It's gettin' to be so dark that one can hardly see the boat, but it seems as if they're about to man the yawl."

"They are, and there goes a lantern into it. And that is Spike himself coming down the brig's side this instant."

"They can only bring a lantern to search this house," exclaimed Rose. "Oh! Harry, you are lost!"

"I rather think the lantern is for the light-house," answered Mulford, whose coolness, at what was certainly a most trying moment, did not desert him. "Spike may wish to keep the light burning, for once before, you will remember, he had it kindled after the keeper was removed. As for his sailing, he would not be apt to sail until the moon rises; and in beating back to the wreck the light may serve to let him know the bearings and position of the reef."

"There they come," whispered Rose, half breathless with alarm. "The boat has left the brig, and is coming directly hither!"

All this was true enough. The yawl had shoved off, and with two men to row it, was pulling for the wharf in front of the house, and among the timbers of which lay the boat, pretty well concealed beneath a sort of bridge. Mulford would not retreat, though he looked to the fastenings of the door as a means of increasing his chances of defence. In the stern-sheets of the boat sat two men, though it was not easy to ascertain who they were by the fading light. One was known to be Spike, however, and the other, it was conjectured, must be Don Juan Montefalderon, from the circumstance of his being in the place of honor. Three minutes solved this question, the boat reaching the wharf by that time. It was instantly secured, and all four of the men left it. Spike was now plainly to be discerned by means of the lantern which he carried in his own hands. He gave some orders, in his customary authoritative way, and in a high key, after which he led the way from the wharf, walking side by side with the Señor Montefalderon. These two last came up within a yard of the door of the house, where they paused, enabling those within not only to see their persons and the working of their countenances, but to hear all that was said ; this last the more especially, since Spike never thought it necessary to keep his powerful voice within moderate limits.

" It 's hardly worth while, Don Wan, for you to go into the light-house," said Spike. " 'T is but a greasy, dirty place at the best, and one's clothes are never the better for dealin' with ile. Here, Bill, take the lantern, and get a filled can, that we may go up, and trim and fill the lamp, and make a blaze. Bear a hand, lads, and I 'll be a'ter ye afore you reach the lantern. Be careful with the flame about the ile, for seamen ought never to wish to see a light-house destroyed."

" What do you expect to gain by lighting the lamps above, Don Esteban ? " demanded the Mexican, when the sailors had disappeared in the light-house, taking their own lantern with them.

" It 's wisest to keep things reg'lar about this spot, Don Wan, which will prevent unnecessary suspicions. But, as the brig stretches in toward the reef to-night, on our way back, the light will be a great assistance. I am short of officers, you know, and want all the help of this sort I can get."

"To be sincere with you, Don Esteban, I greatly regret you are so short of officers, and do not yet despair of inducing you to go and take off the mate, whom I hear you have left on a barren rock. He was a fine young fellow, Señor Spike, and the deed was not one that you will wish to remember a few years hence."

"The fellow run, and I took him at his word, Don Wan. I'm not obliged to receive back a deserter unless it suits me."

"We are all obliged to see we do not cause a fellow-creature the loss of life. This will prove the death of the charming young woman who is so much attached to him, unless you relent and are merciful!"

"Women have tender looks but tough hearts," answered Spike, carelessly, though Mulford felt certain, by the tone of his voice, that great bitterness of feeling lay smothered beneath the affected indifference of his manner; "few die of love."

"The young lady has not been on deck all day; and the Irishwoman tells me that she does nothing but drink water —the certain proof of a high fever."

"Ay, ay, she keeps her room if you will, Don Wan. But she is not about to make a dupe of me by any such tricks. I must go and look to the lamps, however, and you will find the graves you seek in the rear of the house, about thirty yards behind it, you'll remember. That's a very pretty cross you've made, Señor, and the soul of the schooner's skipper will be all the better for settin' it up at the head of his grave."

"It will serve to let those who come after us know that a Christian sleeps beneath the sand, Don Esteban," answered the Mexican, mildly. "I have no other expectation from this sacred symbol."

The two now separated, Spike going into the light-house, little in a hurry, while Don Juan Montefalderon walked round the building to its rear in quest of the grave. Mulford waited a moment for Spike to get a short distance up the stairs of the high tower he had to ascend, when placing the arm of Rose within his own, he opened the door in the rear of the house, and walked boldly toward the Mexican. Don Juan was actually forcing the pointed end of his little cross into the sand, at the head of his countryman's grave, when Mulford and his trembling companion reached the spot. Although night had shut in, it was not so dark that persons could not be recognized at small distances. The Señor Montefalderon was startled at an apparition so sudden and unexpected, when Mulford saluted him by name; but recognizing first the voice of Harry, and then the persons of himself and his companion, surprise, rather than alarm, became the emotion that was uppermost. Notwithstanding the strength of the first of these feelings, he instantly saluted the young couple with the polished ease that marked his manner, which had much of the courtesy of a Castilian in it, tempered a little perhaps, by the greater flexibility of a Southern American.

"I *see* you," exclaimed Don Juan, "and must believe my eyes. Without their evidence, however I could scarce believe it can be you two, one of whom I thought on board the brig, and the other suffering a most miserable death on a naked rock."

"I am aware of your kind feelings in our behalf, Don Juan," said Mulford, "and it is the reason I now confide in you. I was taken off that rock by means of the boat, which you doubtless have missed; and this is the gentle being who has been the means of saving my life. To her and Jack Tier, who is yonder, under the shadows of the house, I owe my not being the victim of Spike's cruelty."

"I now comprehend the whole matter, Don Henriquez. Jack Tier has managed the boat for the Señorita; and those whom we were told were too ill to be seen on deck, have been really out of the brig!"

"Such are the facts, Señor, and from *you* there is no wish to conceal them. We are then to understand that the absence of Rose and Jack from the brig is not known to Spike."

"I believe not, Señor. He has alluded to both, once or twice to-day, as being ill below; but would you not do well to retire within the shade of the dwelling lest a glance from the lantern might let those in it know that I am not alone.''

"There is little danger, Don Juan, as they who stand near a light cannot well see those who are in darkness. Beside, they are high in the air, while we are on the ground, which will greatly add to the obscurity down here. We can retire, nevertheless, as I have a few questions to ask, which may as well be put in perfect security as put where there is any risk.''

The three now drew near the house, Rose actually stepping within its door, though Harry remained on its exterior, in order to watch the proceedings of those in the light-house. Here the Señor Montefalderon entered into a more detailed explanation of what had occurred on board the brig, since the appearance of day, that very morning. According to his account of the matter, Spike had immediately called upon the people to explain the loss of the boat. Tier was not interrogated on this occasion, it being understood he had gone below and turned in, after having the lookout for fully half the night. As no one could, or would, give an account of the manner in which the boat was missing, Josh was ordered to go below and question Jack on the subject. Whether it was from consciousness of his connection with the escape of Jack, and apprehensions of the consequences, or from innate good-nature, and a desire to befriend the lovers, this black now admitted that Jack confessed to him that the boat had got away from him while endeavoring to shift the turns of its painter from a cleet where they ought not to be, to their proper place. This occurred early in Jack's watch, according to Josh's story, and had not been reported, as the boat did not properly belong to the brig, and was an incumbrance rather than an advantage. The mate admired the negro's cunning, as Don Juan related this part of his story, which put him in a situation to throw all the blame on Jack's mendacity in the event of a discovery, while it had the effect to allow the fugitives more time for their escape. The result was, that Spike bestowed a few hearty curses, as usual, on the clumsiness of Jack Tier, and seemed to forget all about the matter. It is probable he connected Jack's abstaining from showing himself on deck, and his alleged indisposition, with his supposed delinquency in this matter of the boat. From that moment the captain appeared to give himself no further concern on the subject, the boat having been, in truth, an incumbrance rather than a benefit, as stated.

As for Rose, her keeping her room, under the circumstances, was so very natural, that the Señor Montefalderon had been completely deceived, as, from his tranquillity on this point, there was no question was the case with Spike also. Biddy appeared on deck, though the widow did not, and the Irishwoman shook her head anxiously when questioned about her young mistress, giving the spectators reason to suppose that the latter was in a very bad way.

As respects the brig and her movements, Spike had got under way as soon as there was light enough to find his course, and had run through the passage. It is probable that the boat was seen ; for something that was taken for a small sail had just been made out for a single instant, and then became lost again. This little sail was made, if made at all, in the direction of the Dry Tortugas, but so completely was all suspicion at rest in the minds of those on the quarter-deck of the Swash, that neither Spike nor the Mexican had the least idea what it was. When the circumstance was reported to the former, he answered that it was probably some small wrecker, of which many were hovering about the reef, and added, laughingly, though in a way to prove how little he thought seriously on the subject at all, " Who knows but the light-house boat has fallen into their hands, and that they 've made sail on *her* ; if they have, my word for it, that she goes, hull, spars, rigging, canvas, and cargo, all in a lump, for salvage."

As the brig came out of the passage, in broad day, the heads of the schooner's masts were seen, as a matter of course. This induced Spike to heave-to, lower a boat, and go in person to examine the condition of the wreck. It will be seen that Jack's presence could now be all the better dispensed with. The examination, with the soundings, and

other calculations connected with raising the vessel, occupied hours. When they were completed, Spike returned
on board, run up his boat, and squared away for the Dry
Tortugas. Señor Montefalderon confirmed the justice of
Jack Tier's surmises, as to the object of this unexpected
visit. The brig had come solely for the chain and anchor
mentioned, and having secured them, it was Spike's intention to get under way and beat up to the wreck again as soon
as the moon rose. As for the sloop-of-war, he believed
she had given him up; for by this time she must know
that she had no chance with the brig, so long as the latter
kept near the reef, and that she ran the constant hazard of
shipwreck, while playing so near the dangers herself.

Before the Señor Montefalderon exhausted all he had
to communicate, he was interrupted by Jack Tier with a
singular proposition. Jack's great desire was to get on
board the Swash; and he now begged the Mexican to let
Mulford take the yawl and scull him off to the brig, and
return to the islet before Spike and his companions should
descend from the lantern of the light-house. The little
fellow insisted there was sufficient time for such a purpose,
as the three in the lantern had not yet succeeded in filling
the lamps with the oil necessary to their burning for a night
—a duty that usually occupied the regular keeper for an
hour. Five or six minutes would suffice for him; and if
he were seen going up the brig's side, it would be easy
for him to maintain that he had come ashore in the boat.
No one took such precise note of what was going on, as
to be able to contradict him; and as to Spike and the
men with him, they would probably never hear anything
about it.

Don Juan Montefalderon was struck with the boldness
of Jack Tier's plan, but refused his assent to it. He
deemed it too hazardous, but substituted a project of his own.
The moon would not rise until near eleven, and it wanted
several hours before the time of sailing. When they returned
to the brig, he would procure his cloak, and scull himself
ashore, being perfectly used to managing a boat in this way,
under the pretence of wishing to pass an hour longer near

the grave of his countryman. At the expiration of that
hour he would take Jack off, concealed beneath his cloak—
an exploit of no great difficulty in the darkness, especially
as no one would be on deck but a hand or two keeping the
anchor-watch. With this arrangement, therefore, Jack Tier
was obliged to be content.

Some fifteen or twenty minutes more passed, during
which the Mexican again alluded to his country, and his
regrets at her deplorable situation. The battles of the 8th
and 9th of May, two combats that ought to, and which will
reflect high honor on the little army that won them, as
well as on that hardly worked, and in some respects hardly
used, service to which they belong, had been just fought.
Don Juan mentioned these events without reserve, and
frankly admitted that success had fallen to the portion of
much the weaker party. He ascribed the victory to the
great superiority of the American officers of inferior rank ;
it being well known that in the service of the "Republic
of the North," as he termed America, men who had been
regularly educated at the military academy, and who had
reached the period of middle life, were serving in the stations of captains, and sometimes in that of lieutenants ; men
who, in many cases, were fitted to command regiments and
brigades, having been kept in these lower stations by the
tardiness with which promotion comes in an army like that
of this country.

Don Juan Montefalderon was not sufficiently conversant
with the subject, perhaps, else he might have added, that
when occasions *do* offer to bestow on these gentlemen the
preferment they have so hardly and patiently earned, they
are too often neglected, in order to extend the circle of
vulgar political patronage. He did not know that when a
new regiment of dragoons was raised, one permanent in
its character, and intended to be identified with the army
in all future time, that, instead of giving its commissions to
those who had fairly earned them by long privations and
faithful service, they were given, with one or two exceptions,
to strangers.

No government trifles more with its army and navy than

our own. So niggardly are the master-spirits at Washington of the honors justly earned by military men, that we have fleets still commanded by captains, and armies by officers whose regular duty it would be to command brigades. The world is edified with the sight of forces sufficient, in numbers, and every other military requisite, to make one of Napoleon's *corps d'armée*, led by one whose commission would place him properly at the head of a brigade, and nobly led, too. Here, when so favorable an occasion offers to add a regiment or two to the old permanent line of the army, and thus infuse new life into its hope deferred, the opportunity is overlooked, and the rank and file are to be obtained by cramming, instead of by a generous regard to the interests of the gallant gentlemen who have done so much for the honor of the American name, and, unhappily, so little for themselves. The extra-patriots of the nation, and they form a legion large enough to trample the "Halls of the Montezumas" under their feet, tell us that the reward of those other patriots beneath the shadows of the Sierra Madre is to be in the love and approbation of their fellow-citizens, at the very moment when they are giving the palpable proof of the value of this esteem, and of the inconstancy of popular applause, by pointing their fingers, on account of an inadvertent expression in a letter, at the gallant soldier who taught, in our own times, the troops of this country to stand up to the best-appointed regiments of England, and to carry off victory from the pride of Europe, in fair field-fights. Alas! alas! it is true of nations as of men, in their simplest and earliest forms of association, that there are "secrets in all families"; and it will no more do to dwell on our own, than it would edify us to expose those of poor Mexico.

The discourse between the Señor Montefalderon and Mulford was interesting, as it ever had been when the former spoke of his unfortunate country. On the subject of the battles of May he was candid, and admitted his deep mortification and regrets. He had expected more from the force collected on the Rio Grande, though, understanding the northern character better than most of his countrymen, he had not been as much taken by surprise as the great bulk of his own nation.

"Nevertheless, Don Henrique," he concluded, for the voice of Spike was just then heard as he was descending the stairs of the light-house, " nevertheless, Don Henrique, there is one thing that your people, brave, energetic, and powerful as I acknowledge them to be, would do well to remember, and it is this—no nation of the numbers of ours can be or ever was conquered, unless by the force of political combinations. In a certain state of society a government may be overturned, or a capital taken, and carry a whole country along with it, but our condition is one not likely to bring about such a result. We are of a race different from the Anglo-Saxon, and it will not be easy either to assimilate us to your own, or wholly to subdue us. In those parts of the country, where the population is small, in time, no doubt, the Spanish race might be absorbed, and your sway established ; but ages of war would be necessary entirely to obliterate our usages, our language, and our religion from the peopled portions of Mexico."

It might be well for some among us to reflect on these matters,—the opinions of Don Juan, in our judgment, being entitled to the consideration of all prudent and considerate men.

As Spike descended to the door of the light-house, Harry, Rose, and Jack Tier retired within that of the dwelling. Presently the voice of the captain was heard hailing the Mexican, and together they walked to the wharf, the former boasting to the latter of his success in making a brilliant light. Brilliant it was, indeed ; so brilliant as to give Mulford many misgivings on the subject of the boat. The light from the lantern fell upon the wharf, and he could see the boat from the window where he stood, with Spike standing nearly over it, waiting for the men to get his own yawl ready. It is true, the captain's back was toward the dangerous object, and the planks of the bridge were partly between him and it ; but there was a serious danger that was solely averted by the circumstance that Spike was so earnestly dilating on some subject to Don

Juan, as to look only at that gentleman's face.   A minute
later they were all in the yawl, which pulled rapidly toward
the brig.

Don Juan Montefalderon was not long absent.   Ten
minutes sufficed for the boat to reach the Swash, for him
to obtain his cloak, and to return to the islet alone, no one
in the vessel feeling a desire to interfere with his imaginary prayers.   As for the people, it was not probable that
one in the brig could have been induced to accompany him
to the graves at that hour ; though everybody but Josh had
turned-in, as he informed Mulford, to catch short naps previously to the hour of getting the brig under way.   As
for the steward, he had been placed on the lookout as the
greatest idler on board.   All this was exceedingly favorable to Jack Tier's project, since Josh was already in the
secret of his absence, and would not be likely to betray his
return.   After a brief consultation, it was agreed to wait
half an hour or an hour, in order to let the sleepers lose
all consciousness, when Don Juan proposed returning to the
vessel with his new companion.

The thirty or forty minutes that succeeded were passed
in general conversation.   On this occasion the Señor Montefalderon spoke more freely than he had yet done of
recent events.   He let it be plainly seen how much he despised Spike, and how irksome to him was the intercourse
he was obliged to maintain, and to which he only submitted
through a sense of duty.   The money known to be in the
schooner was of a larger amount than had been supposed ;
and every dollar was so important to Mexico, at that moment, that he did not like to abandon it, else did he declare, that he would quit the brig at once, and share in the
fortunes of Harry and Rose.   He courteously expressed
his best wishes for the happiness of the young couple, and
delicately intimated that, under the circumstances, he supposed that they would be united as soon as they could
reach a place where the marriage rite could be celebrated.
This was said in the most judicious way possible ; so delicately as not to wound any one's feelings, and in a way to
cause it to resemble the announcement of an expectation,

rather than the piece of paternal advice for which it was really intended. Harry was delighted with this suggestion of his Mexican friend—the most loyal American may still have a sincere friend of Mexican birth and Mexican feelings, too—since it favored not only his secret wishes, but his secret expectations also.

At the appointed moment, Don Juan Montefalderon and Jack Tier took their leave of the two they left behind them. Rose manifested what to Harry seemed a strange reluctance to part with the little steward; but Tier was bent on profiting by this excellent opportunity to get back to the brig. They went, accordingly, and the anxious listeners, who watched the slightest movement of the yawl, from the shore, had reason to believe that Jack was smuggled in without detection. They heard the familiar sound of the oar falling in the boat, and Mulford said that Josh's voice might be distinguished, answering to a call from Don Juan. No noise or clamor was heard, such as Spike would certainly have made, had he detected the deception that had been practised on himself.

Harry and Rose were now alone. The former suggested that the latter should take possession of one of the little bed-rooms that are usually to be found in American dwellings of the dimensions and humble character of the light-house abode, while he kept watch until the brig should sail. Until Spike was fairly off, he would not trust himself to sleep; but there was no sufficient reason why Rose should not endeavor to repair the evil of a broken night's rest, like that which had been passed in the boat. With this understanding, then, our heroine took possession of her little apartment, where she threw herself on the bed in her clothes, while Mulford walked out into the air as the most effective means of helping to keep his eyes open.

It was now some time past ten, and before eleven the moon would rise. The mate consequently knew that his watch could not be long before Spike would quit the neighborhood—a circumstance pregnant with immense relief to him, at least. So long as that unscrupulous and now nearly desperate man remained anywhere near Rose, he felt that she could not be safe; and as he paced the sands, on the off, or outer side of the islet, in order to be beyond the influence of the light in the lantern, his eye was scarcely a moment taken away from the Swash, so impatiently and anxiously did he wait for the signs of some movement on board her.

The moon rose, and Mulford heard the well-known raps on the booby-hatch, which precedes the call of "all hands," on board a merchant-man. "All hands up anchor, ahoy!" succeeded, and in less than five minutes the bustle on board the brig announced the fact, that her people were "getting the anchor." By this time it had got to be so light that the mate deemed it prudent to return to the house, in order that he might conceal his person within its shadows. Awake Rose he would not, though he knew she would witness the departure of the Swash with a satisfaction little short of his own. He thought he would wait, that when he did speak to her at all, it might be to announce their entire safety. As regarded the aunt, Rose was much relieved on her account, by the knowledge that Jack Tier would not fail to let Mrs. Budd know everything connected with her own situation and prospects. The desertion of Jack, after coming so far with her, had pained our heroine in a way we cannot at present explain; but go he would, probably feeling assured there was no longer any necessity for his continuance with the lovers, in order to prevail on Rose to escape from Spike.

The Swash was not long in getting her ground-tackle, and the brig was soon seen with her topsail aback, waiting to cat the anchor. This done, the yards swung round, and the topsail filled. It was blowing just a good breeze for such a craft to carry whole sail on a bowline with, and away the light and active craft started, like the racer that is galloping for daily exercise. Of course there were several passages by which a vessel might quit the group of islets, some being larger and some smaller, but all having sufficient water for a brigantine of the Molly's draught. Determined not to lose an inch of distance unnecessarily, Spike luffed close up to the wind, making an effort to pass out to windward of the light. In order to do this, however, it became necessary for him to make two short tacks within the haven, which brought him far enough to the southward and eastward to effect his purpose. While this was doing, the mate, who perfectly understood the object of the manœuvres, passed to the side of the light-house that was opposite to that on which the dwelling was placed, with a view to get a better sight of the vessel as she stood out to sea. In order to do this, however, it was necessary for the young man to pass through a broad bit of moonlight, but he trusted for his not being seen, to the active manner in which all hands were employed on board the vessel. It would seem that, in this respect, Mulford trusted without his host, for as the vessel drew near, he perceived that six or eight figures were on the guns of the Swash, or in her rigging, gesticulating eagerly, and seemingly pointing to the very spot where he stood. When the brig got fairly abeam of the light, she would not be a hundred yards distant from it, and fearful to complete the exposure of his person, which he had so inadvertently and unexpectedly commenced, our mate drew up close to the wall of the light-house, against which he sustained himself in a position as immovable as possible. This movement had been seen by a single seaman on board the Swash, and the man happened to be one of those who had landed with Spike only two hours before. His name was Barlow.

"Captain Spike, sir," called out Barlow, who was coiling up rigging on the forecastle, and was consequently obliged to call out so loud as to be heard by all on board, "yonder is a man at the foot of the light-house."

By this time, the moon coming out bright through an opening in the clouds, Mulford had become conscious of the risk he ran, and was drawn up, as immovable as the pile itself, against the stones of the light-house. Such an announcement brought everybody to leeward, and every head over the bulwarks. Spike himself sprang into the lee main-chains, where his view was unobstructed, and where Mulford saw and recognized him, even better than he was seen and recognized in his own person. All this time the brig was moving ahead.

24

"A man, Barlow!" exclaimed Spike, in the way one a little bewildered by an announcement expresses his surprise. "A man! that can never be. There is no one at the light-house, you know."

"There he stands, sir, with his back to the tower, and his face this way. His dark figure against the white-washed stones is plain enough to be seen. Living, or dead, sir, that is the mate!"

"*Living* it cannot be," answered Spike, though he gulped at the words the next moment.

A general exclamation now showed that everybody recognized the mate whose figure, stature, dress, and even features, were by this time all tolerably distinct. The fixed attitude, however, the immovable statue-like rigidity of the form, and all the other known circumstances of Harry's case, united to produce a common and simultaneous impression among the superstitious mariners, that what they saw was but the ghostly shadow of one lately departed to the world of spirits. Even Spike was not free from this illusion, and his knees shook beneath him, there where he stood, in the channels of a vessel that he had handled like a top in so many gales and tempests. With him, however, the illusion was neither absolute nor lasting. A second thought told him it could scarcely be so, and then he found his voice. By this time the brig was nearly abreast of where Harry stood.

"You Josh!" called out Spike, in a voice of thunder, loud enough to startle even Mrs. Budd and Biddy in their berths.

"Lor' help us all!" answered the negro, "what *will* come next t'ing aboard dis wessel! Here I be, sir."

"Pass the fowling-piece out of my state-room. Both barrels are loaded with ball; I'll try him, though the bullets *are* only lead."

A common exclamation of dissatisfaction escaped the men, while Josh was obeying the order. "It's no use," "You never can hurt one of them things," "Something will befall the brig on account of this," and "It's the mate's sperit, and sperits can't be harmed by lead or iron," were the sort of remarks made by the seamen, during the short interval between the issuing the order for the fowling-piece and its execution.

"There 't is, Cap'in Spike," said Josh, passing the piece up through the rigging, "but 't will no more shoot *that* thing, than one of our carronades would blow up Gibraltar."

By this time Spike was very determined, his lips being compressed and his teeth set, as he took the gun and cocked it. Then he hailed. As all that passed occurred, as it might be, at once, the brig even at that moment was little more than abreast of the immovable mate, and about eighty yards from him.

"Light-house, there!" cried Spike: "Living or dead, answer or I fire."

No answer came, and no motion appeared in the dark figure that was now very plainly visible, under a bright moon, drawn in high relief against the glittering white of the tower. Spike dropped the muzzle to its aim, and fired.

So intense was the attention of all in the Swash, that a wink of Harry's could almost have been seen, had he betrayed even that slight sign of human infirmity at the flash and the report. The ball was flattened against a stone of the building, within a foot of the mate's body; but he did not stir. All depended now on his perfect immovability, as he well knew; and he so far commanded himself, as to remain rigid as if of stone himself.

"There! one can see how it is—no life in that being," said one. "I know'd how it would end," added another. "Nothing but silver, and that cast on purpose, will ever slay it," continued a third. But Spike disregarded all. This time he was resolved that his aim should be better and he was inveterately deliberate in getting it. Just as he pulled the trigger, however, Don Juan Montefalderon touched his elbow, the piece was fired, and there stood the immovable figure as before, fixed against the tower. Spike was turning angrily to chide his Mexican friend for deranging his aim, when the report of an answering musket came back like an echo. Every eye was turned toward the figure, but it moved not. Then the humming sound of an

advancing ball was heard, and a bullet passed, whistling
hoarsely, through the rigging, and fell some distance to
windward. Every head disappeared below the bulwarks.
Even Spike was so far astonished as to spring in upon deck,
and, for a single instant, not a man was to be seen above
the monkey-rail of the brig. Then Spike recovered himself and jumped upon a gun. His first look was towards
the light-house, now on the vessel's lee-quarter ; but the
spot where had so lately been seen the form of Mulford
showed nothing but the glittering brightness of the white-
washed stones !

The reader will not be surprised to learn that all these
events produced a strange and deep impression on board
the Molly Swash. The few who might have thrown a little
light on the matter were discreetly silent, while all that
portion of the crew which was in the dark, firmly believed
that the spirit of the murdered mate was visiting them, in
order to avenge the wrongs inflicted on it in the flesh.
The superstition of sailors is as deep as it is general. All
those of the Molly, too, were salts of the old school, sea-
dogs of a past generation, properly speaking, and mariners
who had got their notions in the early part of the century,
when the spirit of progress was less active than it is at
present.

Spike himself might have had other misgivings, and
believed that he had seen the living form of his intended
victim, but for the extraordinary and ghost-like echo of
his last discharge. There was nothing visible, or intel-
ligible, from which that fire could have come, and he was
perfectly bewildered by the whole occurrence. An intention to round-to, as soon as through the passage, down
boat and land, which had been promptly conceived when
he found that his first aim had failed, was as suddenly
abandoned, and he gave the command to " board fore-tack " ;
immediately after, his call was to " pack on the brig," and
not without a little tremor in his voice, as soon as he
perceived that the figure had vanished. The crew was not
slow to obey the orders, and in ten minutes the Swash was
a mile from the light, standing to the northward and east-

ward, under a press of canvas, and with a freshening breeze.

To return to the islets. Harry, from the first, had seen that everything depended on his remaining motionless. As the people of the brig were partly in shadow, he could not, and did not, fully understand how completely he was himself exposed, in consequence of the brightness of all around him, and he had at first hoped to be mistaken for some accidental resemblance to a man. His nerves were well-tried by the use of the fowling-piece, but they proved equal to the necessities of the occasion. But, when an answering report came from the rear, or from the opposite side of the islet, he darted round the tower, as much taken by surprise, and overcome by wonder, as any one else who heard it. It was this rapid movement which caused his flight to be unnoticed, all the men of the brig dodging below their own bulwarks at that precise instant.

As the light-house was now between the mate and the brig, he had no longer any motive for trying to conceal himself. His first thought was of Rose, and, strange as it may seem, for some little time he fancied that she had found a musket in the dwelling, and discharged it, in order to aid his escape. The events had passed so swiftly, that there was no time for the cool consideration of anything, and it is not surprising that some extravagances mingled with the first surmises of all these.

On reaching the door of the house, therefore, Harry was by no means surprised at seeing Rose standing in it, gazing at the swiftly receding brigantine. He even looked for the musket, expecting to see it lying at her feet, or leaning against the wall of the building. Rose, however, was entirely unarmed, and as dependent on him for support, as when he had parted from her, an hour or two before.

"Where did you find that musket, Rose, and what have you done with it?" inquired Harry, as soon as he had looked in every place he thought likely to hold such an implement.

"Musket, Harry! I have had no musket, though the report of fire-arms, near by, awoke me from a sweet sleep."

" Is this possible ! I had imprudently trusted myself on the other side of the light-house, while the moon was behind clouds, and when they broke suddenly away, its light betrayed me to those on board the brig. Spike fired at me twice, without injuring me ; when, to my astonishment, an answering report was heard from the islet. What is more, the piece was charged with a ball-cartridge, for I heard the whistling of the bullet as it passed on its way to the brig."

" And you supposed I had fired that musket ? "

" Whom else could I suppose had done it ? You are not a very likely person to do such a thing, I will own, my love; but there are none but us two here."

" It must be Jack Tier," exclaimed Rose, suddenly.

" That is impossible, since he has left us."

" One never knows. Jack understood how anxious I was to retain him with us, and he is so capricious and full of schemes, and he may have contrived to get out of the brig, as artfully as he got on board her."

" If Jack Tier be actually on this islet, I shall set him down as little else than a conjuror."

" Hist ! " interrupted Rose, " what noise is that in the direction of the wharf? It sounds like an oar falling in a boat."

Mulford heard that well-known sound, as well as his companion, and, followed by Rose, he passed swiftly through the house, coming out at the front, next the wharf. The moon was still shining bright, and the mystery of the echoing report, and answering shot, was immediately explained. A large boat, one that pulled ten oars, at least, was just coming up to the end of the wharf, and the manner in which its oars were unshipped and tossed, announced to the mate that the crew were man-of-war's men. He walked hastily forward to meet them.

Three officers first left the boat together. The gold bands of their caps showed that they belonged to the quarter-deck, a fact that the light of the moon made apparent at once, though it was not strong enough to render features distinct. As Mulford continued to advance, however, the three officers saluted him.

"I see you have got the light under way once more," observed the leader of the party. "Last night it was as dark as Erebus in your lantern."

"The light-house keeper and his assistant have both been drowned," answered Mulford. "The lamps have been lit to-night by the people of the brig which has just gone out."

"Pray, sir, what brig may that be?"

"The Molly Swash, of New York; a craft that I lately belonged to myself, but which I have left on account of her evil doings."

"The Molly Swash, Stephen Spike master and owner, bound to Key West and a market, with a cargo of eight hundred barrels of flour, and that of a quality so lively and pungent that it explodes like gunpowder! I beg your pardon, Mr. Mate, for not recognizing you sooner. Have you forgotten the Poughkeepsie, Captain Mull, and her far-reaching Paixhans?"

"I ought to ask your pardon, Mr. Wallace, for not recognizing *you* sooner too. But one does not distinguish well by moonlight. I am delighted to see you, sir, and now hope that, with my assistance, a stop can be put to the career of the brig."

"What, Mr. Mate, do *you* turn against your craft?" said Wallace, under the impulsive feeling which induces all loyal men to have a distaste for treachery of every sort, "the seaman should love the very planks of his vessel."

"I fully understand you, Mr. Wallace, and will own that, for a long time, I was tied to rascality by the opinions to which you allude. But, when you come to hear my explanation, I do not fear your judgment in the least."

Mulford now led the way into the house, whither Rose had already retreated, and where she had lighted candles, and made other womanly arrangements for receiving her guests. At Harry's suggestion, some of the soup was placed over coals, to warm up for the party, and our heroine made her preparations to comfort them also with a cup of tea. While she was thus employed, Mulford gave the whole history of his connection with the brig, his indispo-

sition to quit the latter, the full exposure of Spike's treason,
his own desertion, if desertion it could be called, the loss
of the schooner, and his abandonment on the rock, and the
manner in which he had been finally relieved. It was
scarcely possible to relate all these matters, and altogether
avoid allusions to the schemes of Spike in connection with
Rose, and the relation in which our young man himself
stood toward her. Although Mulford touched on these
points with great delicacy, it was as a seaman talking to
seamen, and he could not entirely throw aside the frankness of the profession. Ashore, men live in the privacy of
their own domestic circles, and their secrets, and secret
thoughts, are "family secrets," of which it has passed into
a proverb to say, that there are always some, even in the
best of these communities. On shipboard, or in the camp,
it is very different. The close contact in which men are
brought with each other, the necessity that exists for opening the heart and expanding the charities, gets in time to
influence the whole character, and a certain degree of frankness and simplicity takes the place of the reserve and
acting that might have been quickened in the same individual, under a different system of schooling. But Mulford
was frank by nature, as well as by his sea-education, and
his companions on this occasion were pretty well possessed
of all his wishes and plans, in reference to Rose, even to
his hope of falling in with the chaplain of the Poughkeepsie, by the time his story was all told. The fact, that Rose
was occupied in another room, most of the time, had made
these explanations all the easier, and spared her many a
blush. As for the man-of-war's men, they listened to the
tale, with manly interest and a generous sympathy.

"I am glad to hear your explanation, Mr. Mate," said
Wallace, cordially, as soon as Harry had done, "and there's
my hand, in proof that I approve of your course. I own
to a radical dislike of a turncoat, or a traitor to his craft,
Brother Hollins"—looking at the elder of his two companions, one of whom was the midshipman who had originally accompanied him on board the Swash—"and am glad
to find that our friend Mulford here is neither. A true-

hearted sailor can be excused for deserting even his own ship, under such circumstances."

"I am glad to hear even this little concession from you, Wallace," answered Hollins, good-naturedly, and speaking with a mild expression of benevolence, on a very calm and thoughtful countenance. "Your mess is as heterodox as any I ever sailed with, on the subject of our duties, in this respect."

"I hold it to be a sailor's duty to stick by his ship, *reverend*, and dear sir."

This mode of address, which was used by the "ship's gentleman" in the cant of the ward-room, as a pleasantry of an old shipmate, for the two had long sailed together in other vessels, at once announced to Harry that he saw the very chaplain for whose presence he had been so anxiously wishing. The "reverend and dear sir" smiled at the sally of his friend, a sort of thing to which he was very well accustomed, but he answered with a gravity and point that, it is to be presumed, he thought befitting his holy office.

It may be well to remark here, that the Rev. Mr. Hollins was not one of the "launch'd chaplains," that used to do discredit to the navy of this country, or a layman dubbed with such a title, and rated that he might get the pay and become a boon companion of the captain, at the table and in his frolics ashore. Those days are gone by, and ministers of the gospel are now really employed to care for the souls of the poor sailors, who so long have been treated by others, and have treated themselves, indeed, as if they were beings without souls, altogether. In these particulars, the world has certainly advanced, though the wise and the good, in looking around them, may feel more cause for astonishment in contemplating what it once was, than to rejoice in what it actually is. But intellect has certainly improved in the aggregate, if not in its especial dispensations, and men will not now submit to abuses that, within the recollections of a generation, they even cherished. In reference to the more intellectual appointments of a ship of war, the commander excepted, for we contend he who directs all ought to possess the most capacity,—in reference to what are ordinarily believed to be the more intellectual appointments of a vessel of war, the surgeon and the chaplain, we well recollect opinions that were expressed to us, many years since, by two officers of the highest rank known to the service. "When I first entered the navy," said one of these old Benbows, "if I had occasion for the amputation of a leg, and the question lay between the carpenter and the doctor, d——e, but I would have tried the carpenter first, for I felt pretty certain he would have been the most likely to get through with the job." "In old times," said the other, "when a chaplain joined a ship, the question immediately arose, whether the mess were to convert the chaplain, or the chaplain the mess; and the mess generally got the best of it." There was very little exaggeration in either of these opinions. But, happily, all this is changed vastly for the better, and a navy-surgeon is necessarily a man of education and experience; in very many instances, men of high talents are to be found among them; while chaplains can do something better than play at backgammon, eat terrapins, when in what may be called terrapin-ports, and drink brandy and water, or pure Bob Smith.[1]

"It is a great mistake, Wallace, to fancy that the highest duty a man owes is either to his ship or to his country," observed the Rev. Mr. Hollins, quietly. "The highest duty of each and all of us is to God; and whatever conflicts with that duty, must be avoided as a transgression of his laws, and consequently as sin."

"You surprise me, reverend and dear sir! I do not remember ever to have heard you broach such opinions before, which might be interpreted to mean that a fellow might be disloyal to his flag."

"Because the opinion might be liable to misinterpretation. Still, I do not go as far as many of my friends on this subject. If Decatur ever really said, 'Our country, right or wrong,' he said what might be just enough, and creditable enough, in certain cases, and taken with the fair lim-

[1] In the palmy days of the service, when Robert Smith was so long Secretary of the Navy, the ship's whiskey went by this familiar sobriquet.

itations that he probably intended should accompany the sentiment ; but, if he meant it as an absolute and controlling principle, it was not possible to be more in error. In this last sense, such a rule of conduct might, and in old times often would, have justified idolatry ; nay, it *is* a species of idolatry in itself, since it is putting country before God. Sailors may not alway be able to make the just distinctions in these cases, but the quarter-deck should be so, *ir*reverend and dear sir.''

Wallace laughed, and then he turned the discourse to the subject more properly before them.

''I understand you to say, Mr. Mulford,'' he remarked, '' that, in your opinion, the Swash has gone to try to raise the unfortunate Mexican schooner, a second time, from the depths of the ocean?''

''From the rock on which she lies. Under the circumstances, I hardly think he would have come hither for the chain and cable, unless with some such object. We know, moreover, that such was his intention when we left the brig.''

'' And you can take us to the very spot where that wreck lies ? ''

''Without any difficulty. Her masts are partly out of water and we hung on to them, in our boat, no later than last night, or this morning rather.''

'' So far, well. Your conduct in all this affair will be duly appreciated, and Captain Mull will not fail to represent it in a right point of view to the government.''

'' Where is the ship, sir? I looked for her most anxiously, without success, last evening ; nor had Jack Tier, the little fellow I have named to you, any better luck ; though I sent him aloft, as high as the lantern in the light-house, for that purpose.''

''The ship is off here to the northward and westward, some six leagues or so. At sunset she may have been a little farther. We have supposed that the Swash would be coming back hither, and had laid a trap for her, which came very near taking her alive.''

''What is the trap you mean, sir—though taking Stephen Spike alive is sooner said than done.''

"Our plan has been to catch him with our boats. With the greater draught of water of the Poughkeepsie, and the heels of your brig, sir, a regular chase about these reefs, as we knew from experience, would be almost hopeless. It was, therefore, necessary to use head-work, and some man-of-war traverses, in order to lay hold of him. Yesterday afternoon we hoisted out three cutters, manned them, and made sail in them all, under our lugs, working up against the trades. Each boat took its own course, one going off the west end of the reef, one going more to the eastward, while I came this way, to look in at the Dry Tortugas. Spike will be lucky if he do not fall in with our third cutter, which is under the fourth lieutenant, should he stand on far on the same tack as that on which he left this place. Let him try his fortune, however. As for our boat, as soon as I saw the lamps burning in the lantern, I made the best of my way hither, and got sight of the brig, just as she loosened her sails. Then I took in my own lugs, and came on with the oars. Had we continued under our canvas, with this breeze, I almost think we might have overhauled the rascal."

"It would have been impossible, sir. The moment he got a sight of your sails, he would have been off in a contrary direction, and that brig really seems to fly, whenever there is a pressing occasion for her to move. You did the wisest thing you could have done, and barely missed him, as it was. He has not seen you at all, as it is, and will be all the less on his guard, against the next visit from the ship."

"Not seen me! Why, sir, the fellow fired at us twice with a musket; why he did not use a carronade is more than I can tell."

"Excuse me, Mr. Wallace; those two shots were intended for me, though I now fully comprehend why you answered them."

"Answered them! yes, indeed; who would not answer such a salute, and gun for gun, if he had a chance. I certainly thought he was firing at us, and having a musket between my legs, I let fly in return, and even the chaplain here will allow that was returning 'good for evil.' But explain your meaning."

Mulford now went into the details of the incidents connected with his coming into the moonlight, at the foot of the light-house. That he was not mistaken as to the party for whom the shots were intended, was plain enough to him, from the words that passed aloud among the people of the Swash, as well as from the circumstance that both balls struck the stones of the tower quite near him. This statement explained everything to Wallace, who now fully comprehended the cause and motive of each incident.

It was now near eleven, and Rose had prepared the table for supper. The gentlemen of the Poughkeepsie manifested great interest in the movements of the Hebe-like little attendant who was caring for their wants. When the cloth was to be laid, the midshipman offered his assistance, but his superior directed him to send a hand or two up from the wharf, where the crew of the cutter were lounging or sleeping after their cruise. These men had been thought of, too ; and a vessel filled with smoking soup was taken to them, by one of their own number.

The supper was as cheerful as it was excellent. The dry humor of Wallace, the mild intelligence of the chaplain, the good sense of Harry, and the spirited information of Rose, contributed, each in its particular way, to make the meal memorable in more senses than one. The laugh came easily at that table, and it was twelve o'clock before the party thought of breaking up.

The dispositions for the night were soon made. Rose returned to her little room, where she could now sleep in comfort, and without apprehension. The gentlemen made the disposition of their persons, that circumstances allowed ; each finding something on which to repose, that was preferable to a plank. As for the men, they were accustomed to hard fare, and enjoyed their present good-luck to the top of their bent. It was quite late, before they had done "spinning their yarns," and "cracking their jokes," around the pot of turtle-soup, and the can of grog that succeeded it. By half-past twelve, however, everybody was asleep.

Mulford was the first person afoot the following morning. He left the house just as the sun rose, and perceiving that the "coast was clear" of sharks, he threw off his light attire, and plunged into the sea. Refreshed with this indulgence, he was returning toward the building, when he met the chaplain coming in quest of him. This gentleman, a man of real piety, and of great discretion, had been singularly struck, on the preceding night, with the narrative of our young mate; and he had not failed to note the allusions, slight as they were, and delicately put as they had been, to himself. He saw, at once, the propriety of marrying a couple so situated, and now sought Harry, with a view to bring about so desirable an event, by intimating his entire willingness to officiate. It is scarcely necessary to say that very few words were wanting, to persuade the young man to fall into his views; and as to Rose, he had handed her a short note on the same subject, which he was of opinion would be likely to bring her to the same way of thinking.

An hour later, all the officers, Harry and Rose, were assembled in what might be termed the light-house parlor. The Rev. Mr. Hollins had neither band, gown, nor surplice; but he had what was far better, feeling and piety. Without a prayer-book he never moved; and he read the marriage ceremony with a solemnity that was communicated to all present. The ring was that which had been used at the marriage of Rose's parents, and which she wore habitually, though not on the left hand. In a word, Harry and Rose were as firmly and legally united, on that solitary and almost unknown islet, as could have been the case had they stood up before the altar of mother Trinity itself, with a bishop to officiate, and a legion of attendants. After the compliments which succeeded the ceremony, the whole party sat down to breakfast.

If the supper had been agreeable, the morning meal was not less so. Rose was timid and blushing, as became a bride, though she could not but feel how much more respectable her position became under the protection of Harry as his wife, than it had been while she was only his betrothed.

The most delicate deportment, on the part of her companions, soon relieved her embarrassment however, and the breakfast passed off without cause for an unhappy moment.

"The ship's standing in toward the light, sir," reported the coxswain of the cutter, as the party was still lingering around the table, as if unwilling to bring so pleasant a meal to a close. "Since the mist has broke away, we see her, sir, even to her ports and dead-eyes."

"In that case, Sam, she can't be very far off," answered Wallace. "Ay, there goes a gun from her, at this moment, as much as to say, 'What has become of all of my boats?' Run down and let off a musket; perhaps she will make out to hear that, as we must be rather to windward if anything."

The signal was given and understood. A quarter of an hour later, the Poughkeepsie began to shorten sail. Then Wallace stationed himself in the cutter, in the centre of one of the passages, signalling the ship to come on. Ten minutes later still, the noble craft came into the haven, passing the still burning light, with her topsails just lifting, and making a graceful sweep under very reduced sail, she came to the wind, and very near the spot where the Swash had lain only ten hours before, and dropped an anchor.

CHAPTER XIII.

" The gull has found her place on shore;
　The sun gone down again to rest;
And all is still but ocean's roar;
　There stands the man unbless'd.
But see, he moves—he turns, as asking where
His mates? Why looks he with that piteous stare? "

DANA.

SUPERSTITION would seem to be a consequence of a state of being, in which so much is shadowed forth, while so little is accurately known. Our far-reaching thoughts range over the vast fields of created things, without penetrating to the secret cause of the existence of even a blade of grass. We can analyze all substances that are brought into our crucibles, tell their combinations and tendencies, give a scientific history of their formation, so far as it is connected with secondary facts, their properties, and their uses ; but in each and all there is a latent natural cause that baffles all our inquiries, and tells us that we are merely men. This is just as true in morals as in physics,—no man living being equal to attaining the very faith that is necessary to his salvation, without the special aid of the Spirit of the Godhead ; and even with that mighty support, trusting implicitly for all that is connected with a future that we are taught to believe is eternal, to " the substance of things *hoped* for, and the evidence of things *unseen*." In a word, this earthly probation of ours was intended for finite beings, in the sense of our present existence, leaving far more to be conjectured than is understood.

Ignorance and superstition ever bear a close, and even a mathematical relation to each other. The degrees of the one are regulated by the degrees of the other. He who knows the least believes the most; while he who has seen the most, without the intelligence to comprehend that which he has seen, feels, perhaps, the strongest inclination to refer those things which to him are mysteries to the supernatural and marvellous. Sailors have been, from time immemorial, more disposed than men of their class on the land, to indulge in this weakness, which is probably heightened by the circumstance of their living constantly and vividly in the presence of powers that menace equally their lives and their means, without being in any manner subject to their control.

Spike, for a seaman of his degree of education, was not particularly addicted to the weakness to which we have just alluded. Nevertheless, he was not altogether free from it; and recent circumstances contributed to dispose him so much the more to admit a feeling which, like sin itself, is ever the most apt to insinuate itself at moments of extraordinary moral imbecility, and through the openings left by previous transgression. As his brig stood off from the light, the captain paced the deck, greatly disturbed by what had just passed, and unable to account for it. The boat of the Poughkeepsie was entirely concealed by the islet, and there existing no obvious motive for wishing to return, in order to come at the truth, not a thought to that effect, for one moment, crossed the mind of the smuggler. So far from this, indeed, were his wishes, that the Molly did not seem to him to go half as fast as usual, in his keen desire to get farther and farther from a spot where such strange incidents had occurred.

As for the men forward, no argument was wanting to make *them* believe that something supernatural had just passed before their eyes. It was known to them all, that Mulford had been left on a naked rock, some thirty miles from that spot; and it was not easy to understand how he could now be at the Dry Tortugas, planted, as it might be, on purpose to show himself to the brig, against the tower, in the bright moonlight, "like a pictur' hung up for his old shipmates to look at."

Sombre were the tales that were related that night among them, many of which related to the sufferings of men abandoned on desert islands; and all of which bordered, more or less, on the supernatural. The crew connected the disappearance of the boat with Mulford's apparition, though the logical inference would have been, that the body which required planks to transport it could scarcely be classed with anything of the world of spirits. The links in arguments, however, are seldom respected by the illiterate and vulgar, who jump to their conclusions, in cases of the marvellous, much as politicians find an expression of the common mind in the prepared opinions of the few who speak for them, totally disregarding the dissenting silence of the million. While the men were first comparing their opinions on that which, to them, seemed to be so extraordinary, the Señor Montefalderon joined the captain in his walk, and dropped into a discourse touching the events which had attended their departure from the haven of the Dry Tortugas. In this conversation, Don Juan most admirably preserved his countenance, as well as his self-command, effectually preventing the suspicion of any knowledge on his part that was not common to them both.

"You did leave the port with the salutes observed," the Mexican commenced, with the slightest accent of a foreigner, or just enough to show that he was not speaking in his mother tongue; "salutes paid and returned."

"Do you call that saluting, Don Wan? To me, that infernal shot sounded more like an echo than anything else."

"And to what do *you* ascribe it, Don Esteban?"

"I wish I could answer that question. Sometimes I begin to wish I had not left my mate on that naked rock."

"There is still time to repair the last wrong; we shall go within a few miles of the place where the Señor Enrique was left; and I can take the yawl, with two men, and go in search of him, while you are at work on the wreck."

"Do you believe it possible that he can be still there?"

demanded Spike, looking suddenly and intently at his companion, while his mind was strangely agitated between hatred and dread. "If he is there, who and what was *he* that we all saw so plainly at the foot of the light-house?"

"How should he have left the rock? He was without food or water; and no man, in all his vigor, could swim the distance. I see no means of his getting here."

"Unless some wrecker, or turtler, fell in with him, and took him off. Ay, ay, Don Wan; I left him that much of a chance, at least. No man can say I murdered my mate."

"I am not aware, Don Esteban, that any one has said so hard a thing of you. Still, we have seen neither wrecker nor turtler since we have been here; and that lessens the excellent chance you left Don Enrique."

"There is no occasion, Señor, to be so particular," growled Spike, a little sullenly, in reply. "The chance, I say, was a good one, when you consider how many of them devils of wreckers hang about these reefs. Let this brig only get fast on a rock, and they would turn up, like sharks, all around us, each with his maw open for salvage. But this is neither here nor there; what puzzles me was what we saw at the light, half an hour since, and the musket that was fired back at us! I *know* that the figure at the foot of the tower did not fire, for my eye was on him from first to last; and he had no arms. You were on the island a good bit, and must have known if the light-house keeper was there or not, Don Wan?"

"The light-house keeper *was* there, Don Esteban—but he was in his *grave*."

"Ay, ay, one, I know, was drowned, and buried with the rest of them; there might, however, have been more than one. You saw none of the people that had gone to Key West, in or about the house, Don Wan?"

"None. If any persons have left the Tortugas to go to Key West, within a few days, not one of them has yet returned."

"So I supposed. No, it can be none of *them*. Then I saw his face as plainly as ever I saw it by moonlight, from aft for'ard.   What is your opinion about seeing the dead walk on the 'arth, Don Wan?''

"That I have never seen any such thing myself, Don Esteban, and consequently know nothing about it.''

"So I supposed; I find it hard to believe it, I do.   It may be a warning to keep us from coming any more to the Dry Tortugas ; and I must say I have little heart for returning to this place, after all that has fell out here.   We can go to the wreck, fish up the doubloons, and be off for Yucatan. Once in one of your ports, I make no question that the merits of the Molly will make themselves understood, and that we shall soon agree on a price.''

"What use could we put the brig to, Don Esteban, if we had her all ready for sea?''

"That is a strange   question to ask in time of war ! Give *me* such a craft as the Molly, with sixty or eighty men on board her, in a war like this, and her 'arnin's should not fall short of half a million within a twelve-month.''

"Could we engage you to take charge of her, Don Esteban?''

"That would be ticklish work, Don Wan.   But we can see.   No one knows what he will do until he is tried.   In for a penny, in for a pound.   A fellow never knows ! Ha ! ha ! ha !   Don Wan, we live in a strange world—yes, in a strange world.''

"We live in strange *times*, Don Esteban, as the situation of my poor country proves.   But let us talk this matter over a little more in confidence.''

And they did thus discuss the subject.   It was a singular spectacle to see an honorable man, one full of zeal of the purest nature in behalf of his own country, sounding a traitor as to the terms on which he might be induced to do all the harm he could to those who claimed his allegiance.   Such sights, however, are often seen ; our own especial objects too frequently blinding us to the obligations that we owe morality, so far as not to be instrumental in effecting even what we conceive to be good, by questionable agencies.   But the Señor Montefalderon kept in view, principally, his desire to be useful to Mexico, blended a little too strongly, perhaps, with the wishes of a man who was born near the sun, to avenge his wrongs, real or fancied.

While this dialogue was going on between Spike and his passenger, as they paced the quarter-deck, one quite as characteristic occurred in the galley, within twenty feet of them—Simon, the cook, and Josh, the steward, being the interlocutors. As they talked secrets, they conferred together with closed doors, though few were ever disposed to encounter the smoke, grease, and fumes of their narrow domains, unless called thither by hunger.

"What *you* t'ink of dis matter, Josh?" demanded Simon, whose skull having the well-known density of his race did not let internal ideas out, or external ideas in, as readily as most men's. "Our young mate *was* at de light-house beyond all controwersy; and how can he be den on dat rock over yonder, too?"

"Dat is imposserble," answered Josh; "derefore I says it is n't true. I surposes you know dat what is imposserble is n't true, Simon. Nobody can't be out yonder and down here at de same time. Dat is imposserble, Simon. But what I wants to intermate to you will explain all dis difficulty; and it do show de raal super'ority of a colored man over de white poperlation. Now you mark my words, cook, and be full of admiration! Jack Tier came back along wid de Mexican gentle'em, in my anchor-watch, dis very night! You see, in de first place, ebberyt'ing come to pass in nigger's watch."

Here the two dark-skinned worthies haw-haw'd to their heart's content; laughing very much as a magistrate or a minister of the gospel might be fancied to laugh, the first time he saw a clown at a circus. The merriment of a negro will have its course, in spite of ghosts, or of anything else; and neither the cook nor the steward dreamed of putting in another syllable, until their laugh was fairly and duly ended. Then the cook made his remarks.

"How Jack Tier comin' back explain der differculty, Josh?" asked Simon.

"Did n't Jack go away wid Miss Rose and de mate, in de boat dat got adrift, you know, in Jack's watch on deck?"

Here the negroes laughed again, their imaginations happening to picture to each, at the same instant, the mystification about the boat; Biddy having told Josh in confidence the manner in which the party had returned to the brig, while he and Simon were asleep; which fact the steward had already communicated to the cook. To these two beings, of an order in nature different from all around them, and of a simplicity and of habits that scarce placed them on a level with the intelligence of the humblest white man, all these circumstances had a sort of mysterious connection, out of which peeped much the most conspicuously to their faculties, the absurdity of the captain's imagining that a boat had got adrift, which had, in truth, been taken away by human hands. Accordingly, they laughed it out; and when they had done laughing, they returned again to the matter before them with renewed interest in the subject.

"Well, how all dat explain dis difficulty?" repeated Simon.

"In dis wery manner, cook," returned the steward, with a little dignity in his manner. "Ebberyt'ing depend on understandin', I s'pose you know. If Mr. Mulford got taken off dat rock by Miss Rose and Jack Tier, wid de boat, and den dey comes here altogedder; and den Jack Tier, he get on board and tell Biddy all dis matter, and den Biddy tell Josh, and den Josh tell de cook—what for you surprise, you black debbil, one bit?"

"Dat all!" exclaimed Simon.

"Dat just all—dat ebbery bit of it, don't I say."

Here Simon burst into such a fit of loud laughter, that it induced Spike himself to shove aside the galley-door, and thrust his own frowning visage into the dark hole within, to inquire the cause.

"What 's the meaning of this uproar?" demanded the captain, all the more excited because he felt that things had reached a pass that would not permit him to laugh himself. "Do you fancy yourself on the Hook, or at the Five Points?"

The Hook and the Five Points are two pieces of tabooed
territory within the limits of the good town of Manhattan,
that are getting to be renowned for their rascality and or-
gies. They probably want nothing but the proclamation
of a governor in vindication of their principles, annexed to a
pardon of some of their unfortunate children, to render both
classical. If we continue to make much further progress in
political logic, and in the same direction as that in which
we have already proceeded so far, neither will probably long
be in want of this illustration. Votes can be given by the
virtuous citizens of both these purlieus, as well as by the
virtuous citizens of the anti-rent districts, and votes contain
the essence of all such principles, as well as of their glorifi-
cation.

"Do you fancy yourselves on the Hook, or at the Five
Points?" demanded Spike, angrily.

"Lor', no, sir!" answered Simon, laughing at each pause
with all his heart. "Only laugh a little at *ghost*—dat all,
sir."

"Laugh at ghost! Is that a subject to laugh at? Have
a care, you black rascal, or he will visit you in your galley
here, when you will least want to see him."

"No care much for *him*, sir," returned Simon, laughing
away as hard as ever. "*Sich* a ghost ought n't to skear
little baby."

"*Such* a ghost? And what do you know of *this* ghost
more than any other?"

"Well, I see'd him, Cap'in Spike; and what a body sees,
he is acquainted wid."

"You saw an image that looked as much like Mr. Mulford, my late mate, as one timber-head in this brig is like
another."

"Yes, sir, he like enough—must say *dat*—so wery like,
could n't see any difference."

As Simon concluded this remark, he burst out into another fit of laughter, in which Josh joined him, heart and
soul, as it might be. The uninitiated reader is not to imagine the laughter of those blacks to be very noisy, or to be
raised on a sharp, high key. They *could* make the welkin

ring, in sudden bursts of merriment, on occasion ; but, at a time like this, they rather caused their diversion to be developed by sounds that came from the depths of their chests. A gleam of suspicion that these blacks were acquainted with some fact that it might be well for him to know, shot across the mind of Spike ; but he was turned from further inquiry by a remark of Don Juan, who intimated that the mirth of such persons never had much meaning to it, expressing at the same time a desire to pursue the important subject in which they were engaged. Admonishing the blacks to be more guarded in their manifestations of merriment, the captain closed the door on them, and resumed his walk up and down the quarter-deck. As soon as left to themselves, the blacks broke out afresh, though in a way so guarded as to confine their mirth to the galley.

"Cap'in Spike t'ink *dat* a ghost!" exclaimed Simon, with contempt.

"Guess if he see *raal* ghost, he find 'e difference," answered Josh. "One look at raal sperit wort' two at dis object."

Simon's eyes now opened like two saucers, and they gleamed, by the light of the lamp they had, like dark balls of condensed curiosity, blended with awe, on his companion.

"You ebber see him, Josh?" he asked, glancing over each shoulder hurriedly, as it might be, to make sure that he could not see "him," too.

"How you t'ink I get so far down the wale of life, Simon, and nebber see sich a t'ing? I see'd t'ree of the crew of the Maria Sheffington, that was drowned by deir boat's capsizin', when we lay at Gibraltar, jest as plain as I see you now. Then—"

But it is unnecessary to repeat Josh's experiences in this way, with which he continued to entertain and terrify Simon for the next half hour. This is just the difference between ignorance and knowledge. While Spike himself, and every man in his brig who belonged forward, had strong misgivings as to the earthly character of the figure they had seen at the foot of the light-house, these negroes laughed at their delusion, because they happened to be in the secret of Mulford's escape from the rock, and of that of his actual presence at the Tortugas. When, however, the same superstitious feeling was brought to bear on circumstances that lay without the sphere of their exact information, they became just as dependent and helpless as all around them ; more so, indeed, inasmuch as their previous habits and opinions disposed them to a more profound credulity.

It was midnight before any of the crew of the Swash sought their rest that night. The captain had to remind them that a day of extraordinary toil was before them, ere he could get one even to quit the deck ; and when they did go below, it was to continue to discuss the subject of what they had seen at the Dry Tortugas. It appeared to be the prevalent opinion among the people, that the late event foreboded evil to the Swash, and long as most of these men had served in the brig, and much as they had become attached to her, had she gone into port that night, nearly every man forward would have run before morning. But fatigue and wonder at length produced their effect, and the vessel was silent as was usual at that hour. Spike himself lay down in his clothes, as he had done ever since Mulford had left him ; and the brig continued to toss the spray from her bows, as she bore gallantly up against the trades, working her way to windward. The light was found to be of great service, as it indicated the position of the reef, though it gradually sunk in the western horizon, until near morning it fell entirely below it.

At this hour Spike appeared on deck again, where, for the first time since their interview on the morning of Harry's and Rose's escape, he laid his eyes on Jack Tier. The little dumpling-looking fellow was standing in the waist, with his arms folded sailor-fashion, as composedly as if nothing had occurred to render his meeting with the captain any way of a doubtful character. Spike approached near the person of the steward, whom he surveyed from head to foot, with a sort of contemptuous superiority, ere he spoke.

"So, Master Tier," at length the captain commenced,

"you have deigned to turn out at last, have you? I hope the day's duty you 've forgotten will help to pay for the lighthouse boat, that I understand you 've lost for me, also."

"What signifies a great clumsy boat that the brig could n't hoist in nor tow?" answered Jack, coolly, turning short round at the same time, but not condescending to "uncoil" his arms as he did so, a mark of indifference that would probably have helped to mystify the captain, had he even actually suspected that anything was wrong beyond the supposed accident to the boat in question. "If you had had the boat astern, Captain Spike, an order would have been given to cut it adrift the first time the brig made sail on the wind."

"Nobody knows, Jack; that boat would have been very useful to us while at work about the wreck. You never even turned out this morning to let me know where that craft lay, as you promised to do, but left us to find it out by our wits."

"There was no occasion for my tellin' you anything about it, sir, when the mast-heads was to be seen above water. As soon as I heard that them 'ere mast-heads was out of water, I turned over and went to sleep upon it. A man can't be on the doctor's list and on duty at the same time."

Spike looked hard at the little steward, but he made no further allusion to his being off duty, or to his failing to stand pilot to the brig as she came through the passage in quest of the schooner's remains. The fact was, that he had discovered the mast-heads himself, just as he was on the point of ordering Jack to be called, having allowed him to remain in his berth to the last moment after his watch, according to a species of implied faith that is seldom disregarded among seamen. Once busied on the wreck, Jack was forgotten, having little to do in common with any one on board, but that which the captain termed the "women's mess."

"Come aft, Jack," resumed Spike, after a considerable pause, during the whole of which he had stood regarding the little steward as if studying his person, and through that his character. "Come aft to the trunk; I wish to catechise you a bit."

"Catechise!" repeated Tier, in an undertone, as he followed the captain to the place mentioned. "It's a long time since I've done anything at *that!*"

"Ay, come hither," resumed Spike, seating himself at his ease on the trunk, while Jack stood near by, his arms still folded, and his rotund little form as immovable, under the plunges that the lively brig made into the head-seas that she was obliged to meet, as if a timber-head in the vessel itself. "You keep your sea-legs well, Jack, short as they are."

"No wonder for that, Captain Spike; for the last twenty years I've scarce passed a twelvemonth ashore; and what I did before that, no one can better tell than yourself, since we was ten good years shipmates."

"So you say, Jack, though I do not remember *you* as well as you seem to remember *me*. Do you not make the time too long?"

"Not a day, sir. Ten good and happy years did we sail together, Captain Spike; and all that time in this very—"

"Hush—h-u-s-h, man, hush! There is no need of telling the Molly's age to everybody. I may wish to sell her some day, and then her great experience will be no recommendation. You should recollect that the Molly is a female, and the ladies do not like to hear of their ages after five-and-twenty."

Jack made no answer, but he dropped his arms to their natural position, seeming to wait the captain's communication, first referring to his tobacco-box and taking a fresh quid.

"If you was with me in the brig, Jack, at the time you mentioned," continued Spike, after another long and thoughtful pause, "you must remember many little things that I don't wish to have known; especially while Mrs. Budd and her handsome niece is aboard here."

"I understand you, Captain Spike. The ladies shall learn no more from me than they know already."

"'Thank'ee for that, Jack; thank'ee with all my heart. Shipmates of our standing ought to be fast friends; and so you'll find me, if you'll only sail under the true colors, my man.''

At that moment Jack longed to let the captain know how strenuously he had insisted that very night on rejoining his vessel; and this at a time, too, when the brig was falling into disrepute. But this he could not do, without betraying the secret of the lovers, so he chose to say nothing.

"There is no use in blabbing all a man knows, and the galley is a sad place for talking. Galley news is poor news, I suppose you know, Jack.''

"I've hear 'n say as much on board o' man-of-war. It's a great place for the officers to meet and talk and smoke in Uncle Sam's crafts; and what a body hears in such places is pretty much newspaper stuff, I do suppose.''

"Ay, ay, that's it; not to be thought of half an hour after it has been spoken. Here's a doubloon for you, Jack; and all for the sake of old times. Now, tell me, my little fellow, how do the ladies come on? Does n't Miss Rose get over her mourning on account of the mate? Are n't we to have the pleasure of seein' her on deck, soon?''

"I can't answer for the minds and fancies of young women, Captain Spike. They are difficult to understand, and I would rather not meddle with what I can't understand.''

"Poh, poh, man; you must get over that. You might be a great use to me, Jack, in a very delicate affair—for you know how it is with women; they must be handled as a man would handle this brig among breakers; Rose, in partic'lar, is as skittish as a colt.''

"Stephen Spike,'' said Jack, solemnly, but in so low a key that it entirely changed his usually harsh and cracked voice to one that sounded soft, if not absolutely pleasant, "do you never think of hereafter? Your days are almost run; a very few years, in your calling it may be a very few weeks, or a few hours, and time will be done with you, and etarnity will commence. Do you never think of a hereafter?"

Spike started to his feet, gazing at Jack intently; then he wiped the perspiration from his face, and began to pace the deck rapidly, muttering to himself, "This has been a most accursed night! First the mate, and now *this!* Blast me, but I thought it was a voice from the grave! Graves! can't they keep those that belong to them, or have rocks and waves no graves?"

What more passed through the mind of the captain must remain a secret, for he kept it to himself; nor did he take any further notice of his companion. Jack, finding that he was unobserved, passed quietly below, and took the place in his berth, which he had only temporarily abandoned.

Just as the day dawned, the Swash reached the vicinity of the wreck again. Sail was shortened, and the brig stood in until near enough for the purpose of her commander, when she was hove-to, so near the mast-heads that, by lowering the yawl, a line was sent out to the fore-mast, and the brig was hauled close alongside. The direction of the reef at that point formed a lee; and the vessel lay in water sufficiently smooth for her object.

This was done soon after the sun had risen, and Spike now ordered all hands called, and began his operations in earnest. By sounding carefully around the schooner when last here, he had ascertained her situation to his entire satisfaction. She had settled on a shelf of the reef, in such a position that her bows lay in a sort of cradle, while her stern was several feet nearer to the surface than the opposite extremity. This last fact was apparent, indeed, by the masts themselves, the lower mast aft being several feet out of water, while the fore-mast was entirely buried, leaving nothing but the fore-topmast exposed. On these great premises Spike had laid the foundation of the practical problem he intended to solve.

No expectation existed of ever getting the schooner afloat again. All that Spike and the Señor Montefalderon now aimed at was to obtain the doubloons. which the former

thought could be got at in the following manner. He knew
that it would be much easier handling the wreck, so far as
its gravity was concerned, while the hull continued submerged. He also knew that one end could be raised with
a comparatively trifling effort, so long as the other rested
on the rock. Under these circumstances, therefore, he proposed merely to get slings around the after body of the
schooner, as near her stern-post, indeed, as would be safe,
and to raise that extremity of the vessel to the surface,
leaving most of the weight of the craft to rest on the
bows. The difference between the power necessary to
effect this much, and that which would be required to raise
the whole wreck, would be like the difference in power
necessary to turn over a log with one end resting on the
ground, and turning the same log by lifting it bodily in
the arms, and turning it in the air. With the stern once
above water, it would be easy to come at the bag of doubloons, which Jack Tier had placed in a locker above the
transoms.

The first thing was to secure the brig properly, in order
that she might bear the necessary strain. This was done
very much as has been described already, in the account
of the manner in which she was secured and supported in
order to raise the schooner at the Dry Tortugas. An anchor
was laid abreast and to windward, and purchases were
brought to the masts, as before. Then the bight of the
chain brought from the Tortugas was brought under the
schooner's keel, and counter-purchases, leading from both
the fore-mast and main-mast of the brig, were brought to
it, and set taut. Spike now carefully examined all his
fastenings, looking to his cables as well as his mechanical
power aloft, heaving in upon this, and veering out upon that,
in order to bring the Molly square to her work; after which
he ordered the people to knock-off for their dinners. By
that time, it was high noon.

While Stephen Spike was thus employed on the wreck,
matters and things were not neglected at the Tortugas.
The Poughkeepsie had no sooner anchored, than Wallace
went on board and made his report. Captain Mull then

sent for Mulford, with whom he had a long personal conference. This officer was getting gray, and consequently he had acquired experience. It was evident to Harry, at first, that he was regarded as one who had been willingly engaged in an unlawful pursuit, but who had abandoned it to push dearer interests in another quarter. It was some time before the commander of the sloop-of-war could divest himself of this opinion, though it gradually gave way before the frankness of the mate's manner, and the manliness, simplicity, and justice of his sentiments. Perhaps Rose had some influence also in bringing about this favorable change.

Wallace did not fail to let it be known that turtle-soup was to be had ashore; and many was the guest our heroine had to supply with that agreeable compound, in the course of the morning. Jack Tier had manifested so much skill in the preparation of the dish, that its reputation soon extended to the cabin, and the captain was induced to land, in order to ascertain how far rumor was or was not a liar, on this interesting occasion. So ample was the custom, indeed, that Wallace had the consideration to send one of the ward-room servants to the light-house in order to relieve Rose from a duty that was getting to be a little irksome. She was "seeing company" as a bride, in a novel and rather unpleasant manner; and it was in consequence of a suggestion of the "ship's gentleman" that the remains of the turtle were transferred to the vessel, and were put into the coppers, *secundum artem*, by the regular cooks.

It was after tickling his palate with a bowl of the soup, and enjoying a half hour's conversation with Rose, that Captain Mull summoned Harry to a final consultation on the subject of their future proceedings. By this time the commander of the Poughkeepsie was in a better humor with his new acquaintance, more disposed to believe him, and infinitely more inclined to listen to his suggestions and advice, than he had been in their previous interviews. Wallace was present in his character of "ship's gentleman," or, as having nothing to do, while his senior, the first lieutenant, was working like a horse on board the vessel, in the execution of his round of daily duties.

At this consultation, the parties came into a right understanding of each other's views and characters. Captain
Mull was slow to yield his confidence, but when he did
bestow it, he bestowed it sailor-fashion, or with all his heart.
Satisfied at last that he had to do with a young man of
honor, and one who was true to the flag, he consulted
freely with our mate, asked his advice, and was greatly
influenced in the formation of his final decision by the opinions that Harry modestly advanced, maintaining them, however, with solid arguments, and reasons that every seaman
could comprehend.

Mulford knew the plans of Spike by means of his own
communications with the Señor Montefalderon. Once acquainted with the projects of his old commander, it was
easy for him to calculate the time it would require to put
them in execution, with the means that were to be found
on board the Swash. "It will take the brig until near
morning," he said, "to beat up to the place where the
wreck lies. Spike will wait for light to commence operations, and several hours will be necessary to moor the brig,
and get out the anchors with which he will think it necessary to stay his masts. Then he will hook on, and he may
partly raise the hull before night return. More than this
he can never do; and it would not surprise me were he
merely to get everything ready for heaving on his purchases
to-morrow, and suspend further proceedings until the next
day, in preference to having so heavy a strain on his spars
all night. He has not the force, however, to carry on such
duty to a very late hour; and you may count with perfect
security, Captain Mull, on his being found alongside of the
wreck at sunrise the next day after to-morrow, in all probability with his anchors down, and fast to the wreck. By
timing your own arrival well, nothing will be easier than
to get him fairly under your guns, and once under your
guns, the brig must give up. When you chased her out of
this very port, a few days since, you would have brought
her up could you have kept her within range of those terrible shells ten minutes longer."

"You would then advise my not sailing from this place immediately," said Mull.

"It will be quite time enough to get under way late in the afternoon, and then under short canvas. Ten hours will be ample time for this ship to beat up to that passage in, and it will be imprudent to arrive too soon; nor do I suppose you will wish to be playing round the reef in the dark."

To the justice of all this Captain Mull assented; and the plan of proceedings was deliberately and intelligently formed. As it was necessary for Mulford to go in the ship, in order to act as pilot, no one else on board knowing exactly where to find the wreck, the commander of the Poughkeepsie had the civility to offer the young couple the hospitalities of his own cabin, with one of his state-rooms. This offer Harry gratefully accepted, it being understood that the ship would land them at Key West, as soon as the contemplated duty was executed. Rose felt so much anxiety about her aunt, that any other arrangement would scarcely have pacified her fears.

In consequence of these arrangements, the Poughkeepsie lay quietly at her anchors until near sunset. In the interval her boats were out in all directions, parties of the officers visiting the islet where the powder had exploded, and the islet where the tent, erected for the uses of the females, was still standing. As for the light-house island, an order of Captain Mull's prevented it from being crowded in a manner unpleasant to Rose, as might otherwise have been the case. The few officers who did land there, however, appeared much struck with the ingenuous simplicity and beauty of the bride, and a manly interest in her welfare was created among them all, principally by means of the representations of the second lieutenant and the chaplain. About five o'clock she went off to the ship, accompanied by Harry, and was hoisted on board in the manner usually practised by vessels of war which have no accommodation-ladder rigged. Rose was immediately installed in her state-room, where she found every convenience necessary to a comfortable though small apartment.

26

It was quite late in the afternoon, when the boatswain and his mate piped " All hands up anchor, ahoy ! " Harry hastened into the state-room for his charming bride, anxious to show her the movements of a vessel of war on such an occasion. Much as she had seen of the ocean, and of a vessel, within the last few weeks, Rose now found that she had yet a great deal to learn, and that a ship of war had many points to distinguish her from a vessel engaged in commerce.

The Poughkeepsie was only a sloop-of-war, or a corvette, in construction, number of her guns, and rate ; but she was a ship of the dimensions of an old-fashioned frigate, measuring about one thousand tons. The frigates of which we read half a century since were seldom ever as large as this, though they were differently built in having a regular gun-deck, or one armed deck that was entirely covered, with another above it ; and on the quarter-deck and forecastle of the last of which were also batteries of lighter guns. To the contrary of all this, the Poughkeepsie had but one armed deck, and on that only twenty guns. These pieces, however, were of unusually heavy calibre, throwing thirty-two pound shot, with the exception of the Paixhans, or Columbiads, which throw shot of even twice that weight. The vessel had a crew of two hundred souls, all told ; and she had the spars, anchors, and other equipments of a light frigate.

In another great particular did the Poughkeepsie differ from the corvette-built vessels that were so much in favor at the beginning of the century ; a species of craft obtained from the French, who have taught the world so much in connection with naval science, and who, after building some of the best vessels that ever floated, have failed in knowing how to handle them, though not always in that. The Poughkeepsie, while she had no spar, or upper deck, properly speaking, had a poop and a topgallant-forecastle. Within the last were the cabins and other accommodations of the captain ; an arrangement that was necessary for a craft of her construction, that carried so many officers, and so large a crew. Without it, sufficient space would not be had for the uses of the last. One gun of a side was in the main cabin, there being a very neat and amply spacious after-cabin between the state-rooms, as is ordinarily the case in all vessels from the size of frigates up to that of three-deckers. It may be well to explain here, while on this subject of construction, that in naval parlance a ship is called a single-decked vessel, a two-decker, or three-decker, not from the number of decks she actually possesses, but from the number of gun-decks that she has or of those that are fully armed. Thus a frigate has four decks ; the spar, gun, berth, and orlop (or haul-up) decks ; but she is called a "single-decked ship," from the circumstance that only one of these four decks has a complete range of batteries. The two-decker has two of these fully armed decks, and the three-decker three; though, in fact, the two-decker has five, and the three-decker six decks. Asking pardon for this little digression, which we trust will be found useful to a portion of our readers, we return to the narrative.

Harry conducted Rose to the poop of the Poughkeepsie, where she might enjoy the best view of the operation of getting so large a craft under way, man-of-war fashion. The details were mysteries, of course, and Rose knew no more of the process by which the chain was brought to the capstan, by the intervention of what is called a messenger, than if she had not been present. She saw two hundred men distributed about the vessel, some at the capstan, some on the forecastle, some in the tops, and others in the waist, and she heard the order to "Heave round." Then the shrill fife commenced the lively air of "The girl I left behind me," rather more from a habit in the fifer, than from any great regrets for the girls left at the Dry Tortugas, as was betrayed to Mulford by the smiles of the officers, and the glances they cast at Rose. As for the latter, she knew nothing of the air, and was quite unconscious of the sort of parody that the gentlemen of the quarter-deck fancied it conveyed on her own situation.

Rose was principally struck with the quiet that prevailed in the ship, Captain Mull being a silent man himself, and insisting on having a quiet vessel. The first lieutenant was not a noisy officer, and from these two, everybody else on board received their cues. A simple "All ready, sir," uttered by the first to the captain, in a common tone of voice, answered by a "Very well, sir, get your anchor," in the same tone, set everything in motion. "Stamp and go," soon followed, and taking the whole scene together, Rose felt a strange excitement come over her. There were the shrill, animating music of the fife; the stamping time of the men at the bars; the perceptible motion of the ship, as she drew ahead to her anchor, and now and then the call between Wallace who stood between the knight-heads, as commander-in-chief on the forecastle (the second lieutenant's station when the captain does not take the trumpet, as very rarely happens), and the "executive officer" aft who was "carrying on duty," all conspiring to produce this effect. At length, and it was but a minute or two from the time when the "Stamp and go" commenced, Wallace called out "A short stay-peak, sir." "Heave and pull" followed, and the men left their bars.

The process of making sail succeeded. There was no "letting fall" a fore-topsail here, as on board a merchant-man, but all the canvas dropped from the yards, into festoons, at the same instant. Then the three topsails were sheeted home and hoisted, all at once, and all in a single minute of time; the yards were counter-braced, and the capstan-bars were again manned. In two more minutes it was "Heave and she's up and down." Then "Heave and in sight," and "Heave and pull again." The cat-fall was ready, and it was "Hook on," when the fife seemed to turn its attention to another subject as the men catted the anchor. Literally, all this was done in less time than we have taken to write it down in, and in very little more time than the reader has wasted in perusing what we have here written.

The Poughkeepsie was now "free of bottom," as it is called, with her anchor catted and fished, and her position maintained in the basin where she lay, by the counter-bracing of her yards, and the counteracting force of the wind on her sails. It only remained to "fill away," by

bracing her head-yards sharp up, when the vast mass over-
came its inertia, and began to move through the water.
As this was done, the jib and spanker were set. The two
most beautiful things with which we are accquainted are a
graceful and high-bred woman entering or quitting a draw-
ing-room, more particularly the last, and a man-of-war
leaving her anchorage in a moderate breeze, and when not
hurried for time. On the present occasion, Captain Mull
was in no haste, and the ship passed out to windward
of the light, as the Swash had done the previous night, under
her three topsails, spanker, and jib, with the light sails loose
and flowing, and the courses hanging in the brails.

A great deal is said concerning the defective construction
of the light cruisers of the navy, of late years, and complaints are made that they will not sail, as American cruisers
ought to sail, and were wont to sail in old times. That there
has been some ground for these complaints, we believe;
though the evil has been greatly exaggerated, and some explanation may be given, we think, even in the cases in which
the strictures are not altogether without justification. The
trim of a light, sharp vessel is easily deranged; and officers,
in their desire to command as much as possible, often get
their vessels of this class too deep. They are, generally,
for the sort of cruiser, oversparred, overmanned, and over-
provisioned; consequently too deep. We recollect a case in
which one of these delicate craft, a half-rigged brig, was
much abused for "having lost her sailing." She did, indeed,
lose her fore-yard, and, after that, she sailed like a witch,
until she got a new one! If the facts were inquired into, in
the spirit which ought to govern such inquiries, it would be
found that even most of the much-abused "ten sloops"
proved to be better vessels than common. The St. Louis
the Vincennes, the Concord, the Fairfield, the Boston, and
the Falmouth, are instances of what we mean. In behalf
of the Warren and the Lexington, we believe no discreet
man was ever heard to utter one syllable, except as wholesome crafts. But the Poughkeepsie was a very different
sort of vessel from any of the "ten sloops." She was every
way a good ship, and, as Jack expressed it, was "a good goer."

The most severe nautical critic could scarcely have found a
fault in her, as she passed out between the islets, on the
evening of the day mentioned, in the sort of undress we
have described. The whole scene, indeed, was impressive,
and of singular maritime characteristics.

The little islets scattered about, low, sandy, and unten-
anted, were the only land in sight—all else was the bound-
less waste of waters. The solitary light rose like an aquatic
monument, as if purposely to give its character to the view.
Captain Mull had caused its lamps to be trimmed and lighted
for the very reason that had induced Spike to do the same
thing, and the dim star they presented was just struggling
into existence, as it might be, as the brilliance left by the
setting sun was gradually diminished, and finally disappeared. As for the ship, the hull appeared dark, glossy, and
graceful, as is usual with a vessel of war. Her sails were
in soft contrast to the color of the hull, and they offered the
variety and divergence from straight lines which are thought
necessary to perfect beauty. Those that were set, presented
the symmetry in their trim, the flatness in their hoist, and
the breadth that distinguish a man-of-war ; while those that
were loose, floated in the air in every wave and cloud-like
swell, that we so often see in light canvas that is released
from the yards in a fresh breeze. The ship had an undress
look from this circumstance, but it was such an undress as
denotes the man or woman of the world. This undress
appearance was increased by the piping down of the hammocks, which left the nettings loose, and with a negligent
but still knowing look about them.

When half a mile from the islets, the main-yard was
braced aback, and the main-topsail was laid to the mast.
As soon as the ship had lost her way, two or three boats that
had been towing astern, each with its boat-sitter, or keeper,
in it, were hauled up alongside, or to the quarters, were
" hooked on," and " run up " to the whistling of the call.
All was done at once, and all was done in a couple of minutes. As soon as effected, the main-topsail was again filled,
and away the ship glided.

Captain Mull was not in the habit of holding many consultations with his officers. If there be wisdom in a "multitude of counsellors," he was of opinion it was not on board a man-of-war. Napoleon is reported to have said that one bad general was better than two good ones; meaning that one head to an army, though of inferior quality, is better than a hydra of Solomons, or Cæsars. Captain Mull was much of the same way of thinking, seldom troubling his subordinates with anything but orders. He interfered very little with "working Willy," though he saw effectually that he did his duty. "The ship's gentleman," might enjoy his joke as much as he pleased, so long as he chose his time and place with discretion; but in the captain's presence joking was not tolerated, unless it were after dinner, at his own table, and in his own cabin. Even there it was not precisely such joking as took place daily, not to say hourly, in the midshipmen's messes.

In making up his mind as to the mode of proceeding on the present occasion, therefore, Captain Mull, while he had heard all that Mulford had to tell him, and had even encouraged Wallace to give his opinions, made up his decision for himself. After learning all that Harry had to communicate, he made his own calculations as to time and distance, and quietly determined to carry whole sail on the ship for the next four hours. This he did as the wisest course of making sure of getting to windward while he could, and knowing that the vessel could be brought under short canvas at any moment when it might be deemed necessary. The light was a beacon to let him know his distance with almost mathematical precision. It could be seen so many miles at sea, each mile being estimated by so many feet of elevation, and having taken that elevation, he was sure of his distance from the glittering object, so long as it could be seen from his own poop. It was also of use by letting him know the range of the reef, though Captain Mull, unlike Spike, had determined to make one leg off to the northward and eastward until he had brought the light nearly to the horizon, and then to make another to the southward and eastward, believing that the last stretch would bring him to the reef, almost as far to windward as he desired to be. In furtherance of this plan, the sheets of the different sails were drawn home, as soon as the boats were in, and the Poughkeepsie bending a little to the breeze, gallantly dashed the waves aside, as she went through and over them, at a rate of not less than ten good knots in the hour. As soon as all these arrangements were made, the watch went below, and from that time throughout the night, the ship offered nothing but the quiet manner in which ordinary duty is carried on in a well-regulated vessel of war at sea, between the hours of sun and sun. Leaving the good craft to pursue her way with speed and certainly, we must now return to the Swash.

Captain Spike had found the mooring of his brig a much more difficult task, on this occasion, than on that of his former attempt to raise the schooner. Then he had to lift the wreck bodily, and he knew that laying the Swash a few feet farther ahead or astern could be of no great moment, inasmuch as the moment the schooner was off the bottom, she would swing in perpendicularly to the purchases. But now one end of the schooner, her bows, was to remain fast, and it became of importance to be certain that the purchases were so placed as to bring the least strain on the masts while they acted most directly on the after body of the vessel to be lifted. This point gave Spike more trouble than he had anticipated. Fully one half of the remainder of the day, even after he had begun to heave upon his purchases, was spent in rectifying mistakes in connection with this matter, and in getting up additional securities to his masts.

In one respect Spike had, from the first, made a good disposition. The masts of the brig raked materially, and by bringing the head of the Swash in the direction of the schooner, he converted this fact, which might otherwise have been of great disadvantage, into a circumstance that was favorable. In consequence of the brig's having been thus moored, the strain, which necessarily led forward, came nearly in a line with the masts, and the latter were much better able to support it. Notwithstanding this ad-

vantage, however, it was found expedient to get up pre-
venter-stays, and to give the spars all the additional support
that could be conveniently bestowed. Hours were passed in
making these preliminary, or it might be better to say, secondary arrangements.

It was past five in the afternoon when the people of the
Swash began to heave on their purchases as finally disposed. After much creaking, and the settling of straps
and lashings into their places, it was found that everything
stood, and the work went on. In ten minutes Spike found
he had the weight of the schooner, so far as he should be
obliged to sustain it at all, until the stern rose above the
surface; and he felt reasonably secure of the doubloons.
Further than this he did not intend to make any experiment on her, the Señor Montefalderon having abandoned all
idea of recovering the vessel itself, now so much of the cargo
was lost. The powder was mostly consumed, and that which
remained in the hull must, by this time, be injured by damp-
ness, if not ruined. So reasoned Don Juan at least.

As the utmost care was necessary, the capstan and windlass were made to do their several duties with great caution. As inch by inch was gained, the extra supports of
the masts were examined, and it was found that a much
heavier strain now came on the masts than when the
schooner was raised before. This was altogether owing to
the direction in which it came, and to the fact that the
anchor planted off abeam was not of as much use as on
the former occasion, in consequence of its not lying so
much in a straight line with the direction of the purchases.
Spike began to have misgivings on account of his masts,
and this so much the more because the wind appeared to
haul a little farther to the northward, and the weather to
look unsettled. Should a swell roll into the bight of the reef
where the brig lay by raising the hull a little too rudely
there would be the imminent danger of at least springing
if not of absolutely carrying away, both the principal spars.
It was therefore necessary to resort to extraordinary precautions, in order to obviate this danger.

The captain was indebted to his boatswain, who was

now in fact acting as his mate, for the suggestion of the plan next adopted. Two of the largest spare spars of the brig were got out, with their heads securely lashed to the links of the chain by which the wreck was suspended, one on each side of the schooner. Pig-iron and shot were lashed to the heels of these spars, which carried them to the bottom. As the spars were of a greater length than was necessary to reach the rock, they necessarily lay at an inclination, which was lessened every inch the after body of the wreck was raised, thus forming props to the hull of the schooner.

Spike was delighted with the success of this scheme, of which he was assured by a single experiment in heaving. After getting the spars well planted at their heels, he even ordered the men to slacken the purchases a little, and found that he could actually relieve the brig from the strain, by causing the wreck to be supported altogether by these shores. This was a vast relief from the cares of the approaching night, and indeed alone prevented the necessity of the work's going on without interruption, or rest, until the end was obtained.

The people of the Swash were just assured of the comfortable fact related, as the Poughkeepsie was passing out from among the islets of the Dry Tortugas. They imagined themselves happy in having thus made a sufficient provision against the most formidable of all the dangers that beset them, at the very moment when the best laid plan for their destruction was on the point of being executed. In this respect, they resembled millions of others of their fellows, who hang suspended over the vast abyss of eternity, totally unconscious of the irretrievable character of the fall that is so soon to occur. Spike, as has been just stated, was highly pleased with his own expedient, and he pointed it out with exultation to the Señor Montefalderon, as soon as it was completed.

"A nicer fit was never made by a Lunnun leg-maker, Don Wan," the captain cried, after going over the explanations connected with the shores; "there she stands, at an angle of fifty, with two as good limbs under her as a body could wish. I could now cast off everything, and leave the wreck in what they call ' *statu quo*,' which, I suppose, means on its pins, like a statue. The tafferel is not six inches below the surface of the water, and half an hour of heaving will bring the starn in sight.''

"Your work seems ingeniously contrived to get up one extremity of the vessel, Don Esteban," returned the Mexican ; "but are you quite certain that the doubloons are in her ?''

This question was put because the functionary of a government in which money was very apt to stick in passing from hand to hand was naturally suspicious, and he found it difficult to believe that Mulford, Jack Tier, and even Biddy, under all the circumstances, had not paid special attention to their own interests.

"The bag was placed in one of the transom-lockers before the schooner capsized," returned the captain, "as Jack Tier informs me ; if so, it remains there still. Even the sharks will not touch gold, Don Wan.''

"Would it not be well to call Jack, and hear his account of the matter once more, now we appear to be so near the Eldorado of our wishes?''

Spike assented, and Jack was summoned to the quarter-deck. The little fellow had scarce showed himself throughout the day, and he now made his appearance with a slow step, and reluctantly.

"You 've made no mistake about them 'ere doubloons, I take it, Master Tier?'' said Spike, in a very nautical sort of style of addressing an inferior. "You *know* them to be in one of the transom-lockers ?''

Jack mounted on the breech of one of the guns, and looked over the bulwarks at the dispositions that had been made about the wreck. The tafferel of the schooner actually came in sight, when a little swell passed over it, leaving it for an instant in the trough. The steward thus caught a glimpse again of the craft on board which he had seen so much hazard, and he shook his head and seemed to be thinking of anything but the question which had just been put to him.

"Well, about that gold?" asked Spike, impatiently.

"The sight of that craft has brought other thoughts than gold into my mind, Captain Spike," answered Jack, gravely, "and it would be well for all us mariners, if we thought less of gold and more of the dangers we run. For hours and hours did I stand over eternity, on the bottom of that schooner, Don Wan, holdin' my life, as it might be, at the marcy of a few bubbles of air."

"What has all that to do with the gold? Have you deceived me about that locker, little rascal?"

"No, sir, I 've not deceived you—no, Captain Spike, no. The bag is in the upper transom-locker, on the starboard side. There I put it with my own hands, and a good lift it was; and there you 'll find it, if you 'll cut through the quarter-deck at the spot I can p'int out to you."

This information seemed to give a renewed energy to all the native cupidity of the captain, who called the men from their suppers and ordered them to commence heaving anew. The word was passed to the crew that "it was now for doubloons," and they went to the bars and handspikes, notwithstanding the sun had set, cheerfully and cheering.

All Spike's expedients admirably answered the intended purposes. The stern of the schooner rose gradually, and at each lift the heels of the shores dropped in more perpendicularly, carried by the weights attached to them, and the spars stood as firm props to secure all that was gained. In a quarter of an hour, most of that part of the stern which was within five or six feet of the tafferel rose above the water, coming fairly in view.

Spike now shouted to the men to "Pall!" then he directed the falls to be very gradually eased off, in order to ascertain if the shores would still do their duty. The experiment was successful, and presently the wreck stood in its upright position, sustained entirely by the two spars. As the last were now nearly perpendicular, they were capable of bearing a very heavy weight, and Spike was so anxious to relieve his own brig from the strain she had been enduring, that he ordered the lashings of the blocks to be loosened, trusting to his shores to do their duty. Against this confidence the boatswain ventured a remonstrance, but the gold was too near to allow the captain to listen or reply. The carpenter was ordered over on the wreck with his tools, while Spike, the Señor Montefalderon, and two men to row the boat and keep it steady, went in the yawl to watch the progress of the work. Jack Tier was ordered to stand in the chains, and to point out, as nearly as possible, the place where the carpenter was to cut.

When all was ready, Spike gave the word, and the chips began to fly. By the use of the saw and the axe, a hole, large enough to admit two or three men at a time, was soon made in the deck, and the sounding for the much-coveted locker commenced. By this time, it was quite dark; and a lantern was passed down from the brig, in order to enable those who searched for the locker to see. Spike had breasted the yawl close up to the hole, where it was held by the men, while the captain himself passed the lantern and his own head into the opening to reconnoitre.

"Ay, it's all right!" cried the voice of the captain from within his cell-like cavity. "I can just see the lid of the locker that Jack means, and we shall soon have what we are a'ter. Carpenter, you may as well slip off your clothes at once, and go inside; I will point out to you the place where to find the locker. You 're certain, Jack, it was the starboard locker?"

"Ay, ay, sir, the starboard locker, and no other."

The carpenter had soon got into the hole, as naked as when he was born. It was a gloomy-looking place for a man to descend into at that hour, the light from the lantern being no great matter, and half the time it was shaded by the manner in which Spike was compelled to hold it.

"Take care and get a good footing, carpenter," said the captain, in a kinder tone than common, "before you let go with your hands; but I suppose you can swim, as a matter of course?"

"No, sir, not a stroke; I never could make out in the water at all."

"Have the more care, then. Had I known as much, I would have sent another hand down; but mind your footing. More to the left, man—more to the left. That is the lid of the locker—your hand is on it; why do you not open it?"

"It is swelled by the water, sir, and will need a chisel, or some tool of that sort. Just call out to one of the men, sir, if you please, to pass me a chisel from my tool-chest. A good stout one will be best."

This order was given, and, during the delay it caused, Spike encouraged the carpenter to be cool, and above all to mind his footing. His own eagerness to get at the gold was so great that he kept his head in at the hole, completely cutting off the man within from all communication with the outer world.

"What's the matter with you?" demanded Spike, a little sternly. "You shiver, and yet the water cannot be cold in this latitude. No, my hand makes it just the right warmth to be pleasant."

"It's not the water, Captain Spike—I wish they would come with the chisel. Did you hear nothing, sir? I'm certain I did!"

"Hear!—what is there here to be heard, unless there may be some fish inside, thrashing about to get out of the vessel's hold?"

"I am sure I heard something like a groan, Captain Spike. I wish you would let me come out, sir, and I'll go for the chisel myself; them men will never find it."

"Stay where you are, coward! are you afraid of dead men standing against walls? Stay where you are. Ah! here is the chisel—now let us see what you can do with it."

"I am certain I heard another groan, Captain Spike. I cannot work, sir. I'm of no use here—do let come out, sir, and send a hand down that can swim."

Spike uttered a terrible malediction on the miserable carpenter, one we do not care to repeat; then he cast the light of the lantern full in the man's face. The quivering flesh, the pallid face, and the whole countenance wrought up almost to a frenzy of terror, astonished as well as alarmed him.

"What ails you, man?" said the captain in a voice of thunder. "Clap in the chisel, or I'll hurl you off into the water. There is nothing here, dead or alive, to harm ye!"

"The groan, sir—I hear it again! *Do* let me come out, Captain Spike."

Spike himself, this time, heard what even *he* took for a groan. It came from the depths of the vessel, apparently, and was sufficiently distinct and audible. Astonished, yet appalled, he thrust his shoulders into the aperture, as if to dare the demon that tormented him, and was met by the carpenter endeavoring to escape. In the struggle that ensued, the lantern was dropped into the water, leaving the half-frenzied combatants contending in the dark. The groan was renewed, when the truth flashed on the minds of both.

"The shores! the shores!" exclaimed the carpenter from within. "The shores!" repeated Spike, throwing himself back into the boat, and shouting to his men to "See all clear of the wreck!" The grating of one of the shores on the coral beneath was now heard plainer than ever, and the lower extremity slipped outward, not astern, as had been apprehended, letting the wreck slowly settle to the bottom again. One piercing shriek arose from the narrow cavity within; then the gurgling of water into the aperture was heard, when naught of sound could be distinguished but the sullen and steady wash of the waves of the Gulf over the rocks of the reef.

The impression made by this accident was most profound. A fatality appeared to attend the brig; and most of the men connected the sad occurrence of this night with the strange appearance of the previous evening. Even the Señor Montefalderon was disposed to abandon the doubloons, and he urged Spike to make the best of his way for Yucatan, to seek a friendly harbor. The captain wavered, but avarice was too strong a passion in him to be easily diverted from its object, and he refused to give up his purpose.

As the wreck was entirely free from the brig when it went down for the third time, no injury was sustained by the last on this occasion. By renewing the lashings, everything would be ready to begin the work anew, and this, Spike was resolved to attempt in the morning. The men were too much fatigued, and it was too dark to think of pushing matters any further that night; and it was very questionable whether they could have been got to work. Orders were consequently given for all hands to turn in, the captain, relieved by Don Juan and Jack Tier, having arranged to keep the watches of the night.

"This is a sad accident, Don Esteban," observed the Mexican, as he and Spike paced the quarter-deck together, just before the last turned in; "a sad accident! My miserable schooner seems to be deserted by its patron saint. Then your poor carpenter!"

"Yes, he was a good fellow enough with a saw, or an adze," answered Spike, yawning. "But we get used to such things at sea. It's neither more nor less than a carpenter expended. Good-night, Señor Don Wan; in the morning we'll be at that gold ag'in."

CHAPTER XIV.

"She's in a scene of nature's war,
The winds and waters are at strife;
And both with her contending for
The brittle thread of human life."

MISS GOULD.

SPIKE was sleeping hard in his berth, quite early on the following morning, before the return of light, indeed, when he suddenly started up, rubbed his eyes, and sprang upon deck like a man alarmed. He had heard, or fancied he had heard, a cry. A voice once well known and listened to, seemed to call him in the very portals of his ear. At first he had listened to its words in wonder, entranced like the bird by the snake, the tones recalling scenes and persons that had once possessed a strong control over his rude feelings. Presently the voice became harsher in its utterance, and it said,—

"Stephen Spike, awake! The hour is getting late, and you have enemies nearer to you than you imagine. Awake, Stephen, awake!"

When the captain was on his feet, and had plunged his head into a basin of water that stood ready for him in the state-room, he could not have told, for his life, whether he had been dreaming or waking, whether what he had heard was the result of a feverish imagination, or of the laws of nature. The call haunted him all that morning, or until events of importance so pressed upon him as to draw his undivided attention to them alone.

It was not yet day. The men were still in heavy sleep, lying about the decks, for they avoided the small and crowded forecastle in that warm climate, and the night was apparently at its deepest hour. Spike walked forward to look for the man charged with the anchor-watch. It proved to be Jack Tier, who was standing near the galley, his arms folded as usual, apparently watching the few signs of approaching day that were beginning to be apparent in the western sky. The captain was in none of the best humors with the steward's assistant ; but Jack had unaccountably got an ascendency over his commander, which it was certainly very unusual for any subordinate in the Swash to obtain. Spike had deferred more to Mulford than to any mate he had ever before employed ; but this was the deference due to superior information, manners, and origin. It was commonplace, if not vulgar ; whereas, the ascendency obtained by little Jack Tier was, even to its subject, entirely inexplicable. He was unwilling to admit it to himself in the most secret manner, though he had begun to feel it on all occasions which brought them in contact, and to submit to it as a thing not to be averted.

"Jack Tier," demanded the captain, now that he found himself once more alone with the other, desirous of obtaining his opinion on a point that harassed him, though he knew not why ; "Jack Tier, answer me one thing. Do you believe that we saw the form of a dead or of a living man at the foot of the light-house ? "

"The dead are never seen leaning against walls in that manner, Stephen Spike," answered Jack, coolly, not even taking the trouble to uncoil his arms. "What you saw was a living man ; and you would do well to be on your guard against him. Harry Mulford is not your friend—and there is reason for it."

"Harry Mulford, and living ! How can that be, Jack ? You know the port in which he chose to run."

"I know the rock on which you chose to abandon him, Captain Spike."

"If so, how could he be living and at the Dry Tortugas. The thing is impossible ! "

"The thing is so. You saw Harry Mulford, living and well, and ready to hunt you to the gallows. Beware of him, then ; and beware of his handsome wife ! "

" Wife ! the fellow has no wife ; he has always professed to be a single man ! ''

"The man is married ; and I bid you beware of his handsome wife. She, too, will be a witness ag'in you."

" This will be news, then, for Rose Budd. I shall delight in telling it to her, at least."

" 'T will be no news to Rose Budd. She was present at the wedding, and will not be taken by surprise. Rose loves Harry too well to let him marry, and she not present at the wedding."

"Jack, you talk strangely ! What is the meaning of all this ? I am captain of this craft, and will not be trifled with ; tell me at once your meaning, fellow."

" My meaning is simple enough, and easily told. Rose Budd is the wife of Harry Mulford."

" You 're dreaming, fellow, or are wishing to trifle with me ! ''

" It may be a dream, but it is one that will turn out to be true. If they have found the Poughkeepsie sloop-of-war, as I make no doubt they have by this time, Mulford and Rose are man and wife."

" Fool ! you know not what you say ! Rose is at this moment in her berth, sick at heart on account of the young gentleman who preferred to live on the Florida Reef rather than to sail in the Molly ! ''

" Rose is not in her berth, sick or well ; neither is she on board this brig at all. She went off in the light-house boat to deliver her lover from the naked rock, and well did she succeed in so doing. God was of her side, Stephen Spike ; and a body seldom fails with such a friend to support one."

Spike was astounded at these words, and not less so at the cool and confident manner with which they were pronounced. Jack spoke in a certain dogmatical, oracular manner, it is true, one that might have lessened his authority with a person over whom he had less influence ; but this in no degree diminished its effect on Spike. On the contrary, it even disposed the captain to yield an implicit faith to what he heard, and all so much the more because the facts he was told appeared of themselves to be nearly impossible. It was half a minute before he had sufficiently recovered from his surprise to continue the discourse.

"The light-house boat!" Spike then slowly repeated. "Why, fellow, you told me the light-house boat went adrift from your own hands!"

"So it did," answered Jack, coolly, "since I cast off the painter, and what is more, went in it."

"You! This is impossible. You are telling me a fabricated lie. If you had gone away in that boat, how could you now be here? No, no—it is a miserable lie, and Rose is below!"

"Go and look into her state-room, and satisfy yourself with your own eyes."

Spike did as was suggested. He went below, took a lamp that was always suspended, lighted, in the main cabin, and, without ceremony, proceeded to Rose's state-room, where he soon found that the bird had really flown. A direful execration followed this discovery, one so loud as to awaken Mrs. Budd and Biddy. Determined not to do things by halves, he broke open the door of the widow's state-room, and ascertained that the person he sought was not there. A fierce explosion of oaths and denunciations followed, which produced an answer in the customary screams. In the midst of this violent scene, however, questions were put and answers obtained, that not only served to let the captain know that Jack had told him nothing but the truth, but to put an end to everything like amicable relations between himself and the relict of his old commander. Until this explosion, appearances had been observed between them; but, from that moment, there must necessarily be an end to all professions of even civility. Spike was never particularly refined in his intercourse with females, but he now threw aside even its pretension. His rage was so great that he totally forgot his manhood, and lavished on both Mrs. Budd and Biddy epithets that were altogether inexcusable, and many of which it will not do to repeat. Weak and silly as was the widow, she was not without spirit; and on this occasion she was indisposed to submit to all this unmerited abuse in silence. Biddy, as usual, took her cue from her mistress, and between the two, their part of the wordy conflict was kept up with a very respectable degree of animation.

"I know you—I know you, now!" screamed the widow, at the top of her voice; "and you can no longer deceive me, unworthy son of Neptune as you are! You are unfit to be a lubber, and would be log-booked for an or'nary by every gentleman on board ship. You, a full-jiggered seaman! No, you are not even half-jiggered, sir; and I tell you so to your face."

"Yes, and it is n't *half* that might be tould the likes of yees!" put in Biddy, as her mistress stopped to breathe. "And it's Miss Rose you'd have for a wife, when Biddy Noon would be too good for ye! We knows ye, and all about ye, and can give yer history as complate from the day ye was born down to the prisent moment, and not find a good word to say in yer favor in all that time—and a precious time it is, too, for a gentleman that would marry pretthy, *young* Miss Rose! Och! I scorn to look at ye, yer so ugly!"

"And trying to persuade me you were a friend of my poor, dear Mr. Budd, whose shoe you are unworthy to touch, and who had the heart and soul for the noble profession you disgrace," cut in the widow, the moment Biddy gave her a chance, by pausing to make a wry face as she pronounced the word "ugly." "I now believe you capasided them poor Mexicans, in order to get their money; and the moment we cast anchor in a road-side, I'll go ashore, and complain of you for murder, I will."

"Do, missus, dear, and I'll be your bail, will I, and swear to all that happened, and more too. Och! yer a wretch, to wish to be the husband of Miss Rose, and she so young and pretthy, and you so ould and ugly!"

"Come away—come away, Stephen Spike, and do not stand wrangling with women, when you and your brig, and all that belongs to you are in danger," called out Jack Tier from the companion-way. "Day is come; and what is much worse for you, your most dangerous enemy is coming with it."

Spike was almost livid with rage, and ready to burst out in awful maledictions; but at this summons he sprang to the ladder, and was on deck in a moment. At first, he felt a strong disposition to wreak his vengeance on Tier, but, fortunately for the latter, as the captain's foot touched the quarter-deck, his eye fell on the Poughkeepsie, then within half a league of the Swash, standing in toward the reef, though fully half a mile to leeward. This spectre drove all other subjects from his mind, leaving the captain of the Swash in the only character in which he could be said to be respectable, that of a seaman. Almost instinctively he called all hands, then he gave one brief minute to a survey of his situation.

It was, indeed, time for the Swash to be moving. There she lay, with three anchors down, including that of the schooner, all she had, in fact, with the exception of her best bower, and one kedge, with the purchases aloft, in readiness for hooking on to the wreck, and all the extra securities up that had been given to the masts. As for the sloop-of-war, she was under the very same canvas, as that with which she had come out from the Dry Tortugas, or her three top-sails, spanker, and jib; but most of her other sails were loose, even to her royals and flying-jibs, though closely gathered in to their spars by means of the running gear. In a word, every sailor would know, at a glance, that the ship was merely waiting for the proper moment to spread her wings, when she would be flying through the water at the top of her speed. The weather looked dirty, and the wind was gradually increasing, threatening to blow heavily as the day advanced.

"Unshackle, unshackle!" shouted Spike to the boatswain, who was the first man that appeared on deck. "The bloody sloop-of-war is upon us, and there is not a moment to lose. We must get the brig clear of the ground in the shortest way we can, and abandon everything. Unshackle, and cast off for'ard and aft, men."

A few minutes of almost desperate exertion succeeded. No men work like sailors, when the last are in a hurry, their efforts being directed to counteracting squalls, and avoiding emergencies of the most pressing character. Thus was it now with the crew of the Swash. The clanking of chains lasted but a minute, when the parts attached to the anchors were thrust through the hawse-holes, or were dropped into the water from other parts of the brig. This at once released the vessel, though a great deal remained to be done to clear her for working, and to put her in the best trim.

"Away with this out-hauler!" again shouted Spike, casting loose the main-brails as he did so; "loose the jibs!"

All went on at once, and the Swash moved away from the grave of the poor carpenter with the ease and facility of motion that marked all her evolutions. Then the top-sail was let fall, and presently all the upper square-sails were sheeted home, and hoisted, and the fore-tack was hauled aboard. The Molly was soon alive, and jumping into the seas that met her with more power than was common, as she drew out from under the shelter of the reef into rough water. From the time when Spike gave his first order, to that when all his canvas was spread, was just seven minutes.

The Poughkeepsie with her vastly superior crew, was not idle the while. Although the watch below was not disturbed, she tacked beautifully, and stood off the reef, in a line parallel to the course of the brig, and distant from her about half a mile. Then sail was made, her tacks having been boarded in stays. Spike knew the play of his craft was short legs, for she was so nimble in her movements that he believed she could go about in half the time that would be required for a vessel of the Poughkeepsie's length. "Ready about," was his cry, therefore, when less than a mile distant from the reef, "ready about, and let her go round." Round the Molly did go, like a top, being full on the other tack in just fifty-six seconds. The movement of the corvette was more stately, and somewhat more deliberate. Still she stayed beautifully, and both Spike and the boatswain shook their heads, as they saw her coming into the wind with her sails all lifting and the sheets flowing.

"That fellow will fore-reach a cable's length before he gets about!" exclaimed Spike. "He will prove too much for us at this sport! Keep her away, my man—keep the brig away for the passage. We must run through the reef, instead of trusting ourselves to our heels in open water."

The brig was kept away accordingly, and sheets were eased off, and braces just touched, to meet the new line of sailing. As the wind stood, it was possible to lay through the passage on an easy bowline, though the breeze, which was getting to be fresher than Spike wished it to be, promised to haul more to the southward of east, as the day advanced. Nevertheless, this was the Swash's best point of sailing, and all on board of her had strong hopes of her being too much for her pursuer, could she maintain it. Until this feeling began to diffuse itself in the brig, not a countenance was to be seen on her decks that did not betray intense anxiety; but now something like grim smiles passed among the crew, as their craft seemed rather to fly than force her way through the water, toward the entrance of the passage so often adverted to in this narrative.

On the other hand, the Poughkeepsie was admirably sailed and handled. Everybody was now on deck, and the first lieutenant had taken the trumpet. Captain Mull was a man of method, and a thorough man-of-war's man. Whatever he did was done according to rule, and with great system. Just as the Swash was about to enter the passage, the drum of the Poughkeepsie beat to quarters. No sooner were the men mustered, in the leeward, or the starboard batteries, than orders were sent to cast loose the guns, and to get them ready for service. Owing to the more leeward position of his vessel, and to the fact that she always head-reached so much in stays, Captain Mull knew that she would not lose much by luffing into the wind, or by making half-boards, while he might gain everything by one well-directed shot.

The strife commenced by the sloop-of-war firing her weather bow-gun, single-shotted, at the Swash. No damage was done, though the fore-yard of the brig had a very narrow escape. This experiment was repeated three times, without even a rope-yarn being carried away, though the gun was pointed by Wallace himself, and well pointed, too. But it is possible for a shot to come very near its object and still to do no injury. Such was the fact on this occasion, though the "ship's gentleman" was a good deal mortified by the result. Men look so much at success as the test of merit, though few pause to inquire into the reasons of failures, though it frequently happens that adventurers prosper by means of their very blunders. Captain Mull now determined on a half-board, for his ship was more to leeward than he desired. Directions were given to the officers in the batteries to be deliberate, and the helm was put down. As the ship shot into the wind, each gun was fired, as it could be brought to bear, until the last of them all was discharged. Then the course of the vessel was changed, the helm being righted before the ship had lost her way, and the sloop-of-war fell off again to her course.

All this was done in such a short period of time as scarcely to cause the Poughkeepsie to lose anything, while it did the Swash the most serious injury. The guns had been directed at the brig's spars and sails, Captain Mull desiring no more than to capture his chase, and the destruction they produced aloft was such as to induce Spike and his men, at first, to imagine that the whole hamper above their heads was about to come clattering down on deck. One shot carried away all the weather fore-top-mast rigging of the brig, and would no doubt have brought about the loss of the mast, if another, that almost instantly succeeded it, had not cut the spar itself in two, bringing down, as a matter of course, everything above it. Nearly half of the main-mast was gouged out of that spar, and the gaff was taken fairly out of its jaws. The fore-yard was cut in the slings, and various important ropes were carried away in different parts of the vessel,

Flight, under such circumstances, was impossible, unless some extraordinary external assistance was to be obtained. This Spike saw at once, and he had recourse to the only expedient that remained, which might possibly yet save him. The guns were still belching forth their smoke and flames, when he shouted out the order to put the helm hard up. The width of the passage in which the vessels were was not so great but that he might hope to pass across it, and to enter a channel among the rocks, which was favorably placed for such a purpose, ere the sloop-of-war could overtake him. Whither that channel led, what water it possessed, or whether it were not a shallow *cul de sac*, were all facts of which Spike was ignorant. The circumstances, however, would not admit of an alternative.

Happily for the execution of Spike's present design, nothing from aloft had fallen into the water to impede the brig's way. Forward, in particular, she seemed all wreck; her fore-yard having come down altogether, so as to encumber the forecastle, while her top-mast, with its dependent spars and gear, was suspended but a short distance above. Still, nothing had gone over the side, so as actually to touch the water, and the craft obeyed her helm as usual. Away she went, then, for the lateral opening in the reef just mentioned, driven ahead by the pressure of a strong breeze on her sails, which still offered large surfaces to the wind, at a rapid rate. Instead of keeping away to follow, the Poughkeepsie maintained her luff, and just as the Swash entered the unknown passage, into which she was blindly plunging, the sloop-of-war was about a quarter of a mile to windward, and standing directly across her stern. Nothing would have been easier, now, than for Captain Mull to destroy his chase; but humanity prevented his firing. He knew that her career must be short, and he fully expected to see her anchor; when it would be easy for him to take possession with his boats. With this expectation, indeed, he shortened sail, furling top-gallant-sails, and hauling up his courses. By this time, the wind had so much freshened, as to induce him to think of putting in a reef, and the step now taken had a double object in view.

To the surprise of all on board the man-of-war, the brig continued on, until she was fully a mile distant, finding her way deeper and deeper among the mazes of the reef, without meeting with any impediment! This fact induced Captain Mull to order his Paixhans to throw their shells beyond her, by way of a hint to anchor. While the guns were getting ready,' Spike stood on boldly, knowing it was neck or nothing, and beginning to feel a faint revival of hope, as he found himself getting farther and farther from his pursuers, and the rocks not fetching him up. Even the men, who had begun to murmur at what seemed to them to be risking too much, partook, in a slight degree, of the same feeling, and began to execute the order they had received to try to get the launch into the water, with some appearance of an intention to succeed. Previously, the work could scarcely be said to go on at all; but two or three of the older seamen now bestirred themselves, and suggestions were made and attended to, that promised results. But it was no easy thing to get the launch out of a half-rigged brig, that had lost her fore-yard, and which carried nothing square abaft. A derrick was used in common, to lift the stern of the boat, but a derrick would now be useless aft, without an assistant forward. While these things were in discussion, under the superintendence of the boatswain, and Spike was standing between the knight-heads conning the craft, the sloop-of-war let fly the first of her hollow shot. Down came the hurtling mass upon the Swash, keeping every head elevated and all eyes looking for the dark object, as it went booming through the air above their heads. The shot passed fully a mile to leeward, where it exploded. This great range had been given to the first shot, with a view to admonish the captain how long he must continue under the guns of the ship, and as advice to come to. The second gun followed immediately. Its shot was seen to ricochet, directly in a line with the brig, making leaps of about half a mile in length. It struck the water about fifty yards astern of the vessel, bounded directly over her decks, passing through the main-sail and some of the fallen hamper forward, and exploded about a hundred yards ahead. As usually happens with such projectiles, most of the fragments were either scattered laterally, or went on, impelled by the original momentum.

The effect of this last gun on the crew of the Swash was instantaneous and deep. The faint gleamings of hope vanished at once, and a lively consciousness of the desperate nature of their condition succeeded in every mind. The launch was forgotten, and, after conferring together for a moment, the men went in a body, with the boatswain at their head, to the forecastle, and offered a remonstrance to their commander, on the subject of holding out any longer, under circumstances so very hazardous, and which menaced their lives in so many different ways. Spike listened to them with eyes that fairly glared with fury. He ordered them back to their duty in a voice of thunder, tapping the breast of his jacket, where he was known to carry revolvers, with a significance that could convey but one meaning.

It is wonderful the ascendency that men sometimes obtain over their fellows, by means of character, the habits of command and obedience, and intimidation. Spike was a stern disciplinarian, relying on that and ample pay for the unlimited control he often found it necessary to exercise over his crew. On the present occasion, his people were profoundly alarmed, but habitual deference and submission to their leader counteracted the feeling, and held them in suspense. They were fully aware of the nature of the position they occupied in a legal sense, and were deeply reluctant to increase the appearances of crime ; but most of them had been extricated from so many grave difficulties in former instances, by the coolness, nerve, and readiness of the captain, that a latent ray of hope was perhaps dimly shining in the rude breast of every old sea-dog among them. As a consequence of these several causes, they abandoned their remonstrance, for the moment at least, and made a show of returning to their duty ; though it was in a sullen and moody manner.

It was easier, however, to make a show of hoisting out the launch, than to effect the object. This was soon made apparent on trial, and Spike himself gave the matter up. He ordered the yawl to be lowered, got alongside, and to be prepared for the reception of the crew, by putting into it a small provision of food and water. All this time the brig was rushing madly to leeward, among rocks and breakers, without any other guide than that which the visible dangers afforded. Spike knew no more where he was going than the meanest man in his vessel. His sole aim was to get away from his pursuers, and to save his neck from the rope. He magnified the danger of punishment that he really ran, for he best knew the extent and nature of his crimes, of which the few that have been laid before the reader, while they might have been amongst the most prominent, as viewed through the statutes and international law, were far from the gravest he had committed in the eyes of morals.

About this time the Señor Montefalderon went forward to confer with Spike. The calmness of this gentleman's demeanor, the simplicity and coolness of his movements, denoted a conscience that saw no particular ground for alarm. He wished to escape captivity, that he might continue to serve his country, but no other apprehension troubled him.

" Do you intend to trust yourself in the yawl, Don Esteban?" demanded the Mexican, quietly. " If so, is she not too small to contain so many as we shall make altogether?"

Spike's answer was given in a low voice; and it evidently came from a very husky throat.

" Speak lower, Don Wan," he said. " The boat would be greatly overloaded with all hands in it, especially among the breakers, and blowing as it does; but we may leave some of the party behind."

" The brig *must* go on the rocks, sooner or later, Don Esteban; when she does, she will go to pieces in an hour."

" I expect to hear her strike every minute, Señor; the moment she does, we must be off. I have had my eye on that ship for some time, expecting to see her lower her cutters and gigs to board us. *You* will not be out of the way, Don Wan; but there is no need of being talkative on the subject of our escape."

Spike now turned his back on the Mexican, looking anxiously ahead, with the desire to get as far into the reef as possible with his brig, which he conned with great skill and coolness. The Señor Montefalderon left him. With the chivalry and consideration of a man and a gentleman, he went in quest of Mrs. Budd and Biddy. A hint sufficed for them, and gathering together a few necessaries they were in the yawl in the next three minutes. This movement was unseen by Spike, or he might have prevented it. His eyes were now riveted on the channel ahead. It had been fully his original intention to make off in the boat, the instant the brig struck, abandoning not only Don Juan, with Mrs. Budd and Biddy to their fates, but most of the crew. A private order had been given to the boatswain, and three of the ablest-bodied among the seamen, each and all of whom kept the secret with religious fidelity, as it was believed their own personal safety might be connected with the success of this plan.

Nothing is so contagious as alarm. It requires not only great natural steadiness of nerve, but much acquired firmness, to remain unmoved when sudden terror has seized on the minds of those around us. Habitual respect had prevented the crew from interfering with the movements of the Mexican, who not only descended into the boat with his female companions uninterrupted, but also took with him the little bag of doubloons which fell to his share from the first raising of the schooner. Josh and Jack Tier assisted in getting Mrs. Budd and Biddy over the side, and both took their own places in the yawl, as soon as this pious duty was discharged. This served as a hint to others near at hand; and man after man left his work to steal into the yawl, until every living being had disappeared from the deck of the Swash, Spike himself excepted. The man at the wheel had been the last to desert his post, nor would he have done so then, but for a signal from the boatswain, with whom he was a favorite.

It is certain there was a secret desire among the people of the Swash, who were now crowded into a boat not large enough to contain more than half their number with safety, to push off from the brig's side, and abandon her commander and owner to his fate. All had passed so soon, however, and events succeeded each other with so much rapidity, that little time was given for consultation. Habit kept them in their places, though the appearances around them were strong motives for taking care of themselves.

Notwithstanding the time necessary to relate the fore-going events, a quarter of an hour had not elapsed, from the moment when the Swash entered this unknown channel among the rocks, ere she struck. No sooner was her helm deserted than she broached-to, and Spike was in the act of denouncing the steerage, ignorant of its cause, when the brig was thrown, broadside-to, on a sharp, angular bed of rocks. It was fortunate for the boat, and all in it, that it was brought to leeward by the broaching-to of the vessel, and that the water was still sufficiently deep around them to prevent the waves from breaking. Breakers there were, however, in thousands on every side; and the seamen under-stood that their situation was almost desperately perilous, without shipwreck coming to increase the danger.

The storm itself was scarcely more noisy and boisterous than was Spike, when he ascertained the manner in which his people had behaved. At first, he believed it was their plan to abandon him to his fate : but, on rushing to the lee-gangway, Don Juan Montefalderon assured him that no such intention existed, and that he would not allow the boat to be cast off until the captain was received on board. This brief respite gave Spike a moment to care for his por-tion of the doubloons ; and he rushed to his state-room to secure them, together with his quadrant.

The grinding of the brig's bottom on the coral, announced a speedy breaking up of the craft, while her commander was thus employed. So violent were some of the shocks with which she came down on the hard bed in which she was now cradled, that Spike expected to see her burst asunder, while he was yet on her decks. The cracking of timbers told him that all was over with the Swash, nor had he got back as far as the gangway with his prize, before he saw plainly that the vessel had broken her back, as it is

termed, and that her plank-sheer was opening in a way
that threatened to permit a separation of the craft into two
sections, one forward and the other aft. Notwithstanding
all these portentous proofs that the minutes of the Molly
were numbered, and the danger that existed of his being
abandoned by his crew, Spike paused a moment, ere he
went over the vessel's side, to take a hasty survey of the
reef. His object was to get a general idea of the position
of the breakers, with a view to avoid them. As much of
the interest of that which is to succeed is connected with
these particular dangers, it may be well to explain their
character, along with a few other points of a similar bearing.

The brig had gone ashore fully two miles within the passage she had entered, and which, indeed, terminated at the
very spot where she had struck. The Poughkeepsie was
standing off and on, in the main channel, with her boats
in the water, evidently preparing to carry the brig in that
mode. As for the breakers, they whitened the surface of
the ocean in all directions around the wreck, far as the eye
could reach, but in two. The passage in which the Poughkeepsie was standing to and fro was clear of them, of
course ; and about a mile and a half to the northward
Spike saw that he should be in open water, or altogether
on the northern side of the reef, could he only get there.
The gravest dangers would exist in the passage, which led
among breakers on all sides, and very possibly among
rocks so near the surface as absolutely to obstruct the way.
In one sense, however, the breakers were useful. By
avoiding them as much as possible, and by keeping in the
unbroken water, the boat would be running in the channels
of the reef, and consequently would be the safer. The result
of the survey, short as it was, and it did not last a minute,
was to give Spike something like a plan ; and when he went
over the side, and got into the boat, it was with a determination to work his way out of the reef to its northern edge as
soon as possible, and then to skirt it as near as he could, in
his flight toward the Dry Tortugas.

CHAPTER XV.

" The screams of rage, the groan, the strife,
   The blow, the grasp, the horrid cry,
The panting, throttled prayer for life,
   The dying's heaving sigh,
The murderer's curse, the dead man's fixed, still glare,
And fear's and death's cold sweat—they all are there."

MATTHEW LEE.

IT was high time that Captain Spike should arrive when his foot touched the bottom of the yawl. The men were getting impatient and anxious to the last degree, and the power of Señor Montefalderon to control them was lessening each instant. They heard the rending of timber, and the grinding on the coral, even more distinctly than the captain himself, and feared that the brig would break up while they lay alongside of her, and crush them amid the ruins. Then the spray of the seas that broke over the weather side of the brig fell like rain upon them ; and everybody in the boat was already as wet as if exposed to a violent shower. It was well, therefore, for Spike that he descended into the boat as he did, for another minute's delay might have brought about his own destruction.

Spike felt a chill at his heart when he looked about him and saw the condition of the yawl. So crowded were the stern-sheets into which he had descended, that it was with difficulty he found room to place his feet ; it being his intention to steer, Jack was ordered to get into the eyes of the boat, in order to give him a seat. The thwarts were crowded, and three or four of the people had placed themselves in the very bottom of the little craft, in order to be as much as possible out of the way, as well as in readiness to bail out water. So seriously, indeed, were all the seamen impressed with the gravity of this last duty, that nearly every man had taken with him some vessel fit for such a purpose. Rowing was entirely out of the question, there being no space for the movement of the arms. The yawl was too low in the water, moreover, for such an operation in so heavy a sea. In all, eighteen persons were squeezed into a little craft that would have been sufficiently loaded, for moderate weather at sea, with its four oarsmen and as many sitters in the stern-sheets, with, perhaps, one in the eyes to bring her more on an even keel. In other words, she had twice the weight in her, in living freight, that it would have been thought prudent to receive in so small a craft in an ordinary time, in or out of a port. In addition to the human beings enumerated, there was a good deal of baggage, nearly every individual having had the forethought to provide a few clothes for a change. The food and water did not amount to much, no more having been provided than enough for the purpose of the captain, together with the four men with whom it had been his intention to abandon the brig. The effect of all this cargo was to bring the yawl quite low in the water ; and every seafaring man in her had the greatest apprehensions about her being able to float at all when she got out from under the lee of the Swash, or into the troubled water. Try it she must, however, and Spike, in a reluctant and hesitating manner, gave the final order to "Shove off!"

The yawl carried a lug, as is usually the case with boats at sea, and the first blast of the breeze upon it satisfied Spike that his present enterprise was one of the most dangerous of any in which he had ever been engaged. The puffs of wind were quite as much as the boat would bear; but this he did not mind, as he was running off before it, and there was little danger of the yawl capsizing with such a weight in her. It was also an advantage to have swift way on, to prevent the combing waves from shooting into the boat, though the wind itself scarce outstrips the send of the sea in a stiff blow. As the yawl cleared the brig and began to feel the united power of the wind and waves, the following short dialogue occurred between the boat-swain and Spike.

"I dare not keep my eyes off the breakers ahead," the captain commenced, "and must trust to you, Strand, to report what is going on among the man-of-war's men. What is the ship about?"

"Reefing her top-sails just now, sir. All three are on the caps, and the vessel is laying-to, in a manner."

"And her boats?"

"I see none, sir—ay, ay, there they come from alongside of her in a little fleet! There are four of them, sir, and all are coming down before the wind, wing and wing, carrying their lugs reefed."

"Ours ought to be reefed by rights, too, but we dare not stop to do it : and these infernal combing seas seem ready to glance aboard us with all the way we can gather. Stand by to bail, men ; we must pass through a strip of white water—there is no help for it. God send that we go clear of the rocks !"

All this was fearfully true. The adventurers were not yet more than a cable's length from the brig, and they found themselves so completely environed with the breakers as to be compelled to go through them. No man in his senses would ever have come into such a place at all, except in the most unavoidable circumstances ; and it was with a species of despair that the seamen of the yawl now saw their little craft go plunging into the foam.

But Spike neglected no precaution that experience or skill could suggest. He had chosen his spot with coolness and judgment. As the boat rose on the seas he looked eagerly ahead, and by giving it a timely sheer, he hit a sort of channel, where there was sufficient water to carry them clear of the rock, and where the breakers were less dangerous than in the shoaler places. The passage lasted about a minute ; and so serious was it, that scarce an individual breathed until it was effected. No human skill could prevent the water from combing in over the gunwales ; and when the danger was passed, the yawl was a third filled with water. There was no time or place to pause, but on the little craft

was dragged almost gunwale to, the breeze coming against
the lug in puffs that threatened to take the mast out of her.
All hands were bailing, and even Biddy used her hands to
aid in throwing out the water.

"This is no time to hesitate, men," said Spike, sternly.
"Everything must go overboard but the food and water.
Away with them at once, and with a will."

It was a proof how completely all hands were alarmed
by this, the first experiment in the breakers, that not a man
stayed his hand a single moment, but each threw into the
sea, without an instant of hesitation, every article he had
brought with him and had hoped to save. Biddy parted with
the carpet-bag, and Señor Montefalderon, feeling the importance of example, committed to the deep a small writing-
desk that he had placed on his knees. The doubloons alone
remained, safe in a little locker where Spike had deposited
them along with his own.

"What news astern, boatswain?" demanded the captain,
as soon as this imminent danger was passed, absolutely
afraid to turn his eyes off the dangers ahead for a single
instant. "How come on the man-of-war's men?"

"They are running down in a body toward the wreck,
though one of their boats does seem to be sheering out of the
line, as if getting into our wake. It is hard to say, sir, for
they are still a good bit to windward of the wreck."

"And the Molly, Strand?"

"Why, sir, the Molly seems to be breaking up fast; as
well as I can see, she has broke in two just abaft the fore-
chains, and cannot hold together in any shape at all many
minutes longer."

This information drew a deep groan from Spike, and the
eye of every seaman in the boat was turned in melancholy
on the object they were so fast leaving behind them. The
yawl could not be said to be sailing very rapidly, considering the power of the wind, which was a little gale, for she
was much too deep for that, but she left the wreck so fast
as already to render objects on board her indistinct. Everybody saw that, like an overburdened steed, she had more
to get along with than she could well bear; and, depend-

ent as seamen usually are on the judgment and orders of
their superiors, even in the direst emergencies, the least
experienced man in her saw that their chances of final
escape from drowning were of the most doubtful nature.
The men looked at each other in a way to express their feelings; and the moment seemed favorable to Spike to confer with his confidential sea-dogs in private; but more
white water was also ahead, and it was necessary to pass
through it, since no opening was visible by which to avoid
it. He deferred his purpose, consequently, until this danger
was escaped.

On this occasion Spike saw but little opportunity to
select a place to get through the breakers, though the
spot, as a whole, was not of the most dangerous kind. The
reader will understand that the preservation of the boat at
all in white water was owing to the circumstance that the
rocks all around it lay so near to the surface of the sea as to
prevent the possibility of agitating the element very seriously, and to the fact that she was near the lee side of the
reef. Had the breakers been of the magnitude of those
which are seen where the deep rolling billows of the ocean
first meet the weather side of shoals or rocks, a craft of that
size, and so loaded, could not possibly have passed the first
line of white water without filling. As it was, however,
the breakers she had to contend with were sufficiently formidable, and they brought with them the certainty that the
boat was in imminent danger of striking the bottom at any
moment. Places like those in which Mulford had waded
on the reef, while it was calm, would now have proved fatal
to the strongest frame, since human powers were insufficient long to withstand the force of such waves as did glance
over even these shallows.

"Look out!" cried Spike, as the boat again plunged
in among the white water. "Keep bailing, men—keep
bailing!"

The men did bail, and the danger was over almost as
soon as encountered. Something like a cheer burst out of
the chest of Spike, when he saw deeper water around him,
and fancied he could now trace a channel that would carry

him quite beyond the extent of the reef. It was arrested, only half uttered, however, by a communication from the boatswain, who sat on a midship thwart, his arms folded, and his eye on the brig and the boats.

"There goes the Molly's masts, sir! Both have gone together; and as good sticks was they, before them bomb-shells passed through our rigging, as was ever stepped in a keelson."

The cheer was changed to something like a groan, while a murmur of regret passed through the boat.

"What news from the man-of-war's men, boatswain? Do they still stand down on a mere wreck?"

"No, sir; they seem to give it up, and are getting out their oars to pull back to their ship. A pretty time they'll have of it, too. The cutter that gets to windward half a mile in an hour, ag'in such a sea, and such a breeze, must be well pulled and better steered. One chap, however, sir, seems to hold on."

Spike now ventured to look behind him, commanding an experienced hand to take the helm. In order to do this he was obliged to change places with the man he had selected to come aft, which brought him on a thwart along-side of the boatswain and one or two other of his confidants. Here a whispered conference took place, which lasted several minutes, Spike appearing to be giving instructions to the men.

By this time the yawl was more than a mile from the wreck, all the man-of-war boats but one had lowered their sails, and were pulling slowly and with great labor back toward the ship, the cutter that kept on, evidently laying her course after the yawl, instead of standing on toward the wreck. The brig was breaking up fast, with every probability that nothing would be left of her in a few more minutes. As for the yawl, while clear of the white water it got along without receiving many seas aboard, though the men in its bottom were kept bailing without intermission. It appeared to Spike that so long as they remained on the reef, and could keep clear of breakers—a most diffi-cult thing, however—they should fare better than if in deeper water, where the swell of the sea, and the combing of the waves, menaced so small and so deep-loaded a craft with serious danger. As it was, two or three men could barely keep the boat clear, working incessantly, and much of the time with a foot or two of water in her.

Josh and Simon had taken their seats, side by side, with that sort of dependence and submission that causes the American black to abstain from mingling with the whites more than might appear seemly. They were squeezed on to one end of the thwart by a couple of robust old sea-dogs, who were two of the very men with whom Spike had been in consultation. Beneath that very thwart was stowed another confidant, to whom communications had also been made. These men had sailed long in the Swash, and having been picked up in various ports, from time to time, as the brig had wanted hands, they were of nearly as many different nations as they were persons. Spike had obtained a great ascendency over them by habit and authority, and his suggestions were now received as a sort of law. As soon as the conference was ended, the captain returned to the helm.

A minute more passed, during which the captain was anxiously surveying the reef ahead, and the state of things astern. Ahead was more white water—the last before they should get clear of the reef; and astern it was now settled that the cutter that held on through the dangers of the place was in chase of the yawl. That Mulford was in her Spike made no doubt ; and the thought embittered even his present calamities. But the moment had arrived for something decided. The white water ahead was much more formidable than any they had passed ; and the boldest seamen there gazed at it with dread. Spike made a sign to the boatswain, and commenced the execution of his dire project.

"I say, you Josh," called out the captain, in the authoritative tones that are so familiar to all on board a ship, " pull in that fender that is dragging alongside."

Josh leaned over the gunwale, and reported that there was no fender out. A malediction followed, also so familiar to those acquainted with ships, and the black was told to look again. This time, as had been expected, the negro leaned with his head and body far over the side of the yawl, to look for that which had no existence, when two of the men beneath the thwart shoved his legs after them. Josh screamed, as he found himself going into the water, with a sort of confused consciousness of the truth ; and Spike called out to Simon to "catch hold of his brother-nigger." The cook bent forward to obey, when a similar assault on *his* legs from beneath the thwart, sent him headlong after Josh. One of the younger seamen, who was not in the secret, sprang up to rescue Simon, who grasped his extended hand, when the too generous fellow was pitched headlong from the boat.

All this occurred in less than ten seconds of time, and so unexpectedly and naturally, that not a soul beyond those who were in the secret, had the least suspicion it was anything but an accident. Some water was shipped, of necessity, but the boat was soon bailed free. As for the victims of this vile conspiracy, they disappeared amid the troubled waters of the reef, struggling with each other. Each and all met the common fate so much the sooner, from the manner in which they impeded their own efforts.

The yawl was now relieved from about five hundred pounds of the weight it had carried—Simon weighing two hundred alone, and the youngish seaman being large and full. So intense does human selfishness get to be, in moments of great emergency, that it is to be feared most of those who remained secretly rejoiced that they were so far benefited by the loss of their fellows. The Señor Montefalderon was seated on the aftermost thwart, with his legs in the stern-sheets, and consequently with his back toward the negroes, and he fully believed that what had happened was purely accidental.

"Let us lower our sail, Don Esteban," he cried eagerly, "and save the poor fellows."

Something very like a sneer gleamed on the dark countenance of the captain, but it suddenly changed to a look of assent.

"Good !" he said hastily ; "spring forward, Don Wan, and lower the sail—stand by the oars, men !"

Without pausing to reflect, the generous-hearted Mexican stepped on a thwart, and began to walk rapidly forward, steadying himself by placing his hands on the heads of the men. He was suffered to get as far as the second thwart or past most of the conspirators, when his legs were seized from behind. The truth now flashed on him, and grasping two of the men in his front, who knew nothing of Spike's dire scheme, he endeavored to save himself by holding to their jackets. Thus assailed, those men seized others with like intent, and an awful struggle filled all that part of the craft. At this dread instant the boat glanced into the white water, shipping so much of the element as nearly to swamp her, and taking so wild a sheer as nearly to broach-to. This last circumstance probably saved her, fearful as was the danger for the moment. Everybody in the middle of the yawl was rendered desperate by the account and nature of the danger incurred, and the men from the bottom rose in their might, underneath the combatants, when a common plunge was made by all who stood erect, one dragging over board another, each a good deal hastened by the assault from beneath, until no less than five were gone. Spike got his helm up, the boat fell off, and away from the spot it flew, clearing the breakers, and reaching the northern wall-like margin of the reef at the next instant. There was now a moment when those who remained could breathe, and dared to look behind them.

The great plunge had been made in water so shoal, that the boat had barely escaped being dashed to pieces on the coral. Had it not been so suddenly relieved from the pressure of near a thousand pounds in weight, it is probable that this calamity would have befallen it, the water received on board contributing so much to weigh it down. The struggle between these victims ceased, however, the moment they went over. Finding bottom for their feet, they released each other, in a desperate hope of prolonging life by wading. Two or three held out their arms, and shouted to Spike to return and pick them up. This dreadful scene lasted but a single instant, for the waves dashed one after another from his feet, continually forcing them all, as they occasionally regained their footing, toward the margin of the reef, and finally washing them off it into deep water. No human power could enable a man to swim back to the rocks, once to lee-ward of them, in the face of such seas, and so heavy a blow ; and the miserable wretches disappeared in succession, as their strength became exhausted, in the depths of the Gulf.

Not a word had been uttered while this terrific scene was in the course of occurrence; not a word was uttered for some time afterward. Gleams of grim satisfaction had been seen on the countenances of the boatswain and his associates, when the success of their nefarious project was first assured ; but they soon disappeared in looks of horror, as they witnessed the struggles of the drowning men. Nevertheless, human selfishness was strong within them all, and none there was so ignorant as not to perceive how much better were the chances of the yawl now than it had been on quitting the wreck. The weight of a large ox had been taken from it, counting that of all the eight men drowned ; and as for the water shipped, it was soon bailed back again into the sea. Not only, therefore, was the yawl in a better condition to resist the waves, but it sailed materially faster than it had done before. Ten persons still remained in it, however, which brought it down in the water below its proper load-line ; and the speed of a craft so small was nec-essarily a good deal lessened by the least deviation from its best sailing, or rowing trim. But Spike's projects were not yet completed.

All this time the man-of-war's cutter had been rushing as madly through the breakers, in chase, as the yawl had done in the attempt to escape. Mulford was, in fact, on board it ; and his now fast friend, Wallace, was in com-mand. The latter wished to seize a traitor, the former to save the aunt of his weeping bride. Both believed that they might follow wherever Spike dared to lead. This reasoning was more bold than judicious notwithstanding, since the cutter was much larger, and drew twice as much water as the yawl. On it came, nevertheless, faring much better in the white water than the little craft it pursued, but necessarily running a much more considerable risk of hitting the coral, over which it was glancing almost as swiftly as the waves themselves; still it had thus far escaped, and little did any in it think of the danger. This cutter pulled ten oars; was an excellent sea-boat; had four armed marines in it, in addition to its crew, but carried all through the breakers, receiving scarcely a drop of water on board, on account of the height of its wash-boards, and the general qualities of the craft. It may be well to add here, that the Poughkeepsie had shaken out her reefs, and was betraying the impatience of Captain Mull to make sail in chase, by firing signal-guns to his boats to bear a hand and return. These signals the three boats under their oars were endeavoring to obey, but Wallace had got so far to leeward as now to render the course he was pursuing the wisest.

Mrs. Budd and Biddy had seen the struggle in which the Señor Montefalderon had been lost, in a sort of stupid horror. Both had screamed, as was their wont, though neither probably suspected the truth. But the fell designs of Spike extended to them, as well as to those whom he had already destroyed. Now the boat was in deep water, running along the margin of the reef, the waves were much increased in magnitude, and the comb of the sea was far more menacing to the boat. This would not have been the case had the rocks formed a lee; but they did not, running too near the direction of the trades to prevent the billows that got up a mile or so in the offing from sending their swell quite home to the reef. It was this swell, indeed, which caused the line of white water along the northern margin of the coral, washing on the rocks by a sort of lateral effort, and breaking, as a matter of course. In many places, no boat could have lived to pass through it.

Another consideration influenced Spike to persevere. The cutter had been overhauling him, hand over hand, but since the yawl was relieved of the weight of no less than eight men, the difference in the rate of sailing was manifestly diminished. The man-of-war's boat drew nearer, but by no means as fast as it had previously done. A point was now reached in the trim of the yawl, when a very few hundreds in weight might make the most important change in her favor; and this change the captain was determined to produce. By this time the cutter was in deep water as well as himself, safe through all the dangers of the reef, and she was less than a quarter of a mile astern. On the whole, she was gaining, though so slowly as to require the most experienced eye to ascertain the fact.

"Madam Budd," said Spike, in a hypocritical tone, "we are in great danger, and I shall have to ask you to change your seat. The boat is too much by the stern, now we've got into deep water, and your weight amidships would be a great relief to us. Just give your hand to the boatswain, and he will help you to step from thwart to thwart until you reach the right place, when Biddy shall follow."

Now Mrs. Budd had witnessed the tremendous struggle in which so many had gone overboard, but so dull was she of apprehension, and so little disposed to suspect anything one half so monstrous as the truth, that she did not hesitate to comply. She was profoundly awed by the horrors of the scene through which she was passing, the raging billows of the Gulf, as seen from so small a craft, producing a deep impression on her; still a lingering of her most inveterate affectation was to be found in her air and language, which presented a strange medley of besetting weakness, and strong, natural, womanly affection.

"Certainly, Captain Spike," she answered, rising. "A craft should never go astern, and I am quite willing to ballast the boat. We have seen such terrible accidents to-day, that all should lend their aid in endeavoring to get under way, and in averting all possible hamper. Only take me to my poor, dear Rosy, Captain Spike, and everything shall be forgotten that has passed between us. This is not a moment to bear malice; and I freely pardon you all and everything. The fate of our unfortunate friend, Mr. Montefalderon, should teach us charity, and cause us to prepare for untimely ends.

All the time the good widow was making this speech, which she uttered in a solemn and oracular sort of manner, she was moving slowly toward the seat the men had prepared for her, in the middle of the boat, assisted with the greatest care and attention by the boatswain and another of Spike's confidants. When on the second thwart from aft, and about to take her seat, the boatswain cast a look behind him, and Spike put the helm down. The boat luffed and lurched, of course, and Mrs. Budd would probably have gone overboard, to leeward, by so sudden and violent a change, had not the impetus thus received been aided by the arms of the men who held her two hands. The plunge she made into the water was deep, for she was a woman of great weight for her stature. Still, she was not immediately gotten rid of. Even at that dread instant, it is probable that the miserable woman did not suspect the truth, for she grasped the hand of the boatswain with the tenacity of a vice, and, thus dragged on the surface of the boiling surges, she screamed aloud for Spike to save her. Of all who had yet been sacrificed to the captain's selfish wish to save himself, this was the first instance in which any had been heard to utter a sound, after falling into the sea. The appeal shocked even the rude beings around her, and Biddy chiming in with a powerful appeal to "Save the missus!" added to the piteous nature of the scene.

"Cast off her hand," said Spike, revengefully ; "she'll swamp the boat by her struggles—get rid of her at once ! Cut her fingers off, if she won't let go !"

The instant these brutal orders were given, and that in a fierce, impatient tone, the voice of Biddy was heard no more. The truth forced itself on her dull imagination, and she sat a witness of the terrible scene, in mute despair. The struggle did not last long. The boatswain drew his knife across the wrist of the hand that grasped his own, one shriek was heard, and the boat plunged into the trough of a sea, leaving the form of poor Mrs. Budd struggling with the wave on its summit, and amid the foam of its crest. This was the last that was ever seen of the unfortunate relict.

"The boat has gained a good deal by that last discharge of cargo," said Spike to the boatswain, a minute after they had gotten rid of the struggling woman, "she is much more lively, and is getting nearer to her load-line. If we can bring her to that, I shall have no fear of the man-of-war's men; for this yawl is one of the fastest boats that ever floated."

"A very little now, sir, would bring us to our true trim."

"Ay, we must get rid of more cargo. Come, good woman," turning to Biddy, with whom he did not think it worth his while to use much circumlocution, "your turn is next. It's the maid's duty to follow her mistress."

"I know'd it must come," said Biddy, meekly. "If there was no mercy for the missus, little could I look for. But ye'll not take the life of a Christian woman widout giving her so much as one minute to say her prayers?"

"Ay, pray away," answered Spike, his throat becoming dry and husky, for, strange to say, the submissive quiet of the Irishwoman, so different from the struggle he had anticipated with her, rendered him more reluctant to proceed than he had hitherto been in all of that terrible day. As Biddy kneeled in the bottom of the stern-sheets, Spike looked behind him, for the double purpose of escaping the painful spectacle at his feet, and that of ascertaining how his pursuers came on. The last still gained, though very slowly, and doubts began to come over the captain's mind whether he could escape such enemies at all. He was too deeply committed, however, to recede, and it was most desirable to get rid of poor Biddy, if it were for no other motive than to shut her mouth. Spike even fancied that some idea of what had passed was entertained by those in the cutter. There was evidently a stir in that boat, and two forms that he had no difficulty, now, in recognizing as those of Wallace and Mulford, were standing on the grating in the eyes of the cutter, or forward of the foresail. The former appeared to have a musket in his hand, and the other a glass. The last circumstance admonished him that all that was now done would be done before dangerous witnesses. It was too late to draw back, however, and the captain turned to look for the Irishwoman.

Biddy rose from her knees, just as Spike withdrew his eyes from his pursuers. The boatswain and another confidant were in readiness to cast the poor creature into the sea, the moment their leader gave the signal. The intended victim saw and understood the arrangement, and she spoke earnestly and piteously to her murderers.

"It 's not wanting will be violence!" said Biddy, in a quiet tone, but with a saddened countenance. "I know it 's my turn, and I will save yer sowls from a part of the burden of this great sin. God, and His Divine Son, and the Blessed Mother of Jesus have mercy on me if it be wrong; but I would far radder jump into the saa widout having the rude hands of man on me, than have the dreadful sight of the missus done over ag'in. It 's a fearful thing is wather, and sometimes we have too little of it, and sometimes more than we want—"

"Bear a hand, bear a hand, good woman," interrupted the boatswain, impatiently. "We must clear the boat of you, and the sooner it is done the better it will be for all of us."

"Don't grudge a poor morthal half a minute of life, at the last moment," answered Biddy. "It 's not long that I 'll throuble ye, and so no more need be said."

The poor creature then got on the quarter of the boat, without any one's touching her; there she placed herself with her legs outboard, while she sat on the gunwale. She gave one moment to the thought of arranging her clothes with womanly decency, and then she paused to gaze with a fixed eye and pallid cheek on the foaming wake that marked the rapid course of the boat. The troughs of the sea seemed less terrible to her than their combing crests, and she waited for the boat to descend into the next.

"God forgive ye all, this deed, as I do!" said Biddy, earnestly, and bending her person forward, she fell, as it might be "without hands," into the gulf of eternity. Though all strained their eyes, none of them, Jack Tier excepted, ever saw more of Biddy Noon. Nor did Jack see much. He got a frightful glimpse of an arm, however, on the summit of a wave, but the motion of the boat was too swift, and the water of the ocean too troubled, to admit of aught else.

A long pause succeeded this event. Biddy's quiet submission to her fate had produced more impression on her murderers than the desperate, but unavailing, struggles of those who had preceded her. Thus it is ever with men. When opposed, the demon within blinds them to consequences as well as to their duties; but unresisted, the silent influence of the image of God makes itself felt, and a better spirit begins to prevail. There was not one in the boat who did not, for a brief space, wish that poor Biddy had been spared. With most, that feeling, the last of human kindness they ever knew, lingered until the occurrence of the dread catastrophe which, so shortly after, closed the scene of this state of being on their eyes.

"Jack Tier," called out Spike, some five minutes after Biddy was drowned, but not until another observation had made it plainly apparent to him that the man-of-war's men still continued to draw nearer, being now not more than fair musket-shot astern.

"Ay, ay, sir," answered Jack, coming quietly out of his hole from forward of the mast, and moving aft as if indifferent to the danger, by stepping lightly from thwart to thwart, until he reached the stern-sheets.

"It is your turn, little Jack," said Spike, as if in a sort of sorrowful submission to a necessity that knew no law, "we cannot spare you the room."

"I have expected this, and am ready. Let me have my own way and I will cause you no trouble. Poor Biddy has taught me how to die. Before I go, however, Stephen Spike, I must leave you this letter. It is written by myself, and addressed to you. When I am gone, read it, and think well of what it contains. And now, may a merciful God pardon the sins of both, through the love of His Divine Son. I forgive you, Stephen; and should you live to escape from those who are now bent on hunting you to the death, let this day cause you no grief on my account. Give me but a moment of time, and I will cause you no trouble."

Jack now stood upon the seat of the stern-sheets, balancing himself with one foot on the stern of the boat. He waited until the yawl had risen to the summit of a wave, when he looked eagerly for the man-of-war's cutter. At that moment she was lost to view in the trough of the sea. Instead of springing overboard, as all expected, he asked another instant of delay. The yawl sank into the trough itself, and rose on the succeeding billow. Then he saw the cutter, and Wallace and Mulford standing in its bows. He waved his hat to them, and sprang high into the air, with the intent to make himself seen; when he came down the boat had shot her length away from the place, leaving him to buffet with the waves. Jack now managed admirably, swimming lightly and easily, but keeping his eyes on the crests of the waves, with a view to meet the cutter. Spike now saw this well-planned project to avoid death, and regretted his own remissness in not making sure of Jack. Everybody in the yawl was eagerly looking after the form of Tier.

"There he is on the comb of that sea, rolling over like a keg!" cried the boatswain.

"He's through it," answered Spike, "and swimming with great strength and coolness."

Several of the men started up involuntarily and simultaneously to look, hitting their shoulders and bodies together. Distrust was at its most painful height; and bull-dogs do not spring at the ox's muzzle more fiercely than those six men throttled each other. Oaths, curses, and appeals for help, succeeded; each man endeavoring, in his frenzied efforts, to throw all the others overboard, as the only means of saving himself. Plunge succeeded plunge; and when that combat of demons ended, no one remained of them all but the boatswain. Spike had taken no share in the struggle, looking on in grim satisfaction, as the Father of Lies may be supposed to regard all human strife, hoping good to himself, let the result be what it might to others.

Of the five men who thus went overboard, not one escaped. They drowned each other by continuing their maddened conflict in an element unsuited to their natures.

Not so with Jack Tier. His leap had been seen, and a dozen eyes in the cutter watched for his person, as that boat came foaming down before the wind. A shout of "There he is!" from Mulford succeeded; and the little fellow was caught by the hair, secured, and then hauled into the boat by the second lieutenant of the Poughkeepsie and our young mate.

Others in the cutter had noted the incident of the hellish fight. The fact was communicated to Wallace, and Mulford said, "That yawl will outsail this loaded cutter, with only two men in it."

"Then it is time to try what virtue there is in lead," answered Wallace. "Marines, come forward, and give the rascal a volley."

The volley was fired; one ball passed through the head of the boatswain, killing him dead on the spot. Another went through the body of Spike. The captain fell in the stern-sheets, and the boat instantly broached-to.

The water that came on board apprised Spike fully of the state in which he was now placed, and by a desperate effort, he clutched the tiller, and got the yawl again before the wind. This could not last, however. Little by little, his hold relaxed, until his hand relinquished its grasp altogether, and the wounded man sank into the bottom of the stern-sheets, unable to raise even his head. Again the boat broached-to. Every sea now sent its water aboard, and the yawl would soon have filled, had not the cutter come glancing down past it, and rounding-to under its lee, secured the prize.

CHAPTER XVI.

"Man hath a weary pilgrimage,
　　As through the world he wends;
On every stage, from youth to age,
　　Still discontent attends ;
With heaviness he casts his eye
　　Upon the road before,
And still remembers with a sigh
　　The days that are no more."

SOUTHEY.

IT has now become necessary to advance the time three entire days, and to change the scene to Key West. As this latter place may not be known to the world at large, it may be well to explain that it is a small seaport, situate on one of the largest of the many low islands that dot the Florida Reef, that has risen into notice, or indeed into existence as a town, since the acquisition of the Floridas by the American Republic. For many years it was the resort of few besides wreckers, and those who live by the business dependent on the rescuing and repairing of stranded vessels, not forgetting the salvages. When it is remembered that the greater portion of the vessels that enter the Gulf of Mexico stand close along this reef, before the trades, for a distance varying from one to two hundred miles, and that nearly everything that quits it is obliged to beat down its rocky coast into the Gulf Stream for the same distance, one is not to be surprised that the wrecks, which so constantly occur, can supply the wants of a considerable population. To live at Key West is the next thing to being at sea. The place has sea air, no other water than such as is preserved in cisterns, and no soil, or so little as to render even a head of lettuce a rarity. Turtle is abundant, and the business of "turtling" forms an occupation additional to that of wrecking. As might be expected, in such circumstances, a potato is a far more precious thing than a turtle's egg, and a sack of the tubers would probably be deemed a sufficient remuneration for enough of the materials of calipash and calipee to feed all the aldermen extant.

Of late years, the government of the United States has turned its attention to the capabilities of the Florida Reef, as an advanced naval station; a sort of Downs, or St. Helen's Roads, for the West Indian seas. As yet little has been done beyond making the preliminary surveys, but the day is not probably very distant when fleets will lie at anchor among the islets described in our earlier chapters, or garnish the fine waters of Key West. For a long time it was thought that even frigates would have a difficulty in entering and quitting the port of the latter, but it is said that recent explorations have discovered channels capable of admitting anything that floats. Still Key West is a town yet in its chrysalis state, possessing the promise rather than the fruition of the prosperous days which are in reserve. It may be well to add, that it lies a very little north of the 24th degree of latitude, and in a longitude quite five degrees west from Washington. Until the recent conquests in Mexico it was the most southern possession of the American government, on the eastern side of the continent; Cape St. Lucas, at the extremity of Lower California, however, being two degrees farther south.

It will give the foreign reader a more accurate notion of the character of Key West, if we mention a fact of quite recent occurrence. A very few weeks after the closing scenes of this tale, the town in question was, in a great measure, washed away! A hurricane brought in the sea upon all these islands and reefs, water running in swift currents over places that within the memory of man were never before submerged. The lower part of Key West was converted into a raging sea, and everything in that quarter of the place disappeared. The foundation being of rock, however, when the ocean retired the island came into view again, and industry and enterprise set to work to repair the injuries.

The government has established a small hospital for seamen at Key West. Into one of the rooms of the building thus appropriated our narrative must now conduct the reader. It contained but a single patient, and that was Spike. He was on his narrow bed, which was to be but the precursor of a much narrower tenement, the grave. In the room with the dying man were two females, in one of whom our readers will at once recognize the person of Rose Budd, dressed in deep mourning for her aunt. At first sight, it is probable that a casual observer would mistake the second female for one of the ordinary nurses of the place. Her attire was well enough, though worn awkwardly, and as if its owner were not exactly at ease in it. She had the air of one in her best attire, who was unaccustomed to be dressed above the most common mode. What added to the singularity of her appearance was the fact, that while she wore no cap, her hair had been cut into short, gray bristles, instead of being long, and turned up, as is usual with females. To give a sort of climax to this uncouth appearance, this strange-looking creature chewed tobacco.

The woman in question, equivocal as might be her exterior, was employed in one of the commonest avocations of her sex—that of sewing. She held in her hand a coarse garment, one of Spike's, in fact, which she seemed to be intently busy in mending; although the work was of a quality that invited the use of the palm and sail-needle, rather than that of the thimble and the smaller implement known to seamstresses, the woman appeared awkward in her business, as if her coarse-looking and dark hands refused to lend themselves to an occupation so feminine. Nevertheless, there were touches of a purely womanly character about this extraordinary person, and touches that particularly attracted the attention, and awakened the sympathy of the gentle Rose, her companion. Tears occasionally struggled out from beneath her eyelids, crossed her dark, sun-burnt cheek, and fell on the coarse canvas garment that lay in her lap. It was after one of these sudden and strong exhibitions of feeling that Rose approached her, laid her own little, fair hand, in a friendly way, though unheeded, on the other's shoulder, and spoke to her in her kindest and softest tones.

"I do really think he is reviving, Jack," said Rose, "and that you may yet hope to have an intelligent conversation with him."

"They all agree he must die," answered Jack Tier—for it was he, appearing in the garb of his proper sex, after a disguise that had now lasted fully twenty years, "and he will never know who I am, and that I forgive him. He must think of me in another world, though he is n't able to do it in this; but it would be a great relief to his soul to know that I forgive him."

"To be sure, a man must like to take a kind leave of his own wife before he closes his eyes forever; and I dare say it would be a great relief to you to tell him that you have forgotten his desertion of you, and all the hardships it has brought upon you in searching for him, and in earning your own livelihood as a common sailor."

"I shall not tell him I 've forgotten it, Miss Rose; that would be untrue—and there shall be no more deception between us; but I shall tell him that I forgive him, as I hope God will one day forgive me all my sins."

"It is, certainly, not a light offence to desert a wife in a foreign land, and then to seek to deceive another woman," quietly observed Rose.

"He 's a willain!" muttered the wife, "but—but—"

"You forgive him, Jack—yes, I 'm sure you do. You are too good a Christian to refuse to forgive him."

"I 'm a woman a'ter all, Miss Rose; and that, I believe, is the truth of it. I suppose I ought to do as you say, for the reason you mention; but I 'm his wife—and once he loved me, though that has long been over. When I first knew Stephen, I 'd the sort of feelin's you speak of, and was a very different creatur' from what you see me to-day. Change comes over us all with years and sufferin'."

Rose did not answer, but she stood looking intently at the speaker, more than a minute. Change had, indeed, come over her, if she had ever possessed the power to please the fancy of any living man. Her features had always seemed diminutive and mean for her assumed sex, as her voice was small and cracked; but, making every allowance for the probabilities, Rose found it difficult to imagine that Jack Tier had ever possessed, even under the high advantages of youth and innocence, the attractions so common to her sex. Her skin had acquired the tanning of the sea; the expression of her face had become hard and worldly; and her habits contributed to render those natural consequences of exposure and toil even more than usually marked and decided. By saying "habits," however, we do not mean that Jack had ever drunk to excess, as happens with so many seamen, for this would have been doing her injustice, but she smoked and chewed, practices that intoxicate in another form, and lead nearly as many to the grave as excess in drinking. Thus all the accessories about this singular being partook of the character of her recent life and duties. Her walk was between a waddle and a seaman's roll; her hands were discolored with tar, and had got to be full of knuckles, and even her feet had degenerated into that flat, broad-toed form that, perhaps, sooner distinguishes caste, in connection with outward appearances, than any other physical peculiarity. Yet this being had once been young—had once been even *fair*, and had once possessed that feminine air and lightness of form, that as often belongs to the youthful American of her sex, perhaps, as to the girl of any other nation on earth. Rose continued to gaze at her companion for some time, when she walked musingly to a window that looked out upon the port.

"I am not certain whether it would do him good or not to see this sight," she said, addressing the wife kindly, doubtful of the effect of her words even on the latter. "But here are the sloop-of-war, and several other vessels."

"Ay, she is there; but never will his foot be put on board the Swash ag'in. When he bought that brig I was still young, and agreeable to him; and he gave her my maiden name, which was Mary, or Molly Swash. But that is all changed; I wonder he did not change the name with his change of feelin's.''

"Then you did really sail in the brig in former times, and knew the seaman whose name you assumed?''

"Many years. Tier, with whose name I made free, on account of his size, and some resemblance to me in form, died under my care; and his protection fell into my hands, which first put the notion into my head of hailing as his representative. Yes, I knew Tier in the brig, and we were left ashore at the same time; I, intentionally, I make no question; he, because Stephen Spike was in a hurry, and did not choose to wait for a man. The poor fellow caught the yellow fever the very next day, and did not live eight-and-forty hours. So the world goes; them that wish to live, die; and them that wants to die, live!''

"You have had a hard time for one of your sex, poor Jack; quite twenty years a sailor, did you not tell me?''

"Every day of it, Miss Rose, and bitter years have they been; for the whole of that time have I been in chase of my husband, keeping my own secret, and slaving like a horse for a livelihood.''

"You could not have been old when he left—that is—when you parted.''

"Call it by its true name, and say at once, when he desarted me. I was under thirty by two or three years, and was still like my own sex to look at. All that is changed since; but I was comely then.''

"Why did Captain Spike abandon you, Jack? You have never told me that.''

"Because he fancied another. And ever since that time he has been fancying others, instead of remembering me. Had he got *you*, Miss Rose, I think he would have been content for the rest of his days.''

"Be certain, Jack, I should never have consented to marry Captain Spike.''

"You 're well out of his hands,'' answered Jack, sighing heavily, which was the most feminine thing she had done during the whole conversation,—"well out of his hands, and God be praised it is so. He should have died, before I would let him carry you off the island—husband or no husband.''

"It might have exceeded your power to prevent it under other circumstances, Jack."

Rose now continued looking out of the window in silence. Her thoughts reverted to her aunt and Biddy, and tears rolled down her cheeks as she remembered the love of one, and the fidelity of the other. Their horrible fate had given her a shock that, at first, menaced her with a severe fit of illness; but her strong good sense, and excellent constitution, both sustained by her piety and Harry's manly tenderness, had brought her through the danger, and left her, as the reader now sees her, struggling with her own griefs, in order to be of use to the still more unhappy woman who had so singularly become her friend and companion.

The reader will readily have anticipated that Jack Tier had early made the females on board the Swash her confidantes. Rose had known the outlines of her history from the first few days they were at sea together, which is the explanation of the visible intimacy that had caused Mulford so much surprise. Jack's motive in making his revelations might possibly have been tinctured with jealousy, but a desire to save one as young and innocent as Rose was at its bottom. Few persons but a wife would have supposed our heroine could have been in any danger from a lover like Spike; but Jack saw him with the eyes of her own youth, and of past recollections, rather than with those of truth. A movement of the wounded man first drew Rose from the window. Drying her eyes hastily, she turned toward him, fancying she might prove the better nurse of the two, notwithstanding Jack's greater interest in the patient.

"What place is this, and why am I here?" demanded Spike, with more strength of voice than could have been expected, after all that had passed. "This is not a cabin —not the Swash—it looks like a hospital."

"It is a hospital, Captain Spike," said Rose, gently, drawing near the bed; "you have been hurt, and have been brought to Key West, and placed in the hospital. I hope you feel better, and that you suffer no pain."

"My head is n't right—I don't know—everything seems turned round with me; perhaps it will all come out as it should. I begin to remember—where is my brig?"

"She is lost on the rocks. The seas have broken her into fragments."

"That's melancholy news, at any rate. Ah! Miss Rose! God bless you—I've had terrible dreams. Well, it's pleasant to be among friends; what creature is that—where does *she* come from?"

"That is Jack Tier," answered Rose, steadily. "She turns out to be a woman, and has put on her proper dress, in order to attend on you during your illness. Jack has never left your bedside since we have been here."

A long silence succeeded this revelation. Jack's eyes twinkled, and she hitched her body half aside, as if to conceal her features, where emotions that were unusual were at work with the muscles. Rose thought it might be well to leave the man and wife alone, and she managed to get out of the room unobserved.

Spike continued to gaze at the strange-looking female, who was now his sole companion. Gradually his recollection returned, and with it the full consciousness of his situation. He might not have been fully aware of the absolute certainty of his approaching death, but he must have known that his wound was of a very grave character, and that the result might early prove fatal. Still that strange and unknown figure haunted him; a figure that was so different from any he had ever seen before, and which, in spite of its present dress, seemed to belong quite as much to one sex as to the other. As for Jack—we call Molly, or Mary Swash by her masculine appellation, not only because it is more familiar, but because the other name seems really out of place, as applied to such a person —as for Jack, then, she sat with her face half averted, thumbing the canvas, and endeavoring to ply the needle, but perfectly mute. She was conscious that Spike's eyes were on her; and a lingering feeling of her sex told her how much time, exposure, and circumstances had changed her person, and she would have gladly hidden the defects in her appearance.

Mary Swash was the daughter as well as the wife of a shipmaster. In her youth, as has been said before, she had even been pretty, and down to the day her husband deserted her, she would have been thought a female of a comely appearance rather than the reverse. Her hair in particular, though slightly coarse, perhaps, had been rich and abundant; and the change from the long, dark, shining, flowing locks which she still possessed in her thirtieth year, to the short, gray bristles that now stood exposed without a cap, or covering of any sort, was one very likely to destroy all identity of appearance. Then Jack had passed from what might be called youth to the verge of old age, in the interval that she had been separated from her husband. Her shape had changed entirely; her complexion, was utterly gone; and her features, always unmeaning, though feminine, and suitable to her sex, had become hard and slightly coarse. Still there was something of her former self about Jack that bewildered Spike; and his eyes continued fastened on her for quite a quarter of an hour in profound silence.

"Give me some water," said the wounded man. "I wish some water to drink."

Jack arose, filled a tumbler and brought it to the side of the bed. Spike took the glass and drank, but the whole time his eyes were riveted on the strange nurse. When his thirst was appeased, he asked,—

"Who are you? How came you here?"

"I am your nurse. It is common to place nurses at the bedsides of the sick."

"Are you man or woman?"

"That is a question I hardly know how to answer. Sometimes I think myself each; sometimes neither."

"Did I ever see you before?"

"Often, and quite lately. I sailed with you in your last voyage."

"You! That cannot be. If so, what is your name?"

"Jack Tier."

A long pause succeeded this announcement, which induced Spike to muse as intently as his condition would allow, though the truth did not yet flash on his understanding. At length the bewildered man again spoke,

"Are you Jack Tier?" he said slowly, like one who doubted. "Yes—I now see the resemblance, and it was that which puzzled me. Are they so rigid in this hospital that you have been obliged to put on woman's clothes in order to lend me a helping hand?"

"I am dressed as you see, and for good reasons."

"But Jack Tier run, like that rascal Mulford; ay, I remember now; you were in the boat when I overhauled you all on the reef."

"Very true; I was in the boat. But I never run, Stephen Spike. It was *you* who abandoned *me*, on the islet in the Gulf, and that makes the second time in your life that you left me ashore, when it was your duty to carry me to sea."

"The first time I was in a hurry, and could not wait for you; this last time you took sides with the women. But for your interference, I should have got Rose, and married her, and all would now have been well with me."

This was an awkward announcement for a man to make to his legal wife. But after all Jack had endured, and all Jack had seen during the late voyage, she was not to be overcome by this avowal. Her self-command extended so far as to prevent any open manifestation of emotion, however much her feelings were excited.

"I took sides with the women, because I am a woman myself," she answered, speaking at length with decision, as if determined to bring matters to a head at once. "It is natural for us all to take sides with our kind."

"You a woman, Jack! That is very remarkable. Since when have you hailed for a woman? You have shipped with me twice, and each time as a man, though I've never thought you able to do seaman's duty."

"Nevertheless, I am what you see; a woman born and edicated; one that never had on man's dress until I knew you. You supposed me to be a man, when I came off to you in the skiff to the eastward of Riker's Island, but I was then what you now see."

"I begin to understand matters," rejoined the invalid, musingly. "Ay, ay, it opens on me; and I now see how it was you made such fair weather with Madam Budd and pretty, pretty Rose. Rose *is* pretty, Jack; you must admit that, though you be a woman.''

"Rose is pretty—I do admit it; and what is better, Rose is good.'' It required a heavy draft on Jack's justice and magnanimity, however, to make this concession.

"And you told Rose and Madam Budd about your sex; and that was the reason they took to you so on the v'y'ge?''

"I told them who I was, and why I went abroad as a man. They know my whole story.''

"Did Rose approve of your sailing under false colors, Jack?''

"You must ask that of Rose herself. My story made her my friend; but she never said anything for or against my disguise.''

"It was no great disguise after all, Jack. Now you're fitted out in your own clothes, you 've a sort of half-rigged look; one would be as likely to set you down for a man under jury-canvas, as for a woman.''

Jack made no answer to this, but she sighed very heavily. As for Spike himself, he was silent for some little time, not only from exhaustion, but because he suffered pain from his wound. The needle was diligently but awkwardly plied in this pause.

Spike's ideas were still a little confused; but a silence and rest of a quarter of an hour cleared them materially. At the end of that time he again asked for water. When he had drunk, and Jack was once more seated, with his side-face toward him, at work with the needle, the captain gazed long and intently at this strange woman. It happened that the profile of Jack preserved more of the resemblance to her former self, than the full face; and it was this resemblance that now attracted Spike's attention, though not the smallest suspicion of the truth yet gleamed upon him. He saw something that was familiar, though he could not even tell what that something was, much less to what and whom it bore any resemblance. At length he spoke.

"I was told that Jack Tier was dead,'' he said; "that

he took the fever, and was in his grave within eight-and-forty hours after we sailed. That was what they told me of him."

"And what did they tell you of your own wife, Stephen Spike,—she that you left ashore at the time Jack was left?"

"They said she did not die for three years later. I heard of her death at New Orleans, three years later."

"And how could you leave her ashore—she, your true and lawful wife?"

"It was a bad thing," answered Spike, who, like all other mortals, regarded his own past career, now that he stood on the edge of the grave, very differently from what he had regarded it in the hour of his health and strength. "Yes, it *was* a very bad thing; and I wish it was ondone. But it is too late now. She died of the fever, too—that's some comfort; had she died of a broken heart, I could not have forgiven myself. Molly was not without her faults—great faults, I considered them; but, on the whole, Molly was a good creatur'."

"You liked her, then, Stephen Spike?"

"I can truly say that when I married Molly, and old Captain Swash put his da'ghter's hand into mine, that the woman wasn't living who was better in my judgment, or handsomer in my eyes."

"Ay, ay, when you *married* her; but how was it a'terwards?—when you was tired of her, and saw another that was fairer in your eyes?"

"I desarted her; and God has punished me for the sin! Do you know, Jack, that luck has never been with me since that day. Often and often have I bethought me of it; and sartain as you sit there, no great luck has ever been with me, or my craft, since I went off, leaving my wife ashore. What was made in one v'y'ge, was lost in the next. Up and down, up and down the whole time, for so many, many long years, that gray hairs set in, and old age was beginning to get close aboard—and I as poor as ever. It has been rub and go with me ever since; and I have had as much as I could do to keep the brig in motion, as the only means that was left to make the two ends meet."

"And did not all this make you think of your poor wife —she whom you had so wronged?"

"I thought of little else, until I heard of her death at New Orleens—and then I gave it up as useless. Could I have fallen in with Molly at any time a'ter the first six months of my desartion, she and I would have come together again, and everything would have been forgotten. I knowed her very nature, which was all forgiveness to me at the bottom, though seemingly so spiteful and hard."

"Yet you wanted to have this Rose Budd, who is only too young, and handsome, and good for you."

"I was tired of being a widower, Jack; and Rose is wonderful pretty. She has money, too, and might make the evening of my days comfortable. The brig was old, as you must know, and has long been off the insurance offices' books; and she could n't hold together much longer. But for this sloop-of-war, I should have put her off on the Mexicans; and they would have lost her to our people in a month."

"And was it an honest thing to sell an old and worn-out craft to any one, Stephen Spike?"

Spike had a conscience that had become hard as iron by means of trade. He who traffics much, most especially if his dealings be on so small a scale as to render constant investigations of the minor qualities of things necessary, must be a very fortunate man, if he preserve his conscience in any better condition. When Jack made this allusion, therefore, the dying man—for death was much nearer to Spike than even he supposed, though he no longer hoped for his own recovery—when Jack made this allusion, then, the dying man was a good deal at a loss to comprehend it. He saw no particular harm in making the best bargain he could; nor was it easy for him to understand why he might not dispose of anything he possessed for the highest price that was to be had. Still he answered in an apologetic sort of way.

"The brig was old, I acknowledge," he said, "but she was strong, and might have run a long time. I only spoke of her capture as a thing likely to take place soon, if the

Mexicans got her; so that her qualities were of no great account, unless it might be her speed—and that you know was excellent, Jack."

"And you regret that brig, Stephen Spike, lying as you do on your death-bed, more than anything else."

"Not as much as I do pretty Rose Budd, Jack; Rosy is so delightful to look at!"

The muscles of Jack's face twitched a little, and she looked deeply mortified; for, to own the truth, she hoped that the conversation had so far turned her delinquent husband's thoughts to the past, as to have revived in him some of his former interest in herself. It is true, he still believed her dead; but this was a circumstance Jack overlooked—so hard it is to hear the praises of a rival, and be just. She felt the necessity of being more explicit, and determined at once to come to the point.

"Stephen Spike," she said steadily, drawing near to the bedside, "you should be told the truth, when you are heard thus extolling the good looks of Rose Budd, with less than eight-and-forty hours of life remaining. Mary Swash did not die, as you have supposed, three years a'ter you desarted her, but is living at this moment. Had you read the letter I gave you in the boat, just before you made me jump into the sea, *that* would have told you where she is to be found."

Spike stared at the speaker intently; and when her cracked voice ceased, his look was that of a man who was terrified as well as bewildered. This did not arise still from any gleamings of the real state of the case, but from the soreness with which his conscience pricked him, when he heard that his much-wronged wife was alive. He fancied, with a vivid and rapid glance at the probabilities, all that a woman abandoned would be likely to endure in the course of so many long and suffering years.

"Are you sure of what you say, Jack? You would n't take advantage of my situation to tell me an untruth?"

"As certain of it as of my own existence. I have seen her quite lately—talked with her of you—in short, she is now at Key West, knows your state, and has a wife's feelin's to come to your bedside."

Notwithstanding all this, and the many gleamings he had had of the facts during their late intercourse on board the brig, Spike did not guess at the truth. He appeared astounded, and his terror seemed to increase.

" I have another thing to tell you," continued Jack, pausing but a moment to collect her own thoughts. " Jack Tier —the real Jack Tier—he who sailed with you of old, and whom you left ashore at the same time you desarted your wife, did die of the fever, as you was told, in eight-and-forty hours a'ter the brig went to sea."

"Then who, in the name of Heaven, are you? How came you to hail by another's name as well as by another's sex ? "

" What could a woman do, whose husband had desarted her in a strange land ? "

" That is remarkable ! So you 've been married ? I should not have thought that possible ; and your husband desarted you, too. Well, such things do happen."

Jack now felt a severe pang. She could not but see that her ungainly—we had almost said her unearthly appearance —prevented the captain from even yet suspecting the truth ; and the meaning of his language was not easily to be mistaken. That any one should have married *her*, seemed to her husband as improbable as it was probable he would run away from her as soon as it was in his power after the ceremony.

"Stephen Spike," resumed Jack, solemnly, "*I* am Mary Swash—*I* am your wife ! "

Spike started in his bed ; then he buried his face in the coverlet, and he actually groaned. In bitterness of spirit the woman turned away and wept. Her feelings had been blunted by misfortune and the collisions of a selfish world ; but enough of former self remained to make this the hardest of all the blows she had ever received. Her husband, dying as he was, as he must and did know himself to be, shrunk from one of her appearance, unsexed as she had become by habits, and changed by years and suffering.

30

CHAPTER XVII.

" The trusting heart's repose, the paradise
Of home, with all its loves, doth fate allow
The crown of glory unto woman's brow."

MRS. HEMANS.

IT has again become necessary to advance the time ; and
we shall take the occasion thus offered to make a few
explanations touching certain events which have been
passed over without notice.

The reason why Captain Mull did not chase the yawl of
the brig in the Poughkeepsie herself, was the necessity of
waiting for his own boats that were endeavoring to regain
the sloop-of-war. It would not have done to abandon them,
inasmuch as the men were so much exhausted by the pull
to windward, that when they reached the vessel all were relieved from duty for the rest of the day. As soon, however,
as the other boats were hoisted in, or run up, the ship filled
away, stood out of the passage and ran down to join the
cutter of Wallace, which was endeavoring to keep its position, as much as possible, by making short tacks under close-
reefed lugs.

Spike had been received on board the sloop-of-war, sent
into her sick bay, and put under the care of the surgeon and
his assistants. From the first, these gentlemen pronounced
the hurt mortal. The wounded man was insensible most of
the time, until the ship had beat up and gone into Key West,
where he was transferred to the regular hospital, as has
already been mentioned.

The wreckers went out the moment the news of the calamity of the Swash reached their ears. Some went in

quest of the doubloons of the schooner, and others to pick up anything valuable that might be discovered in the neighborhood of the stranded brig. It may be mentioned here, that not much was ever obtained from the brigantine, with the exception of a few spars, the sails, and a little rigging ; but, in the end, the schooner was raised, by means of the chain Spike had placed around her, the cabin was ransacked, and the doubloons were recovered. As there was no one to claim the money, it was quietly divided among the conscientious citizens present at its revisiting "the glimpses of the moon," making gold plenty.

The doubloons of the yawl would have been lost but for the sagacity of Mulford. He too well knew the character of Spike to believe he would quit the brig without taking the doubloons with him. Acquainted with the boat, he examined the little locker in the stern-sheets, and found the two bags, one of which was probably the lawful property of Captain Spike, while the other, in truth, belonged to the Mexican government. The last contained the most gold, but the first amounted to a sum that our young mate knew to be very considerable. Rose had made him acquainted with the sex of Jack Tier since their own marriage ; and he at once saw that the claims of this uncouth wife, who was so soon to be a widow, to the gold in question, might prove to be as good in law as they unquestionably were in morals. On representing the facts of the case to Captain Mull and the legal functionaries at Key West, it was determined to relinquish this money to the heirs of Spike, as, indeed, they must have done under process, there being no other claimant. These doubloons, however, did not amount to the full price of the flour and powder that composed the cargo of the Swash. The cargo had been purchased with Mexican funds ; and all that Spike or his heirs could claim was the high freight for which he had undertaken the delicate office of transporting those forbidden articles, contraband of war, to the Dry Tortugas.

Mulford by this time was high in the confidence and esteem of all on board the Poughkeepsie. He had frankly explained his whole connection with Spike, not even attempting to conceal the reluctance he had felt to betray the brig after he had fully ascertained the fact of his commander's treason. The manly gentlemen with whom he was now brought in contact entered into his feelings, and admitted that it was an office no one could desire, to turn against the craft in which he sailed. It is true, they could not and would not be traitors, but Mulford had stopped far short of this ; and the distinction between such a character and that of an informer was wide enough to satisfy all their scruples.

Then Rose had the greatest success with the gentlemen of the Poughkeepsie. Her youth, beauty, and modesty told largely in her favor ; and the simple, womanly affection she unconsciously betrayed in behalf of Harry touched the heart of every observer. When the intelligence of her aunt's fate reached her, the sorrow she manifested was so profound and natural, that every one sympathized with her grief. Nor would she be satisfied unless Mulford would consent to go in search of the bodies. The latter knew the hopelessness of such an excursion, but he could not refuse to comply. He was absent on that melancholy duty, therefore, at the moment of the scene related in our last chapter, and did not return until after that which we are now about to lay before the reader. Mrs. Budd, Biddy, and all of those who perished after the yawl got clear of the reef, were drowned in deep water, and no more was ever seen of any of them ; or, if wreckers did pass them, they did not stop to bury the dead. It was different, however, with those who were first sacrificed to Spike's selfishness. They were drowned on the reef, and Harry did actually recover the bodies of the Señor Montefalderon, and of Josh, the steward. They had been washed upon a rock that is bare at low water. He took them both to the Dry Tortugas, and had them interred along with the other dead at that place. Don Juan was placed side by side with his unfortunate countryman, the master of his equally unfortunate schooner.

While Harry was absent and thus employed, Rose wept much and prayed more. She would have felt herself almost alone in the world, but for the youth to whom she

had so recently, less than a week before, plighted her faith
in wedlock. That new tie, it is true, was of sufficient importance to counteract many of the ordinary feelings of
her situation ; and she now turned to it as the one which
absorbed most of the future duties of her life. Still she
missed the kindness, the solicitude, even the weaknesses of
her aunt ; and the terrible manner in which Mrs. Budd had
perished made her shudder with horror whenever she thought
of it. Poor Biddy, too, came in for her share of the regrets.
This faithful creature, who had been in the relict's service
ever since Rose's infancy, had become endeared to her, in
spite of her uncouth manners and confused ideas, by the
warmth of her heart and the singular truth of her feelings.
Biddy, of all her family, had come to America, leaving behind her not only brothers and sisters, but parents living.
Each year did she remit to the last a moiety of her earnings,
and many a half-dollar that had come from Rose's pretty
little hand had been converted into gold, and forwarded on
the same pious errand to the green island of her nativity.
Ireland, unhappy country ! at this moment what are not
the dire necessities of thy poor ! Here, from the midst of
abundance, in a land that God has blessed in its productions
far beyond the limits of human wants, a land in which famine was never known, do we at this moment hear thy groans,
and listen to tales of suffering that to us seem almost incred-
ible. In the midst of these chilling narratives, our eyes fall
on an appeal to the English nation, that appears in what it
is the fashion of some to term the first journal of Europe (!)
in behalf of thy suffering people. A worthy appeal to the
charity of England seldom fails ; but it seems to us that one
sentiment of this might have been altered, if not spared.
The English are asked to be "forgetful of the past," and to
come forward to the relief of their suffering fellow-subjects.
We should have written "mindful of the past," in its stead.
We say this in charity, as well as in truth. We come of
English blood, and if we claim to share in all the ancient
renown of that warlike and enlightened people, we are
equally bound to share in the reproaches that original mis-
government has inflicted on thee. In this latter sense, then,

thou hast a right to our sympathies, and they are not with-
held.

As has been already said, we now advance the time eight-
and-forty hours, and again transfer the scene to that room
in the hospital which was occupied by Spike. The approaches
of death, during the interval just named, had been slow but
certain. The surgeons had announced that the wounded
man could not possibly survive the coming night; and he
himself had been made sensible that his end was near. It
is scarcely necessary to add that Stephen Spike, conscious
of his vigor and strength, in command of his brig, and bent
on the pursuits of worldly gains, or of personal gratifica-
tion, was a very different person from him who now lay
stretched on his pallet in the hospital of Key West, a dying
man. By the side of his bed still sat his strange nurse,
less peculiar in appearance, however, than when last seen
by the reader.

Rose Budd had been ministering to the ungainly exter-
nals of Jack Tier. She now wore a cap, thus concealing the
short, gray bristles of hair, and lending to her countenance a
little of that softness which is a requisite of female character. Some attention had also been paid to the rest of her
attire; and Jack was, altogether, less repulsive in her exterior than when, unaided, she had attempted to resume the
proper garb of her sex. Use and association, too, had contributed a little to revive her woman's nature, if we may so
express it, and she had begun, in particular, to feel the sort
of interest in her patient which we all come in time to entertain toward any object of our especial care. We do not
mean that Jack had absolutely ever ceased to love her husband; strange as it may seem, such had not literally been the
case; on the contrary, her interest in him and in his welfare had never ceased, even while she saw his vices and de-
tested his crimes; but all we wish to say here is, that she
was getting, in addition to the long-enduring feelings of a
wife, some of the interest of a nurse.

During the whole time which had elapsed between Jack's
revealing her true character, and the moment of which we
are now writing, Spike had not once spoken to his wife.

Often had she caught his eyes intently riveted on her, when he would turn them away, as she feared, in distaste; and once or twice he groaned deeply, more like a man who suffered mental than bodily pain. Still the patient did not speak once in all the time mentioned. We should be representing poor Jack as possessing more philosophy, or less feeling, than the truth would warrant, were we to say that she was not hurt at this conduct in her husband. On the contrary, she felt it deeply; and more than once it had so far subdued her pride as to cause her bitterly to weep. This shedding of tears, however, was of service to Jack in one sense, for it had the effect of renewing old impressions, and, in a certain way, of reviving the nature of her sex within her,—a nature which had been sadly weakened by her past life.

But the hour had at length come when this long and painful silence was to be broken. Jack and Rose were alone with the patient, when the last again spoke to his wife.

"Molly—poor Molly!" said the dying man, his voice continuing full and deep to the last, "what a sad time you must have had of it after I did you that wrong!"

"It is hard upon a woman, Stephen, to turn her out, helpless, on a cold and selfish world," answered Jack, simply, much too honest to affect a reserve she did not feel.

"It was hard, indeed; may God forgive me for it, as I hope ye do, Molly."

No answer was made to this appeal; and the invalid looked anxiously at his wife. The last sat at her work, which had now got to be less awkward to her, with her eyes bent on her needle,—her countenance rigid, and, so far as the eye could discern, her feelings unmoved.

"Your husband speaks to you, Jack Tier," said Rose, pointedly.

"May yours never have occasion to speak to you, Rose Budd, in the same way," was the solemn answer. "I do not flatter myself that I ever was as comely as you, or that yonder poor dying wretch was a Harry Mulford in his youth; but we were young and happy, and respected once, and loved each other, yet you see what it's all come to!"

Rose was silenced, though she had too much tenderness in behalf of her own youthful and manly bridegroom to dread a fate similar to that which had overtaken poor Jack. Spike now seemed disposed to say something, and she went to the side of his bed, followed by her companion, who kept a little in the background, as if unwilling to let the emotion she really felt be seen, and, perhaps, conscious that her ungainly appearance did not aid her in recovering the lost affections of her husband.

"I have been a very wicked man, I fear," said Spike, earnestly.

"There are none without sin," answered Rose. "Place your reliance on the mediation of the Son of God, and sins even far deeper than yours may be pardoned."

The captain stared at the beautiful speaker, but self-indulgence, the incessant pursuit of worldly and selfish objects for forty years, and the habits of a life into which the thought of God and the dread hereafter never entered, had encased his spiritual being in a sort of brazen armor, through which no ordinary blow of conscience could penetrate. Still he had fearful glimpses of recent events, and his soul, hanging as it was over the abyss of eternity, was troubled.

"What has become of your aunt?" half whispered Spike, "my old captain's widow. She ought to be here; and Don Wan Montezuma—where is he?"

Rose turned aside to conceal her tears, but no one answered the questions of the dying man. Then a gleaming of childhood shot into the recollection of Spike, and, clasping his hands, he tried to pray. But, like others who have lived without any communication with their Creator through long lives of apathy to His existence and laws, thinking only of the present time, and daily, hourly sacrificing principles and duty to the narrow interests of the moment, he now found how hard it is to renew communications with a being who has been so long neglected. The fault lay in himself, however, for a gracious ear was open, even over the death-bed of Stephen Spike, could that rude spirit only bring itself to ask for mercy in earnestness and truth. As his companions saw his struggles, they left him for a few minutes to his own thoughts.

"Molly," Spike at length uttered, in a faint tone, the voice of one conscious of being very near his end, "I hope you will forgive me, Molly. I know you must have had a hard, hard time of it."

"It is hard for a woman to unsex herself, Stephen; to throw off her very natur', as it might be, and to turn man."

"It has changed you sadly—even your speech is altered. Once your voice was soft and womanish, more like that of Rose Budd's than it is now."

"I speak as them speak among whom I've been forced to live. The forecastle and steward's pantry, Stephen Spike, are poor schools to send women to l'arn language in."

"Try and forget it all, poor Molly! Say to me, so that I can hear you, 'I forget and forgive, Stephen.' I am afraid God will not pardon my sins, which begin to seem dreadful to me, if my own wife refuse to forget and forgive, on my dying bed."

Jack was much mollified by this appeal. Her interest in her offending husband had never been entirely extinguished. She had remembered him, and often with woman's kindness, in all her wanderings and sufferings, as the preceding parts of our narrative must show; and though resentment had been mingled with the grief and mortification she felt at finding how much he still submitted to Rose's superior charms, in a breast as really generous and humane as that of Jack Tier's, such a feeling was not likely to endure in the midst of a scene like that she was now called to witness. The muscles of her countenance twitched, the hard-looking, tanned face began to lose its sternness, and every way she appeared like one profoundly disturbed.

"Turn to Him whose goodness and marcy may sarve you, Stephen," she said, in a milder and more feminine tone than she had used now for years, making her more like herself than either her husband or Rose had seen her since the commencement of the late voyage; "my sayin' that I forget and forgive cannot help a man on his death-bed."

"It will settle my mind, Molly, and leave me freer to turn my thoughts to God."

Jack was much affected, more by the countenance and manner of the sufferer, perhaps, than by his words. She drew nearer to the side of her husband's pallet, knelt, took his hand, and said solemnly,—

"Stephen Spike, from the bottom of my heart, I do forgive you ; and I shall pray to God that he will pardon your sins as freely and more marcifully than I now pardon all, and try to forget all that you have done to me."

Spike clasped his hands, and again he tried to pray ; but the habits of a whole life are not to be thrown off at will, and he who endeavors to regain, in his extremity, the moments that have been lost, will find, in bitter reality, that he has been heaping mountains on his own soul, by the mere practice of sin, which were never laid there by the original fall of his race. Jack, however, had disburdened her spirit of a load that had long oppressed it, and, burying her face in the rug, she wept.

"I wish, Molly," said the dying man, several minutes later, "I wish I had never seen the brig. Until I got that craft, no thought of wronging human being ever crossed my mind."

"It was the Father of Lies that tempts all to do evil, Stephen, and not the brig, which caused the sins."

"I wish I could live a year longer—*only* one year ; that is not much to ask for a man who is not yet sixty."

"It is hopeless, poor Stephen. The surgeons say you cannot live one day."

Spike groaned, for the past, blended fearfully with the future, gleamed on his conscience with a brightness that appalled him. And what is that future, which is to make us happy or miserable through an endless vista of time? Is it not composed of an existence, in which conscience, released from the delusions and weaknesses of the body, sees all in its true colors, appreciates all, and punishes all. Such an existence would make every man the keeper of the record of his own transgressions, even to the most minute exactness. It would of itself mete out perfect justice, since the sin would be seen amid its accompanying facts,— every aggravating or extenuating circumstance. Each man would be strictly punished according to his talents. As no one is without sin, it makes the necessity of an atonement indispensable, and, in its most rigid interpretation, it exhibits the truth of the scheme of salvation in the clearest colors. The soul, or conscience, that can admit the necessary degree of faith in that atonement, and in admitting, *feels* its efficacy, throws the burden of its own transgressions away, and remains forever in the condition of its original existence, pure, and consequently happy.

We do not presume to lay down a creed on this mighty and mysterious matter, in which all have so deep an interest, and concerning which so very small a portion of the human race think much, or think with any clearness when it does become the subject of their passing thoughts at all. We too well know our own ignorance to venture on dogmas which it has probably been intended that the mind of man should not yet grapple with and comprehend. To return to our subject.

Stephen Spike was now made to feel the incubus-load which perseverance in sin heaps on the breast of the reckless offender. What was the most grievous of all, his power to shake off this dead weight was diminished in precisely the same proportion as the burden was increased, the moral force of every man lessening in a very just ratio to the magnitude of his delinquencies. Bitterly did this deep offender struggle with his conscience, and little did his half-unsexed wife know how to console or aid him. Jack had been superficially instructed in the dogmas of her faith, in childhood and youth, as most persons are instructed in what are termed Christian communities,—had been made to learn the Catechism, the Lord's Prayer, and the Creed,—and had been left to set up for herself on this small capital, in the great concern of human existence, on her marriage and entrance on the active business of life. When the manner in which she had passed the last twenty years is remembered, no one can be surprised to learn that Jack was of little assistance to her husband in his extremity. Rose made an effort to administer hope and consolation, but the terrible nature of the struggle she witnessed induced her to send for the chaplain of the Poughkeepsie. This divine prayed with the dying man ; but even he, in the last moments of the sufferer, was little more than a passive but shocked witness of remorse, suspended over the abyss of eternity in hopeless dread. We shall not enter into the details of the revolting scene, but simply add that curses, blasphemy, tremulous cries for mercy, agonized entreaties to be advised, and sullen defiance were all strangely and fearfully blended. In the midst of one of these revolting paroxysms, Spike breathed his last. A few hours later, his body was interred in the sands of the shore. It may be well to say in this place, that the hurricane of 1846, which is known to have occurred only a few months later, swept off the frail covering, and that the body was washed away to leave its bones among the wrecks and relics of the Florida Reef.

Mulford did not return from his fruitless expedition in quest of the remains of Mrs. Budd, until after the death and interment of Spike. As nothing remained to be done at Key West, he and Rose accompanied by Jack Tier, took passage for Charleston in the first convenient vessel that offered. Two days before they sailed, the Poughkeepsie went out to cruise in the Gulf, agreeably to her general orders. The evening previously Captain Mull, Wallace, and the chaplain passed with the bridegroom and bride, when the matter of the doubloons found in the boat was discussed. It was agreed that Jack Tier should have them ; and in her hands the bag was now placed. On this occasion, to oblige the officers, Jack went into a narrative of all she had seen and suffered, from the moment when abandoned by her late husband down to that when she found him again. It was a strange account, and one filled with surprising adventures. In most of the vessels in which she had served, Jack had acted in the steward's department, though she had frequently done duty as a fore-mast hand. In strength and skill she admitted that she had often failed ;

but in courage, never. Having been given reason to think her husband was reduced to serving in a vessel of war, she had shipped on board a frigate bound to the Mediterranean, and had actually made a whole cruise as a ward-room boy on that station. While thus employed, she had met with two of the gentlemen present,—Captain Mull and Mr. Wallace. The former was then first-lieutenant of the frigate, and the latter a passed-midshipman; and these capacities both had been well known to her. As the name she then bore was the same as that under which she now "hailed," these officers were soon made to recollect her, though Jack was no longer the light, trim-built lad he had then appeared to be. Neither of the gentlemen named had made the whole cruise in the ship, but each had been promoted and transferred to another craft, after being Jack's shipmate rather more than a year. This information greatly facilitated the affair of the doubloons.

From Charleston the travellers came north by railroad. Harry made several stops by the way, in order to divert the thoughts of his beautiful young bride from dwelling too much on the fate of her aunt. He knew that home would revive all these recollections painfully, and wished to put off the hour of their return until time had a little weakened Rose's regrets. For this reason, he passed a whole week in Washington, though it was a season of the year that the place is not in much request. Still, Washington is scarce a town at any season. It is much the fashion to deride the American capital, and to treat it as a place of very humble performance with very sounding pretensions. Certainly, Washington has very few of the peculiarities of a great European capital, but few as these are, they are more than belong to any other place in this country. We now allude to the distinctive characteristics of a capital, and not to a mere concentration of houses and shops within a given space. In this last respect, Washington is much behind fifty other American towns, even while it is the only place in the whole Republic which possesses specimens of architecture on a scale approaching that of the higher classes of the edifices of the old world. It is totally deficient in churches,

and theatres, and markets ; or those it does possess are, in
an architectural sense, not at all above the level of village
or country-town pretensions, but one or two of its national
edifices do approach the magnificence and grandeur of the
old world. The new Treasury Buildings are unquestionably, on the score of size, embellishments, and finish, *the*
American edifice that comes nearest to first-class architecture
on the other side of the Atlantic. The Capitol comes next,
though it can scarce be ranked, relatively, as high. As for
the White House, it is every way sufficient for its purposes
and the institutions ; and now that its grounds are finished,
and the shrubbery and trees begin to tell, one sees about it
something that is not unworthy of its high uses and origin.
Those grounds, which so long lay a reproach to the national
taste and liberality, are now fast becoming beautiful, are already exceedingly pretty, and give to a structure that is des-
tined to become historical, having already associated with
it the names of Jefferson, Madison, Jackson, and Quincy
Adams, together with the *oi polloi* of the later Presidents, an
entourage that is suitable to its past recollections and its
present purposes. They are not quite on a level with the
parks of London, it is true ; or even with the Tuileries or
Luxembourg, or the Boboli or the Villa Reale, or fifty more
grounds and gardens of a similar nature, that might be
mentioned ; but, seen in the spring and early summer, they
adorn the building they surround, and lend to the whole
neighborhood a character of high civilization that no other
place in America can show, in precisely the same form, or
to the same extent.

This much have we said on the subject of the White
House and its precincts, because we took occasion, in a former work, to berate the narrow-minded parsimony which
left the grounds of the White House in a condition that was
discreditable to the Republic. How far our philippic may
have hastened the improvements which have been made, is
more than we shall pretend to say ; but having made the
former strictures, we are happy to have an occasion to say
(though nearly twenty years have intervened between the expressions of the two opinions) that they are no longer merited.

And here we will add another word, and that on a subject

that is not sufficiently pressed on the attention of a people, who, by position, are unavoidably provincial. We invite those whose gorges rise at any stricture on anything American, and who fancy it is enough to belong to the great Republic to be great in itself, to place themselves in front of the State Department, as it now stands, and to examine its dimensions, material, and form with critical eyes ; then to look along the adjacent Treasury Buildings, to fancy them completed, by a junction with new edifices of a similar construction to contain the department of state ; next to fancy similar works completed for the two opposite departments ; after which, to compare the past and present with the future as thus finished, and remember how recent has been the partial improvement which even now exists. If this examination and comparison do not show, directly to the sense of sight, how much there was and is to criticise, as put in contrast with other countries, we shall give up the individuals in question as too deeply dyed in the provincial wool ever to be whitened. The present Trinity Church, New York, certainly not more than a third-class European church, if as much, compared with its village-like predecessor, may supply a practical homily of the same degree of usefulness. There may be those among us, however, who fancy it patriotism to maintain that the old Treasury Buildings were quite equal to the new, and of these intense Americans we cry their mercy !

Rose felt keenly on reaching her late aunt's very neat dwelling in Fourteenth Street, New York. But the manly tenderness of Mulford was a great support to her, and a little time brought her to think of that weak-minded, but well-meaning and affectionate relative, with gentle regret rather than with grief. Among the connections of her young husband she found several females of a class in life certainly equal to her own, and somewhat superior to the latter in education and habits. As for Harry, he very gladly passed the season with his beautiful bride, though a fine ship was laid down for him, by means of Rose's fortune, now much increased by her aunt's death, and he was absent in Europe when his son was born,—an event that occurred only two months since.

The Swash, and the shipment of gunpowder, were thought of no more in the good town of Manhattan. This great emporium—we beg pardon, this great commercial emporium—has a trick of forgetting, condensing all interests into those of the present moment. It is much addicted to believing that which never had an existence, and of overlooking that which is occurring directly *under its nose*. So marked is this tendency to forgetfulness, we should not be surprised to hear some of the Manhattanese pretend that our legend is nothing but a fiction, and deny the existence of the Molly, Captain Spike, and even of Biddy Noon. But we know them too well to mind what they say, and shall go on and finish our narrative in our own way, just as if there were no such raven-throated commentators at all.

Jack Tier, still known by that name, lives in the family of Captain Mulford. She is fast losing the tan on her face and hands, and every day is improving in appearance. She now habitually wears her proper attire, and is dropping gradually into the feelings and habits of her sex. She never can become what she once was, any more than the blackamoor can become white, or the leopard change his spots ; but she is no longer revolting. She has left off chewing and smoking, having found a refuge in snuff. Her hair is permitted to grow, and is already turned up with a comb, though constantly concealed beneath a cap. The heart of Jack, alone, seems unaltered. The strange, tiger-like affection that she bore for Spike, during twenty years of abandonment, has disappeared in regrets for his end. It is succeeded by a most sincere attachment for Rose, in which the little boy, since his appearance on the scene, is becoming a large participator. This child Jack is beginning to love intensely ; and the doubloons, well invested, placing her above the feeling of dependence, she is likely to end her life, once so errant and disturbed, in tranquillity and a home-like happiness.

THE END.

www.ingramcontent.com/pod-product-compliance
Lightning Source LLC
Chambersburg PA
CBHW011119050726
47495CB00020B/2712